Also by Robert J. Shade

The Forbes Road Series:
Forbes Road
Conestoga Winter
The Camp Follower Affair
Lord Dunmore's Folly

The Rebellion Road Series:
Pursuit Through Chaos
Fight From Bonniecrest Manor

FREEDOM
AT
GWYNN'S ISLAND

Freedom At Gwynn's Island

A Rebellion Road Novel

ROBERT J. SHADE

Sunshine Hill Press

Sunshine Hill Press, LLC
2937 Novum Road
Reva, VA 22735

ISBN-13: 979-218-05504-2

Artwork with specific permission:

Front Cover: *Route Step* by Bryant White

(www.whitehistoricart.com)

Freedom At Gwynn's Island is a work of fiction. With the exception
of historical people and places and events in the narrative, all names,
characters, places, and incidents are used fictitiously. Any resemblance to
current events, places, or to living persons is entirely coincidental.

MAJOR CHARACTERS

Historical	Description
John Murray, 4th Earl of Dunmore	Royal governor of Virginia
James Wood	Frederick County representative to Convention of Virginia; member, Committee of Safety
Jean Moncure Wood	Wife of James Wood
Angus McDonald	Master of Glengarry Manor, militia major, member of Frederick County Committee of Safety
Anna McDonald	Wife of Angus
Andrew Lewis	Commanding general of Virginia Army
Patrick Henry	Governor of Virginia
Dorothea Dandridge	Fiancée of Patrick Henry
William Daingerfield	Colonel of 7th Virginia Regiment
Thomas Posey	Captain in 7th Virginia Regiment
William Howe	General commanding British Army in North America
James Paterson	Lieutenant colonel, adjutant general to General Howe
William Gardiner	Captain, military secretary to General Howe
Elizabeth Loring	Wife of British commissary general, "friend" of General Howe
Thomas Stirling	Lieutenant colonel commandant of 42nd Foot (Black Watch)
William Grayson	Colonel, Continental Army; aide to George Washington
Caleb Gibbs	Captain of Washington's Life Guard
Andrew Snape Hammond	Captain of HMS *Roebuck* and senior officer of Royal Navy Squadron

Fictional	Description
Wend Eckert	Gunsmith, captain of Frederick County Light Foot
Peggy McCartie Eckert	Wend's wife
Henry Johann Eckert	Wend's son with Abigail Gibson
Bernd Eckert	Wend's son with Peggy
Joshua Baird	Militia scout of Frederick County
Alice Downy Baird	Common-law wife of Joshua
Simon Donegal	Distiller of whiskey, former corporal of 77th Highlanders, company sergeant of Frederick County Light Foot
Sally Porter Donegal	Simon's wife
Billy Wood	Servant to Eckert family, private in Frederick County Light Foot
Mary Fraser	Matron of the hospital, 42nd Foot (Black Watch)
Charles McDonald	Major, 42nd Foot (Black Watch)
Barrett Penfold Northcutt	Lieutenant colonel commandant of King's Loyal Virginia Legion
Reginald Welford	Major in King's Loyal Virginia Legion
Aubrey Harbridge	Senior adviser to Lord Dunmore
Dudley Fellows	Secretary to Lord Dunmore
Wesley Proctor	Lieutenant commanding HMS *Raven*
Colleen Alison McGraw	Proprietress of the Red Vixen Sutler Company
Geoffrey Fairfield	Lieutenant commanding 1st Troop Palmetto Light Horse
Reese Newkirk	First lieutenant of Frederick County Light Foot
Shay O'beirne	Second lieutenant of Frederick County Light Foot
Edward Childers	Ensign of Frederick County Light Foot
Thomas Wilder	Sergeant in Frederick County Light Foot
Henry Flannagan	Sergeant in Frederick County Light Foot
Jonathan Rhys	Traveling ironmonger
Melinda	Former African slave with Dunmore's forces

CONTENTS

PART I
WELFORD'S RAID

CHAPTER ONE

THE FLOATING COLONY

Just south of where the Elizabeth River flows into Hampton Roads lay a fleet of more than one hundred vessels, large and small, riding to their anchors in the choppy waters generated by the gusty March winds. Anchored together at the northern end of the assemblage was a small squadron of Royal Navy warships, the largest of which was a graceful forty-four-gun frigate. The balance of craft was a mix of large and small merchants ranging from single-masted coasting sloops to three-masted trading vessels. One of the largest was a broad-beamed former East India Company ship, located near the center of the assemblage. Painted in large gold letters across its stern was the name *Dunmore.*

The man for whom the ship was named stood at the taffrail, clothed in a heavy overcoat and cocked hat, hands clasped behind his back and feet spread wide to steady himself against the motion of the deck. John Murray, 4th Earl of Dunmore, royal governor of Virginia, stared out at the vessels surrounding him with a scowl on his face, brooding about the wretched state of affairs. The fleet, with the inclusion of a few patches of land in the tidewater, constituted the practical remains of what had once been England's largest colony in North America. The rest of Virginia was held in this year of 1776 by the deplorable pack of rebels who stood in opposition to their rightful king, His Majesty George III.

Dunmore could see many of his loyalist followers on the decks of the ships, some sitting in groups or standing by the rails, others walking about the decks for a measure of exercise. There were individuals, couples, and families, all refugees from their rightful homes. On some ships the people were virtually all black Africans, former slaves who had been freed by his proclamation of last November and had fled to his fleet from the plantations where they had been held in bondage.

Dunmore raised his eyes and looked eastward to the land beyond the ships, where the ruins of the city of Norfolk lay. Much of the destruction had been done on the very first day of 1776 by the guns of his warships when they had bombarded the parts of the town held by the defiant rebels. Then the so-called patriots had burned the loyalist portions of the city in reprisal. After contemplating the wrecked town for a moment, he turned and looked at the eastern bank of the Elizabeth and could see the more rural land of the Portsmouth area. Near the mouth of the river, at a place called Tucker's Point, was a wooden stockade within which was a garrison of his own troops and to which local farmers brought meat, flour, and vegetables to sell for consumption by the fleet.

At that moment the governor was distracted by a call from the masthead. "Deck there! Ship coming into the anchorage!" Turning toward the taffrail, Dunmore looked out at the mouth of the river and could see a small, two-masted ship rounding the point on the Norfolk side, coming into the river from Hampton Roads. He saw that it was flying the union flag. As he watched, a string of naval signal flags was hoisted smartly from a yardarm on the mainmast. Soon a responding hoist was raised on the frigate. Clearly the new ship was a naval vessel. Presently it tacked into a position near the flagship and with great alacrity and precision took in its sails and dropped anchor.

As the governor watched, he was approached by Howser, his steward. "My lord, we are ready to serve your midday meal in the great cabin."

Dunmore nodded. "Ah yes, Howser. I shall be down promptly."

He looked back at the new arrival and could see a boat being hoisted out. Dunmore bit his lips. Most likely the ship was carrying dispatches. But from where? From Lord Germain, the secretary for North America in London? Or from General Howe in Boston, commander of all forces in North America? He shrugged. Captain Hammond, commander of the frigate and senior officer of the naval squadron, would appraise him soon enough. With that thought the governor went below for his meal, reflecting that he did indeed have quite an appetite.

—m—

The meal in the *Dunmore*'s great cabin was nearly finished. As usual the governor was dining with his two closest aides. The chief counselor, Aubrey Harbridge, a razor-thin, balding man in his fifties, who sat on his right hand, had been with Dunmore since his days as governor of New York. After five years Dunmore trusted him implicitly. Young Dudley Fellows, his personal secretary, sat to the left. Fellows was the opposite of Harbridge, tending toward corpulence but with a prodigious thatch of brown hair. However, Fellows was highly industrious, had a nice turn of phrase when writing, and did so with a fine round hand.

Also at the table on this occasion were officers of the ship. Jacob McCabe, the master of the Dunmore, sat next to Harbridge. He had been the ship's captain in the merchant service, and now that the ship had been drafted into the colony's use, he had remained in charge. Navy Lieutenant Jared Coble, from Hammond's frigate, HMS *Roebuck*, was seated next to McCabe. He had been seconded to supervise the operation of the ship's twelve six-pounders, along with a party of navy seaman from various ships of the naval squadron. Across from Coble sat Captain Thomas Slidell, who led the detachment of Royal Marines that had been assigned to the former merchant ship.

The stewards had just served the dessert when there was a tap on the door. Howser walked over and swung it open to admit the mate of the watch. The officer doffed his cap and strode to the bottom of the table.

"My lord," said the mate, "there's a boat headed our way from the *Roebuck*. Captain Hammond is embarked, and there's another officer with him." He paused, then continued, "They should arrive shortly."

Dunmore nodded. "Thank you, sir. Please have them shown here immediately upon their arrival."

The officer withdrew. Dunmore said, "Well, now we shall know what news that schooner brought."

Harbridge thought a moment, then responded, "I would hope it is a response from General Howe in Boston regarding the additional troops you requested." He shook his head. "My God, what we could do with a full battalion of regular foot."

Dunmore nodded. "Absolutely, Aubrey. The colonials are still recruiting and organizing their regiments. Would that we could strike a powerful blow before they do so. It would encourage the numerous gentry with loyalist sympathies who have hesitated to show their hand to join us."

Fellows spoke up. "I am told Captain Hammond considers that Colonel Northcutt and his King's Loyal Virginia Legion are in an increasingly precarious position at Strawbridge Plantation. He cites reports that the rebels are gathering troops to challenge them."

Lieutenant Coble spoke up. "Hammond has drawn up plans to evacuate Northcutt's troops if necessary."

Dunmore's lips tightened. "Evacuation? I'm not worried about that, Coble. Northcutt has also got the Queen's Loyal Regiment with him and a detachment of the Ethiopians. All told, there are over three hundred well-organized troops, along with a significant battery of artillery. I think we have no immediate worry about their position."

"Indeed," added Harbridge. "Besides, we would be foolish to withdraw them; they're in an excellent location to send out raiding parties to gather supplies for us and to find African recruits for the Ethiopian Regiment."

Dunmore nodded. "Quite correct, Aubrey. In any case, we must have a toehold on the land here in the tidewater. Without troops on the soil of Virginia, we'll have no credibility with those who remain loyal to the crown." He shook his head. "In fact, we must soon find a way to increase our presence ashore, or they will give up."

He had just finished speaking when there was a tap on the door. Howser opened it, peered into the passage, then opened wide to admit two naval officers. Captain Andrew Spade Hammond of the frigate *Roebuck*, hat under his arm, led the way in, followed by a youngish, razor-thin lieutenant also carrying his hat.

The captain said, "Good afternoon, Your Lordship."

Dunmore nodded. "Glad to see you, Andrew." He motioned toward the other officer. "And whom have you brought with you?"

"Sir, this is Lieutenant Commanding Wesley Proctor, of His Majesty's Schooner *Raven*, newly arrived from Boston."

Proctor bowed his head momentarily and simply said, "Afternoon, Lord Dunmore."

The governor acknowledged the lieutenant and said, "I take it we have news from Lord Howe? Dispatches?"

"Indeed, sir," said Hammond. Meanwhile, Proctor proffered a leather case.

Dunmore signaled to Fellows, who rose, walked over to the lieutenant, and accepted the dispatches.

Harbridge cleared his throat. "Lieutenant, are you aware of what is in the dispatches? Perhaps there is news of Lord Howe sending the reinforcements we requested?"

Proctor looked at Hammond. For his part, the captain took a deep breath and said, "I regret to say the dispatches contain rather distressing news."

The governor cocked his head. "Distressing news? Pray tell, please explain."

Hammond looked over at the lieutenant and motioned for him to speak.

Proctor took a deep breath and said, "Sir, it is my sad duty to report that Boston has fallen to the rebels. When I departed, Howe was in the process of evacuating the city. He and all his forces were preparing to sail to Halifax."

A look of shock swept over Dunmore's face.

Harbridge partially rose from his seat. "Good God! Can such things be?"

Proctor shrugged. "I'm afraid so. General Howe intends to land in Halifax, reorganize and resupply his force, and await the strong reinforcements even now enroute from England. Unofficially, it is expected that he will eventually descend on New York City."

Fellows said, "I find it hard to understand how our forces could have been driven from Boston. With the rebel army surrounding the city, did it become too hard to provide provisions to our men?"

Proctor shook his head. "No, that wasn't the problem. We were able to keep them adequately supplied by sea." He paused and looked around the table. "The truth is, the colonists brought heavy guns to the city and emplaced them on a high ridge overlooking Boston. A hill called Dorchester Heights."

Harbridge asked, "That is hard to imagine. Where would they get such guns?"

The lieutenant sighed. "They brought them from the fortress Ticonderoga, on the New York lakes."

A startled look came over Dunmore's face. "My God, I visited Ticonderoga when I was governor of New York. That's hundreds of miles from Boston. Many days of travel, in good weather. How the devil could the colonists have transported heavy guns through winter weather, over numerous streams and rivers, to Massachusetts? I hardly find that credible."

The lieutenant responded, "My lord, they used the weather conditions to their favor. Spies told us that they put the ordnance on sledges and pulled them with teams of oxen through the snow and over the ice of rivers." He pursed his lips a moment as he sought to recall something, then continued, "The effort was led by a man named Knox. If you could believe it, before the insurrection he was the proprietor of a bookstore."

Dunmore looked puzzled. "We are stymied militarily by a *bookseller*?"

Fellows asked, "Couldn't the army have stopped them from emplacing the guns? Surely a rapid advance of our troops could have disrupted their activity."

Proctor shook his head. "The truth is, the rebels took us by surprise. With incredible speed, they constructed the gun emplacements in one night. We were faced with a fait accompli." He shrugged. "And the guns were supported by strong lines of infantry, in trenches also dug overnight. Although some of the senior officers wanted to attack the position and drive the colonials from the hill, General Howe considered success quite problematic and feared another bloodbath on the order of Bunker Hill. Instead, he elected to negotiate a withdrawal."

Hammond shook his head. "The upshot of all this is that we have very little presence in the thirteen colonies which are in revolt. A few forts along the shores of the great lakes." The captain thought a moment, then said "And of course, we hold naval superiority. Our blockade of the coast is becoming more effective every day, and additional ships are on the way from England."

Dunmore stood up, throwing his napkin onto the table. He clasped his hands behind his back and began pacing back and forth across the rear of the cabin. Then he turned to the naval officer. "You are wrong, Andrew! Wrong in one important aspect: we hold a critical position here in Virginia!"

Hammond pursed his lips and then sighed. "Critical, indeed, Your Lordship. But I must say, *tenuous.* We have but two small footholds on the land, and our adversaries are clearly preparing to challenge us in both places."

"You are being too pessimistic, Hammond. Colonel Northcutt assures me he can hold his position! And he has never let me down or misstated his situation."

Hammond took a deep breath but said nothing.

Dunmore resumed pacing for a long interval. Then he stopped and raised a finger. "The fact is, now is the time for us to reassert ourselves here in Virginia. We must prepare to put the insurrectionists off balance, take steps to increase our forces, and look to reclaim more land."

Not sure what Dunmore intended, Hammond said noncommittally, "A noble goal, Your Lordship."

Dunmore paced some more, then turned to back to the table. "Harbridge, we must call a council of war. We must assemble all our commanders, assess our position, and then make a plan to take the offensive."

Harbridge nodded slowly. "Yes, Your Lordship, I understand. I shall prepare summonses for all of them."

"Exactly, Harbridge. We must meet as soon as possible." Dunmore turned to Hammond. "And my respects to you, Captain. Please take action to arrange water transport to get Northcutt and the commanders of the Queens Loyal Virginians and the Ethiopian Regiment here."

Hammond nodded. "Of course, my lord. As soon as Mr. Harbridge has prepared his dispatches to them."

"Excellent, Hammond. And thank you for your prompt delivery of the dispatches brought by Lieutenant Proctor."

Taking that for dismissal, Hammond made a slight bow and motioned toward Proctor. "With your permission, we shall withdraw to our ships and wait for your instructions."

McCabe excused himself from the table, saying that he would escort the naval officers to their boat. The two other offices, Coble and Slidell, also took leave in order to pursue their duties.

Once the others had left, Dunmore sat down at the table and took a deep drink from his wine glass. Then he looked at his two aides with a glint in his eyes. "Gentlemen, with the withdrawal of Howe from Boston, we have a rare opportunity. Virginia can take the stage as the main theater of action against this rebellion! But time is of the essence. We must marshal our forces and strike a telling blow at these impudent colonists."

Harbridge and Fellows exchanged glances. Then Harbridge asked, "Does Your Lordship have some idea of what form this offensive could take?"

Dunmore bit his lip. "Only in general. I need to talk with Northcutt. He is always thinking ahead, and his plans have most often born useful fruit." He thought a moment, then said, "Get a dispatch out to him today, explaining our estimate of the situation, and summoning him here as soon as practicable."

Harbridge nodded "Your Lordship, it will be done immediately."

—⟋⟋⟋—

It took a few days to get all the key commanders together, such that it was a week later when the *Dunmore*'s great cabin was actually the scene of a council of war. Dunmore stood looking out the windows that spread across the rear of the cabin, cigar in hand, contemplating the scene on the Elizabeth River and waiting for the attendees to enter the space and take their places. Harbridge sat at the table, looking through some papers and notes.

The cabin door swung open, and Fellows entered. "Your Lordship, all the attendees have arrived."

Dunmore turned and nodded to his secretary. "Then by all means, have them come in."

The governor's chair was placed at the head of the table. He would be flanked on the right by Captain Hammond, with Harbridge on his left. Lieutenant Colonel Barrett Penfold Northcutt was placed next to Hammond, while Lieutenant Colonel Ellegood, commandant of the Queen's Loyal Virginians, would be seated beside Harbridge. The officer in charge of the detachment of the 14th Foot, Captain Samuel Leslie, was adjacent to Northcutt. Opposite Northcutt was Major Thomas Byrd of the Ethiopians. Finally Captain Johnston Sidwell, senior officer of all the marines in the squadron, had taken a place across from Leslie. Two other men were in the room. The secretary, Fellows, sat at a small writing table, recording the proceedings. The other was the second in command of the King's Loyal Virginia Legion, Major Reginald Welford, whom Northcutt had brought along. The major walked over to the settee that ran along the windows at the rear of the cabin and settled there.

Dunmore walked to the head of the table and motioned for his subordinates to take their seats. Seating himself, he looked around the table and said, "Welcome, gentlemen. I've been looking forward to this meeting ever since word was received of the evacuation of Boston."

He motioned to Howser, who brought out a humidor, and offered cigars to the men, then lit a taper and assisted those who had chosen to smoke in igniting their tobacco.

Then the governor continued, "As preface to our discussion, I'd like to make the point that Howe's departure for Halifax leaves us as the only major force directly confronting the rebels."

There were nods around the table. The governor continued, "So I would say that there is a burden on us to redouble our efforts to keep Virginia in the hands of its rightful government. Today we must assess our position and find the most advantageous strategy for that goal. I'll ask each of you for your ideas."

There were universal nods around the table.

Dunmore motioned to Hammond. "Captain, as the senior officer present, please give us your assessment of the situation."

Hammond stared down at the cigar in his hand momentarily, then looked around the table and finally at the governor. "Right now our forces are dispersed widely. We are here in the Elizabeth River, with some troops ashore close by in a stockade at Tucker's Point.

Northcutt's regiment, along with Ellegood and a detachment of the Ethiopians, is on the peninsula, and Leslie and his 14th, along with the field detachment of marines, under Sidwell, and another portion of the Ethiopians, is down at Lynnhaven Inlet to the east of Norfolk." He paused and cleared his throat. "I believe each of these forces is under serious threat."

Dunmore exhaled smoke from his cigar. "How so, my dear Hammond? In particular, are you saying that we here at the anchorage are at risk?"

"Yes, my lord. I am in contact with several loyal men ashore who act as informers. Over the last few days, they have all reported that the rebels are discussing a plan to attack with fireships. They may be gathering vessels for the purpose around the bend at the small shipyard in Gosport. If it materializes, we have little capability to counter such an attack." He sighed. "Think of the terror such an assault would spread among the civilians we have aboard all these ships, not to mention all the actual casualties which could result."

Dunmore, cigar in hand, motioned toward the naval officer. "So, Andrew, what is your recommendation?"

"Let me precede that with a more general discussion. It is becoming increasingly difficult to keep all the ships and our land positions provisioned. Fewer and fewer farmers are willing to bring supplies to the receiving station at Tucker's Point, particularly as rebel armed presence increases." He paused, then said, "And of course, you are aware of the losses we are taking from the smallpox. Every night, virtually every ship is depositing bodies into the river. You get the reports."

The governor nodded. "Yes, the reports are dreadful." He thought a moment and turned to Captain Leslie, the senior officer of the 14th Foot. "How is your position? Do you concur with Hammond that you are in jeopardy?"

Leslie quickly glanced at the naval captain, then said, "Your Lordship, at the moment things are quiet, but the rebels are gathering their forces. Troops of a Virginia regiment are in the area, and militia units are drilling in preparation to assist them. I would agree with a decision to move to a more secure location and the concentration of our military assets."

Sidwell of the marines spoke up. "We have a little more than two hundred regular troops between the Fourteenth and my marines. There are perhaps one hundred Ethiopians with us. Sooner or later the rebels will be able to overwhelm us. I would say a move to evacuate our position would be quite discrete."

Hammond resumed speaking. "Based on all that, my recommendation is that we find a place where we can concentrate our forces and move both our military assets and our civilian supporters into camps ashore." Hammond looked around the table. "That would allow us respite to train the loyalist forces, particularly the Ethiopian Regiment. It is split up, with detachments with Northcutt and Leslie, while the remainder are on ships here in the river, where they can get no realistic drilling. Moreover, we could isolate and treat our smallpox victims in a hospital and build up our stocks of provisions."

Dunmore pulled on his cigar, considering what the naval commander had said. There was an extended silence while he thought. Finally he turned to Northcutt. "Well, Colonel, what is your view?"

Northcutt shrugged. "Our position is secure at the present. There are rebel patrols, but no concentration of force." He paused to gather his thoughts. "We are able to move out of our defense lines to scour the countryside for provisions and recruit for all our units." He turned to Ellegood and asked, "Do you agree with that assessment?"

Ellegood hesitated a moment, then looked at Hammond and the governor. Finally he spoke. "I would second what Northcutt has said. We are comfortable in our position."

Northcutt motioned toward the naval captain. "I understand the rationale behind Captain Hammond's desire to consolidate our force and the danger to the fleet here in the Elizabeth, but I fear that a withdrawal of our land forces from their positions would be a sign of weakness and encourage the insurrectionists." He waited a moment, then looked at Leslie of the 14th and continued, "Particularly after the setback in the action at Great Bridge in December, which forced the evacuation of Norfolk and led to our current situation."

Leslie, who had commanded at the battle, bristled, his face turning red. He looked at Dunmore and quickly said, "We were greatly outnumbered at Great Bridge. It is on the record that our troops fought heroically. We withdrew in good order, which was all that could have been expected."

Northcutt had been taking a draw on his cigar and quickly expelled the smoke. "My dear Leslie, let me assure you I meant no disparagement of the performance of either you or our troops at the battle. I was simply stating the regrettable truth that the outcome encouraged the rebels." He raised a finger and looked at the governor. "Given that setback, I think that we should be discussing a way to take the offensive so as to curb the confidence of our opponents."

Hammond stiffened in his chair. Then he said, with heat in his voice, "Northcutt, I am in full support of offensive action at the earliest moment. But I strongly maintain that that cannot occur until we consolidate our forces and are ready to operate from a secure base, adequately supplied. Attempting to take the offensive now, from our dispersed positions, would only lay us open to defeat in detail." He shook his head. "I reiterate, we must withdraw the fleet from the Elizabeth, find a good defensive position, and bring all our forces together before we can conceive and undertake a strike at the enemy."

Dunmore held up his hand to calm matters. "Gentlemen, gentlemen!" He paused and looked in turn at Hammond and Northcutt. "We are here to calmly discuss matters; there is no need for raised voices."

Hammond cleared his throat. "There is one other thing to consider. Our eventual plan for offensive campaigning is predicated on the actions of Colonel Connolly, who we all know has traveled to the Ohio Country to raise the tribes there in support of the king. He will advance with a mixed force of warriors and army detachments from the outposts along the lakes. We need a consolidated force to carry out our role in the overall plan."

The governor nodded. "That is quite true, Captain." Then a concerned look came over his face. "We have heard nothing of Connolly's progress. I had expected some word by way of courier before this." He stood up and walked over to the gallery of windows across the ship's stern, for a long moment looking out at the fleet around them. He took a long pull on his cigar, then carefully exhaled the smoke, which wafted up toward the cabins overhead.

Finally he turned and faced the men at the table. "Gentlemen, we've had a valuable discussion. You have provided me with a significant amount of information and given me your frank opinions on how we should proceed in the immediate future. I intend to take some time to consider what you have said and form my own thoughts." He pointed in the general direction of Hammond with his cigar. "Captain, do you have any suggestions on where we might concentrate our forces if we decide to implement your plan?"

Hammond nodded. "No precise idea as of yet. It should be either an island near the shore or a peninsula which could be easily defended yet provide us access to the interior when we are ready to move against the rebels. There are numerous spots along the coast of the Chesapeake which would be suitable. I would like to send an expedition, consisting of my smallest vessel, the fourteen-gun *Otter*, along with a small, shallow draft tender, to survey the coast to the north of here. That will take some time, and then I shall be able to offer you some precise locations from which to choose."

The governor thought a moment, then said, "Make preparations for such a survey expedition, and I shall give you my decision very shortly."

"Yes, my lord, we shall make ready."

"Excellent, Hammond. Now we shall adjourn while I consider all that has transpired and take a decision. We shall reconvene in due course."

—◆—

An hour after the council of war had ended, Dunmore sat in another meeting. This one was more informal and intimate, consisting of his immediate staff—Harbridge and Fellows—plus Northcutt and Welford.

The stewards had poured rum all around, and the smoke from cigars wafted throughout the cabin.

The governor leaned back in his chair and looked around at his companions. "Well, gentlemen, it was obvious that our compatriots from His Majesty's navy and army came prepared to speak as one."

Northcutt looked down at the cigar in his hand. "Yes, Your Lordship, I would wager Hammond had a meeting of all of them aboard his ship to work out the idea of consolidating the forces in one location. It was all too pat to reflect anything else." He took a drag on his cigar and then continued, "That's why I made sure to say that we felt secure in our position on the peninsula. I want to preserve room to maneuver, and I damn well wasn't going to let Hammond think he was running the show."

Dunmore smiled broadly. "I rather thought that was what you were up to, Barrett. And I totally agree. Hammond wants to dominate the naval and military picture, and I have no intention of letting him do so." Then he asked, "So in truth, what is your actual situation?"

"We're secure—for the moment. However, we have loyalist spies who tell us that the rebel government in Williamsburg intends to move against us when they have fully organized and trained units. We are prepared to resist, and I think we could successfully hold out for a significant period. However, in fact we have cleared the surrounding country of provisions, and most of the blacks who are disposed to join us have come to camp." He shrugged. "There is little to gain by remaining where we are, and if attacked, we will obviously suffer losses which I would not like to sustain. So, in reality, I have no objection to relocating to another position to consolidate our strength at the appropriate time."

The governor nodded. "Yes, I can't deny it will be expedient to leave in due course. I'll shortly authorize Hammond to send out his expedition to find such a place." He thought a moment. "Meanwhile, I do wish we would get some word from Connolly or from Howe that our plan for the Indian insurrection in the Ohio Country is moving forward."

Northcutt and Welford looked at each other. Northcutt took a deep breath. "I am afraid we do have some news about Connolly."

Dunmore's face brightened momentarily, but then a cloud came over his countenance. "You say you're afraid? Pray tell, what does that mean?"

It was Welford who spoke up. "I regret to say that we have a report that Colonel Connolly has been captured by the rebels."

The governor sat in stunned silence. Then he said slowly, "A report? One single report? How reliable is that information—can it be verified, or is this just some rumor?"

Welford replied, "I'm afraid, my lord, it is from a spy who has direct knowledge."

Northcutt quickly said, "Governor, we just received the information from the spy himself, who has recently arrived at our camp. In fact, we brought him along to give you the report personally."

"He's here aboard ship? Well, summon him immediately!"

Welford went to get the man in question. A silence, as heavy as the cloud of cigar smoke, hung over the cabin as the remaining men waited.

In short order the major returned with another man. He was sharp-faced, black-haired, and of medium height, with a wiry build. His clothing was that of a tradesman.

Welford motioned toward the newcomer. "My lord, this is Mr. Jonathan Rhys, of Fredericksburg. He's an ironmonger by trade and a loyal subject of the rightful government of Virginia."

Rhys, who appeared very nervous, bowed his head briefly. "Very proud to meet Your Lordship, sir. Very proud indeed." He looked around the great cabin and then added, "Never thought I'd be talkin' to the governor himself."

"Well, Mr. Rhys, here you are, and it's a pleasure to meet someone of great loyalty who understands his duty. Now I am told you have some information to relate to us."

Welford quickly said, "Rhys, tell him what you know about Colonel Connolly and how you found out about what happened to him."

"Aye, sir, that I will." Rhys wrinkled up his face and said, "To start, my place is just outside the town of Fredericksburg. But I peddle my goods out of my wagon, traveling all over the country 'round there and northward into Culpeper County and Frederick County. I often get all the way up to Winchester itself." He paused to gather his thoughts. "And that's where I heard about what happened to Colonel Connolly. It was in a tavern at Winchester, a place called the Golden Buck."

The governor and Northcutt exchanged glances. "Yes, Mr. Rhys, we're all quite familiar with that establishment."

"Well, I was in there on court day last month, havin' a little libation, as it were. I was standin' at the counter, and right next to me was a table with five or six men. They was all listening to a fellow called Baird, who was talkin' about the takin' of Connolly."

Northcutt asked sharply, "Joshua Baird?"

Rhys nodded. "Why, yes, that was his name. He's a tall, rail-thin man with a thatch of brown hair and a stubble beard."

The governor nodded. "Yes, Rhys, we know Baird. He was a scout for us during the Indian war in Ohio last year."

"Well, sir, like I said, he was tellin' the story of how a group of men from the 1st Virginia Regiment and some Maryland cavalry hunted down and caught Connolly. They had been sent by Patrick Henry, who was the colonel of the regiment at that time. Baird said they took Connolly and most of the men with him at a creek called the Conococheague, just west of a place in Maryland named Elizabethtown. It was late November, in the middle of a snowstorm, the way Baird put it."

Dunmore turned to Northcutt. "Now, Barrett, how the devil did Henry find out about Connolly's plan?"

Northcutt sighed. "It appears the rebels obtained that dispatch which I sent you in late October and which went missing. The one which mentioned that Connolly was about ready to leave, sir. Rhys says that it fell into the rebels' hands in Williamsburg and was forwarded to Henry, who was organizing a regiment at Culpeper."

The governor looked puzzled. "How did Baird know about all this? Was he repeating a story he had heard?"

"Oh no, sir, Governor," Rhys replied. "He was there at the takin' of Connolly."

Dunmore looked puzzled. "You said it was men from Patrick's regiment. But Baird is too old for that service, and besides, he's got a game leg."

Rhys shrugged. "He was there because he had come down from Winchester to Culpeper, where the 1st Virginia was, with a gunsmith called Eckert who was delivering muskets to the regiment. And Henry sent Eckert along with his own men because he knew John Connolly and none of the soldiers did."

Dunmore's face turned red, and he looked at Northcutt. "Eckert? The German gunsmith? The one who was a lieutenant on my staff last year?"

Barrett Northcutt sighed and said in a resigned tone, "Indeed, sir. The man is like a bad penny."

There was a prolonged silence, the governor's face set. Finally he waved at Rhys. "Continue your story, sir."

"Well, it turns out this Eckert fellow was the real spirit behind the hunt for Connolly and his men. Pushing the soldiers until they caught the colonel and his men at that ford on the Conococheague. It was right in the middle of a snowstorm. They captured most of the men, but three got away. They were men who had come east from the Ohio Country to help Connolly."

Welford interjected, "It was Munger and his men, Lord Dunmore, who had joined Connolly in Fredericktown. They escaped while Connolly was negotiating surrender."

Rhys nodded. "Yes, sir, that's the truth. Anyway, the rebels took the captured men back to hold in a tavern in Elizabethtown. But the next night, Munger and the other two men came back and tried to rescue Connolly and the others. They failed, but Colonel Connolly was able to give them dispatches explaining the plan and containing the names of loyal men in Pittsburgh and the Ohio Country who were ready to help with raising the tribes."

Dunmore's face brightened. "So even with John Connolly in captivity, there's still a chance something will come of our plan? John always told me Munger was very capable."

Northcutt took a deep breath. "Regrettably, my lord, that is not the case." He motioned to Rhys. "Continue, sir."

Rhys looked around the room. "Aye, sir. Well, after Munger got the dispatches, he and his men headed for Pittsburgh along the Braddock Road. Eckert and the First Virginia men pursued." He shook his head. "There was a long chase, but the rebels caught up with Munger at a place called Dunbar's Camp. Had something to do with General Braddock's old army."

The governor said impatiently, "Yes, yes, Rhys. We all know that place. Continue—what happened at Dunbar's Camp?"

"There was a gunfight, sir. And Munger and all his men were killed. All except one, a very young lad who Eckert let go back to his farm."

Welford said, "And Eckert captured Connolly's dispatches. They laid out the entire plan and listed the names of our allies at Pittsburgh and in the Ohio Country. He sent all the correspondence to Williamsburg, so the rebels have the information. We must assume that they will take the loyalists into custody."

"Good God!" The muscles of Dunmore's face tightened, and his eyes showed raw anger. He was silent for a long moment, then looked at Rhys. "Well, sir, we thank you for your loyalty and your information."

Northcutt raised a finger. "My lord, there's additional news." He motioned toward Rhys. "Tell him what else you learned about Eckert."

"Ah, yes sir." The ironmonger thought a second. "Eckert is making muskets for the rebels, sir. He's expanded his shop and put on more apprentices and is turnin' out muskets on the king's short land pattern at a rapid rate. In Winchester they call his place the Musket Plantation." Rhys put his hand to his chin. "And there's somethin' else I heard. Last year, Winchester sent a company of riflemen to Washington's army, under a captain called Morgan. Daniel Morgan. He be a wagoner. But Morgan and a goodly number of the men were captured in the attempt to take Quebec, and more were killed. So the town is planning to recruit a new company for the rebel army." He paused and looked around the cabin. "And the rumor is the Committee of Safety wants to make Eckert its captain." He shrugged. "But I heard Baird say Eckert is resisting the idea. Takes the position he can better serve Virginia by turning out muskets." He raised both hands with the palms upward. "That's all I heard, Your Lordship."

Dunmore nodded. "That is indeed interesting, Rhys."

The ironmonger said, "Thank, you, Your Lordship. I just want to be of help to yourself and the cause of the Crown."

"Indeed you have. And once again, we thank you." The governor waved his hand in dismissal.

Welford showed Rhys out.

The governor took a deep pull on his cigar, then blew his smoke upward. Then he exploded in anger. "Damn that man Eckert! After all that we have done for him! We enriched him with a lucrative contract to overhaul hundreds of muskets from the armory in Williamsburg, we gave him a lieutenant's commission in the militia, we made him an aide de camp on my staff for the war in Ohio last year, and we gave him a land grant in Ohio!"

Northcutt added, "Not to mention offering him a captaincy in my regiment and an even bigger land grant to raise a company for our service."

"Yes, Northcutt, and this is how he pays us back! By turning on us and throwing in his lot with the rebels." He thought a moment. "And it seems indisputable that last year he killed our good friend Richard Grenough over some grudge from years ago."

Northcutt took a sip of his rum. "All quite correct, my lord. I'm not sure of the details, but for some reason, he held Grenough responsible for the death of his parents and siblings. Be that as it may, I would propose that it is time that we deal Mr. Wendelmar Eckert a good measure of retribution. Violent retribution."

The governor stared at Northcutt for a long moment, a puzzled expression on his countenance. Finally he said, "Barrett, I would find that very satisfying, satisfying indeed. But just how do you propose we would we do that, given our physical location and the current military situation?"

Northcutt motioned toward Welford. "Reginald and I have worked out a plan. Daring in its concept, but we believe it has a very good chance of success."

Dunmore took a deep drink from his cup, then said, "Come on, Northcutt, we are here in the Tidewater. Eckert's place is just east of Winchester, in the Valley. I would say near two hundred miles from here and on the far side of the Blue Ridge. I find it hard to understand how you would reach out and attack Eckert. But out of curiosity, I am quite ready to listen to your idea."

Northcutt smiled and turned to Welford. "Lay out the plan, Reginald."

Welford rose from his seat and unrolled a large square piece of parchment on the table. On it was a crude map of the territory between the Tidewater and Winchester. He said, "I've drawn this up over the last few days." Welford looked around the cabin at the other men. "This scheme started out as a plan to attack a rather large weapons manufactory just outside Fredericksburg. Rhys had told us about it in an earlier visit to our camp, and Barrett and I thought it would make an inviting target for an offensive raid. However, when Rhys came back a few days ago, he told us that the rebels have established the camp of a newly formed regiment right alongside the musket establishment, thus making our planned attack far too dangerous."

Dunmore nodded. "Most certainly."

Welford continued. "But of course, Rhys also brought us the news of Eckert's capture of Connolly, and so it occurred to us to contemplate an attack on Eckert's musket plantation instead."

Northcutt spoke up. "My lord, doing so would serve two purposes. First, we would destroy a source of arms which are flowing to the regiments which the rebels are raising. This would be a significant accomplishment because they are particularly short of muskets and bayonets for their foot battalions. And second, it would demonstrate that even in our current situation, we still have the power to strike the rebels effectively."

Dunmore's face lit up. "By God, it damn well might offset the loss at Great Bridge and inspire some men with loyal sympathies to come forward and join us." ·

Northcutt smiled. "Precisely, sir. A successful blow would undoubtedly help recruiting." He waved to Welford. "Continue, Reggie."

The major said, "My lord, we have received messages through Rhys that there is significant loyalist sympathy on plantations around Fredericksburg. A planter called Dalton Crosswell, whose estate is on the Rappahannock River, has in fact secretly organized a group of men who are ready to act on behalf of the king, only waiting for the proper project and the right moment."

Dunmore perked up. "Why, I know Crosswell. I met him in Williamsburg after I first arrived from New York in '72." He turned to Harbridge. "And hasn't he been in the Burgesses?"

Harbridge responded, "Indeed, sir. As a matter of fact, he maintains a residence in the capital and has been in attendance at several balls at the palace. He was widowed a few years back and remarried to a much younger and quite attractive lady. His holdings include several other farms beside the place on the James."

The governor thought all that over for a moment, then nodded to Welford. "So how does Crosswell figure in your plans?"

"His plantation, just south of Fredericksburg, would be the base from which we could move against Eckert." Welford pointed to the map. "Myself and four of the men from the legion, good horsemen all, would travel by small boat up the Rappahannock to Crosswell's estate, where he would provide us with mounts."

Harbridge said sharply, "You're going to attack with only five men?"

Welford laughed. "No, that's just the core of our force. Crosswell and his son, Lindsey, are recruiting a group of other loyalists to ride with us. I expect to have a total of between fifteen and twenty men for the raid. A troop that size should be perfectly adequate for the service."

Harbridge screwed up his face. "So presumably you're going to ride from the Crosswell plantation up to Eckert's place. Won't a body of twenty men look suspicious?"

Welford shook his head. "We'll ride in small groups of two or three men each, taking different routes northward. Then we'll assemble in the rural area at Ashby's Ferry on the Shenandoah, a few miles south of Eckert's place. Rhys in his wagon will go ahead and scout Eckert's farm, getting the layout and ascertaining their routine. He'll meet us at the ferry, and we'll make final plans for the attack with him then. Afterward our men will retreat to their homes singly or in small groups."

"Thank you." Northcutt turned to the governor. "My lord, that's the plan. I believe it is entirely feasible and if put into action, would provide us with a way of achieving a credible demonstration of our ability to strike back against the rebels, even over a considerable distance."

Dunmore's fingers played on the table as he considered the proposal. After nearly a minute, he said, "It does appear to have a fair chance of success." Then he looked over to Welford. "How long would it take you to get started?"

"Rhys could leave within a day of your approval. It will take him near ten days to get to Eckert's farm. We would leave five or six days after his departure."

The governor nodded. "I shall give your proposal my immediate consideration." He motioned to Northcutt. "You and Welford and Rhys remain onboard tonight, and I shall give you my answer tomorrow."

Dunmore and Harbridge stood together at the ship's taffrail, enjoying after-dinner cigars. It was a moonlit night, and the lights of the anchored ships reflected against the waters of the Elizabeth River. They were discussing the content of the two meetings earlier in the day.

The governor said, in a contemplative tone, "Aubrey, I rather like Welford's plan to hit the Eckert place. If successful, it would bolster the spirits of our forces and followers." He took a puff on his cigar. "Not to mention, punishing Eckert would give me a large measure of satisfaction."

Harbridge thought a moment and then replied, "Actually, my lord, it has occurred to me that Welford's proposed raid and Hammond's plan to relocate to a land base could be made to complement each other."

"Complement each other? How so?"

"My lord, ultimately, we must accede to Hammond. There's no question that we need to move ashore to facilitate the health of our people and to conduct military operations."

"Yes, yes, Aubrey. I agree."

"Well, sir, if we simply leave our anchorage here and move to a new location, our people might see it as a retreat and the concession of a victory, at least a symbolic one, to the rebels. The dissident government in Williamsburg would certainly play it that way. Newspapers would proclaim that we were driven from a position where we can affect affairs in Norfolk. But if we can show some success, even if relatively minor, our departure to a new base could then credibly be portrayed as part of a larger plan to begin an offensive campaign."

Dunmore took a long pull on his cigar, then exhaled the smoke in a stream, which dissipated in the night air. He turned to Harbridge. "By God, sir, that makes sense. And in any case, we need some success after this long winter of stalemate." He paused a minute, then said in a determined voice, "Have Fellows draft an order to Northcutt authorizing the raid on Eckert and another to Hammond approving his expedition to locate a land base of operations."

Harbridge replied, "Consider it done, my lord."

The governor stared into the darkness with a look of determination on his face. "Damn, Aubrey, we stumbled at Great Bridge. But now it's time for us to take back the initiative. I am quite optimistic that these two actions constitute the beginning of the road back to our control of Virginia."

Harbridge nodded. "Indeed, sir. Taken together, they will give us some momentum."

Chapter Two

ECKERT RIDGE

Wend Eckert, dressed for town in his black coat, gray breaches, knee-length boots, and dark gray hat, rode a tall stallion into Winchester from the Battletown Road. The master gunsmith and owner of the farm that local people called Eckert Ridge turned onto Market Street with the horse at the trot and guided the animal down the street to the Golden Buck Inn, where he entered the establishment's yard and dismounted. A stable boy came out to take the mount.

"Nice looking black, Mr. Eckert. Powerful legs."

Wend smiled. "He comes out of an extraordinary mare of the same color, sired by an excellent hunter." He handed the reins to the attendant. "The mare carried me through many long journeys and several fights. He's young, and I've just started riding him, but I expect he'll live up to his mother."

The boy grinned approvingly. "I should say so, sir." He asked, "What do you call him?"

"So far, just Sonny. Not very formal, but accurate."

"Sonny it is, sir. Will he be here long?"

"Just a couple of hours. I'll be riding back to my place later today. Water him, and give him a handful of oats."

"Aye, sir."

Wend handed the boy a coin and then walked to the inn's front door and entered the common room. Inside, the proprietor, Bush, was standing next to the bar, looking around at his clientele. Eckert joined him. "Hello, Phillip. I'm supposed to meet with the Committee of Safety. Have they convened yet?"

"Indeed, Wend, they've been at it for nearly an hour. They're in the big room at the end of the hall."

Eckert nodded. "Well, before I face the esteemed gentlemen of the committee, I need some refreshment." He waved to one of the barmen. "Do you have any of Donegal's whiskey available?"

The barman nodded. "Sure enough, Mr. Eckert. Have it to you in a minute."

Wend took out a coin to pay with. He said to Bush, "A little fortification for what lays ahead."

Bush laughed. "I would say that's a prudent measure. But pretty ironic, having to pay for spirits distilled on your own farm."

Wend shot him a glance and crooked grin. "Well, you could let me have it for free, seeing how this stuff makes you a lot of money."

Bush laughed and shook his head. "My friend, that will be the day!" Still grinning, he left the counter and headed toward the cook room.

Eckert quickly downed the whiskey, then motioned to the barkeep to refill it. "I'll need some to take with me into the meeting."

When the cup had been refilled, he took it in his left hand and strode through the common room toward the hall, waving to several acquaintances as he walked.

A loud voice with a Highland accent called out from one table. "Ach na, Eckert, when you come out of the meeting, sure and we'll be calling you *captain*, I'm thinkin'."

Wend looked at the table to see Angus McDonald's retainer, Even McLeod, who had fought with Angus at Culloden over thirty years ago and now helped run his plantation. He was seated with several other men, who all had grins on their faces. "Don't even say that, Even! I'm a gunsmith, not a soldier."

There was laughter from several tables, and McLeod shot back, "Seems I remember you leading a brisk little fight or two during Dunmore's War last year. Na I'm sayin' the committee will give you the company!"

"And I'll damn well give it right back to them!" Wend said as he entered the hall that led to the meeting rooms at the rear of the inn. There was more laughter behind him. Presently he reached the door to the last room, which was also the largest. He could hear voices within. Dreading what was about to transpire, he pushed open the door and stepped into the room.

James Wood, who represented Winchester and Frederick County at the legislature in Williamsburg and was the chairman, sat at the head of the table, leaning back in his chair. The committee included Angus McDonald, major of the county militia, whose plantation, Glengarry, was not far from Wend's farm, Reverend Thruston, Smith the sheriff, and Rutledge, who had been the county lieutenant under the royal administration. Four other prominent men rounded out the assemblage. Wend noticed that every man had a cup at hand and most held a pipe or cigar. A cloud of acrid tobacco smoke hovered above the table.

"Ah, Wend, glad to see you." Wood motioned to a chair at the opposite end of the table. "Take a seat and join us."

Moving deliberately, Wend took his place at the bottom of the table. Conversation had stopped, and the nine men were staring at him as he seated himself. Wend thought, *Sure feels like we're about to have an inquisition.*

Wend took the initiative and broke the silence. "Well, gentlemen, you summoned me here, *ostensibly* to relate my progress in manufacturing muskets for Virginia's forces. Shall I proceed with that report?"

Wood nodded. "Yes, please do so."

"Well, you know that we had been restoring old muskets from the stocks in the armory at Williamsburg, under a contract from the royal government. When the insurrection began, we had a hundred of those in hand on which work was in progress. We finished those up and delivered them to the First Virginia Regiment. Obviously our former governor, Lord Dunmore, was less than pleased."

The men around the table nodded and smiled; one or two laughed outright. Wood commented, "I daresay you're right about that." Wend continued, "We then began producing new muskets on the same model, specifically the King's Arm Short Land Pattern."

Reverend Thruston nodded. "Yes, yes, Eckert. We all remember that."

"All right, gentlemen, although we had never produced new muskets before and we were feeling our way to some degree, we were able to make a lot of twenty-five during the three-month period from October to December of last year." He paused and gathered his thoughts. "We learned much doing that and were able to figure ways to speed production." He shrugged. "Now, in the three months since then, we've been able to assemble close to fifty firelocks and should be able to ship that number next month. To further speed things up, I've taken on new apprentices and hired other workers. Right now we're building an addition to the shop. It will double the size of our workspace. Finally, we built a small forge, and I have begun casting my own parts for making locks, so we have to depend less on the forge down at Fredericksburg and Zane's place out to the west of town." Wend looked up and down the table. "Taken together, all these enhancements will soon give us the ability to produce both a greater number of muskets and do so with more dispatch."

Wood said, "A very complete report. I might say that I have talked with Colonel Daingerfield, the commander of the 7th Virginia Regiment, which is only partially formed and was the recipient of that first lot of twenty-five firelocks. He was most satisfied with the quality of the arms. I might add, he hopes you can provide more for his battalion as a number of his men are completely unarmed."

Wend shrugged. "As I said, we are working as fast as possible."

Angus McDonald raised a hand. "A question, Wend. Is there any problem which would slow your ability to deliver muskets as early as possible? In other words, anything which the committee could help you with?"

Wend waved a hand. "The potential holdup is bayonets and cartridge boxes. Zane's makes the bayonets and Handel's Leather Shop makes the boxes. If they fall behind, it will delay my shipment, as we must send out complete stands of arms. So they must be encouraged to keep pace with my production."

Rutledge took his pipe out of his mouth. "We'll keep after them, Eckert. Virginia needs muskets as fast as possible."

Wend nodded. "I appreciate that." Wend raised his hands, palm up, to indicate he was finished. Then he took a sip of his whiskey. As he did so, he thought, *And now we'll get to the real business of this meeting.*

Silence spread around the room, members of the committee looking toward Wood. Momentarily, the chairman cleared his throat, took a sip of his libation, and then said, "Wend, we have something else to discuss with you."

Wend put his cup to his lips, sighed, and then said, "I feared you might."

Wood ignored his comment and continued, "Since learning of the decimation of Dan Morgan's rifle company at Quebec, we have been determined to send a replacement to Washington's army."

"I've heard that mentioned."

"Yes, I expected you were aware of that," Wood said. "Well, we have now received authorization from the government in Williamsburg to recruit such a company." He held up a sheet of parchment.

Wend shrugged and said blandly and with as much lack of interest in his voice as he could manage, "I would anticipate you'll have no trouble finding volunteers. There's much sentiment to avenge the loss of Morgan and his men."

Reverend Thruston cleared his throat. "Finding volunteers would be facilitated by having the right captain. Someone with recognized experience and the admiration of the type of men who we would like to recruit."

Angus McDonald raised a finger. "Wend, we are worried that recruiting might not be as easy as you believe. Morgan took the very best of the riflemen in the county. And we are aware that a good many likely men have joined companies from other counties. There may be some difficulty in raising the full one hundred men specified for the company."

Rutledge added, "The best way to ensure that we can recruit the full number is to appoint a man who the men know has experience and whom they admire and want to serve under."

Wend said laconically, "Well, there are plenty such men here in Frederick County. I should say you won't have trouble choosing a captain and the other officers."

There was silence in the room. Several members of the committee exchanged glances. Finally James Wood raised a hand. "Let us stop bandying words. Wend, the committee has discussed these matters at great length. Put succinctly, we believe you are the best man to recruit and lead the new company."

There was a round of "Aye" and "Hear! Hear!" from other members.

Wend said nothing, simply staring ahead. Soon the other men quieted.

Finally Wend said slowly, "Gentlemen, I am honored by your assertion. Honored, indeed. But I think it highly impractical. It is indisputable that my real value to the cause is my knowledge of firelocks and the ability to produce muskets. Our forces are in desperate need of military weapons. It makes far more sense for me to remain at Eckert Ridge, expanding my production facilities and supervising and training the men of my gun-making shop." He paused and looked around the table. "In fact, I am quite surprised that you gentlemen—even for a moment—considered me for this captaincy."

Wood smiled tightly. "Come, sir, you are too modest. Everyone here knows you have quite a valiant record over the course of several conflicts."

McDonald nodded and said, "Let us look back. As a very young man, you volunteered to serve as a scout with Bouquet in his march to lift the siege of Fort Pitt during the Pontiac War of '63. Your heroism at Bushy Run is very well-known."

Wend shrugged. "That was nothing but the action of a lovesick youth. I volunteered because I wanted to find a young girl who had been taken prisoner by the Mingo. It was the best way to get to the Ohio Country."

Rutledge grinned. "Come now, Eckert. The story of how, after the first day of battle, you crawled out into the night to find the route for Bouquet's men to flank the Indians is a matter of record. And how while behind enemy lines, in the moonless blackness, you fought and killed a warrior with your knife."

"I had no choice. The other scouts had been disabled during the day's fighting. I was the only one left." Wend paused, then continued, "And killing that warrior was a matter of pure chance. He had no idea I was there."

Rutledge shook his head. "Your actions as a lieutenant in last year's war against the Ohio tribes were no accident."

"I was dragooned into that by the governor's henchman, Barrett Northcutt. He threatened to take away my musket contract if I didn't serve."

McDonald said, "And in that war, you performed superbly leading detachments in my battalion. You won two desperate fights against war parties."

"I blundered my way through both, and fortune smiled on me."

Angus shook his head. "In the first instance, you saved women and children while leading the rear guard on the march back to Wheeling Island from the massacre at Hart's Store. You drove off a war party which outnumbered you three to one with a daring bayonet attack."

"Damn it, Angus, that was desperation, not daring. If we hadn't charged, we'd have been dead within minutes."

Rutledge added, "Well, you safely escorted all the wounded back from the raid on Wakatamica, including fighting off an attack by Mingoes and Shawnee near the Ohio itself."

"The fact is, I stumbled into an ambush. We were in desperate straits until my scouts Joshua Baird and Simon Kenton came back and tricked the Indians into thinking a major force was attacking."

Wood grinned at Wend. "You know as well as I that Indians always start a fight with an ambush. And during the skirmish, you captured their leader, so the others ran off."

Wend sighed and simply remained silent. All the others stared at him for a long moment.

Rutledge spoke up again. "Beyond the matter of your valor, we also know that your background would facilitate recruitment. You are of German heritage and speak the language, so men of that community would find you attractive. And then your wife is Irish, so you also have a foot in that camp."

Wend stared at the former county lieutenant for a long moment. Then he took a pull of his whiskey, grinned, and said, "Rutledge, I should love to be there if you were to call my wife *Irish* to her face. Indeed, I assure you your regret would be immediate, physical, and longstanding. She, like most of her strain, considers herself lowland Scot, or Ulster Scot, if you must recall her family's time in Ireland. And I can, from experience, say that she does indeed have the well-known Ulster Scot temper, fast to rise and long to burn."

Rutledge's face reddened. He bit his lip, and he looked sheepishly around the table. After a moment he turned back to Wend and said, "Please accept my apology for those thoughtless words. I, like every man here, admire your wife for her virtue, grace, and remarkable beauty. My words were taken without thought."

Wend nodded and responded dryly, "Oh yes, I am sure of that."

Silence was palpable around the table. Finally James Wood coughed into his hand, then laughed and said, "Wend, that self-deprecating description of your military record was droll, but it won't work." He waved his finger at Eckert and said, "We know the truth." Wood rose from his place and picked up a piece of parchment that had been lying on the table in front of him. He walked down to where Wend sat and placed the paper in front of the gunsmith.

"Here is a captain's commission from Virginia. Take it with you, and reflect in the solitude of your home where your duty lies. Consider that the men who go to war from Frederick County deserve a worthy, war-tested leader when facing the enemy. Ponder the matter seriously, and give us your answer within the week."

Wend picked up the commission, stared at it for a few seconds, then carefully rolled it up and tucked it into a pocket. "Well, gentlemen, I shall take this with me and think on it as you have requested. However, I suggest that you harbor no optimism that I will change my mind."

—m—

The sun was low, the evening shadows well advanced by the time Wend brought Sonny up the drive at the trot to Eckert Ridge Farm. He was pleased to note that the young stallion still had lots of energy, even after the round trip to Winchester.

Wend looked with pride at the establishment, which had the appearance of a small village and where more than thirty people lived and worked. Twelve years before, when he and Peggy had arrived, there had been only open fields and forest. Now, at the crest of the drive, on the right, was his own residence, a spacious, two-story, white-painted center-hall house with a covered porch that extended completely across the front. Close behind it was the log cabin that had been the Eckert's' first home and now served as the cookhouse for the main residence and the living quarters for their family of servants.

Directly across the drive from the house was Wend's workshop, with the rifling machine out front sheltered by a lean-to roof. An addition to the back of the shop was framed out, with the roof partially installed.

Wend dismounted and led the horse along the drive toward the stable. Various buildings were on either side as he walked. First on the left, or south side, was the long building which everyone called "the barracks." The near end was a set of rooms that housed Simon Donegal; his wife, Sally; and the children. The other side contained a long bunkroom for Wend's apprentices and farmworkers and a kitchen that served them. Wend looked beyond the barracks to the nearly finished house, which was sited on a nicely wooded patch of land. It was Simon and Sally's new residence and similar in size and appearance to Wend's house. A slight difference was the front porch, which only extended about three-quarters of the way across the front. After a year of living in the barracks apartment with two children, Sally was thrilled with the idea of having her own home.

On the north side, across from the barracks, was the small cottage that housed Wend's journeyman assistant, Wilhelm Hecht, and his family. Wend could see Hecht's children playing in the rear yard. The eight-year-old, Jebediah, or Jebby, stopped and waved at him as he passed by.

Next along the left, set well back from the drive, was the distillery where Donegal produced his special blend of strong whiskey. He and Wend had gone into the business in late 1774, after returning from Dunmore's campaign against the Ohio tribes. It had rapidly become one of the major sources of income for both.

Just past the distillery were the working buildings of the farm. There was a stable, a large hay barn, and a long shed that housed the farm's vehicles—wagons, carts, plows, and the elegant, black-painted one-horse chaise that was Peggy Eckert's beloved ride.

Beyond the working farm buildings, right at the end of the drive, was another residence. The two-story house sheltered Joshua Baird and his common-law wife, Alice Downy. Joshua was a hunter and former British army scout who had worked for Colonel Henry Bouquet of the Royal American Regiment during General Forbes's 1758 campaign to take the Forks of the Ohio from the French. In 1763 he had been the chief scout for Bouquet's expedition to relieve Fort Pitt during Pontiac's War. It was he who, in 1759, had taken the newly orphaned and seriously injured Wend Eckert to live with his sister and her husband, Reverend Carnahan, in Sherman Mill, a small town north of Carlisle.

As Wend led Sonny past the barracks, Jacob Specht, the farm's top hand and master of the horse, came out, wiping his mouth. He joined Wend and asked, "How did he do, Mr. Eckert? This bein' his first time out for a serious ride, an' all that?"

Wend smiled. "Sonny was as good as you could expect, Jacob. He obeyed well and responded to every command." He thought a second. "Just before coming into Winchester, I let him out, and I tell you, his speed and power were impressive. And it didn't seem to wind him one bit."

"That's wonderful, Mr. Eckert. You should start to use him regular-like now." Specht looked over at Wend. "I'm goin' to start training him on the jumps. Look at the muscles in those long legs, sir. He'll float over every fence in the county."

Wend nodded. "I believe you're right. And if we work him consistently, I think he can be ready for the races at Angus McDonald's fair next year."

"Ah yes, sir! Indeed! And I vow we'll take the cup!"

Eckert laughed. "I'll hold you to that, Jacob!"

They had reached the stable. Specht reached over and took Sonny's reins. "Here, sir, I'll get him grained and rubbed down, then let him out into the pasture."

Wend nodded, then reached up and detached the holsters of his saddle pistols from Sonny's pommel and slung them over his right shoulder. "Good evening, Jacob. See you tomorrow."

Wend turned and walked back up the drive toward the residence. As he passed the barracks, he could hear the loud conversation and laughter of the farmhands and apprentices. The smell of their food also wafted out, arousing his appetite.

He was almost to the house when he was surprised to notice a light shining from the workshop. Then he remembered that Andrew Horner, his senior apprentice, had just taken up sleeping in the shop, in search of privacy now that the barracks were crowded with new apprentices and workers for the distillery.

Wend walked over and entered the shop to find Horner sitting at one of the workbenches beside a lantern. In his hands was a sheet of paper, and he was so engrossed in reading it that he didn't notice Wend's approach until he was right beside the young man.

"What's that which has you so interested, Andrew?"

Startled, the apprentice looked up. "Oh, good evening, sir." He pointed to the paper. "Post rider came by today."

"Is that a letter from your parents across the ocean in Hesse?"

Horner smiled. "No, sir. It's from Emily Crider. You remember her, sir. One of the girls in Widow McGraw's tavern at Fredericktown in Maryland."

"Indeed I do. A pretty lass with fair hair. She has a beautiful singing voice. And you were quite taken with her." Wend looked down at the letter to see closely spaced lines in a fair round hand. "She seems to have much to say."

"Yes, sir. There's a lot of news. The widow has sold her tavern and is going north to be a sutler with Washington's army."

Wend nodded. "Yes, she mentioned to me her intention to do that when we were there last fall. She had already procured wagons and was building up a stock of supplies for sale."

"Aye, sir. Emily writes about the wagons and all the provisions." Horner bit his lip. "And she's taking all the girls with her."

There was a long silence. Finally Wend said in a gentle tone, "You must know what Emily will be doing."

Horner bit his lip. "The same thing she was doing at the tavern." He hesitated a second, then said, "The girl's had a hard life, sir. She lost her parents in an Indian raid. She started working for Widow McGraw to escape from abuse by her aunt's husband."

"I know that, but selling her favors in an army camp will be far more intensive than doing so in a small-town tavern. She will become hardened, and many of her charms will soon fade. After a few months, Andrew, she'll be a different girl."

Horner stared up at Wend for a moment, then shook his head. "I don't believe it, sir. Not Emily. She's hardy, and she's basically a good person." He assumed a thoughtful look, then abruptly changed the subject. "Did they offer you the captain's commission, Mr. Eckert?"

Wend laughed. "Everyone seems to know they were going to do it." He sighed, "Yes, Andrew, they asked me to accept a commission and recruit a company."

An eager look came into Horner's eyes. "So you'll be taking it up to join Washington?"

"Well, the company will join the army, but I won't be going with it. I didn't accept the captaincy."

Disappointment spread over the lad's face.

Before he could say anything, Wend said, "So I'm not going to join the army, and neither are you, if you were thinking of that as a way to find Miss Crider. We're both needed here to produce muskets. It's just as important. It is our real duty."

The apprentice stared ahead without speaking.

Wend said in a businesslike tone, "In the morning I'll check today's work. But for right now, I must go to the house for dinner. You have a good evening, Andrew." He turned and walked toward the door.

The apprentice said, "Good night, sir." His voice was barely audible and carried an unmistakable tone of disappointment.

Wend crossed the drive and ascended the steps to the porch, swung open the door, and stepped into the hall of the house. Looking to the left, he could see the cook, Wilma, and her daughter Liza laying the table for supper. He turned right into the parlor to see Peggy sitting at one end of a settee, a cup in her hand. Even in an everyday gown, she looked radiant, with her raven hair, high-cheekboned face, blue eyes, and fair complexion. Wend had become accustomed to the way men stared at her when she walked into a room. He had married her when she was twenty and the undisputed beauty of Sherman Valley. Now, twelve years later, in maturity, she had grown even more ravishing despite the rigors of bearing three children.

Wend hung his pistols on a rack beside the door and walked into the room. Peggy looked at him with a crooked smile on her face and remarked, "Well, my dear, should I call you *Captain* now?"

Wend didn't answer; instead he simply pulled the rolled commission from his pocket and handed it to her.

Peggy unrolled the sheet and quickly scanned the words. "So you accepted after all?"

Wend had walked over to the liquor cabinet. He took out a pewter cup and poured himself a generous portion of Donegal's whiskey.

He took a sip, then turned back to Peggy and said, "No, actually I turned them down."

Peggy raised her eyebrows, then waved the commission. "So why do you have this?"

"The esteemed members of the Committee of Safety wouldn't take no for an answer. James Wood insisted that I take it with me and think over my decision. They urged me to reconsider my duty to the cause and all that. I'm supposed to answer within a week."

"Well, Wend, of course I will support what you finally decide, but you know where I stand."

"Yes, I know you want me to take the command. You've made that clear enough."

"How could I feel any other way, considering how the Ulster people were treated by the British?"

Wend grinned. He put his hand to his forehead as if trying hard to remember something. "Now, my dear, as I seem to recall, you were born in a small village in the backcountry of Pennsylvania. The British didn't actually have much chance to mistreat you."

Peggy bristled. "Damn you, Wend! I've heard many stories from my grandfather and father! When I was a child, I used to sit on the floor by the fire while they talked about the old times and how our family came to America. We were unwelcome in our homeland of low-land Scotland and forced to Ireland simply because of our religion. And we weren't treated much better in Ireland. Only here in the colonies, in the border country, have we found relative freedom! That's a matter of fact, and one I won't forget! By God, it is my family's heritage!"

Wend smiled to himself, thinking how easy it was to get Peggy riled up on this subject. But then it was a trait she shared with most of the Ulster Scots. He looked at her and knew by the set of her jaw and the fire in her eyes that she was not through.

Peggy exclaimed, "I'll not be happy until the British have no say in our government and there are no redcoats in Virginia or in any of the colonies, for that matter." She paused to take a drink of her whiskey. "And I do think that if we are to be successful, we need the best men to lead our soldiers. Like everyone else in Frederick County, I think there is no better man to lead the new company than you!"

Wend looked down at his cup. "And if I go off to the army, what happens to the production of muskets, which I would remind you, my dear, is our main source of income?"

Peggy had a ready answer. "Wilhelm Hecht and the apprentices would keep production going for the year you were away. You have things set up well. And Wilhelm is highly competent in managing the work, as you've told me often enough. And let's be frank, he actually was the one who put out the first lot of new muskets while you were off chasing that despicable Colonel John Connolly last fall."

"Yes, it seems I'm just a superfluous appendage."

"Oh, stop it, Wend! Sometimes you can be so contrary and infuriating! The point is, you've worked hard to get things organized and the shop can function quite efficiently for the year you would be away." She gave him a knowing look. "And anyway, I'll be here to watch out for the work. I remind you, my dear husband, that I have been keeping the accounts and ledgers for the shop for over ten years now. And by doing that, I've learned a lot about the trade."

Wend sat down in a wing chair in front of the fireplace. He drank deeply of his whiskey. "I hesitate to bring this up, Mrs. Eckert, but I must remind you that we are indeed talking about my participation in a war, and the fact is, my absence could easily become quite permanent."

"If that Mingo chief Wolf Claw and Matt Bratton and that rat Richard Grenough couldn't kill you, I think there is little to fear from the British."

Wend looked around the side of the chair to the settee. "Might I draw it to your attention that musket balls tend to be rather random in whom they hit. And the captain is supposed to be out front of his company in battle."

Peggy feigned not to hear. She said, "There's also the matter of our standing with our friends here in Winchester and the county. We are friends with the most important people in the area and the largest landowners, which is quite an accomplishment for a trade and farming family."

Wend grinned. "I don't flatter myself that I've had anything to do with that. You struck up a friendship with Anna McDonald, and that led to your association on a regular basis with Jean Wood and other ladies of the gentry. I'm known mostly as Peggy Eckert's husband or that backwoods fellow who escorts you to parties."

"Oh please, Wend. You are also known and respected as the best rifleman and best gunsmith in Frederick County. And as an aide to Lord Dunmore last year during the war."

Wend looked around at Peggy again. "Don't let Dan Morgan hear you call me the best rifleman in the county."

Peggy grimaced. "You are known and admired throughout the county for your bravery in war. That's why everyone wants you to be the captain."

"Everyone but me. But luckily it is my choice that counts."

"Stop being so contrary! You know what I mean. The important point is that if you turn down the commission, many people will question your patriotism."

"But not my ability to make muskets."

"They're going to say you are a typical German tradesman, more interested in advancing his business than enthusiastically supporting the cause!"

"Well, it happens that I am a typical German tradesman. I like to mind my trade and avoid politics. It makes for a longer, safer, and more profitable life."

"Wend, damn you! You know what I mean."

Wend rose from the chair and faced his wife. "Sooner rather than later, people are going to realize that producing weapons is as patriotic and important as marching off to the army." He raised a finger to make a point. "And you, more than anyone else, well know that we have cut out profit to the bone for the muskets we are providing to the Virginia forces. I call that true patriotism."

Peggy set her jaw and was about to reply when a loud ringing interrupted the conversation.

Wilma was standing at the bottom of the stairs, bell in hand. She shouted upward, "All you young ones, come on down! Food is on the table!" Then she walked to the parlor door and announced, rather unnecessarily, "Miss Peggy, we be ready for the meal."

Meanwhile there was the pounding of numerous feet running down the stairs accompanied by laughing voices as the four Eckert children hurried to the dining room.

By the time Wend and Peggy entered, the children stood by their places at the table. To say that the four siblings were a diverse group would be an understatement. As Wend took his place at the head of the table, to his right sat Johann. His features were strikingly similar to Wend's. The boy was the product of a tryst in 1759 between Wend and Abigail Gibson, the daughter of a Philadelphia lawyer. Her father and she had been traveling with the Eckert family on their way to Fort Pitt. She had been orphaned in the same Indian raid in which Wend's family had been killed but had been taken as hostage wife of the Mingo war captain who had led the raiding party. In 1760 she had given birth to Wend's son. In the previous year, during the course of Dunmore's War, events had led to Wend visiting Abigail's village. She had taken the heartrending decision to send the boy back east with his natural father, so that he could experience European life. Now, a year later, the other children had not only accepted Johann but held him in awe for his life with the Mingo, the mannerisms which it had imparted on him, and for the fact that at sixteen he was as skilled a woodsman and hunter as Joshua Baird himself.

On Wend's left sat eleven-year-old Bernd. He was a tall, strapping lad, already almost as tall as Johann. He believed he was Wend's son, but in fact he was the product of a liaison between Peggy and her former fiancé, Matt Bratton, a wagoner from Sherman Valley who had been the main henchman of the influential and duplicitous merchant and Indian trader Richard Grenough. The war party that had killed Wend's family in 1759 had come east from the Ohio Country to receive illegal arms and powder from Grenough. It had ambushed the Eckert-Gibson caravan on Forbes Road because Wend, while hunting, had discovered the trader's pack train and its illicit cargo en route to meet the Indians. Wend had held Grenough responsible for his family's death and had finally exacted the full measure of vengeance on both Grenough and Bratton the previous year. Their remains lay in the Shenandoah River near Ashby's Ferry. Wend and Peggy were determined that Bernd would never find out his true parentage.

Only the youngest two children had been parented jointly by Wend and Peggy. The two girls sat on either side of their mother. Elise, at nine, was named for Wend's sister, who had died at the hands of the Mingo war party. Seated at her mother's right hand, she was a brown-haired girl with features from both her parents. She had a willowy frame, a high-cheekboned face, and brown hair. She was showing the promise of real beauty.

Six-year-old Ellen was named for Peggy's sister and was definitely going to be a copy of her mother, with raven hair, large blue eyes, and high cheekbones.

Wend motioned to Johann to say the blessing. It was the family custom to rotate the duty among the children so they would learn the proper words. Johann, who had only been introduced to the white man's religion a year ago, had the most difficult time. Everyone patiently listened as he struggled to find the right words. Finally he finished and said, "Amen."

Then Wend waved for everyone to sit down.

Wilma, who had been standing by the sideboard, announced, "We be haven' venison pie tonight. Fresh made from the buck young Mr. Johann brought in yesterday."

Peggy turned to Ellen. "Now you mind to eat some of the meat. I don't want to see you just scooping up the gravy and crust. You need the meat to grow up tall and strong."

The little girl made a face but said nothing.

Wend asked, "Where did you get the buck, Johann? Was Joshua with you?"

Wilma interjected, "Mr. Eckert, it was a big one! And he was by himself."

Johann smiled. "I trailed it down along the creek. Almost to Widow Callow's place before I caught up with it."

Wend raised his eyebrows. "You brought the deer back by yourself, on foot, all that way?"

Wilma said, "Yes, sir, he did! Came to the cookhouse with that ole buck hangin' over his shoulders. Didn't even look winded."

Johann looked around the table sheepishly. "Well, actually I was carrying the deer along the road and a man in a wagon gave me a ride. Carried me all the way to the foot of our drive."

Wend asked, "That was charitable. Someone we know?"

The boy wrinkled his face. "No, sir. He was an ironmonger. Had his wagon full of pans and pots and all that." He thought a second. "Said his name was Rhys."

Peggy looked up from her plate. "Oh, I think I know him, from court days. He sets up on the square with the other merchants. But he's from down near Fredericksburg." She paused, thought a second, then continued, "That's funny; what's he doing here now? Court day is not for a fortnight."

Johann swallowed the food he had in his mouth and then spoke. "Mother Eckert, he was quite talkative as we rode along. He mentioned to me that the war has cut into his business at court days around here. So he's making calls at farms and homesteads to sell more things."

Wend raised his eyebrows. "Well, why didn't he stop in here, as long as he was helping you with the deer?"

Peggy nodded. "Yes, you know, I should think that Sally Donegal would be interested in looking over his wares, what with moving into the new house."

Johann said, "He said he was going straight up to Battletown Crossroads because there were a lot of homesteads right around the inn. He said he would be coming to the farmsteads down here along the Ashby Ford Road soon enough."

"Well, then," Peggy responded, "I'll be sure to warn Sally that he'll be coming. She'll want to think about what she needs." Then she looked over the table and announced, "You children finish your pie, or you'll not get any of the sweets."

Wilma joined in, "Yes, we got a nice apple pie for dessert, so you want to listen to your mother."

The gray light of false dawn was illuminating the buildings of Eckert Ridge when Wend left the house, its other occupants still asleep, and crossed the drive to the shop. It was his practice to arrive well before any of the other workers so that he could accurately assess the progress of the previous day and plan out the schedule for his men and himself. Now things were complicated by the presence of the sleeping Andrew Horner, who had laid out a pallet and blankets in a corner and was still fast asleep. Wend put the candle lamp he carried down on his desk and quietly walked over to the part of the building where musket construction was carried out. He counted thirty-nine finished firelocks lined up on the wall, waiting to be boxed. He moved to the apprentice workbenches and saw five more in various stages of fabrication. Two were simply stocks being carved; the other three were further along.

He inspected the carving work on the two stocks and found some problems. The carving was being done by the two new apprentices, and Wend resolved to have Horner spend some more time with them. Horner was a gifted carver; it had been his family trade in Germany. The youth had come to Eckert Ridge as a redemptioner farmhand who would repay his passage to Virginia by three years' work in the fields. But when Wend discovered his skill with wood, he quickly took him on as an apprentice. Horner took to the trade eagerly and proved a fast learner. Now Wend considered him essentially a journeyman. He was in fact the leader of the other apprentices, working right under Wend and Wilhelm Hecht, the journeyman manager of the shop.

Wend went back to his desk and contemplated his own day's work. Because he had been concentrating on the musket fabrication, he was behind schedule on some important projects. After getting the shop started, he planned to personally work on a sporting fowler he had promised to Charles Gerson, the proprietor of a gun shop in Alexandria. Gerson had also ordered a brace of Wend's special light-weight pistols, and they had not even been started.

As he was pondering the day ahead, the shop door opened and Wilma's son Billy came in, carrying Wend's breakfast on a tray.

"Good mornin', Mr. Eckert! I got you some fine eggs and some sausage. And some hot coffee."

Billy was nearly twenty, of above-average height, and always friendly. Wend looked down at the tray and immediately realized how hungry he was. He reached for his fork, anticipating the first bite.

At the same time, Billy spoke up. "Mr. Eckert, sir, I got a question."

Wend put the fork down. "Yes, Billy—what is it?"

"I hear the county is goin' to raise another company for the war. To join General Washington's army up north fightin' the British. And I heard you was to be the cap'n."

Wend raised his finger. "One, Billy, you are right about the county raising a new company for the war." He raised a second finger. "But two, I am not going to be the captain. I have turned the offer of a commission down. I plan to stay right here making muskets and other firelocks."

There was a decided look of disappointment in the youth's face. "Well, my real question is this, Mr. Eckert: Could I join up with this company and be a soldier?"

Wend, who was again about to take his first bite of sausage, put the fork down for the second time. He was not sure what to say. He had no certainty what the state's policy was on black soldiers. Dunmore had made soldiers out of African slaves, a move that had made him the most hated man in Virginia. But Billy was free—he had been for five years, since the Eckerts had purchased the whole family from an estate and, through the efforts of James Wood in the Burgesses, had had them receive their writ of manumission. That was why the whole family had taken the last name of *Wood*. Wend thought a moment; he had never seen any blacks in the militia.

"Billy," he said, "that's a good question. I'll tell you what, next time I see Mr. Rutledge, the county lieutenant, or Mr. Wood, I'll ask. They should know."

"Thank ya, Mr. Eckert. I sure would like to know if I can go."

"Now, Billy, why on earth do you want to go off as a soldier?"

"Well, like everyone else, I want to have Virginia be free of the British." He shrugged and smiled sheepishly, "And I been thinkin' that I want to get away from this county, leastways for a little while. Lived here my whole life. I'm thinkin' to see more places."

Wend smiled. *All young men wanted to wander, sooner or later.* "Have you mentioned this to your ma and pa?"

"Didn't want to say anything till I knew if'n I could go to the army."

Grinning, Wend answered, "Well, I'll find out the answer, and I won't say anything to Wilma or Albert."

Billy smiled and said, "Thank you, Mr. Eckert."

And with that he headed back to the cookhouse.

There was a cough, and Horner said, "Mornin', Mr. Eckert." He was buttoning up his shirt.

"Guess we woke you up, Andrew."

"Time for me to be up anyway, sir. Got to get down to the barracks for some food before work starts."

"Yes, when you are finished, come talk to me. I want you to work with some of the younger apprentices on their carving. And I need to talk with Wilhelm and you about expediting finishing up this lot of fifty muskets. There's a new regiment forming, and the Committee of Safety wants us to get them off as soon as possible."

Horner nodded. "I'll get back from breakfast posthaste." Then he turned and departed for the barracks.

Wend sighed. He had tossed and turned the night before worrying about Horner. He was afraid the lovesick lad would decide to take things into his own hands and go in search of Emily Crider. The fact was, Horner was in all but name a qualified journeyman, and the lad knew it. Now Billy's request about becoming a soldier had rekindled his worries about Horner taking off for Washington's army. The two were of an age—a restless age. Then, suddenly, a thought occurred to him, an idea about what might keep Horner focused on the shop and gunsmithing. It was rather momentous, and Wend decided to think things over for a day or two before taking action.

On a bright day in the first week of April, the entire population of Eckert Ridge was gathered in front of the Donegal family's new house to celebrate its completion. In addition, people from neighboring farms had come to help enjoy the festivities. Tables from the barracks had been set up and loaded with food contributed from each household, and libations of all types were also present in great supply. Three fiddlers and a flutist were busy providing music to the scene, led by Elijah McCartney, one of Abby Morgan's wagoners. He was quite adept at the violin and directed the other musicians in their version of popular tunes. In addition to Abby, Dan Morgan's wife, whose farm was just to the north, the Widow Callow had come over with her hands and their families. Many of the attendees had brought gifts to help fit out the house, for the Donegals had little in the way of domestic furnishings. Various people were in the process of coming forward to present their items to the couple.

Wend stood to one side, watching the festivities and reflecting on what had led to this occasion. Sally had lost her first husband—Frank Potter—and indeed her cabin and most of her possessions to a Shawnee war party in 1774 during the early stage of what would soon be called Dunmore's War. The couple had had a farmstead south of Braddock Road in western Pennsylvania. Early one evening, while preparing the evening meal, she had looked out the window in horror to see her husband die under a warrior's hatchet. Losing not a moment, she had grabbed up her new baby and four-year-old daughter, climbed out through the rear window of the cabin, and run down a slope to Little Pebble Creek, which flowed just behind their cabin. Thus had begun a harrowing attempt to escape the pursuing war party that had lasted through the cold spring night. It had ended only when Sally and her children arrived at dawn at a point where Braddock Road forded the creek. An exhausted Sally had dropped to the ground, believing they had eluded the Indians. But within a few minutes, her hopes had been dashed when the warriors appeared out of the woods. In despair, Sally had accepted that she and her children were doomed when suddenly Wend, Donegal, and Joshua had come riding down the road to drive off the war party. They had quickly been joined by two wagons carrying muskets Wend had reconditioned for use by the militia garrison at Fort Pitt. They had loaded the three refugees into a wagon and taken them to Ransome's Tavern, a tiny village just a few miles west of Little Pebble Creek. There a shopkeeper and his wife had taken in Sally and her children, and then, the next morning Wend and his caravan had continued on westward, considering the incident closed.

But the story wasn't over. Donegal, a man in his thirties with years of soldiering behind him, had taken a liking to young Louisa and baby Henry and even more of a liking to their mother. Dunmore's War, in which Donegal served as the sergeant major of Winchester's battalion, had brought him back in contact with Sally and her family and had led to a marriage proposal, which had been accepted. Once the war was over, Donegal had married Sally, fourteen years his junior, and then had brought his new family to Eckert Ridge, where they had been ensconced in the cramped apartment at the end of the barracks while a suitable dwelling was constructed.

Now, as Wend watched, people were presenting the couple with old but serviceable furniture from their own homes and in some cases, new items. One of the latter was carried forward by Wilhelm Hecht and Andrew Horner. It was a sizable storage cabinet with two doors, suitable for a parlor or hall. It was made of beautifully grained oak, stained and oiled to perfection. It had been assembled and finished by the men of the gun shop.

Sally exclaimed, "Oh, how lovely! I've n'er seen anything of its like! It shall have pride of place in our hall!" She hugged the two men.

Peggy came forward, carrying a large package wrapped in paper. She placed it on the cabinet. "Sally, I think you'll need this for your windows."

Sally opened the package to find a large roll of patterned fabric. "Oh, material for curtains! And so pretty! I'm so grateful! I was worried about how I would obtain all I needed, what with so many other things to buy! You have thought of the perfect gift!"

The gift-giving had ended, and Donegal, standing next to Sally, raised his hands for attention. "Na, all of you, it's a wonderful thing you've done for us. We are both excited to live in this lovely home. It is the first proper house each of us has ever had. What with me bein' in the army for years and Sally livin' all her life in log cabins, we're gonna feel like gentry once we get moved in." He put his arm around his wife's waist and beamed at the assemblage.

Wend thought Sally had never looked prettier, her golden hair shining in the sunlight and a gleam in her blue eyes.

Then Simon spoke up again. "But we also got some other news to tell you." He looked down at his wife's face. "Sally is about to honor me with an addition to our family! A brother or sister for Louisa and Henry!"

Widow Callow laughed loudly. "So Donegal has been workin' hard to fill up that grand new house of his!"

There was laughter and a great cheer from the crowd. As it died down, Joshua Baird spoke up in a loud voice. "Now a man who makes an announcement like that better be ready to provide some strong libation to all his friends so they can celebrate properly!"

Donegal grinned broadly. "Na, do you think a good Highlander like myself would ever ha' dreamed of not havin' some good spirits ready?" He waved to a table where one of the men from his distillery stood. On cue, the man reached under the table and placed several jugs on top of it. Donegal announced, "Na you all are invited to partake of the best whiskey in the county to help celebrate the good fortune of the Donegal family!"

There was another cheer, followed by an immediate rush to the table, and soon enough the party became increasingly raucous.

Presently Donegal, having made the rounds of his guests to thank them for their generosity, joined Eckert. "Ah, lad, it's a great day!" He shook his head. "In my soldiering days, I would never have thought a livin' in such a grand house. And isn't my bride such a bonny young lass?"

Wend put his hand on the former corporal of the 77th Highlanders' shoulder. "Indeed, Simon, it's a great day for the Donegal family and Eckert Ridge." He grinned. "But you're going to have to increase your distilling to make up for all the whiskey they're downing here today."

A thoughtful look came over the Scotsman's face. "Na, I'm havin' to do that anyway. The stuff is gettin' very popular around here. I'm havin' trouble makin' enough for all the taverns which are askin' for it."

"Well, my friend, you do make the best whiskey in the county. But there's another reason it's so popular. The British blockade has cut off most of the rum which used to come up from Jamaica and other islands in the West Indies. The tavern keepers don't have much choice 'cept to buy whiskey for their customers."

Donegal shrugged. "So we'll work hard to supply the county with the liquor. And do it before others can start makin' whiskey in large amounts."

"Yes, we should do that immediately. And we've got the advantage of having your formula, which makes ours better than anyone else's." Wend hesitate and put his hand on Donegal's arm. "But I've been thinking about something beyond that which could be very profitable for us."

Simon looked at Wend with narrowed eyes. "And na, what could that be?"

"I think we should both increase production *and* expand the sale of our whiskey to towns beyond the county."

Donegal stared at his friend for a long moment. "And just where would you be talkin' about?"

"Places we can get to easily by wagons, specifically using Morgan's freight wagons. I've thought of Wills Creek to the north, Alexandria to the east, maybe some places in Maryland, such as Fredericktown. There are good roads to all those places."

Donegal put his hand to his chin. "I see what you mean. But we'd have to run the distillery at full blast all the time. I'd have to put more men on."

Wend nodded. "At the very first, it would be a gamble. But we could do it one town at a time, to reduce the risk. Go to one place and sell all the taverns in the area, then when business there is secure, move on to another."

"Aye, I see what your thinkin'. Let me consider on it for a while, and we'll talk again in a few days."

As they were talking, Jacob Specht walked over to join them. He pointed down the slope toward the Ashby Ferry Road. "Mr. Eckert, there's a wagon coming up the drive."

Wend and Donegal turned to look. Donegal said, "Na who could that be?"

Wend scrutinized the wagon. It was a fairly large wagon with a canvas cover pulled by a two-horse team. A wiry-framed, black-haired man drove the horses from a seat at the front. "I haven't any idea. It's not anyone from around here."

The three of them walked along the drive, almost down to the gun shop, as the wagon continued to come up the slope. Presently the wagon arrived in front of them and the driver pulled up the horses.

"Hello, gentlemen. My name is Rhys. Jonathan Rhys. I'm an iron-monger by trade and thought to show some of my wares to the good ladies of this establishment." He waved toward the party. "But I seem to have come at an inconvenient time for that purpose."

Wend said, "Indeed, sir. Tomorrow would be a better day." Then he had a thought. "Why don't you stay the night? Camp if you would, and I'm sure the ladies of the farm would be interested in looking over your wares tomorrow."

Donegal waved toward his house. "We're celebrating the finish of my new home." He motioned toward where Sally stood with some other women. "My beautiful wife—the blond lady there—would certainly be interested in some of your cooking pans."

Rhys glanced at the ladies, "Ah yes, you are indeed fortunate, Mr. Donegal." He turned back to Wend. "I'm much obliged by your offer. Just tell me where you'd like me to stay."

Wend turned to Specht. "Jacob, show Mr. Rhys that spot near the small pasture down past Joshua's house. That would be a good place for him to camp. And the creek is just down the hill from there, for him to draw water."

"And," added Donegal, "come back over here and join us in a bit of whiskey when you've tended to your animals. There's na doubt we'll still be at it."

Wend looked back at the party and laughed. "I'm certain things will go on as long as the whiskey holds out."

Rhys smiled. "Now that's right kindly of you. I'll be along soon as I've settled my animals."

CHAPTER THREE

FLAMES ON THE RIDGE

It was well past midnight on the night of the party. Wend, lying in bed beside Peggy, stared over at the hearth and saw there was still a glow of embers and an occasional flicker of actual flame. It had been one of those nights when Peggy had signaled her desire for lovemaking by leaving her sleeping cap off, her long raven hair falling beautifully over her shoulders. And, undoubtedly stimulated by the excitement of the party and dancing, she had served him with even more than her usual passion. Her efforts had artfully aroused him to maximum performance, and in consequence, Wend was physically exhausted and should have easily dropped off to deep sleep.

But instead he was fitful and restless.

Suddenly Peggy's sleepy voice came from beside him. "What is it that is bothering you? You've been wiggling around ever since our lovemaking. You usually drop off like a rock."

Wend sighed. "Well, you do have a way of exhausting me." Then he said, "I'm worried about Andrew Horner."

"Worried? Why in the world?"

"He got a letter from that tart he met at Widow McGraw's tavern in Fredericktown, in Maryland. The widow took her and all the other girls up to Washington's army."

"You mean..."

"Yes, my dear, she's selling her favors to the soldiers. But that hasn't stopped Andrew from pining away for her. His mind's not on his work, and he was really disappointed when I told him I wasn't going to lead a company to the army. Obviously he was hoping to go along so he could search out dear Miss Emily."

Peggy laughed. "But last I heard, my dearest, you were encouraging him to court the Haldorf girl—that blonde, Frieda. As you said, a pretty German lass with wide hips. Perfect for childbearing. You were even letting him use the chaise to ride her around in grand style. What went wrong?"

Wend shook his head. "The girl doesn't seem to know her business. I had hoped by now she would have had him up in the loft of a barn somewhere with their clothes off. *Honey for the bear.* But he's seen her several times, and nothing seems to be happening." Wend sighed again. "It's depressing to think that an intelligent youth like Andrew is besotted over a tart, beautiful as she may be."

Peggy giggled loudly, then placed her hand over her mouth until her mirth subsided. Then she said in a voice dripping with irony, "Imagine that, a serious-minded German gunsmith falling in love with an Ulster Scot prostitute." She paused for effect. "Let me see, where have we heard of that before?"

"Stop it, Peggy! What you did was very limited. You slipped away to your father's barn only with traveling men who visited Sherman Mill. You didn't do it with men who lived in the valley. There were those who suspected what you were doing, but no one said it out loud."

Peggy laughed again. "Are you sure about that?"

"Well, that's what you told me."

"Do you always believe everything a harlot tells you?"

Wend didn't answer directly. Instead, he continued, "And you did it because you wanted to make money to escape from living in the backwoods. But Emily is going to be taking on all comers, and everyone will know what she is."

Peggy was quiet for a long moment. Then she said, "Wend, you're skirting the real reason you're upset about this. This isn't just about that tart. Andrew has been with you for years, always loyal and diligent in his work. He works with you on your most important firelocks. You've come to think of him as family. Dare I say, like another son? The truth is you can't bear the idea of working without him around, not only for the help he gives you but also the companionship."

"He's a wonderful gunsmith, and he takes much of the load off of me so I can manage the work of Hecht and the other apprentices." Wend sighed. "But he can't get his mind off going to the army. I've watched him the last couple of days, and I can see the idea is hanging over him, in his thoughts all the time. He's distracted as he works. I fear he's going to come up to me any day and say that he wants to leave."

"You can't do much about it except try to talk him out of it."

"Well, I do have an idea of something that may keep him around."

Peggy rose slightly and looked at her husband in the dim light. "Now what would that be?"

"I've got an order for a brace of pistols from Gerson in Alexandria. The special lightweight ones." Wend paused a moment. "I'm thinking of having him carve the stocks and as he does so, teaching him the secret curve of the handles which makes them so comfortable to hold and easy to aim."

"My God, Wend, that's the secret your father gave you! You are the only one who knows the proper shape and angle! For heaven's sake, that should be kept only in the family!" She pushed herself up on an elbow. "You see, I'm right! You are about to treat Andrew like one of your sons. That secret must be taught only to Bernd and Johann!"

Wend quietly said, "I'll think about it for a few days. I know it's a desperate measure."

Peggy answered with a determined tone in her voice, "Wend, don't consider it at all. You *must* think of your children. I almost wish Andrew *would* leave; then you would be forced to depend more on Johann and Bernd. That would be good for them and good for our family."

Wend realized this had quickly become one of those times when there is only one answer to a wife. So he simply said, "Yes, dear."

With the sun low in the western sky and the shadows long, Wend said good night to Wilhelm Hecht as the journeyman followed the other workers out of the shop. Wend planned to work a little longer. He had started carving the stocks of the pistols for Gerson's store. But as he settled in at his bench, Donegal strode in through the door, a jug in hand. And just behind him was the lanky figure of Joshua Baird.

Wend asked, "What's this?"

Joshua responded, "We're running from the women. Sally and Alice been working to fix up the new house all day, and they pressed us into service, movin' things from the barracks and then shifting them all over the house. And what other chores they could think of, which was a mighty lot. We finally escaped and came here to hide out."

Wend laughed. "Aren't you worried they'll come after you?"

Donegal shook his head. "Ah na, they've realized it's time to get supper ready. So we got some time until they'll be callin' for us." He held up the jug. "Time to take some medicine against the aches and pains from all the work."

Wend put his tools down. "All right, you pull some chairs out to the lean-to, and we'll sit beside the rifling machine." He grabbed three cups from a shelf above his desk.

The three men each drew a full cup from the jug, and all was quiet for a minute as they savored the robust flavor of Donegal's whiskey.

It was Joshua who broke the silence. He wiped his mouth with his hand, then asked Wend, "So you've made up your mind to send back that commission to the committee?"

Wend shrugged. "I made up my mind the day I met with them at the Golden Buck. Wilma and the cook for the barracks are driving into Winchester day after tomorrow, and I'll send the commission in with them." He motioned back toward the shop. "I've got to concentrate on finishing up this lot of muskets. I promised we'd ship fifty by the end of the month. And then we get started on another batch."

Donegal took a sip of whiskey and said, "Na, I'm not a wee bit interested in this war. The thing is, the three of us have spent more than enough time on the war trail. Seven years in the 77th Highlanders for me against the French and the tribes, and Joshua did as much time scouting for Bouquet and the 60th. And then we all marched with Bouquet to relieve Fort Pitt, when Joshua took that ball in his left leg. And that's not mentioning that little skirmish Dunmore put on in late '74 when we went right into the middle of the Ohio Country." He took a deep breath and then another pull on his cup. "I say we done enough soldiering and we earned the right to sit this one out and tend to our business. We keep the whiskey and firelocks flowin' to those what can make good use of them."

Joshua said, "I'll drink to that: whiskey and firelocks."

All three raised their glasses.

Wend said, "There's something else I've been thinking about, especially since this offer of a captaincy came up."

Donegal cocked his head, "And na what would that be?"

"If we did go to the army, chances are sooner or later we'd find ourselves facing men we knew from the old days. Men from the 77th, the Black Watch, and the Royal Americans. Men we respect, men we marched with and charged with at Bushy Run. I don't fancy the idea of leveling a firelock at any of them."

The other two men nodded. Donegal said, "Aye, I've thought of that myself. I dunna relish the idea of pullin' the trigger against someone like Captain McDonald or Captain Stirling. And many a man in the ranks I knew would be a sergeant by now and standin' in line against us." He looked down at his cup and continued, "Yes, it's best we stay here and mind our work and our families."

Wend smiled at Donegal. "Especially you, Simon. With a pretty new wife and children and your first very own baby on the way."

Simon grinned from ear to eat. "Na, when I was a corporal in the old 77th, gettin' into trouble with the likes of Bob Kirkwood, I n'er dreamed of bein' married to a fine woman like Sally or havin' my own little ones. Thought I'd spend my life as a single man, probably ended up layin' dead on some desolate field with a ball in me. Now look, here I am almost a proper gentleman with a family."

Wend said, "Well, Sally looks as happy as you with the new house and new baby."

"Aye, and new cookware. She spent a long time with that iron-monger Rhys earlier today." Donegal grimaced. "And spent a lot of money. She bought some cook pans and a big pot."

Joshua raised his eyebrows and laughed. "That couldn't 'ave been all that expensive. You're just bein' a cheap Scotsman about it all!"

The Highlander nodded. "You'd be right, Joshua, if that's all she had purchased. Na, it turns out that Rhys was carrying a set of pewter tableware. Plates and serving dishes and all. And Sally falls in love with it, sure enough. So she put it on me that she had to have the whole lot, so we could set a proper table. Kept up at it till I couldn't but say yes. That's what cost a pretty penny!"

Smiling, Wend added, "Looks like Mr. Rhys had a good day." He motioned toward the drive. "I saw him headin' down to the road in his wagon in the middle of the afternoon."

Joshua looked bemused for a moment. "You know, that Rhys is a strange bird. He spent a goodly amount of time walking 'round the farm, lookin' at things and askin' questions. Specht talked with him at the party and said he asked how many people were livin' here on the ridge and how many were grown men. And how many families. Also asked what the routine was as far as what went on during the day. Funny kind of questions to be askin'."

Wend shrugged. "He was probably just trying to figure how many people would be interested in his wares and when the best time to approach them was."

Joshua added, "And then, just afore he left, Alice said, he walked down to our house and stared off into the fields and woods down to the south. Can't think of no reason he'd do that." He shrugged. "Like I said, he's a funny man."

Wend took a sip, then remarked, "Well, in any case, he's gone." He turned to Donegal and grinned. "And he's got a goodly amount of your coin. So if he's a bit strange, he also knows how to make money."

Donegal shook his head. "I'll not argue with you on that."

Just then little six-year-old Louisa came skipping up the drive and said to Donegal, "Father, mother says it's time for supper. Time for you to come home before it gets cold." Then she turned and raced back toward the new house.

Donegal picked up his jug and stood up. "One thing I've learned in my short time as a married man is not to be late for supper! Women seem to take that very badly." With a wave, he headed off toward home.

Joshua also got up. "Yeah, time for me to go too. Alice will have the meal ready, and I'm thinkin' yours is close to bein' on the table."

Wend picked up the chairs and carried them back inside the shop. Then he went over to his bench and began cleaning up and restowing his tools. As he was doing so, Horner came back from his meal at the barracks.

Wend looked up and said, "You're back early. Didn't you like what was on the table?"

"No, sir, that's not it. The food was fine. But I ate fast cause I wanted to talk with you alone before you went over to the house for the night."

A sense of foreboding swept over Wend. "Oh, what's on your mind, Andrew?"

The youth bit his lip and hesitated a few seconds, as if searching for the right words. Finally he spoke. "Sir, I want your permission to leave. To go out on my own."

Wend sucked in his breath. "Let me guess, Andrew, you want to go up to Washington's army?"

A tight smile formed on Horner's lips. "Yes, sir."

It was what Wend had dreaded, but now that it was out in the open, the words hit Wend hard. He was momentarily speechless.

Horner hurried to fill the void. "Sir, I want to find Emily. I hope to save her from the life she's going to have to live up there."

Wend finally found words. "Andrew, if you join the army, your time won't be your own. Your officers won't let you wander around looking for Emily. And as a private, you'll find it hard to keep her, even if you do locate her."

"I wasn't planning to actually join the army."

Bewildered, Wend asked, "Well, what did you *plan* to do?"

"I thought to work as a contractor—as a gunsmith. I'm sure they need people to keep the firelocks in order. After our work here, I know how to maintain muskets as well as anyone."

Wend thought for a moment. "Well, I can't deny that. But you're even more important to us here, since we're trying to build muskets as fast as possible. And at this moment, you know we're struggling to get this lot of muskets out by the end of the month." He gave the lad a hard look. "You'd be leaving us shorthanded just when we need everyone."

Horner shook his head. "I won't leave until we finish this lot of muskets and they've been shipped out."

"Yes, but we need to make many more muskets, Andrew. You are a key man in our shop."

Horner sighed deeply. "I know, sir, and I feel bad about leaving. You have taught me so much over the last few years, and not just about gun making. But by the Father Above, I love Emily and I want to save her from the life she's being forced to live. The truth is, she wrote that she was very unhappy about what she was about to do but she didn't think she had any choice. She says she owes a lot to Widow McGraw for saving her from a bad situation with her aunt's husband. If I find her, perhaps I can give her that choice."

Wend was at a loss for words. He stared silently at his apprentice for a long time. "Andrew, it will be a couple of weeks until we finish this batch of muskets and get them ready to ship. Meanwhile, I want you to think hard about what you are doing. We will talk again soon."

Horner nodded. "Yes, sir. But there's something else I want to tell you."

"Yes, Andrew? And what would that be?"

"Sir, Billy wants to leave also. He wants to go join the army or work as a laborer. We want to travel together."

Wend raised his eyebrows. "Well, the two of you are going to have a long walk."

"Actually, sir, we figured to ride."

"Ride? How? Where are you going to get horses?"

"Well, it turns out that the Widow Callow has an old cart. It's been sitting in her shed for many years and needs repairs. The widow says we can have it if we can fix it. So Billy and I thought to give it a try."

Wend answered in a frustrated tone, "All right, Andrew, so perhaps you've got a cart—if it can be fixed. But you'll need at least one horse. Now just where do you plan to get that?"

"The widow's got a horse she'll sell. A gelding. Old, but he looks to have some years in him yet. She's giving us a good price because she really doesn't need him. You know I've got some money put aside. Turns out it's enough for the horse and buying some provisions to travel."

Wend's temper was rising. He said, more harshly and sarcastically than he intended, "Well, you've got things all planned out, don't you?"

Horner, reacting to Wend's tone, didn't say anything immediately. Instead, he stood silent, looking a little sheepish. Then he took a deep breath and said in a quiet and calm voice, "Sir, I knew you'd be unhappy, but this means a lot to me, and I have to do it. I just haven't been able to get that girl out of my mind. Please understand."

Wend didn't trust himself to speak. Instead, he just nodded and walked past Andrew out the door, then over to the house.

As he arrived in the hall, Peggy came out of the dining room. "You're quite late tonight. Supper is on the table, and everyone is at their places."

Wend shook his head. "I can't eat right now. Start without me. I'm going into the parlor for a drink."

Concern spread over Peggy's face. "What's the matter? You have a dreadful expression on your face. I've never seen you like this."

"I'll tell you what's the matter. Andrew just told me he's planning to leave. Exactly what I've been worried about has come to pass."

He strode over to the liquor cabinet and poured himself a full cup of whiskey and downed half of it in one gulp. He stiffened as the liquid burned its way down his throat.

Peggy disappeared into the dining room but came back after a few seconds. "I told them to go ahead without us for now."

Wend took another pull on the cup. "He intends to leave after we finish this lot of muskets."

Peggy thought a minute, then offered, "That will be some weeks. Maybe he'll reconsider. After all, he just got that letter from the girl."

"I don't think there's much chance. He's besotted with dear Miss Crider."

Peggy crossed her arms. "Then you'll just have to get used to working without him. As we said last night, you'll have to make more use of your own two sons. As far as I'm concerned, that's not a bad outcome." She turned to head back to the dining room. "I've got to get back to the table before the children get out of hand."

Wend held up his hand. "Oh, by the way, there's something else you should know about. Billy plans to go with Andrew. He wants to try to join the army."

Peggy spun on her heel. "What did you say?"

"You heard me. Billy intends to leave with Andrew. Mrs. Callow has given them a cart and will sell them an old nag. They've conspired together and have this all planned."

"*Good Lord!* What shall I do? Billy is such a help around the house—chores, repairs, and helping with the garden." She thought a moment. "Do Wilma and Albert know about this?"

"I don't have a clue." Wend looked up at his wife, smiling for the first time since he had come into the house. "But it seems we are both about to share in the loss."

Peggy stamped her foot. "I shall talk to his parents about this. Surely they will have something to say about his leaving."

Wend shrugged. "He's a grown man, my dear. I'm not sure they can stop him."

Peggy stood for a moment, gritting her teeth. Then she spun about and started to leave. She looked back and said over her shoulder, "I shall have Wilma save you a plate. I think when your anger recedes, you will find you are hungry."

After leaving Eckert Ridge in midafternoon on the day after the party, Rhys drove his team as hard as he dared south along the Ashby Ferry Road, wanting to make good time but taking care not to wear out the animals. He was quite familiar with the route and knew that he would have to hurry if he wanted to make the rendezvous with Welford's troop by nightfall. That is, he thought, if the royalist men had indeed arrived according to the general plan the major had discussed with him on board the *Dunmore*.

Dusk was gathering as he arrived at the ford of a small creek. Rhys knew it emptied into the Shenandoah, which was about a mile eastward. He drove down the slope to the edge of the stream and pulled up to let the horses drink their fill. After they had had enough, he slapped the reins and carefully drove the heavily loaded wagon through the water and up the far bank. The land between the stream and the river was heavily forested but spotted with clearings used for overnight camp by travelers. He expected to find Welford in one of those clearings.

Rhys traveled on, with darkness settling in but no sign of the camp. He thought, *Has something held up Welford and the others?* The plan was for them to be traveling in small groups, but in any case, some of them should have arrived by now. Anxiety arose within him as he was within a quarter mile of the ferry landing and had seen no indication of a camp. He tapped the horses' backs with the reins to increase speed. Then he rounded a curve in the road and breathed a sigh of relief. In a fair-sized clearing, he could see three fires. A rough wagon track turned off the main road leading toward the clearing, and he turned the team onto it and proceeded about a hundred yards. The woods parted, and he was gratified to see what he had hoped for. A least a score of men sat around the fires, and off to one side was a long picket line tethering riding horses. The men were joking and laughing, with many holding cups and others smoking pipes or cigars.

As he entered the clearing, all the men turned to look at him, and one rose from his seat by the fire. Rhys immediately recognized the tall, lean figure of Major Reginald Welford. The ironmonger pulled up his team, and Welford came over and stood beside the wagon. He had a cup in hand. He took a sip, then asked, "All right, Rhys. Have you got what we need?"

Rhys smiled and said, "Indeed, Major. Most certainly. I got the layout of the farm and all the other information you wanted. Let me take care of my animals, and I'll be ready to draw it all out for you." He pointed to the cup in Welford's hand. "And if that's some good West Indies rum, I'd like a bit to help shake off the dust of my travels and make it easier to talk."

Welford nodded. "It is, and you shall have a generous portion."

Twenty minutes later, Rhys joined Welford beside his fire. It was now quite dark, and the flickering flames of the fire formed an oasis of light in the forest. Welford handed the promised cup of rum to the Welshman. "So let's hear what you have, sir."

Rhys took a sip, then said, "Right, sir. I'll start with the details of the farm."

The men of the troop gathered around. Rhys had picked up a stick on his way from the picket line. Now he waved the men back, until he had a piece of open dirt in front of him. He looked around at the faces; the men stared back at him with intense interest. He nodded to Welford and said to the group in general, "Now pay attention, gentlemen, because you will need to have this firmly in your mind when you attack."

They all quieted down as he drew the course of the drive and then began marking in the houses and working buildings of Eckert Ridge in great detail. Then he described the important structures—such as the gunsmith shop, distillery, and barns. Finally he marked a spot to the southwest of the farm. "Gentlemen, this marks a small patch of woods just below the Eckert farm. A small stream runs from the main road past it and then loops up around the farm itself. I would propose that you use that as your assembly point and the place from which to launch the attack."

Following Rhys's comments, Welford looked around the troop and announced, "Now, men, we'll spend the night here, resting ourselves and the horses and making sure our weapons are ready. Tomorrow, in the morning, I will brief you on the specific plan for the attack itself. Then we will proceed northward in small groups to avoid suspicion, although in reality most of the way is very thinly populated. The idea will be to arrive at that small patch of woods Rhys has identified just at dark, and there we can safely spend the night and launch our strike in the early hours of the next day."

Wend stepped out onto the front porch into the deep morning darkness that prevails just before first light. He felt a breeze from the west, which made for a slight chill in the air, but he reflected it had lost the sharp bite of late winter and in fact contained a hint of spring. He stopped a moment to look up at the sky. The heavens were clear, the last stars still visible. The day ahead would be sunny. He looked down along the drive through the farm and saw the only lights were those emanating from the kitchen window of the barracks. The cook would undoubtedly be well along in his preparations for the men's breakfast.

Then suddenly Wend stopped still, his eyes frozen on a spot in the distance. He blinked, unsure he had actually seen anything. But he swore there had been the merest flicker of light down across the fields to the southwest, as if a fire had momentarily flared up. He continued to stare at the spot, but all was dark, with no further sign of light. He shrugged. He knew there was nothing there but woods and fields. After a moment he decided that it could only have been a trick of his mind. Wend shrugged again and went down the steps and hurried across the drive to the workshop.

When he arrived, he found Horner up and dressed. The young man had lit a fire in the hearth and was feeding it wood. He turned to Wend. "Sir, I'm just about to leave for breakfast down at the barracks. When I get back, it should be light enough for you to examine the musket carving that was done yesterday. We made some real progress."

Wend nodded. "Yes, I saw the apprentices busy at it all day." He thought of something. "And we need to do some test firings early this morning. I believe you have two muskets ready and also that pair of horse pistols for Caleb Markey?"

Horner had walked to the door as Wend was talking. He turned around and said, "Yes, sir. I loaded all those pieces last night after supper. I'll put up targets, and we'll be ready for the test."

Wend waved his agreement, and Andrew left for the Barracks. Wend went to his desk, picked up a candle, and lit it from the hearth. Then he walked over to the wall beside his desk, where the firelocks in question hung on brackets, and made a preliminary examination. Everything looked in order. He was particularly pleased with the quality of the finish on the wood of the pistols. Markey, a wealthy planter whose property lay just west of the Battletown Inn, would certainly be very pleased when he saw them and ready to pay the premium price Wend was asking.

Wend carried the candle back to his desk, sat down, and began going through a stack of bills and receipts for the work of the shop that started at the beginning of the month. After his review they would go to Peggy, who would assemble all the data into proper accounts and make an assessment of the financial implications of the month's work. He was at it for quite a while, losing track of time. Then his concentration was broken by voices outside, and he looked up to see Horner and two other apprentices, Hardt and Schmidt, entering the shop. Looking through the doorway, he could see that the first dim light of day had appeared.

After greeting the new arrivals, Wend went back to his paperwork, and Horner got the two apprentices, who were both young and relatively new to the shop, started on their work with the musket manufacturing. Suddenly Wend heard the loud barking of a dog, which was soon joined by several other members of Eckert Ridge's extensive pack of canines. The barking was somewhat distant and seemed to be coming from the western side of the farm. But the barking persisted and grew in volume as more dogs joined in the chorus.

Wend looked over at the apprentices on the other side of the shop and asked, "Now what do you imagine has got the dogs all stirred up?"

Horner said, "I'll take a look." He walked over to the door, looked out, and stood staring for a moment. Then he turned to Wend with a distressed look on his face and said in an urgent tone, "Sir, come here and take a look!"

Irritated, Wend got up and strode to the door. Horner pointed down toward Joshua's house at the far end of the drive.

Wend stared through the half-light and then was stunned by what he saw. There were many orbs of light, at least a score, moving rapidly up toward the farm from the southwest. He squinted and realized to his horror that they were torches, each carried in the hand of a mounted man. The men and their mounts, partially illuminated by the flickering flames, looked ghostly in the near-darkness. Wend stood frozen for a few moments, unable to discern what it all meant. Then the troop rode close by Joshua's house and two men broke off. One vigorously tossed a torch onto the front porch, the flames licking up before the door. The second smashed his torch through the pane of a window. It ended up half-inside. Fire was soon spreading in the residence and climbing up the exterior wall.

Understanding rapidly flowed over Wend. He turned to Horner. "God above! Somebody's attacking the farm!" He looked inside the shop, thinking what to do. Then he shouted, "Andrew, get the muskets and the pistols. Right now!" He turned to the two apprentices, who stood puzzled about what was happening. "You two, be ready to reload! Get powder and balls!"

Suddenly a bell began ringing loudly. Wend realized it was the fire bell, which was positioned by the barracks door. *Somebody else had realized what was happening!* He stepped outside and looked down at the barracks to make out Jacob Specht standing beside the bell, furiously slamming the clapper back and forth with its rope.

The mob of riders had now turned up the drive, and its members were tossing torches into the working farm buildings as they rode. Wend saw one go into the stable and another into the hay barn. He thought, *Thank God all the horses are out in the pasture.*

The pack of farm dogs had turned and was running ahead of the riders, still barking as they went. Wend laughed at them in spite of himself.

Wend looked across the drive to his house and saw that Johann, partially dressed, had come out onto the porch in response to the bell and was staring at the approaching riders.

Wend yelled at the boy, "Get my pistols and rifles. Then gather all the women and children and lead them out the back and down the hill to the creek. Hide in the woods!"

Johann nodded, looked one more time at the horsemen, and disappeared back into the house.

Horner arrived at the door and handed Wend a musket and one of the pistols. He had armed himself the same way. He also carried a rifle, which he leaned up against the door frame. The young man said in a calm voice, "It's too far to fire now." He paused and took a deep breath, then said grimly, "But they'll be within range soon enough."

He had just finished speaking when a shot rang out. Wend saw one of the riders toward the rear of the troop crumple, then fall from his horse. The animal kept running along with the others.

Horner asked, "Who was that shooting?"

Wend responded quietly, "Joshua, no doubt. Coming out of his place and firing from behind them."

Now most of the farmyard buildings were burning and the riders were approaching the barracks. Several men rode right up to the building and smashed torches through the windows.

"I pray," said Horner, "all the hands have got out of there."

Wend nodded. "Pray God."

Two of the horsemen approached William Hecht's cottage and tossed torches into the dwelling.

Wend looked closely and saw the Hechts running out of the back of the house. Hecht had a rifle in hand. He turned back and fired at one of the riders. Wend couldn't determine if he hit anyone, but some of the raiders saw the journeyman and rode toward him, pistols in hand. Momentarily they fired in his direction. Smoke from the now-burning house obscured the entire scene, so Wend could not see the results of their shots or what happened to the Hechts.

Meanwhile a group of men broke off and galloped up toward the distillery and the Donegal house. The area was not visible from where Wend was, but he heard repeated shots from different-caliber guns.

Horner turned to look at Eckert. "Sir, I think Donegal is shooting at them."

Wend responded, "Damned right. I'll be surprised if he doesn't go after them with his broadsword."

Horner looked at the pack of riders as they moved along the drive. "Sir, they'll be here momentarily."

Wend took a deep breath and put a hand on the young man's shoulder. "Andrew, I believe the shop is the main target of this attack. Nothing else makes any sense. They're going to try and destroy this building and all the muskets."

"We'll make them pay for it, sir." Horner went over to the front window of the shop, pushed the shutters open, and called to the other apprentices. "Get over here." He handed Schmidt a musket and gave Hardt his pistol. Then he reached over and picked up the rifle. "You two take a shot at riders as soon as they're in range, then start reloading for Mr. Eckert and myself."

Wend looked around at the apprentices. Horner had been under fire the year before during Dunmore's War and had been with him *in* the pursuit of John Connolly. Wend could see a calmness about him and knew he would be steady. But the two younger men had never seen any combat. Eckert could see the fear manifest in their faces. He said, "Listen now, lads. We're outnumbered, so make every ball count. These men are all on horses. That gives us a bit of an advantage in this situation. If you don't think you can hit the rider, put the ball into the horse. That's almost as good, because it will either leave the rider hard on the ground or trying to control an injured horse. If he's thrown, we can deal with him there, where he'll probably be stunned by the fall. Now, we're going to try to hold the shop, but if I tell you to run, don't hesitate—just run out the back."

Suddenly Horner called out, "My God, sir, look at the porch of your house!"

Wend turned to see a sight that stopped him cold. Peggy was there, still dressed in her night clothes. She was carrying the pistols from his saddle holsters. As he watched, she started screaming epithets in the general direction of the raiders. It started with the words "You bastards!" and got more sailor-like as she went on.

Horner stood in shock at what he was hearing. He said in a startled voice, "Good Lord! Where did she learn such words?"

Wend turned to his apprentice and said, "Andrew, if you ever do marry Emily Crider, always keep this in mind: never—*under any circumstances*—anger an Ulster-Scot tavern maid."

He looked back to the house and saw that Peggy, still screaming out curses, had gone to her knees and was bracing one of the pistols over the railing as she aimed at the riders. Then, behind her, he saw Johann emerge, rifle in hand. Wend shook his head and sighed. "Apparently no one is listening to me today."

Turning back toward the horsemen, Wend saw that they were now at point-blank musket range. He called out to his companions, "All right, pick your man and shoot!"

From beside him Andrew fired immediately. One of the leading men slumped against his horse's neck and dropped his torch. The horse carried the wounded man past the shop and down the drive.

Wend aimed his musket at another rider and pulled the trigger. The ball hit him in the chest, and he slid off his mount and went to the ground in a heap. Wend dropped the long gun and picked up the large, heavy horse pistol and braced the barrel over his left arm as he looked for a target.

Wend's eyes settled on a rider in a red military coat with blue facings. He suddenly realized it was an officer's coat of the 60th— the Royal Americans. He looked up at the rider's face and instantly recognition flowed through him: *Major Reginald Welford.* Late of His Majesty's 1st Guards, late of the 60th, late of General Gage's staff, currently serving Lord Dunmore, and above all one of the most arrogant and despicable officers in the British Army. As Wend watched, Welford, who was still carrying a torch, tossed it onto the roof of the lean-to that sheltered the rifling machine. He reached down and pulled a pistol out of his saddle holster. At the same time, he called out to other men to fire the shop.

Wend quickly took aim and fired. But Welford's horse moved, and the ball only knocked the officer's hat into the air.

Welford saw Wend, and a tight smile spread over his lips. He instantly pulled on the reins to still his horse, aimed, and fired. Wend felt a hammer blow, followed by searing heat on the left side of his head, and then suddenly everything went black.

CHAPTER FOUR
AFTERMATH

Horner and the other apprentices, all sooty and exhausted, stood in a group looking at the burned-out gunsmith shop. Flames were still flaring up occasionally. It was nearly noon, and they had been working hard since dawn, when the troop of raiders had completed their destructive sweep through the farm and ridden down the drive, pursued by gunfire from residents.

Horner, assisted by Schmidt and Hardt, had pulled the limp Eckert, his head bloody from a long wound along the left side of his head, out of the shop as the flames were taking hold.

After the gunsmith went down, the raiders had thrown seven or eight torches into the shop nearly simultaneously. Horner and the others had been able to throw back a couple of the torches, but there had been no question about saving the building. However, the contents were another thing. After getting Wend to safety, they had begun darting into the shop and grabbing everything that could move. Soon the three were joined by the other apprentices, who had run up from the barracks. Horner set the new arrivals busy grabbing the finished muskets from the storage area before the flames got to most of them. Several were scorched, but that was the extent of it. Horner was also able to get a lot of the tools out, but his crowning achievement was saving the rifling machine. He and three others manhandled the heavy device far enough out into the drive that the flames consuming the lean-to couldn't reach it.

Immediately after the raiders left, Johann and Bernd had run over from the house to help their father, only to find him unconscious. They had carefully picked Wend up and carried him back to their home.

Horner, standing in the middle of the drive, looked at the Eckert house now and smiled. It stood, scorched in a few places but structurally intact. And much of that was due to the bold actions of Mrs. Eckert. She and Johann had crouched behind the railing, firing at the raiders, and she had actually hit one of the men, who dropped his torch, crouched over his saddle, and rode away down the drive. But two men had got in close and tossed torches at the house. One had landed on the porch, but Peggy had grabbed a broom and used it to literally sweep the torch back down onto the ground. A few flames had taken hold on the railing and a support post for the roof, but she used the broom to swat them out. The other torch had smashed through the window of the dining room, but Wilma and Billy had been inside and smothered it with blankets before the flames did much damage.

Now Horner looked along the drive and at the rest of the farm for the first time and paused to assess the extent of the destruction.

He was shocked.

Many of the important buildings of Eckert Ridge were smoking ruins. The walls of the barracks still stood, but its roof had been burned off. Beyond that, most of the farmyard barns and sheds were burned out. Some buildings did remain intact. Andrew saw that Wilhelm Hecht's house stood slightly burned. It looked like the raiders hadn't expended much effort on it. Horner thought, *Probably saving torches for the shop.* Horner looked over at Donegal's new house. It also looked almost untouched; it was some distance to the south of the drive, actually beyond the barracks. *Probably saved for the same reason as Hecht's cottage or perhaps by Donegal's stand.* He had heard repeated shots emanating from there during the raid. Then he stared in surprise—the distillery stood intact. He realized it was set back from the central drive, even farther back than the Donegal house. That had probably spared it.

As he stared, Horner saw Jacob Specht coming from the direction of the Donegal house. He was hurrying, almost running, smoke from the barracks swirling around him. In a few seconds, he was near Horner. Andrew flagged him down. "Why the hurry, Jacob?"

"Got to get Mrs. Eckert to come down to the Donegal place."

"I think she's busy taking care of Mr. Eckert. A ball grazed the side of his head, and he's still unconscious."

"I need her to help with Donegal."

Horner was puzzled. "Help with Donegal?" He laughed. "When did that Highlander need help from a woman?"

Specht stopped and turned to the apprentice, a grim look on his face. "Haven't you heard?"

"I haven't heard anything. Been too busy with the shop. Heard what?"

The master of the horse took a deep breath. "Donegal was firing at the riders from his porch with rifle and pistols. Sally was behind him reloading his firelocks. She took a pistol ball in the chest from a rider who came in close and was aiming at Donegal. She bled out and died before Donegal could do anything. Now he's got her laid out in the parlor, and he's damn well gone crazy. Won't let anyone near him or the body. He's got a pistol and that great broadsword of his at hand. The two kids are wailing, with nobody to take care of them."

Horner was immediately filled with rage. "God above! The poor woman. Who are these bastards that would shoot at a woman?"

"Who they were is a damn good question! But the worst part for Donegal is she was pregnant."

Andrew gasped. "God, yes, I forgot! So Donegal lost his wife and his own child."

"That's it, Horner. I think that's why he's takin' it so hard." Specht looked up at the house. "I'm thinkin' only Mrs. Eckert will be able to deal with him. She's got a way about her."

"You'll get no argument about that from me." He pointed toward the Eckerts' porch. "She shot a man with one of Mr. Eckert's pistols. That was just before she picked up a broom and swept the torch he had thrown right off the porch before the flames could fairly catch hold." He raised his eyebrows. "And all the while, she was screaming out words I have never heard a woman use before or for that matter, even a man."

Specht nodded, a crooked smile on his lips. "You don't have to tell me. I've seen her mad before." He stopped and looked back at Horner. "But then I also seen her dressed all up like a fine lady talkin' to people of the gentry like she was one of them. Like I say, she's got a way about her."

With that, he turned and hurried up the steps to the house.

In only a minute, he came back out, followed by Mrs. Eckert, Wilma, and Billy. They all ran down the steps. Peggy looked at Horner. "Andrew, you come with us!" Then she was off toward the Donegal place.

Horner followed behind. Peggy had only gone a few steps when she stopped and looked at Specht. "Do we have many people hurt? And dead?"

Specht replied, "Ma'am, we got two of the farmhands who were injured. One took a ball in his shoulder, the other got burned by a flaming beam which fell on him while tryin' to get stuff out of the barracks. As far as dead, you know about Mrs. Donegal. And there's little Jebediah Hecht, ma'am; he got shot in the back tryin' to run down to the woods by the creek. Ball was probably meant for Wilhelm, who was tryin' to cover his family while they escaped.

"Good Lord! Not Jebby? He was only eight."

"Sorry, Mrs. Eckert, but I saw him lyin' on the ground, with his mother sittin' beside him cryin', with Wilhelm trying to console her."

Peggy's face turned red. A fierce look came over her face. "Jacob, send a rider to Winchester to let Sheriff Smith know what's happened, and then fetch Doctor Harmon posthaste." She paused a minute as a thought struck her. "Have we still got saddles and harness? Or did the tack building get burned out?

"No, ma'am. I guess they didn't think that little shack was important. All the leather's still fine."

"Good. You go get someone mounted and on his way!"

Specht hurried off, and Peggy resumed her march, followed by her entourage. Shortly they were at the Donegal house.

The two children were huddled together on the porch, still in their nightclothes. Louisa had tears running down her face, but she was trying to console Henry, who was sobbing uncontrollably.

Peggy led the group up the steps, where Wilma stopped to gather up the children and shepherd them over to the Eckert house. The others went into the front hall, where they immediately stopped, frozen by what they beheld in the parlor.

Horner knew he would never forget what he saw.

Sally Donegal's body was laid out on the floor, arms crossed over her chest. She was covered in blood from the chest down to the waist.

Her face was white as a bedsheet, her mouth was open wide, but her eyes were nearly closed, just a slit showing.

But what shocked Horner most was Donegal.

The Highlander was on his knees, his pistol on the floor by his right hand and his broadsword on the left. His hands were clasped in front of him; he was wringing them constantly, and his body was rocking backward and forward. Horner had always thought of him as the hardest of men: battle-seasoned former corporal of a Highland regiment, veteran of border wars, a man who had seen all the evil and death there was to witness. But here he was sobbing, copious tears flowing down his powder-stained face and periodically groaning and whimpering like a child as he cried.

They all stood there staring for a long moment, and their silence became palpable. Then Donegal sensed their presence. He slowly turned his head toward the hall, and his eyes opened. At first they were unfocused, as if not really registering what he was seeing. Then recognition spread across his face.

He sighed deeply, his chest heaved, and then he said in a quiet voice, "Ah na, Peggy, she's dead. She had but a moment to know what happened and no chance to say a word. The bastards, whoever they might be, shot her down like an animal. Shot a woman."

Peggy moved slowly, hesitantly forward until she was beside the kneeling Scot. Then she gently put her hand on his shoulder and whispered, "We've come to take care of her, Simon." She paused and looked into his eyes. "That is, if you're ready."

He sobbed once again, then he slowly nodded. "There's na more to be done."

Peggy gave him her hand, and he rose to his feet. Then she led him like a child out of the room. As they went, she said quietly to Horner, "Get a blanket." And she motioned back to Sally's body.

Horner ran upstairs and pulled a blanket off a bed in one of the rooms, then returned to the parlor and, with Billy's assistance, wrapped it tightly around Sally's body.

As they were doing so, something occurred to Andrew. "Billy," he said, "we're going to have to find some place to put all these bodies until we can get them buried. There's Sally and Jebby and then the raiders who were shot."

Just as they finished covering Sally, Horner heard the sound of hoofbeats, and he looked out the window to see Charlie Sowers, one of the hands, riding out at the trot. He thought, *When Charlie gets to Winchester and the word spreads about what's happened, there's going to be the devil to pay.* It came to him that the flames that had destroyed the buildings of Eckert Ridge would be nothing compared to the burning fury of the people of Winchester.

—⁂—

The first response to the attack didn't come as a result of Charlie Sower's ride into Winchester. It came much sooner and from a much closer place.

With the help of Johann, Bernd, and Billy, Peggy had gotten the still unconscious Wend out of the parlor and up to their room and into bed. She had dressed the heavily bleeding wound along the side of his head the best she could, taken his clothes off, and done everything she could to make him comfortable. Now she could only wait for him to open his eyes or for the doctor to arrive. But as she sat beside her husband, she soon realized Wend wasn't her only responsibility. Thinking back on what she had seen while tending to Donegal, she realized that someone must take charge to pull things together throughout the farm. And *she* was mistress of Eckert Ridge.

Peggy rose from her chair, went downstairs, and found Wilma trying to restore order in the dining room.

"Wilma, I've got to go out and see what's happening around the farm. Please send Liza up to sit with Wend. Send for me if he wakes up."

With that, she left the house, determined to make sure that everyone was working to begin the recovery. First, she walked over to the burned-out shop, noticing with relief that the rifling machine had been dragged out into the drive and that that piece of vital equipment at least was safe. She saw that Horner had the apprentices organizing the muskets and tools that had been saved.

Peggy stood watching and listening for a few moments. She realized that the most important items from the shop had been recovered. She thought, *Wend certainly had it right regarding how valuable Andrew was to their operations.* She decided that the lead apprentice had things under control at the shop. Turning, she was starting to walk down the drive to find Specht and take a look at what was left of the farmyard buildings when she heard Horner calling her.

"Mrs. Eckert! There's a wagon and a rider coming up the drive! Looks like Mrs. Morgan and some of her hands!"

Peggy turned around to look down the hill. She squinted against the bright light and sure enough made out Abbey Morgan seated in a small wagon drawn by a team. Two of the wagoners from the Morgan freight line were with her. Elijah McCartney drove the wagon, and Jake Cather, the lead teamster, rode out ahead on horseback. The two men were carrying rifles.

Soon the newcomers had pulled up in front of the wrecked workshop. Abby jumped down from the wagon. Peggy noted she was in her workday clothes, an old patched gown with an apron and a white cap over her head.

"My God, Peggy! We saw the smoke and thought one of your buildings had caught fire. But then it got thicker and spread wide, and I knew more than one building was burning. So I got Jake to rig the team and we headed over here. We had just got out onto the Ashby Ferry Road when your man Sowers came riding up and told us what had happened!" She looked down the drive at the ruins of the farm, with considerable smoke still rising. "But he didn't no way tell the whole story! Good Lord, everything is burned out! Who would have done this, and why?"

With rage written large on her face, Peggy responded, "I damn well know who did it: Dunmore's loyalists, that's who. It must be because of the muskets!" She pointed at the shop. "Horner says they made sure it would be destroyed. They threw torch after torch in there."

Abby looked around. "*Horner* thinks? What does Wend say? Where is he?"

"Upstairs in the house." Peggy motioned with her hand. "Lying unconscious with a wound along the side of his head."

Abby was quiet for a minute. Then she asked softly, "Who else did they hurt?"

Peggy sighed. "Sally is dead. So is the Hecht's boy, Jebediah."

Shock registered across Abby's face. "Women and children dead? Sally and Jebby? Good God, what kind of men were these?"

"I don't know who precisely they were. Two of them are dead. Joshua got one and so did Wend, before they hit him."

Horner spoke up. "Mrs. Eckert put a pistol ball in one of them, shooting from the porch, but he managed to stay on his horse."

Abby looked at her in shock and put a hand on her shoulder. "Good girl! But my God, Peggy, why weren't you in the house or down in the woods?"

"You know me better than that, Abby. They damn well weren't going to burn my house down. And they sure tried."

Abby was about to answer when Horner, pointing westward along the drive, said, "Mrs. Eckert, look at that, down in the farm buildings."

Everyone turned and looked toward the farmyard.

They saw two figures pushing through the wafting layers of smoke, walking toward them with saddled horses in hand. One was tall, lean, angular and walked with a limp on his left leg: Joshua Baird, dressed in his hunting shirt, leggings, and wide-brimmed hat with the left side turned up over a bucktail. He was leading his long-legged, powerful hunter, Beau. Beside him was a youth, also thin but not quite as tall as Baird, similarly dressed in hunting clothes with a floppy hat atop his head. It was Johann Eckert, walking beside Joshua with the long stride gained from years of living in the forest. He was leading young Sonny. Both carried rifles in the crook of their arm and had pistols hung in holsters before the saddles of the animals. Saddlebags and bedrolls were lashed to the rear of the saddles.

Abby Morgan remarked, "Looks like Joshua's got some sort of hunt in mind."

Jake grinned broadly. "Yes, ma'am! And he ain't goin' after no four-legged creatures either!"

Meanwhile the pair had arrived at the place where the little group stood.

An angry expression came over Peggy's face. "Damn your bones, Joshua Baird! Where the hell do you think you're going? We've got to start putting things back together, and just like every other time there's hard work to do, you're skedaddling out with some flimsy excuse."

"There ain't no excuse. And we're just doin' another kind of work. Johann and me are goin' to find the men who did this. That's just as important as cleaning up." He waved his hand around at the group and back down toward the farm. "And you got plenty of men to get started on what you got to do."

Peggy stamped her foot. "Are you planning to take on that whole mob of men—near twenty with just the two of you?" She looked over at Johann. "And why do you think you can take Wend's son—and my stepson—on this fool's errand?" She turned to Johann. "You go back and unsaddle. There's much work to do here, and besides, we need you to help to take care of your father."

Joshua rolled his eyes skyward. "Now, Peggy, you've known me since you was a little girl in Reverend Carnahan's school back at Sherman Mill. Afore you even started bein' a maid at your father's tavern. So you know I ain't ridin' out to do anything foolish and we ain't goin' to a fight. We're goin' on a *scout*. To find out who those men were and where they came from and why nobody knew anything about them. That's what we need to know before we lay out a reckoning for what they did. And we got to find out now while the trail is fresh."

Abby looked at her friend and put a hand on her arm. "He's makin' sense, Peggy. We got to find out exactly who did this, besides that they're just royalists. And Joshua's the best scout in Frederick County, even with that wrecked leg of his."

Joshua retorted, "Abby, I could have gone all day without you talkin' about my leg. And it don't slow me down for this kind of work."

Peggy shot back sarcastically, "No, it just keeps you from doing any hard work around the farm."

The scout sighed deeply and looked at the heavens. "Now, lass, don't use that McCartie temper of yours on me."

Peggy stood silent for a moment. Then she stamped a foot and said, "All right, do what you will, Joshua. But Johann stays here. I'll not have Wend waking up to find his son has been hurt or worse. Take someone else with you."

Joshua looked over at Johann. "Now look, Peggy, the Sprout is the best man here on the Ridge for the job we got to do. After livin' in the forest most of his life, he knows how to read sign better than anyone." He shrugged and grinned. "Leastways, 'cept me." He put his hand on Johann's shoulder. "And he's 'bout the same age as when I took out Wend on the war trail the first time. If his pa was awake, he'd be proud for him to come out with me."

Johann spoke for the first time. "Mother Eckert, I'm old enough. And I want to help find the men who did this to our farm and hurt father. It is a son's duty." He paused and looked his stepmother in the eye. "And you know father rode to avenge his family after they were killed. I must do the same with these men."

Peggy stood silent, her chin jutting out.

Joshua stepped close to Peggy and said in a soft, reassuring tone, "Now, darlin', you know he's right. Deep down you know Wend would want him to go. And I vow I'll not let any harm come to him."

Peggy jabbed a finger at Joshua. "That's an empty vow! Who knows what will happen."

Baird continued, "And in any case, the Sprout can take care of himself." He turned to Johann. "Let's mount. The day's wasting, and we got a ways to go and a lot to do."

Baird swung up into the saddle, doffed his hat to Peggy and Abby, and then the two were off down the drive at the gallop, the noise of their powerful mounts' pounding hooves echoing over the ridge.

❧

After Joshua and Johann departed, Peggy and Abby turned and walked along the drive through the burned-out buildings. Specht accompanied them. They stopped by the barracks, now simply walls standing with the roof burnt out and collapsed.

Peggy stopped and looked over the ruin, worry written across her face. "We've got to find a way to shelter all the hands and apprentices. And I've got to do that before nightfall." She thought for a time. "Maybe we could find enough canvas for tents." She turned to Specht. "Do you think we still have anything to make tents?"

Specht sighed. "Can't think of anything. Had it all stored in one of the sheds which is burned out."

Abby shook her head. "Canvas ain't gonna do, even if you can get your hands on some. Still too many cold and rainy spring nights ahead. They'd be fightin' the mud all the time." She pointed at the Donegal house. "That's your answer. With Sally dead, there's plenty of room in there for all the single men. That's your new barracks, leastways for now."

Peggy slowly nodded. "You're right." She looked back up at the main house and sighed. "But I'll have to clear it with Donegal, when he starts being rational again. He's still deeply lost in mourning. Right now he's sitting up in my parlor, soaking himself in whiskey. He's still out of this world."

"You just do it, and he'll have to accept it when he shakes himself back to reality. There really ain't no choice."

Peggy shrugged. "I guess you're right. After all, he lived in the barracks before Sally came."

Abby pointed to the distillery, which was sited just to the west of the house. "Look, it hasn't been touched."

Peggy shrugged. "They probably didn't have time to get to it; they rode through fast, and I don't think they expected so much resistance. Anyway, Horner thinks they were saving enough torches to make sure of the gun shop."

Abby looked at Peggy. "But do you know what that means?"

Peggy was puzzled for a moment, then it hit her. "Why, if we can get that running, we still have a source of income! It will help us keep going until the shop can be rebuilt."

"That's it. And it will give somethin' for Donegal to do, help pull his mind off Sally."

The two women started walking again until they came to the remnants of the barns and farm sheds. Peggy shook her head. "Look, all the hay is a loss. And we've got weeks until the grass starts growing and gets high enough to feed the horses."

Specht spoke up. "That ain't the worst of it. We lost a lot of the grain—oats for the animals." He shook his head. "They're goin' to have a rough spring, just when they normally build up their weight and strength."

Abby put her hand on Peggy's shoulder. "We'll bring you a couple loads of hay from our stock. I got some to spare."

Specht looked relieved. "We'd greatly appreciate that, ma'am. That's been on my mind ever since the raid."

"Yes, Abby, that's very kind of you. It will keep us going for a while at least." Then a thought hit Peggy. A look of extreme distress came over her face. She turned to Specht. "Jacob! What about my chaise? Did it get burned with the wagon shed?"

The master of the horse grinned broadly. "Ma'am, that's the first thing I thought about! Frederick County wouldn't be the same without you runnin' around the roads in that little cart. No, ma'am, that was what I did right after I rang the fire bell this mornin'. I ran around behind the stable so those loyalists wouldn't see me and went directly to the wagon shed. They had the roof on fire, but I got your chaise out first thing and parked it in the woods. It's safe as can be!"

"Bless you, Jacob!" Peggy grinned from ear to ear. Then a more serious thought hit her, and the grin was replaced by a look of concern. "What about the wagons? We'll need those badly."

"After I hid the chaise, I got to work on those, Mrs. Eckert. Charlie Sowers came to join me, and we manhandled two of the wagons out of the shed afore the fire got to them. And like I said, the harness shack is safe, so we're in good shape at least that ways."

"So we lost one wagon and a cart?"

"Yes, ma'am, fire was too hot when we got to them two."

Peggy looked over at Abby. "Well, things could be worse."

A new female voice said, "Yes, it could be a damned sight worse."

Peggy and Abby looked around to see Alice Downy approaching. Her face was soot-stained, as was her clothing.

"Alice, you look a sight!" exclaimed Peggy. "But how's your house?"

Alice pointed over her shoulder. "See for yourself. They started a fire, but Joshua and I got to it with blankets before it could get fairly started. Scorched the side of the house and part of my sewing room, but that's all." She looked up the drive and said, "Before he left, Joshua told me about Sally and the Hecht boy."

As she looked up the drive, her eyebrows raised and she nodded. "We got some more company."

Everyone turned around to see a wagon and team stopped beside the wreckage of the shop. The occupants were talking to Horner.

Peggy said, "It's Edna Callow and some of her Africans."

As she spoke, the black driver of the wagon slapped the reins on the horses' back and the wagon started coming toward them. Edna waved her hand toward the little group, and Peggy waved back. The wagon arrived in a minute, and the Widow Callow jumped down. "God above, Peggy! This is terrible." She paused a moment and said, "I was wonderin' what all the smoke was about and had just about decided to come look when Joshua and Johann came ridin' by and told us what was toward. We harnessed the team and came right away!" She pointed to the men in the back of the wagon. "My men are here to help you clean up and get things in order!"

Peggy nodded. "Edna, we're very grateful."

Widow Callow looked around. "Where are Wend and Donegal? They leaving it up to the women?"

The other three looked at each other. Then Peggy responded, "Edna, Wend has a head wound. He's unconscious. I've called the physician. And Donegal is beside himself mourning Sally. He might as well be unconscious like Wend."

Edna Callow straightened up. "You mean a soldier of the British Army, a Highlander at that, can't put his grief aside to get started on puttin' things back together? While he leaves the women to do the work?"

Peggy nodded. "Edna, he really is beside himself."

Edna straightened her back. "Where is Corporal Donegal?"

"He's in my house, sitting in the parlor. Staring straight ahead and drinking hard."

"Let me go see him. By God, I didn't spend twenty and more years as an army wife, a captain's lady, to stand by and see a Highlander not able to put aside his personal grief when duty is a-callin'."

Peggy waved back at the house. "Of course, Edna. Go see what you can do. There are some things we need to talk to him about so we can make decisions."

—∿—

It was late afternoon when the two scouts reached Ashby's Ferry on the Shenandoah. As they arrived, the ferry was just coming into the landing on the near side of the river; it carried a blue Conestoga with a six-horse team on its deck. Joshua and Johann dismounted and eased the girths on their mounts as they waited for the boat to make its landing. After the wagon disembarked, the two led their horses up onto the flatboat's deck and tied them off to a rail. The trip would take only a few minutes.

Joshua turned to Johann and pointed to buildings that stood on the far bank. "Sprout, the house on the right is Ashby's place. He runs the ferry business out of there. That's a tavern across the road from Ashby's home. We'll talk to Ashby first, then go over to the tavern to see what the proprietor knows."

Ashby himself came to greet the ferry and collect their fares. He put out his hand, but Joshua held his up to pause the transaction.

"Ashby, my name's Baird. Joshua Baird. I'm scouting for Angus McDonald's battalion of the Frederick County Militia."

The ferryman raised an eyebrow and made a very exaggerated puzzled face. He looked back and forth at the two men before him. "Scouting? Scouting around here? For God's sake, why?"

"There's been a raid by Royalists. They burned down a farm called Eckert Ridge."

"Eckert Ridge? I heard of a fellow named Eckert. He's a German gunsmith. And supposed to be a crack shot. Lives up the road here toward Battletown Crossroads."

"That's the one. He's been making muskets for the Virginia forces. We think the attack was because of that."

"Hell, Baird, the only Royalists which are fightin' that I know about are down in the Tidewater near Norfolk. How the devil would they get up around here?"

"Now, Ashby, that's exactly the point." Joshua pointed back toward the ferry barge. "We figure there's a good chance they'd have to come through here." He turned around and pointed across the river. "Now it happens we found a place where a lot of men camped. It's 'bout a quarter mile up the road, round a bend. There were the ashes of several fires, hoof marks, and other signs showin' there was a picket line with more than twenty horses tied up. And wagon tracks goin' in and out of the camp."

Ashby shrugged. "That's a lot of men."

"Yes, and now you know why we're talkin' to you. You seen a big group of men comin' through here?"

The ferry proprietor shook his head. "No. I damn well would have noticed a troop of riders." Then he paused, lost in thought. "Wait a minute!" He nodded. "Now you mention it, there has been a lot of riders comin' across, not together, mind you, but over several days. In twos and threes. Didn't have any reason to think upon it till now."

Joshua and Johann exchanged glances. "You seen anything else outside the normal?"

Ashby shook his head. "Naw. Just the usual traffic. Mostly freight wagons and some peddlers." He pointed back toward the ferry again. "There's been some riders goin' south today. But not nearly enough to explain all the people you're lookin' for."

Johann turned to Joshua. "I'm thinking they probably broke up and went south different ways. Some of them may be going down the Valley to LeHewtown to cross the Blue Ridge through the gap which starts there."

"Yeah." Baird nodded. "You're probably right about that, Sprout."

Ashby had his hand up to his chin and was staring off into the distance. "Were any of those loyalists hurt in the raid?"

"Yeah, at least one we know about was wounded. Shot while ridin' but managed to stay on his horse."

The ferry proprietor froze a minute, then held up his finger. "Well, Baird, now you say that, I did see somethin' which roused my curiosity."

Joshua said impatiently, "Well, spit it out, man."

"There was a wagon that crossed about an hour ago. Driven by that Welsh ironmonger; I think Rhys is his name."

Joshua and Johann quickly looked at each other. "You sayin' Rhys crossed today?"

"Yeah, like I said, about an hour ago." Ashby waved his finger again. "But that wasn't what roused my attention. I walked by the rear gate of the wagon, and I thought I saw movement under blankets and canvas tarpaulins which were piled up in the bed. Like someone layin' in there tryin' to hide." He shrugged his shoulders. "Didn't think a whole lot about it, wasn't really sure what I had seen."

"You say anything to Rhys about that?"

"Nope, weren't any of my business. I charge for wagons by one fee, not how many people are with it. And like I said, wasn't sure about it."

Joshua reached out, a coin in his hand. "Here's your fare for our crossing. And you've been very helpful."

They led their horses off a short distance.

Johann said, "I don't think we need to ask any questions at the tavern. We found out what we wanted. He worked to tighten his girth."

Joshua sighed. "Nope, we don't." He looked winsomely at the tavern. "But I hate to have to pass up a bit of libation." Joshua tightened Beau's girth. "Now we know why that damned ironmonger was here before court day. And if Rhys is an hour ahead, in a wagon, we ought to be able to catch up before dark, if we push the horses."

"We pushed them hard on the way down here."

"Beau will take it and so will that big colt of yours. He's strong, and if I'm any judge of horses, someday he'll be more powerful than old Beau here." He looked at Johann. "And Sprout, if we don't run down that wagon by dark, we'll take him while he's campin' or at a tavern, if that's where he stops. But either way, Rhys don't know it now, but as God is my witness, that bastard is goin' to have a very uncomfortable night."

Edna Callow walked into the Eckert's parlor. Alice Downy had come with her. The two stood looking at Simon Donegal as he sat in misery, slumped over in an armchair, pewter cup of whiskey in hand, staring sightlessly into the distance. He took no notice of the two women.

Widow Callow took the initiative. In a parade-ground voice, she called out, "Corporal Donegal!"

Simon continued staring, but a grimace came over his face.

Edna looked at Alice Downy and shook her head. "He needs a shock to come out of this." She looked around the room, then walked over to the fireplace and picked up a three-foot stick serving as a poker. She walked over to Donegal and without the slightest hesitation, swung the switch and whipped the cup out of the Highlander's hand without actually striking any flesh.

Alice raised her eyebrows. She said in a calm voice, "Damn, Edna, that was deft. I thought you were going to take off a finger or two."

"Got plenty of practice at this thing with young soldiers over the years. Able to smack just about where I want." She looked back at Donegal "Now are you going to listen to me, or do I have to whack you alongside the head to get your attention?"

The Highlander was looking down at his hand, where the cup had formerly resided, his eyes wide in astonishment. Then he turned to look at the women. "Leave me be. They killed my woman. A man's got a right to mourn."

Edna shook her head. "Not when the farm's been burnt down around us and there's a powerful amount of work to be done." She smacked the stick down on the wooden arm of a chair. "There needs to be a man out there to take charge. All the work is bein' run by women and apprentices. You're one of the owners, and there's no one else to take charge."

"Go talk to Wend. Why isn't he out there?"

Alice said, "Simon, Wend's been shot. Shot in the head. He's out like a light. And my Joshua has ridden out to scout the men who did this. But poor Wilhelm Hecht is over cleanin' up the gun shop, and he lost his boy."

Donegal's brow furrowed. "Ah na, they killed little Jebby?"

Alice nodded. "That's a fact. But like I said, it ain't keepin' Wilhelm from his duty."

Widow Callow said in her harsh, parade-ground voice, "That's right, Wilhelm Hecht is working through his grief. Everyone knows that boy was the light of his life. But I'll tell you, I never thought I'd see a corporal of the 77th, and a Highland man, to boot, using his grief as a reason not to get on with things. There'll be a time to grieve and a time for revenge, but right now we have to start setting things right on Eckert Ridge."

"Na it sounds to me like things are gettin' done. Leave me be."

Alice said, "Not likely, Simon. There's one thing that's got to be done, and you're the only one who can do it. And it will mean everything to Eckert Ridge."

Now Donegal turned and stared at Alice. "An' what will that be?"

It was Edna who answered. "You've got to get the distillery back operating. Turnin' out whiskey. And you're the only one who knows how to do it properly."

A bemused Simon said, "They didn't burn it?"

"Didn't touch it," responded Edna, "nor the grain storage huts beside it."

Donegal shrugged. "What are you so worked up about? They burned down the farm. Na what's suddenly so important about makin' whiskey?"

Edna smacked the stick down smartly again on the chair's arm, causing Donegal to jump. "Don't you get it, you big dolt? The farm's goin' to need money to get built back up. The gun shop has got to be rebuilt and ain't gonna be ready to work for weeks. You need to turn out batches of whiskey to pay for rebuildin'; that's why! There'll be a need for lumber and other supplies. Even a wild Highlander ought to be able to figure that out! Particularly one who's smart enough to make spirits."

Alice came over and put her hand on Donegal's shoulder. She said, in a manner far gentler than Edna's hard tones, "And there's somethin' else to do. You got to start takin' care of Louisa and little Henry. Sally was their mother, but you're the one who has got to take care of them now. They have come to think of you as their father."

Donegal looked at Alice and slowly nodded, understanding flowing into his eyes. "Aye, you're right about that." He rose to his feet. "Where are the little ones?"

Alice replied, "Right here in this house. Wilma's lookin' over them since the raid."

Edna said, "There's somethin' else to think about. Your barracks are all burnt down. There's no place for the hands and apprentices to live." She looked over at Alice and then back to Donegal. "So we were thinkin' of puttin' them up in your house; it's big enough to hold all of them. And your cookhouse could be used to feed them."

Alice interjected, "I say you and the children come live with Joshua and me. There's plenty of room. And I can look over the little ones while you are workin'."

A scowl came over the Highlander's face. "Aye, take the house. That was Sally's pride and joy, but I canna live there anymore. I'd be thinkin' of her every minute. Her spirit would haunt me in the night." He shrugged. "Aye, we'll come live with you, Alice."

Edna grabbed Donegal by the arm. "Good! That's settled. Now let's go over to the distillery and see what it's going to take to get things going."

Donegal nodded, and the three of them set off immediately.

Two hours after they left the ferry, dusk was rapidly settling in. The two scouts had relentlessly urged the horses on, not taking any rest or dismounting to walk.

Johann turned to the older man. "These horses are feeling the pace, Joshua. Sonny is tiring; I can sense it."

"Yeah, Beau's heart isn't in it after all this time." He looked around. "But we gone a fair piece. Rhys can't be far now."

It turned out that Joshua was prescient. The two were amid heavy forestation, and as they rode around a sharp bend, to their surprise, they sighted a wagon with a two-horse team pulled off beside the track. It was a mere forty or fifty yards ahead. Rhys stood beside the team.

What was even more surprising was that two riders were sitting their horses alongside the wagon.

Rhys looked up at the new arrivals, and immediately recognition came over his face. He shouted at the riders while pointing at Joshua and Johann.

The two mounted men turned their horses and spurred toward the scouts. At the same time, they pulled out pistols.

"Oh, shit!" Exclaimed Joshua. "Shit, shit!" He looked over at Johann. "Our horses are too tired to outrun them. We ain't got any choice!" He reached down to draw a firelock. "Get your pistols out!"

Johann was already pulling a firelock out of the saddle holster.

Pistols in hand, both men spurred toward their armed opponents.

The two loyalists closed to within fifteen feet and fired almost simultaneously.

As they shot, Sonny, startled by the noise, reared up on his hind legs, dumping Johann to the ground, where the youth lay momentarily stunned.

Beau, trained to the pistol, stood rock steady. Joshua quickly aimed and shot the rider who had fired at Johann. The man dropped off his horse and lay still on the ground. Joshua heard the sound of another shot and felt the hot wind of a ball whipping passed his head. He pulled out his second pistol, steadied Beau, carefully aimed, and shot the second loyalist. The man sat still in his saddle for a long moment, staring into the distance. Then fell right over and landed on the ground headfirst.

Joshua dismounted, checked both loyalists to ensure they were dead, then walked over to where Johann lay, trying to catch his breath.

The youth said, "I'm sorry, Joshua. I lost control of Sonny. I wasn't any use to you."

"It weren't you. That horse ain't never heard gunfire before. They got to be trained to it." He looked over the lad. "In case you don't realize it, you been shot in the left shoulder."

Johann quickly looked over and saw the tear in his hunting shirt. He reached over with his right hand and felt the wound. Blood covered his hand. But he quickly said, "I'll be all right; it just grazed along my arm."

Joshua sighed deeply and shook his head. "Yeah, at the moment I ain't worried about you. We'll bandage that up when we get a chance. It's me that's in big hurt."

"What do you mean? Have you been hit?"

"Hit? Hell no. That ain't it. But after that argument back at the Ridge just afore we left, your stepma sees that wound, she's gonna grab a pitchfork and chase me up and down the drive callin' me every name she can think of. I'm gonna be on her bad side for months."

Johann laughed. "I can't believe you are worried about that!"

"I've known Peggy since she was at her ma's skirts. We get back, she's gonna give me hell." Joshua held out his hand to Johann. "Come on, get up." Once the youth was on his feet, he continued, "You round up all the horses. I'll drag these bodies into the bush so travelers don't see them while we go to deal with Rhys and find out who he's got in that wagon."

A half hour later, in the gathering dusk, they rode off again. They nursed their horses, moving at the best pace. It was just before actual dark that they caught sight of Rhys's wagon.

Rhys saw them at the same time and slapped the reins down on his team. The wagon took off along the road, the ironmonger frantically using the whip to urge his horses to even greater effort. The wagon bounced along over the rough road.

Joshua said, "We got to ask for everything these horses got left." With that, he spurred Beau, and the hunter responded. Johann kicked Sonny and slapped him on the flank.

Both horses, tired as they were, found their last reserves of strength and came to the gallop.

The wagon was running furiously on a rough roadway cut along the side of a low ridge. Rhys, in near panic, kept leaning out and looking back around the canvas cover to glimpse at his pursuers.

Perhaps it was that distraction that led to the accident.

As Joshua and Johann watched, the wagon swerved to the left slightly and both wheels on that side ran off the cleared track. The wagon slipped over the edge of the hill, the bed leaning precariously and bouncing on the rough ground and low vegetation beside the road as the team continued to race ahead. The situation could not persist. In a few seconds, the wagon went over, separating from the tongue of the hitch. The unbound team ran on while Rhys was ejected from his seat into the bush. The wagon came to rest on its side, the right wheels spinning in the air.

Moments later the pursuers arrived. Joshua called out, "Sprout, you go look in the wagon and see who or what be in there that Rhys was protectin'. I'll check on that Welsh bastard."

Joshua walked over to where the ironmonger lay. Rhys was crumpled up against the base of a tree, unconscious. Careful examination showed that although he had some cuts and bruises, he was still quite alive. Joshua grabbed him by his coat and dragged him over close to the wagon. He cut a length of rope from the lashing used to secure the canvas cover and then tied the Welshman to a small tree.

As he was finishing, Johann called out urgently, "Joshua, come here. In the wagon, quick!"

Joshua carefully began climbing into the sidewise wagon bed. Pain from his injured hip ran up and down his leg, and he inadvertently groaned as he raised it high to step into the wagon.

Johann looked at him. "Are you all right?"

"Of course. Just moved my leg the wrong way. Now tell me what's got you all excited."

The youth pulled back a blanket to reveal a young lad, perhaps a year older than Johann. He was bleeding profusely, and though his eyes were closed, he was groaning, gasping for breath, and blood was issuing from his mouth.

Johann pointed toward the boy's torso. "He's got a ball in his side. That's why he was in the wagon. But he got busted up a whole lot more when the wagon went over. All the iron pots and frying pans broke loose and battered him all over." He pointed toward his head. "Took a bad blow on the side of the head." He motioned to the lad's bloody mouth. "And it a sure thing he's bleeding inside."

Joshua thought a moment. "I'd say that's the one Peggy hit with her pistol. Wounded bad, so he couldn't ride. Looks like Rhys was tryin' to get him to a doctor." He looked over the youth, then at Johann, shook his head, and said in a low voice, "He ain't goin' to make it. All we can do is get him out of this mess and make him comfortable."

With considerable difficulty, the two slowly, carefully worked the boy out of the wreck and laid him in blankets retrieved from the wagon. Although semiconscious, he screamed and groaned as they moved him.

When they had finished, Joshua looked around, then said, "Sprout, you go gather fixins for a fire. I'll get the saddles off the horses and give them grain. Then we'll cook for ourselves. We'll spend the night here."

"What if someone comes along and starts asking questions?"

Joshua shook his head. "Ain't likely. Dark has come on, and everyone has mostly settled in for the night, just like us. We'll be out of here before people start comin' by in the mornin'."

While Johann was out gathering wood, Rhys came to. He looked at Joshua and said, "Baird, what are you going to do with me?"

Joshua glanced at him, then went back to sorting through the provisions they had brought with them. "Rhys, just bide your time. We'll be dealin' with you presently. And I'll give you a piece of advice: you don't want to hurry what's comin'." He looked over at the boy in the blanket. "By the way, that lad you was carrying is dying. Got busted up when the wagon went over. I don't 'spect he'll last out the night."

They built their cook fire close by the wounded boy, both to provide him the comfort of some heat and so they could easily keep an eye on him.

Night was well on when they finished their meal. Joshua motioned to Johann and led him behind the wrecked wagon, out of Rhys's sight.

Joshua said, "Be still now and listen." He had a handful of ashes from the fire, and he started spreading it in a pattern on the lad's forehead and cheeks.

"Joshua, what are you doing?"

"I'm puttin' Indian war paint on you. Want to make you look like a Mingo warrior."

"No Mingo would put markings on that looked like this, and he sure wouldn't do it with soot."

"You know it, and I know it, but Rhys don't know it. We're about to give that damned spy the scare of his life."

"What are you planning?"

"We're goin' to *intimidate* him, that's what."

"Intimidate?" replied Johann with a puzzled expression.

Joshua smiled broadly. "*Intimidate.* That's a gentry-type word I learned from Colonel Henry Bouquet himself, God rest his soul. Big word that means *scare the hell out of somebody.* When we marched into the Ohio Country in '65, Henry put on a big show by parading all his soldiers in front of the tribal chiefs, to get them to sign a treaty. He convinced them they didn't have a chance in battle." He paused and looked back in the direction of where the ironmonger was tied to a tree on the other side of the wagon. "Now we're goin' to *intimidate* Rhys into tellin' us all he knows about the raid."

"All right, so how are we going to *intimidate* Rhys?"

"You just act like a Mingo warrior and follow what I say. You'll get the idea. Right now, get some wood and pile it up in front of Rhys as if you was goin' to start a fire."

Joshua went back around the wagon to find the wounded boy groaning. The scout kneeled by him and saw by the flickering light of the fire that the lad's eyes were open. They fixated on Joshua, and then he started to mumble in very low tones. Joshua went to his knees and cupped a hand to his ear.

The boy, gasping for breath, started to talk in broken phrases. "I can't move. I'm bad hurt inside. I know I'll die. I beg of you, tell my mother and father what happened to me, Please, it's a dying wish, sir. Get word to them."

Joshua bent even lower. "What's your name, boy?"

"Crosswell, sir. Lindsey Crosswell."

"Where do I find your parents?"

"River View Landing Plantation, on the James, just below Fredericksburg. My father is Dalton Crosswell."

"Yes, we'll find a way to get him word. Nobody can say Joshua Baird won't help a man in a bad way. Now you try to stay still." Joshua put a comforting hand on his shoulder. "We'll see how you are in the morning," he lied. But he thought, *Boy ain't got much time left.*

Now Johann came in with a load of wood. He dropped it just in front of Rhys and started to lay it properly for a fire.

Rhys looked down at the firewood, then up at the lad. His eyes opened wide as he saw the markings on his face. "Baird, what the hell is he doing?"

Joshua, sitting casually at the fire with a metal cup in his hand, responded, "What does it look like he's doing? Building a fire, of course."

"It's right at my feet! I'll roast like a piece of meat!"

Joshua reached for a canteen and poured some whiskey into the cup. "You got that right, Rhys. That's the whole purpose: a slow roast. Gives you lots of time to contemplate your sins before you meet the Almighty."

The flickering cook fire illuminated a look of disbelief and horror on the ironmonger's face. "Why is that boy all marked up like that? He looks like some savage from the Ohio Country."

Baird took a sip of the whiskey. "You know, Rhys, I got to hand it to you. That's a pretty smart thing to say. And it turns out, you're right as rain." He looked over at Johann. "Now this here is Eckert's boy. A son by another woman besides his wife. From an 'affair of the heart,' as the gentry like to say. His mother's a fine-lookin' blond English woman from Philadelphia. *Real fine lookin'*, Rhys. One thing about Eckert, he always gets the good-lookin' women. But the point is, she's a hostage of the Mingo, captured right at the end of the French war. Lives in a village up northwest of the Forks of the Ohio. The lad lived as a Mingo for sixteen years afore he came back to stay with Eckert after Dunmore's War last year. His Mingo stepfather was a war captain, and he brought him up as a warrior." Joshua smiled meaningfully at the spy. "Knows all about Mingo ways." He paused for effect, then added, "Includin' torture. Seen it happen many times."

A look of horror spread over Rhys's face. "You're not going to…"

"Oh yes, of course we are, Rhys. We want the story of how that raid on Eckert Ridge came about, who was leading it, how they got up here. We figured out what your part was. You was the spy, gettin' the lay of the land."

"I ain't tellin' you nothin'."

Joshua looked over at Johann, who now was standing with an impassive face in the wavering light, his arms crossed in front of him. "All right, Sprout, start convincing Mr. Rhys here."

Johann nodded, then bent over and picked up a relatively straight stick, about three feet long. He took out his knife and quickly carved one end into a sharp point. Then he heated the point in the fire until it started to glow red hot.

As he was doing it, Joshua commented, "Now Rhys, we're goin' to light that fire in front of you. That ain't goin' to be particularly pleasant. But while it's scorchin' you and workin' its way closer to you, the lad here is going to entertain you with that hot stick in sensitive parts of your body. That will help you mostly forget about the roastin'."

Rhys sucked his breath in. "I say you wouldn't dare do this. You're just trying to scare me."

Joshua shrugged. "Look, Rhys, we damn well know you were a spy. Now the truth is, you're goin' to die for it. But you got a choice. You can tell us what we want to know here and now, and we'll take you back to Winchester alive. You'll get a fair trial and then a Christian hanging in the square, with Reverend Thruston sayin' words just afore they drop you."

Joshua rose to his feet, then pulled a burning stick from the cook fire and applied it to the kindling in front of Rhys. The flames took easily. He looked down at the growing fire. "Now's your chance, Welshman. The comfort of a hangin' or torture by fire."

Rhys stood looking between the fire in front of him and the glowing stick in Johann's hand. Horror registered in his eyes. But he still said nothing.

Joshua shrugged and took another pull of whiskey. "All right, lad, he's all yours."

Johann approached, put the point of the stick into the new fire to heat it up further. The tip began glowing, with small flames flaring up. Then he held it close alongside Rhys's face. The heat turned his skin red, and sweat began pouring down his face.

The Welshman shrieked. "Stop! Stop! I'll tell you what you want! Just make him go away!"

"Now you're makin' sense, Rhys." Joshua took a stick and pushed the fire back a little distance from the ironmonger but didn't put it out.

"Rhys, you answer all my questions, I'll put out the fire and the lad will get rid of his burning stick. But that won't happen till you tell us the whole story. If I get the feelin' you're holding back, we'll give you more encouragement with the fire." He smiled demonically. "Now start talkin'."

CHAPTER FIVE

THE COMMISSION

At midafternoon Peggy mounted the steps of her own porch and gratefully settled into one of the wooden chairs. The mistress of Eckert Ridge was dog-tired but satisfied with what had been accomplished since the raid. She had organized the people of the farm and got them started at pulling down the burned-out buildings and raking through the ashes to recover any iron artifacts that could be salvaged. The barracks cook and Wilma had set up shop in Donegal's cookhouse and managed to get everyone something to eat at midday. She looked over at the distillery and was gratified to see smoke coming from the chimney; there, Edna Callow was riding herd on Donegal as he made preparations to restart whiskey production. It occurred to her that she ought to go inside, sit down at her desk, and start calculating the state of their finances in light of the need to rebuild. Undoubtedly it would be grim, even with the money that Donegal's spirits could contribute. And she had to check on Wend. She sighed deeply, suddenly overwhelmed by what lay before her. She thought, *I'll just sit here a while and recover my strength and rest my mind. It's been racing since the raid.*

"Now, Lassie, will ya na come awake and greet your neighbors?"

Peggy opened her eyes to see the burly figure of Angus McDonald standing in front of the porch, reins to his mount in one hand. Behind him was his wife, Anna, who was far younger than her husband, as well as Peggy's closest friend, mounted sidesaddle on her bay filly. The McDonalds' retainer, Even McCleod, had slipped off his horse and was standing by Anna, ready to help her dismount. Peggy sighed and had a momentary flash of anger at herself for having dropped off and wondered how long she had been sleeping.

Angus climbed the steps, his face grim. "Na, Peggy, it's a terrible thing they did to you. Sowers stopped at Glengarry to let us know on his way into town, and he told us about Wend. How's the lad doing?"

Peggy motioned upward. "He's upstairs in bed, still unconscious."

"Well, lass, the good doctor should be here soon." He looked around the farm. "Lord above, Sowers didn't tell us the half of it." He shook his head. "But when he got into Winchester, he roused a bee's nest. The whole town is angry. James Wood sent a messenger out to our place. Rutledge is calling out a half company of militia. They'll be out here tomorrow morning, just in case there's more danger."

Peggy frowned and threw up her hands. "For God's sake, Angus, it's too late for militia."

The planter made a calming motion with his hand. "Now, now, Peggy, that's most likely true. But when they're not doing guard duty, they'll be extra hands to help you clean up. Rutledge had that in mind."

Her anger subsided, and she nodded. "Well, that will be helpful."

"And as soon as they can manage, James Wood and the Committee of Safety will ride over to see what can be done and talk things over with you and Wend; that is, if he's in condition to speak with them."

As he finished, Anna came running up the steps, leaned over, and hugged Peggy. "Oh, I was so worried about you!" She stood back up and looked down at Peggy. "Good Lord, you are a sight! You've soot all over your face and clothing! My God, what you've been through!" She paused a moment and then said in a quiet tone, "And we are so, so sorry to hear about Sally Donegal and that little boy." She shook her head. "How terrible!"

Peggy looked up at her friend. "Yes, but it's worse. I don't think you know. Sally was with child."

Anna stood stunned. "Simon must be devastated!"

"There's no consoling him. But Edna Callow got him back working in the distillery, if for no other reason than to take his mind off things."

Angus said, "Now we came to see things for ourselves but also to see what we can help you with. Now, lass, is there anything you need right now?"

Peggy thought a moment. "Yes, yes, there is! Wilhelm Hecht and Horner are worried about sheltering all the things that were in the gunsmith shop. The muskets, the tools, the supplies. Do you have any canvas you could loan us to make a shelter? If we had enough to make a canopy, we could protect everything from the weather and maybe even set up an improvised workshop."

"Why, indeed we do, and you shall have it immediately!" He turned to McCleod. "Even, ride back to the plantation posthaste, and have the overseer get together a goodly amount from the storehouse and send it here by wagon." He thought a moment. "And have him also send coils of rope. They'll need that to rig the canvas." He turned back to Peggy. "You shall have it in the morning. And whatever else you think of that we can provide." He turned to Peggy. "Na, lass, I'm going to walk around your place and see if there's anything else we at Glengarry can help you with." He turned and started walking down the drive toward the remains of the farm building.

Anna sat down in a chair beside Peggy. "Now, if you're up to it, you must tell me all of what happened here."

—ɷ—

The McDonalds had just left to ride back to their place and dusk was falling on the long, terrible day at Eckert Ridge when young Liza came running down the steps, visibly excited. "Miss Peggy! Miss Peggy! Doctor Harmon! He be waking up! He's moving around and groanin'!"

Peggy and the doctor, who was in his early sixties, with graying hair, were sitting in the parlor, talking about the condition of all the wounded on Eckert Ridge. Harmon had ridden in with Sowers just after the McDonalds and had first looked at Wend, then gone round to look at the two hands who had been seriously hurt. Now Peggy sprang up and ran up the stairs, followed by Harmon at a more dignified pace.

Wend lay in bed, a bandage wrapped around the top of his head. Spots of blood were showing through the white of the bandage, just above his left ear. Peggy came in and sat on the side of the bed. The doctor arrived moments later and stood looking down at Wend, who was indeed groaning, his legs writhing. One arm moved and dangled over the side of the mattress.

Then, after a particularly loud groan, Wend's eyes opened. For a moment he looked straight up at the ceiling, then his eyes moved around the room, and he looked in turn at Peggy and the physician. At first they were glazed with incomprehension, but in a few seconds, they focused in recognition of the people standing around him.

Peggy said, "Oh, God be thanked!"

Wend looked around again, and an expression of extreme distress spread over his face. He took a deep breath and proclaimed, "Christ! My head hurts like hell!"

Harmon laughed gently. "My dear Mr. Eckert, you should be very thankful for that."

Wend stared at him for a moment, then said, "Thankful? I should be thankful that my head is damn well splitting open?"

"Indeed, Eckert. If the ball that grazed your head had passed a fraction of an inch more to the left, you would be eternally beyond feeling pain."

Wend looked at him for a long moment. "Well, Doctor, it still hurts like hell."

Harmon nodded. "I'm sure it does. But of course that will go away with time." He walked over to his leather case, which sat on a chair in the corner. He came back with a bottle containing a dark-colored liquid. Turning to Liza, who stood in the door, he said, "Could you get a cup?"

Peggy motioned toward Liza, who nodded and headed down the stairs.

Wend threw his legs over the side of the bed and started to rise.

Harmon put a hand on him, pressing him back down to the bed. "Eckert, what in the devil do you think you're doing?"

"I've got to tend to the farm. There's bound to be much to do."

Harmon laughed. "You're in no shape for that. And in any case, your good wife and the farm's people have been at it all day."

Peggy said, "For God's sake, Wend, stay in bed. Horner and Hecht and Specht and the others have been at work since the raid ended at dawn. We've made plans and taken care of our people. You must take care of yourself."

"What about the shop? And the muskets?" Then something struck him. "Oh my God! What about the rifling machine?"

Peggy put her hand on Wend's shoulder to calm him. "The shop's burnt to the ground, but Horner saved almost everything which is important: the muskets are mostly safe, your tools, and he dragged the rifling machine away from the shop before the flames got to it."

Wend sagged back in relief. "Thank God!"

Peggy said quietly, "But there's bad news. Some of our people are dead." She told him about Sally and the Hechts' boy.

Tears came to Wend's eyes, momentarily to be replaced by a hard-as-stone expression. "Those bastards! What kind of men are they, to shoot women and children?" He was silent a moment, then asked, "What about Donegal? How's he taking this?"

Peggy sighed. "Not very well, at least at first. But Widow Callow gave him a stern talking to, army style, and we've set him to work making whiskey. He fired up the distillery just a little while ago."

Wend said, "Distilling whiskey? After what happened today? Why in the world would you do that at this moment?"

"Because, my dear husband, it takes Simon's mind off his grief and more importantly, we need the money. You aren't going to be selling any rifles or pistols for quite some time. We need a source of funds to rebuild."

Wend was quiet for a moment. "How bad is it?"

"Besides the destruction of the shop, most of the farm buildings are gone. The barracks are burnt out. Luckily, the houses are intact despite the fact that they tried to burn them, so we have shelter."

Wend gritted his teeth. "We must get to work and rebuild as soon as possible."

Harmon crossed his arms. "Eckert, your women and your hands have made a good start on all that. But you, sir, have a more important task at hand. You must take care to heal yourself. That means remaining in bed. If you tried to move now, you would find yourself dizzy and unstable. I believe that condition will persist for some time. You must remain here for several days and let the body do its work. There is no other choice for you." Harmon stood up. "Now, you are not the only one on Eckert Ridge who needs my attention. You have a man, Dunn by name, who has severe burns from being caught in the fire of the barracks. And another, Dorner, who took a ball in his shoulder. I began treating both earlier, but now I must check on them. All three of my patients are going to need continuing care."

Peggy nodded. "Indeed. You must stay with us here in the house. I'll have Wilma set you up in the spare room."

—ɯ—

Dawn was in the sky when Peggy tiptoed into the bedroom to check on Wend. She need not have bothered. Her husband was sitting up in bed, eyes wide open.

"What are you doing awake, dear? You need as much sleep as you can get if you are going to recover."

Wend responded, "I've slept myself out for now." He raised a hand toward Peggy. "The question is, Why are you awake? You must be exhausted after what you took on yesterday."

"I slept for a little in a chair in the parlor." She made a worried face. "But I'm so anxious about how we can possibly find the resources to rebuild the farm, I just couldn't stay asleep."

Wend shrugged. "We built it once. We can do it again."

Peggy sat down in a chair and wrung her hands. "Wend, we built this place over ten years. And we didn't have a score of people to feed and pay." She shook her head in frustration. "Since I couldn't sleep, I lit a candle and went through the ledgers. The sad truth is, we don't have the money to rebuild. We likely will have to send some hands away. Because of all the money we've spent setting up to make the muskets and expanding the shop before it was destroyed, we just don't have much cash."

"Well, we have those fifty muskets. You said Horner saved them and only a few will have to be repaired from fire damage. We'll get paid for those. And you said Donegal was going to be distilling again soon. That will bring in more money."

"Yes, yes, but damn it, Wend, it's not enough! And you know the government: it will take forever to get the money for those muskets from Williamsburg. I'm telling you again, we'll have to let people go and rebuild slowly and on a smaller scale."

Wend raised a finger. "Before the raid, Donegal and I were talking about expanding the area in which we sell the whiskey. Maybe we can do that, and that would bring in more money."

Peggy raised her hands impatiently. "But you don't understand! It will take more money to do that! And I'm telling you, we hardly have enough to rub together!" She sighed and balled her hands into fists.

Wend thought a moment. "We'll try to get a loan. There are people in Winchester who have money. Our name is worth something; we can use the farm for security. And everybody knows there's going to be a good market for musket sales." He bit his lips. "I hate the idea of going around, hat in hand, begging, but I'll do it if I must."

There was a deep silence in the room. Neither of them liked the prospect.

Finally Wend said, "You told me Angus was going to send over canvas today. First thing have Wilhelm Hecht and Horner rig a shelter for a temporary shop, and then have them get started on making sure all the muskets are ready to ship. Once we send them off, I can show we're still in business and get someone to advance money based on our money receivable from the government. It won't be a lot, but it will be a start."

Peggy said adamantly, "Of course we'll do that, but it won't be adequate." She stood up. "We'll talk about this more when you feel better. Now I'll send Wilma up with some food, and then you try to get some more rest."

The sun was high in the sky, and Peggy was standing with Wilhelm Hecht and Andrew Horner near the ruins of the gun shop. They were watching several of the apprentices unloading canvas and rope from the McDonald's wagon, which had arrived shortly before, driven by one of the plantation's hands and escorted on horseback by Even McCleod. Earlier in the day, some of Abby Morgan's teamsters had brought two wagons of hay, and Specht was supervising farmhands who were forking the hay into a large stack by the remains of the barn. McCleod had mentioned that he and his wagoner had passed a column of militia en route to Eckert Hill. Earlier Doc Harmon had looked in at Wend and stated that he was doing as well as could be expected. The physician had then gone off to Donegal's house to treat the two injured hands. With all this going on, Peggy's spirits were the highest they'd been since the raid.

Wilhelm turned to Peggy. "Mrs. Eckert, we may be able to get started on rebuilding the shop sooner than expected."

"Rebuilding the shop soon? I don't see how—where would you get the milled wood you need?"

Hecht said, "I found a pile of leftover planks stacked behind Donegal's house. It's enough to start work at least, until we can get a full supply." He turned and asked, "Speaking of that, perhaps tomorrow I could ride over to Dorman's sawmill and order the rest of what we need for the shop."

Peggy bit her lip. There was no money to pay for an order that size. "Let's wait a few days and get more organized and be sure how much we need. I'll let you know when to go."

Hecht shrugged. "Yes, ma'am. I was just thinkin' it will take a while for Dorman to cut and mill all that we'll need. And we should get him started."

Peggy was about to repeat her admonition to wait, but just then the conversation was interrupted by Horner, who said, "Mrs. Eckert, look over at the house."

She turned and was startled to see Wend, steadied by Liza and Billy, step out through the front door onto the porch. They helped him settle into one of the chairs. Aghast, she exclaimed, "Oh, for God's sake!" and hurried across the drive to the house.

Wend grinned broadly. "Hello, Mrs. Eckert. I came out to see how you were handling things and give you advice."

"We are doing as well as could be expected. And when I want advice from a man wounded in the head, I will ask him. But what in God's name are you doing here? You know the doctor told you to stay in bed."

"Sleep would not come, and I couldn't just lay there anymore. The boredom was killing me. And besides, the pain in my head isn't nearly as bad. That medicine seems to be helping."

Peggy turned to Liza and said angrily, "You *know* he is supposed to rest in bed. Why did you help him?"

Liza shook her head. "Now, Mrs. Eckert, I told him what you said, but he wouldn't take no for an answer. What was I supposed to do?"

"Don't scold her, Peggy. I can rest here just as easily as in the bedroom. And I can see what's going on, which makes me feel better than lying upstairs and worrying."

Peggy, hands on hips, was about to respond in a scathing tone when she was stopped by the sound of a drum cadence, almost immediately joined by the shrill tone of a fife playing a merry tune. She looked down the drive and saw a small detachment of troops marching up the incline in a column of twos, an officer in the lead. A wagon pulled by a team followed behind. She said, "Well, there's the militia that the Committee of Safety sent." She contemplated the sight for a moment, then continued, "I hope that wagon is carrying their rations, for we can't feed them. It's all we can do to feed our own people."

Wend looked at the marching men. "Well, at least it's some labor to help clean up."

In a few moments, the detachment arrived, and the young officer in charge ordered the halt in front of the house and had his men ground arms. He walked to the foot of the porch steps and doffed his hat. He looked at Wend. "Captain Eckert, I believe?" Then he said, "I'm Ensign Childers, sir. Edward Childers. Here with a half company by direction of Mr. Rutledge, the county lieutenant."

Wend nodded by way of identification and casual return of the ensign's salute. "It's *Lieutenant* Eckert, Mr. Childers."

Childers replied, "Lieutenant? I had heard you were commissioned a captain. To lead the new rifle company, sir."

Wend said crossly. "Mr. Childers, be informed that I have *not* accepted that honor." Then he asked, "What are your orders?"

Childers drew himself up. "Put out guards to prevent any recurrence of the raid which took place here and beyond that, place my men at your disposal to help in any way possible."

Peggy asked, "How long are you to stay?"

The ensign replied, "Indefinitely. I was told the Committee of Safety would determine that." He looked around. "Where would you like for me to set up camp?"

Peggy pointed down the drive to the Baird house. "You see that house at the end of the drive?"

Childers turned to look. "Indeed, ma'am."

"Take your men just beyond that, and you'll come to an open clearing which will make a good campground. The creek runs not far away, down a small slope, so you'll have good water."

"Thank you. That will serve very well." Then he said, "Ah yes—I am to inform you that representatives of the Committee of Safety will arrive in the afternoon to view the damage and discuss the situation with you." Childers touched his hat to Peggy and then to Wend. Then he took his place at the head of the detachment and led his men off along the drive.

Peggy looked up at Wend and said, "That's just what we need: the gentlemen of the Committee of Safety walking around, gawking at all the damage, getting in the way. What are they coming here for—just to satisfy their curiosity?"

Wend thought before answering. "I suspect the esteemed men of the committee want to discuss how long it will take to restart musket production. They will undoubtedly make some offer to help, although it will simply be a gesture, for there's nothing they can actually do." Then, to Peggy's surprise, he laughed out loud. He held up a finger. "But one thing is sure, Peggy: given the need to rebuild the shop and the farm, they'll have to give up any idea of me recruiting and leading a company. That would be impossible with everything here to do."

It was a couple of hours after midday, and Wend was now ensconced in the most comfortable upholstered chair in the parlor. After being awake all morning and for dinner, he had finally become drowsy. But just as he was drifting off, Bernd came in the front door. He had been working with the rest of the apprentices helping set up the canvas workshop.

Leaning in through the parlor entrance, he called out, "Father, there's a bunch of people riding up the drive. Horner says it must be the Committee of Safety."

Wend shook himself awake. "Where's your mother?"

"She's down at the distillery, seeing how Mr. Donegal is getting along with the whiskey distillery."

"Go run and fetch her, son. She'll want to be here when we talk with the committee."

As soon as Bernd had left, Wend called for Liza, who appeared momentarily. "Visitors coming, Liza. Please meet them at the door and show them in here."

Wend looked out the window and saw that the men of the committee were dismounting in front of the porch. In a very short time, ushered by Liza, the men filed into the room. The group included most of the committee, led by James Wood, Angus McDonald, and Reverend Thruston. Then he was surprised to note that Issac Zane, who ran an iron furnace and forge to the south of Winchester, at a place called Marlborough, was present. He also noted Charles Dorman, proprietor of the most prominent sawmill in the area. Wend's curiosity was aroused because neither was a member of the committee.

Greetings had just been finished when Peggy arrived, somewhat breathless from hurrying up from the distillery. As she swept into the parlor, Wend, as usual, was amused to see that the reaction of the assembled men was universal—all faces turned in her direction, their expression showing appreciation of her beauty and sense of presence. He noted that even in a soiled workday gown, apron, and cap, she looked spectacular.

Peggy made the merest curtsy to the men and said, "We welcome you to Eckert Ridge and wish it could have been under more favorable circumstances."

James Wood went over and took her hand. "Mrs. Eckert, permit me to express, on behalf of the committee, our deep regret for what has occurred. Please understand, we came as soon as we could gather together and make certain arrangements. And I must say, what we have seen, in our brief time here, is so much more devastating than we could have ever imagined."

Rutledge, standing just behind Wood, exclaimed bellicosely, "By God, Mrs. Eckert, rest assured we shall find out who committed this atrocity and visit retribution on them!"

There was a murmur of agreement from around the room.

Wend cleared his throat. "Gentlemen, I know exactly who led this attack. It came directly from Lord Dunmore."

Wood looked over at Wend. "Well, of course, it was done on behalf of Dunmore and the royal authority. But surely it came from a closer source than the tidewater, where Dunmore has his forces? I fear that it may even have come from somewhere in this county, meaning we have an active cabal of loyalists among us."

Wend looked around the room. "Actually, I know precisely who led the raid. It was the man who served me this from a distance of fifteen feet." He pointed to the wound on his head. "His name is Major Reginald Welford, of the 60th Foot, the Royal Americans, now seconded to one of Dunmore's regiments. He was even wearing a uniform coat of the 60th."

Wood cocked his head as if trying to recall something. "Welford? Where have I heard that name before?"

Angus McDonald stepped forward and answered. "I know the man. Know him to my deep regret. He was sent down from General Gage's staff to work as an aide to Dunmore last year during the war. In my role as brigade major for Dunmore's force, I had to work with him frequently. He's an arrogant twit."

Wood nodded. "Yes, now I remember hearing his name."

Wend said, "I know quite a bit about him; I first met the man during Pontiac's War. He was originally a lieutenant in the Guards in London but was exiled to the 60th at Fort Pitt in 1764 for indiscretions with a major's wife. Angus is right: he combines arrogance with disdain for colonists. During Bouquet's campaign against the Ohio tribes in 1765, he shot Baird's horse out of hand simply because it had a minor wound. Believe me, Joshua still bears a blood grudge against him." Wend paused, looking around at all the men. "But the important point is that Welford is with Dunmore's forces. So it is clear that this raid had a direct connection to the former governor and was at least in part mounted from the tidewater."

Wood looked puzzled. "Why would they go to so much effort over so long a distance to strike this farm?"

Rutledge interjected, "Undoubtedly it had something to do with the muskets."

Wend nodded. "I don't doubt you are correct, sir. But there's more to it than that. I believe Dunmore and his close adviser Northcutt intended to punish me and my family for diverting the colony's muskets to patriot forces and for turning down a commission in the loyalist forces that they offered me. They feel I should have remained loyal to the Crown because of the contract I had to refurbish muskets over the years."

"Quite possible, Eckert," responded Wood. And numerous other heads around the room nodded. "But we shall never settle the question at this moment. Instead, we need to think about how you are to restore your shop and resume musket production. It is essential to the Virginia forces."

"Indeed." Reverend Thruston spoke up. "To that end, we are willing to assist you in reconstruction."

Wood nodded his agreement. "Here is what we intend..."

At that moment Andrew Horner strode into the room. He looked around for Peggy and said in an excited voice, "Mrs. Eckert, Joshua and Johann are comin' up the drive. They just passed the militia guard down at the road." He stopped to catch his breath. "And they got someone with them. And a whole string of horses that look like they're carrying packs."

Peggy motioned to the committee men. "Joshua left right after the raid to try and find out who staged it and how it was done. Let us go see what he has to say."

She turned and headed for the porch, followed by a rush of committeemen.

Wend, left behind in the hurried departure, called out to Horner, "Andrew, for God's sake, help me get out to a chair on the porch."

By the time Horner had gotten Wend to the porch and helped him settle in a chair, Joshua and his caravan were approaching the house. Peggy and most of the committee had descended the stairs to the drive and stood waiting. As he pulled up his horse at the house, Joshua looked over and, seeing Wend, grinned and gave him a wink and a little salute. Wend waved back.

Joshua and Johann dismounted. Joshua looked around at all the men gathered in front of the steps and grinned mischievously. "Why, damned nice of you all to come see us arrive. Makes me feel real welcome."

Peggy was in no mood to joke. She pointed to Rhys, who was mounted on one of his team horses, and tied up. "Why is he here, and what do you have under the canvas on those other horses?"

Baird, enjoying the moment, grinned again and said, "Now Miss Peggy, you just be patient, and I'll tell all of you a very interesting story. A story about how all this came to be and who did it." He swept his arm around in a motion that took in the destruction.

Meanwhile, Thruston pointed at Rhys and said, "I've seen that man. He's an ironmonger who sells his wares at court day! I've spoken to him in passing. Why do you have him tied up?"

"Reverend, I have him tied up because he's a spy for Lord Dunmore. He was here before the raid to scout out the lay of the farm so the raiders would know where everything was. Now the Sprout here"— he nodded toward Johann—"and I caught up with him a bit south of Ashby's Ferry and with just a little gentle persuasion, made him real happy to spill the beans about the raid."

Joshua went over to the horse that was carrying Rhys, whose hands were tied, and yanked the man to the ground. Then he dragged him over in front of the assembled committee and placed him on his knees. He said, "Now Rhys and I are goin' to tell you all about the raid." He grabbed the ironmonger by his collar and shook him. "Ain't we, Mr. Rhys?"

Rhys took a deep breath and nodded. "Yes, yes."

"First thing, this raid was cooked up by a certain bastard named Major Reginald Welford, with the personal approval of Lord Dunmore himself. And the governor's henchman Barrett Penfold Northcutt was in on it." Joshua waved toward Wend. "They wanted to punish Eckert for keepin' their muskets and more'n that, stop him from makin' more."

Many of the committeemen turned and looked at Wend.

Joshua was speaking again. "Now Welford and several other men from the King's Loyal Virginia Legion, Northcutt's regiment, came by boat up the James River to a plantation called River View Landing, which is owned by a man named Dalton Crosswell. He be the leader of a local ring of loyalists down near Fredericksburg."

Wood spoke up in a shocked tone. "Why, I know that man—he was a member of the Burgesses. I've shared libations and dined with him several times. I find this incredible."

"Well, ain't no doubt about it. James, take a look at this." Joshua walked over to one of the horses and pulled the canvas cover off its load to reveal the body of a young man. He grabbed the boy's hair and pulled his head up so all could see his features.

Wood stepped forward for a closer look. "My God! It is Crosswell's son! I saw him at Williamsburg with his father more than once."

"Yep, that's who it be. His name is Lindsey. He was shot by Mrs. Eckert during the raid and wounded so bad he couldn't ride no more. Rhys was carrying him to a doctor when we caught up with him. Then Rhys decided to try to run from us and ended up wrecking his wagon. The lad was busted up so much when the wagon turned over, he died within a few hours."

Joshua walked to the other two horses and pulled the covers off, exposing the other two dead royalists. "These gentlemen, part of the troop which raided here, were escorting the wagon and tried to stop us." Joshua smiled. "As you can see, they lost the gunfight."

Wood stared at the men, then turned back to Baird. "So several men, including Welford, came by boat up to Crosswell's plantation and were joined by others recruited by him and his son?"

"That's it exactly, James. Then they rode in small groups up to Ashby's Ferry so they wouldn't raise any suspicions. That's where Rhys joined them and gave Welford the word on Eckert Ridge. Rhys had also picked out a spot—a patch of woods just a half mile south of here, where they could spend the night before the raid and then light their torches just afore dawn the day of the raid." He smacked Rhys on the back of the head. "Ain't that the way it happened?"

Rhys nodded. "Yes."

Joshua continued, "They wanted to make sure to destroy the main buildings of the farm and particularly the gun workshop. But Welford hoped to do it without casualties. So the plan was just to make one fast ride along the drive, from west to east, tossing torches as they went. But they didn't count on so many people being up so early. I put a ball in one of them after they rode past my house, and Wend and his apprentices hit a couple more. And then, of course, Peggy put a ball into young Crosswell as he threw a torch onto the porch."

Wood turned to Peggy and said, "My compliments, Mrs. Eckert."

All the other committeemen followed suit.

"Now one more important thing." Joshua turned to look at Wend in his chair on the porch. "Welford thinks he killed Wend. After the raid he was bragging to his men about how he shot him right smack in the forehead." He reached down and shook Rhys. "Ain't that true?"

Rhys took a deep breath and nodded. "Welford said blood sprayed all over; no one could have survived."

Angus McDonald said, "So Dunmore will think Eckert paid with his life for what he considers treason."

Wood put his hand to his chin. "That's quite interesting. You know, it may be useful for Dunmore and Northcutt and Welford to keep thinking Wend is deceased." Then Wood turned to his fellow committeemen. "We'll take Rhys with us when we return to Winchester. He'll be tried as a spy."

Peggy spoke up. "James, I beseech you to take those dead men with you. I don't want them buried anywhere near Eckert Hill. I don't want our dead to have to share the same ground with them!"

Reverend Thruston nodded to Peggy. "Mrs. Eckert, we will gladly oblige your request."

Peggy responded, "Thank you, Reverend. I appreciate your understanding." She thought a moment, then said, "Gentlemen, why don't you accompany me on a short tour of the farm, and I will show you the details of what these despicable men did."

While Peggy led the visitors around the farm, Wend, aided by Horner, went back into the parlor. Joshua came with them. After Horner had departed, Baird walked over to the liquor cabinet and poured himself a generous cup of whiskey. He took a deep sip, turned to Wend, and said, "I've been thinking about nothing more than havin' some of Donegal's stuff since last night. I ran out of it the first night out on the road."

Wend nodded. "You did good work out there, Joshua. And you showed up just at the right time to tell the committee the details."

"Well, we was lucky. We got to Ashby's in good time so that Rhys and his guards weren't that far ahead of us." He took another sip, then continued, "By the way, thought you'd want to know, your boy did well out there. First shot of our little skirmish, that damned colt Sonny bucked him off. Didn't faze him one bit, nor did the fact a ball grazed his left shoulder. He got right to his feet, shook it all off, and was a real help bringing down Rhys's wagon and then scaring the hell out of him that night so he spilled everything to us. Lad's going to be good on the warpath."

"Thanks for telling me that, Joshua."

Baird pointed to Wend. "What kind of drink is that you got in your hand?"

"It's a syrup the doctor has me drink. Has coffee and some other stuff in it. He says it will help ease the pain in my head."

"Is it working?"

"Damn, who knows, Joshua? My head still hurts like hell. Well, maybe it has eased a bit. But this syrup tastes like shit."

Joshua turned back to the cabinet. "Damn, take some of the whiskey. It can't hurt, and I'll wager it will ease the pain a lot faster than some blasted potion from the apothecary shop." He poured a cup and handed it to Wend.

Wend took a deep pull on the whiskey. He laughed and said, "You know, I think I feel better already!"

Joshua chuckled. Then his face turned serious. "We need to have a little talk. A talk about revenge. We got to serve Welford and Northcutt with serious vengeance. Rhys says those two are the ones who really put this war party together."

Wend sighed. "In due time I'll think about that. Anyway, they're hundreds of miles away in the Tidewater. Right now I've got to concentrate on rebuilding the farm. And Peggy says we don't have the money to do it." He waved a hand. "When I'm able, I'll have to go into Winchester and try to get credit."

Joshua raised a finger. "Just a minute. I'll be right back. Got to get something from my saddlebag."

The scout was back in a couple of minutes. He was carrying two small bags.

Wend took a sip of his whiskey. "What's that?"

Baird held up one bag and shook it. There was the tinkle of metal. "This here is Rhys's money from selling his iron stuff." He did the same with the second bag, which again tinkled with the sound of metal coins. "This one is money Northcutt paid Rhys to do his spyin'. Not a whole lot—seems Rhys is a cheap spy." He shrugged. "Put together, it still ain't that much, but it's somethin' to get started with in rebuildin'. Or at least enough to keep goin' till you get that loan money."

"Thanks, Joshua. But you ought to take some of it; you did the work."

"Shit, Alice and I got what we need, which ain't much. I make some huntin' for the taverns and inns around here. We all benefit from the farm, so that's where it needs to go." He walked over to the liquor cabinet and stuffed the bags into a drawer. "Here, when all these committee people are gone, tell Peggy where it's at. Sure enough she'll want to count it up."

—⁂—

Their tour of the farm having been completed, Peggy led the members of the committee back to the house and into the parlor. She came over and stood beside Wend's chair. Joshua was leaning against the wall next to the liquor cabinet, contentedly consuming another cup of whiskey.

As leader, James Wood took a seat close to Wend. "Well, Eckert, the damage to your farm is beyond what I would have dreamed." He smiled at Peggy. "But you should be very proud of the work Mrs. Eckert and your people have done in starting to recover."

Wend said, "I'm always proud of Mrs. Eckert and never surprised at what she can accomplish when she puts mind to a matter. She is a very determined woman." He shrugged. "However, the actual rebuilding of the shop and the farm buildings will take time and financial resources, funds which I don't have. I shall have to find someone willing to extend me amounts necessary for the purpose. We shall have to put the farm up for security."

Wood glanced around the room at the other members of the committee, then turned back to Wend. "My dear Wend, we have already considered your situation. And the fact that this disaster is solely the result of your support of Virginia's great cause. We have also considered the urgent need for arms, which in this part of Virginia, only you have been able to meet."

Thruston spoke up. "The fact is, Eckert, we have discussed the matter and are prepared to fully support you in your effort to rebuild as rapidly as possible."

Wend looked at Peggy and then around the room. "To what level does that support extend?"

Wood said, "We intend to supply whatever it takes to restore your shop and your farm buildings." He waved his hand to the place where Dorman and Zane stood together.

Dorman nodded. "As we inspected the property, I made an estimate of the milled lumber which will be required. It will be forthcoming from my mill on an expedited basis." He looked over to Zane and nodded.

Zane raised a finger. "I am prepared to supply the nails and other iron fittings you need with the highest priority."

Wood smiled and nodded at the two men. "Thank you, gentlemen." He turned back to Wend. "Other members of the committee will provide skilled labor as needed to help you and your men reconstruct the farm. We propose to start immediately, so that musket production can resume at the earliest moment."

Wend replied, "I am overwhelmed. However, I still must find funds to repay these merchants for the wood, metal, and services."

Wood shook his head. "No, Eckert, you don't understand. Let me make myself clear: the goods and services will be donated to you, on behalf of the cause."

Puzzled, Wend said, "And you are not asking for any repayment from me?"

A smile spread over Wood's face. "Well, that is not *quite* correct. But we are not asking anything from you that the committee has not already requested."

Wend stared at Wood for a long moment. "Nothing you haven't already requested?"

Then understanding dawned on him. "Oh, I see."

Wood grinned and put it into words. "I assume that somewhere in this room is a captain's commission to raise a rifle company and serve as its commander for one year. We ask merely that you accept that responsibility and service, and you will have discharged any debt to the committee and the people of Frederick County."

There was a long silence as Wend considered his position. He had the feeling of a mouse cornered by a cat. But he thought of one thing to say. "What about musket production? You just said that was the main reason you were extending all this assistance. I must be here to supervise the work."

Angus McDonald spoke up. "Now, Wend, that would be ideal. But we all know you have a good man in Wilhelm Hecht. And in truth, he and your apprentices turned out muskets of excellent quality while you were out hunting John Connolly and his men last fall." He raised a finger and waved it back and forth. "You canna deny that. And you can manage the rebuilding of the shop and the restarting of musket making while you recruit and train your company."

Wood nodded. "Angus is quite correct. You'll only be gone for a year. Hecht should be able to handle it for that time." He smiled triumphantly. "Now, what's your answer, Wend? It seems an easy choice to me."

Peggy put her hand on Wend's shoulder. He looked up into her eyes and knew he had no choice. "My dear, go over to the secretary and fetch the commission."

Peggy, happiness in her eyes, quickly walked over, opened the desk, picked up the paper, dipped a quill in the ink well, and returned. She laid the commission on the table next to Wend's chair and handed him the quill.

Wend looked around the room. "Two conditions, gentlemen: I shall have the right to name my own officers and sergeants. And second, I will be able to organize the company according to my own ideas."

Wood looked around at his compatriots, who all nodded. He turned back to Wend. "That's agreed, Eckert."

Wend wrote out his acceptance and signed his name to the commission.

McDonald grinned broadly. "Na that that's done, I propose we toast our new captain and the success of his company on the field of arms"—he looked over at Baird—"with some of that fine whiskey which Joshua has been imbibing all this time." He turned to Peggy. "That is, if the lovely mistress of Eckert Ridge is amenable?"

Peggy laughed. "She is indeed! Let me call Wilma to bring enough cups, and you all shall have a round of the best whiskey in Frederick County."

PART II

THE FREDERICK COUNTY LIGHT COMPANY

Chapter Six

SPRING BEGINNINGS

Lord Dunmore was positively ebullient. He sat at the head of the table in his flagship's great cabin, cigar in hand, as Major Reginald Welford recounted the story of the successful raid on Eckert Ridge. Also in the cabin were his aides, Aubrey Harbridge and Dudley Fellows, as well as Lieutenant Colonel Barrett Northcutt and Captain Andrew Spade Hammond of the naval squadron.

Welford finished by summing things up. "So, Your Lordship, we can definitely say that we have destroyed the musket manufacturing capability at Eckert Ridge. There will be no more firelocks coming from there for a long time, if ever. The building was entirely in flames when we rode off, and the rest of the plantation was substantially destroyed."

Dunmore took a pull on his cigar and grinned. "Excellent, Major. You have accomplished your mission with precision and great daring."

"Thank you, sir. And there's one more important thing: I can vouch for the fact that Eckert himself is dead. The traitor has received his due."

Hammond looked skeptical. He cleared his throat. "If I may be so bold, how can you be so sure, Major? You yourself have indicated that the raid consisted of one very rapid, mounted sweep through the plantation. You would hardly have had time to verify that this Eckert fellow was in fact dead."

Welford displayed a self-satisfied grin. "The truth, sir, is that I personally shot him with a pistol at about the same distance I am from you now. The ball struck his head, and blood sprayed in all directions.

Eckert dropped to the ground like a sack of flour. That, Captain, is why I am certain of his demise."

Northcutt smiled and then said to the naval officer, "My dear Andrew, Reggie is a dead shot with the pistol, whether standing or mounted. Captain, be assured you'd not want to wager against him, nor, dare I say, encounter him on the dueling field."

Hammond snapped, "I am not one to find myself in such a position."

Northcutt simply shrugged and smiled in response.

Harbridge moved to change the subject. "And what were your losses, Major?"

Welford shrugged. "Two men killed, shot from their horses." He thought a moment. "Two minor wounded, and one man seriously hurt by a shot to the torso. Regrettably, that was Crosswell's son, Lindsey."

Dunmore stiffened. "Crosswell's son? Damn! That is unfortunate. We are much indebted to Dalton Crosswell for his support, which was critical to mounting this endeavor. We may need to again call on his good offices in the future as our operations grow in scope." He reflected a moment. "I hope you took care to provide appropriate medical treatment for the lad."

"Indeed, sir. We dressed his wound at our camp near Ashby's Ferry, then sent him to a doctor near Fredericksburg in the ironmonger Rhys's wagon. I even provided an escort of two men to ensure no one interfered with the transport. I'm confident that young Crosswell will receive excellent care and will be returned to the comfort of his family's plantation."

"Excellent, Major Welford." The governor smiled and looked around at his advisers. "Now we must capitalize on the major's brilliant action." Then he turned to Fellows. "Draft a broadside announcing the success of our raid on the rebel nest of Frederick County. Then we will have it distributed by our agents throughout the tidewater area."

The secretary nodded. "It will be done immediately, sir."

Northcutt said, "My Lord, in my opinion, this strike will go a long way toward erasing memory of the debacle at Great Bridge."

Dunmore said, "Absolutely, Barrett!" Then he motioned with his cigar toward the naval captain. "Andrew, Northcutt is quite correct. In fact, I am confident the effect will be to inspire and embolden our supporters. Most importantly, with this victory in hand, I feel that we are now in a position to take your advice to move from our anchorage here in the Elizabeth to a site on land. A place where we can consolidate and supply our forces, more completely train our soldiers, and treat the ailing. You spoke of finding an island or easily defended peninsula for that purpose. Now is the time to identify such a location."

Hammond nodded. "Certainly; I will dispatch HMS *Otter*, our smallest, most-shallow-draft vessel, along with a small tender, to search the coast from here up to the mouth of the Potomac. Having studied the charts, I have several places in mind which might serve our purpose. The *Otter* will sail tomorrow to begin the necessary reconnaissance."

The governor smiled. "Excellent, Andrew. Pray the *Otter* will rapidly complete her mission and we can finally leave this wretched place."

Hammond took on a reflective look. "I am sure she will. He motioned toward Northcutt. "Meanwhile, our compatriots on land should consolidate and minimize their positions in preparation for withdrawal. I will assign transports, and we will be ready to embark them immediately after the new base has been identified."

Northcutt stared at the senior naval officer for a long moment and took a long drag on his cigar. Finally he exhaled and said, "I beg to differ somewhat with your last statement, Hammond. I believe we will be better served by doing just the opposite."

The captain stiffened. "The opposite? Surely there can be no objection to preparing for an orderly extraction of your command on the York and the 14th Foot at Lynnhaven?"

Northcutt looked at Dunmore and shrugged. "I am all for a well-planned embarkation when the time comes. However, I submit that the *Otter*'s reconnaissance will take weeks, given the vagaries of the wind and the number of locations which should be investigated. In the meantime, I believe our forces ashore should operate in as aggressive a manner as possible, for two reasons. First, that would be consistent with capitalizing on the success of Welford's raid, and in any case, we don't want to show our hand with regard to the pending withdrawal. Second, we should use the time to move through the countryside foraging for supplies and, where possible, gathering recruits." He looked around the table. "I maintain we are quite capable of moving quickly from offense to a well-conceived withdrawal and embarkation when the moment arrives."

Dunmore considered for a moment, then waved his cigar toward Hammond. "My dear Andrew, I rather like Barrett's concept. If we take an offensive stance while all the while planning to depart, we will keep the rebels off balance. And they'll have to keep their forces dispersed over a wide area to protect plantations and villages, rather than being able to concentrate in front of our enclaves. Such a tactic may actually lead to a safer situation as we embark the troops."

Hammond shot an irritated glance at Northcutt, then turned to the governor and made a brief nod. "Naturally, Lord Dunmore, I defer to your judgment."

"Good," said the governor. "Then we're all in agreement."

There was a tap on the door, and Howser, the steward, peeked into the cabin. "Sir, we're ready to lay the midday meal."

Dunmore waved his hand to the table. "That will be fine, Howser. We have finished here." He stood up and looked over at Hammond. "Won't you join us for the meal, Andrew?"

The captain replied, "Sir, much as I enjoy your fare, and the company of all present, I must decline. I should return to my ship and complete orders for the *Otter*'s expedition, in order to facilitate her timely departure." He made a small bow and said, "With your permission, Lordship, I will withdraw."

The governor responded, "Certainly, Andrew, and Godspeed to the *Otter* and her crew."

An hour later Dunmore, his aides, Northcutt, and Welford were completing dinner. Conversation among the subordinates had been lively and about virtually anything other than the war. The governor, on the other hand, had been relatively silent, thoughtful, altogether seeming distracted. As the stewards came in to clear the table, he suddenly raised a hand, then motioned toward the two junior men. "Gentlemen, I have some business to transact with Mr. Harbridge and Colonel Northcutt. I would ask if you could entertain yourself elsewhere for a few minutes."

Welford said, "Of course, sir" and rose to depart.

Fellows stood up. "Governor, I will go to my cabin and begin drafting the broadside about our successful raid."

After the two had departed and the stewards had withdrawn, Dunmore picked up the wooden humidor and offered cigars to the other two while taking one for himself.

The three men were silent for a couple of minutes while lighting their tobacco.

Then Dunmore said, "Gentlemen, as Welford's briefing progressed and then later over dinner, some thoughts on our situation and how we should proceed occupied my mind."

Harbridge responded, "I rather thought you looked preoccupied."

The governor said nothing for a long moment, the two advisers staring at him. Finally he spoke. "I've been trying to make an honest, critical evaluation of our position and strength. The inevitable conclusion is that we need more troops. *Disciplined* troops. Even if we have more men come in and join us as a result of Welford's raid, it is not likely to be enough for us to go on the offensive, at least not on the scale we need to defeat the rebellion here in Virginia. We were counting on John Connolly to bring down a significant number of men: loyal militia, the companies of regulars which Gage had promised to send with him, and of course the Ohio tribal warriors. But now that plan is dashed."

Harbridge spoke up. "Perchance you are not being optimistic enough, sir. Once we are seen to be at an established land station, instead of isolated here on ships, enthusiasm and recruitment may fill up our muster roles."

Dunmore shook his head. "I think we indeed will get more men, but I doubt they will be sufficient to give us superiority over the rebels. That report we got from a sympathizer just a few days ago said that they now have seven full-strength battalions formed or forming. That could be nearly six thousand men. In addition, they can turn out large numbers of militia very rapidly, for what they are worth."

Northcutt raised his hand. "Yes, my lord, they have the numbers. But I have seen with my own eyes that they are poorly equipped. Many men are carrying unsuitable arms, such as fowling pieces. They're scrambling to produce muskets or obtain them from overseas markets. Few have bayonets. Some companies are all riflemen, excellent sharpshooters but not particularly good on the defense or in the charge since they can't mount bayonets." He paused a second, then added, "And their training is miserable. Many of their officers have no knowledge of tactics." He waved his hand. "I maintain that we shouldn't overestimate our foe."

Dunmore pointed at Northcutt with his cigar. "Barrett, I don't often disagree with you, but in this case, I must point out that even if everything you say is quite true—and I'm sure it is—the rebels can simply overwhelm us with numbers. Even poorly trained and equipped troops can prevail over a far smaller number of better trained and equipped forces if the differential is as wide as this one." He paused, looking at each man in turn, and then continued, "Being honest, when we add all our effective men together, we have less than half a battalion. And while our loyalist troops are enthusiastic, the only fully trained men are the three weak companies of the 14th Foot and the marines from Hammond's squadron, which amount to another two companies."

Harbridge raised his hands. "My lord, we simply must make do with what we have and can recruit in the future. We have already requested troops from General Howe and been turned down."

"Yes," said Northcutt, "we will have to continue our current tactics. Raiding and attacks on the enemy where he is weak. We may not triumph, but we keep the colors of the king visible, and if the enemy's fortunes are reversed in the future and our recruitment gains momentum, we may have the opportunity for decisive action."

Dunmore shook his head. "That's not good enough, gentlemen. We need to severely punish the rebels and soundly defeat them on the battlefield if we are actually to hold Virginia for the Crown. And I say we can do that with one full-strength battalion of regulars."

Harbridge raised his eyebrows. "But, sir, since we have already been turned down for that by Howe himself, how would you expect that decision to be reversed?"

"I have been contemplating that fact for several days, Aubrey." He smiled. "I have come to the conclusion that, by simply sending a dispatch, we asked in the wrong way." He raised a finger. "When we presented our plan for the Indian uprising, we sent Connolly to Boston to meet with Gage personally. He was able to forcefully make the case, and Gage not only approved it, he also assigned troops in significant numbers to march with Connolly's forces coming from the Ohio Country. He also diverted the companies of the 14th to us here."

Harbridge assumed a thoughtful look. "I see where you are going, sir. You intend to send someone to Halifax to make our case directly to Howe."

Dunmore pulled on his cigar, then quickly blew the smoke upward toward the ceiling of the cabin. "Precisely, Aubrey. An articulate envoy can lay out the situation, apprise the general of how, after Welford's raid, we are positioned to take the offense, particularly if a good battalion were here to stiffen our forces. And possibly tip the scales in our favor. A verbal argument is much stronger and more nuanced than simple written words. And an envoy can answer questions which might be raised and perhaps sway the decision process."

Harbridge grinned. "And it is much harder to say no to a person than a written proposal." He smacked his hand on the table and exclaimed enthusiastically, "Certainly it is worth a try!"

Northcutt was looking suspiciously over his cigar at Dunmore. "Have you someone in mind for this mission?"

Dunmore's eyes sparkled. "I've thought very hard about the qualifications of the man we send. It must be someone with a persuasive way of speaking who can marshal the proper arguments and logically present them in the best light. It must be someone with a personable manner, and finally, the envoy must be of sufficient rank that his words will carry weight with a general officer."

A cloud came over Northcutt's face. "Whom do you consider to fit that description?"

Dunmore laughed. "Why, Barrett, it is you, of course! You're the perfect man for the job."

"What about my regiment? My duties here?"

"Welford can take charge in your absence. You have barely a hundred men. And Reginald has certainly proven himself capable of independent command." Dunmore shrugged. "And there's another important factor which led to my choice."

Northcutt cocked his head. "What would that be, sir?"

"You mentioned once, some time ago, in passing, that your father's estate is near Howe property and that your father had some relationship with the Howe family."

"True, but I would not say it is particularly close." Northcutt thought a minute. "But now that you bring it up, my brother is a major in the 23rd Foot. General Howe was the proprietary colonel until last year."

Dunmore beamed. "There you are! You have some relationship with Howe."

"Albeit very tenuous, sir. We can't put too much stock in that." Northcutt paused, then asked, "When will you send me?"

"We'll not send you until we know where our base of operations ashore will be. The fact that our force is ashore instead of aboard ship in this wretched anchorage will add credibility to our appeal. So your journey will not begin for some time yet."

"How do you intend I get to Halifax?"

"Why, by sea, of course. Hammond has kept that dispatch schooner HMS *Raven* with his squadron. I intend to prevail upon him to transport you to Halifax and back. It actually should be a quick trip. I understand the *Raven* is quite swift."

Northcutt made an anxious face, which Dunmore noted. "Now, my dear Barrett, I've never seen such concern on your face. Are you that loath to assume this assignment?"

"Sir, it is not the *assignment* that bothers me. It will be my honor to make your case to General Howe." He paused for a moment. "It is the *journey itself* to which I do not look forward. You see, sir, I am a terrible sailor, something which I learned very well when I crossed the Atlantic to come to the colonies. The motion of a ship at sea is something which I—and my stomach—found most disagreeable. I was a shadow of my former self due to lack of food by the time the ship arrived in New York." He sighed and added, "And the *Raven* is much smaller than the vessel in which I crossed the ocean."

Dunmore laughed and looked over at Harbridge. "Come now, Barrett, then this trip will give you the opportunity to demonstrate the sacrifices which you are willing to make for your king, your governor, and Virginia!"

Then both the governor and Harbridge looked in amusement at Northcutt, whose face was a portrait of extreme distress.

Just at dawn, on an April day, Colleen Alison McGraw, dressed in traveling attire, stood in the common room of the Red Vixen Inn of Fredericktown and took one final look around. Her long auburn hair was put up and largely covered by a broad-brimmed hat she had selected to keep as much of the sun off her face as possible. Froman, the German man who had purchased the inn from her, stood leaning against the counter, his portly wife, who was beside him, patiently watching Colleen.

At that moment Charlie Farley, the cook's son, pushed through the front door. "Mother sent me in to get your baggage, Mrs. McGraw."

Colleen waved him toward the hall door. "Yes, the last of it is packed and ready. Put it in the first wagon."

The youth nodded. "Yes, ma'am," he said and headed into the hallway.

Colleen turned to the new proprietor. "Well, Mr. Froman, the Red Vixen is all yours. I sincerely wish your ownership will be as profitable as was mine."

"*Ja*, Mrs. McGraw," Froman said. "I have no doubt we will find it so." He held up a wooden sign, which read, "Froman's Ordinary." He said, "That is the establishment's new name."

His wife, a dour look on her face, added, "*Ja*, a new name, and..." She hesitated momentarily, then said in a deprecating tone, "a new reputation."

Colleen couldn't help but laugh. "Well, the *Red Vixen* certainly had an excellent reputation with its *particular* clientele." She paused and gave the couple a meaningful look. "I sincerely hope your reputation will be as high with yours."

Then a thought hit her. As Charlie came out carrying her bag, she said to him, "Lad, after you load that in the wagon, come back and take down the Red Vixen sign from beside the door, and put that in the wagon also." Colleen looked back at the Fromans. "We'll use that when we're with the army. It always was a distinctive and meaningful name, and our new patrons will certainly appreciate it!" She smiled broadly and gave a nod to the couple. "Good day, and good fortune."

And with that, she turned and left the inn to its new owners.

In the yard Colleen looked over a formidable assemblage of wagons, horses, and people. Four blue-painted Conestogas, each with a six-horse team, stood ready to depart. They carried the extensive inventory of goods that would be sold to soldiers. Two smaller farm wagons, with single teams, were also in the yard; they would carry Colleen's people and their personal items. A herd of additional horses, constituting relief teams, were standing together, watched over by a young boy. Five comely young women—Colleen's tavern maids—were talking and laughing, waiting to climb into one of the farm wagons.

Colleen called out to Edna Farley, a woman in her mid-fifties, who served as her strong right arm. She stood hands on hips, supervising the whole scene. Next to her was Elijah Lynch, the head teamster. "Edna, I'm going over to pay my respects to Georgie before we leave."

Edna turned and said, "I'll come with you."

The two women walked the short distance to a small cemetery surrounded by a white fence. Inside was a stone with the name George McGraw.

The two women stood silent for a minute. Then Colleen sighed and said, "Well, Georgie, the time has come for us to finally part. But I'll never deny my good fortune stems from the day I met you."

Edna said, "Indeed, you owe him a debt."

The younger woman shrugged. "He was the opportunity for fortune, not the cause. The real fortune was made after he passed. Come, Edna, you know the story."

Edna looked knowingly at Colleen. "I well know that you had no real wifely love for him."

"I make no bones about it. For me, our marriage was from the beginning a business partnership. He was a newly widowed, lonely, middle-aged man traveling to Philadelphia to get an indentured maid for his tavern. He stopped at the Proud Rooster, where I was a seventeen-year-old indentured maid, sold into servitude by my drunkard mother. Out of his loneliness, he paid me to sleep with him, and he told me in his grief how he had just lost his wife." Colleen pointed to the gravestone beside Georgie's, on which was engraved the name Patricia McGraw. "I saw my opportunity." She smiled to herself. "By then I was very experienced with men, and in bed that night, I gave him the best performance of my life." She laughed. "And maybe the best of his life! But more important, I listened to his story and showered him with understanding and sympathy." Colleen paused and sighed. "In the morning he thanked me, paid me handsomely, and went on his way without saying much. I thought my efforts had been for naught, except for the coins." She smiled. "But it had worked. On his way home, he stopped at the tavern and told me he would buy out my indenture if I married him. I was exultant!"

"The man was twenty-two years older than you."

"Yes, and corpulent and balding. There was never any question of love, but by God, it got me away from the Proud Rooster and its proprietor, whom I hated. And I disciplined myself to make him a good wife, keeping him warm at night, pleasuring him when he wanted it, and being affable company. I assure you, he never had any complaint on that measure. And after my experience at the Proud Rooster, I knew how to run an inn or tavern. So I was a good workmate."

Edna said, "He taught you to read and write and how to do numbers."

"Yes, that is what I owe him the most for; after a couple of years, I kept the accounts, so I learned that end of the business. And then when the lung fever took him that winter, I was ready to start making some real money at the Red Vixen. I found the right girls, and soon the good men of Fredericktown were beating a path to my door with coin in hand." She looked over at Edna and put a hand on her arm. "And of course, I hired you to cook and run the inn itself. Probably one of my smartest moves!"

Edna shook her head. "I'll not deny that. And now you're gambling all the money you made, and the money from selling the inn, on this venture to be a sutler to the army."

Colleen made a tight smile. "I know you've always been skeptical, but it will work out. You'll see, between the girls and the supplies and liquor we'll sell, we'll make even more money."

The older lady sighed. "I hope you are right."

Just then a bright young voice interrupted, "Mrs. McGraw! Mrs. McGraw! Mr. Lynch says we're all ready to start out! He says we mustn't dally if we're going to make it up the ridges to the South Mountain Inn by nightfall."

Colleen looked around to see Emily Crider, her golden hair all but covered by a traveling bonnet, an excited expression on her face, standing behind them. "All right, Emily, tell Lynch we'll be there directly."

Emily smiled broadly, "Yes, ma'am!" She turned and almost skipped back toward the wagons.

Colleen turned to Mrs. Farley. "Good Lord, I've never seen her so excited. I guess she's looking forward to the trip."

"She's looking forward to something which excites her even more."

"What the devil do you mean?"

"Yesterday she got a letter. She's been like that ever since."

Colleen's face wrinkled in puzzlement. "I wonder what was in it to make her so ebullient?"

Edna replied, "I made it my business to find out. She told Faith what it was all about, and I pulled it out of Faith."

"Well, don't hold your tongue."

"You remember the young apprentice that was with that gunsmith Eckert and his party last fall?"

"How could I forget? He took on that backcountry lout who wanted to take Emily upstairs on her day off. The apprentice tried to fight him but was getting the worst of it until we pulled out the pistol and told him to get out."

"Well, you remember how Emily felt toward the apprentice."

"Yes, she slept with him for a couple nights until he left. I didn't mind; it made her happy. It was a passing fancy, and I knew he was going to leave and never see her again. I mean, Winchester is one hundred miles away in another colony. Besides, a good-looking boy like that must have girls closer to home."

"Well, you couldn't be more wrong about that. Faith says they've been corresponding with each other."

"Oh shit."

"Yeah, and last month she wrote and told Andrew—Andrew Horner; that's the lad's name, if you remember—that we were about to leave for the army."

"All right, that should put more distance between them. So why is Emily so happy?"

"Horner wrote back that he's made arrangements to leave Eckert's place and become a gunsmith for the army. He's got a horse and cart and will leave in a fortnight from the time he wrote the letter."

Colleen sucked in her breath. "Damn! Damn! Damn! She's my youngest, freshest, sweetest-looking girl. And she sings like an angel.

I've been counting on her to pull in good customers." Her face muscles tightened, and her lips pursed. "Finding girls like that is hard as hell! I've spent a year teaching her how to please a man before and after they get in bed. Now I'm going to be fretting all the time, waiting for that lad to show up and lure her away."

Edna put her hands on her hips. "My God, Colleen, I've never seen you so upset. You usually take everything calmly and simply put your mind to solving the problem. Now just think on it. There are all sorts of things which can happen till they would be able to get together. The army's big, and it will be spread out, with units located in different places. It will take him a while to find her. And accidents happen; he may never make it to the army. So just calm down. You need to be thinking about managing our journey and getting started with business once we get to New York."

Colleen stood staring into the distance for a long moment, then took a deep breath. "Yes, you're right. We'll deal with Emily's love affair when the young man shows up." A determined look came over her face. "And if he thinks he's going to just sweep in and take my best girl, he's got another thing coming. He's going to find out how hard a woman I am." She looked back at the wagons and horses. "Let's go. Lynch is right—we've got to start up the mountain and make the crest today. I want to be down to Elizabethtown by tomorrow night and start out on the Great Wagon Road northward the day after that."

Wend Eckert, moving with great care, walked out onto the porch of the house and, grasping the rail in case one of the dizzy spells came on, gingerly took the steps down to the ground. It was his first solo trip out of the house since the day of the raid. He was determined to make a walking inspection of the farm, to check out the progress in rebuilding.

The April day was warm, enhanced by the early afternoon sunlight. Wend walked across the drive to the workshop. Horner was supervising the construction work, having organized the apprentices for the task. They were nearly finished framing out the building.

In the open area behind the shop, some carpenters sent over by the Committee of Safety were working on shaping trusses for the roof.

Wend saw that Hecht, over in the canvas-covered temporary shop, was working with one apprentice to restore the muskets that had been scorched in the fire.

Meanwhile, Andrew had seen Wend and had joined him in looking at the construction work.

Wend motioned toward the shop. "You've made great progress. And from what I can see, it will be larger and better laid out than the original."

Horner smiled in pride. "Yes, sir. In a way, those loyalists did us a favor, giving us a chance to make a bigger shop on a more useful design." He furrowed his brow. "We'll be ready to raise the trusses for the roof in just a couple days."

After a little more discussion with the apprentice, Wend walked down the drive to see what else was in progress. He passed the burned-out barracks, which were still untouched since the men had shelter in the Donegal house. Wend, Peggy, and Specht had decided that the farm buildings would take priority. Now Wend could see the lead hand himself directing work on the new hay barn. Erection of the walls was well underway. Another crew was working on pulling down the charred walls of the stable—it would be the next building to be reconstructed. Specht told him that the wall frames would be fully in place in two days, and then they would be ready for the carpenters to fabricate the trusses.

After inspecting the farm area, Wend started to walk back to the house. Then he noticed smoke coming out of the distillery. He realized he hadn't seen Donegal in days, so he turned and walked over to the building.

As he entered, his nose was pleasantly assaulted by the pungent aroma of alcohol. Donegal and his two assistants, all wearing aprons and tight-fitting caps, were busily engaged in draining a completed batch of the product into a barrel. Wend waited by the door until they had finished.

Finally Donegal looked up and noticed his partner. "Well, na, lad, you're sure and looking better than the last time I saw you."

"I can walk all right, but I get dizzy spells. Doctor says those will stop in a few days."

"Aye, that's good. It was a close call you had."

Wend nodded. "Indeed, Simon." He motioned toward the door, and the two walked outside. "I've got something important to talk about with you."

Donegal pulled his cap off. "Well, speak your peace. We have to clean up everything to start getting ready for the next batch."

Wend said, "I'm grateful for what you are doing. It's providing the only source of money we have until I can get the shop fully working."

The Highlander shrugged. "You came here just to tell me that?"

Wend laughed. "No, my old friend. I wanted to talk about the company I will be raising."

"Yes, the Committee of Safety got their way in the end, didn't they? So much for your wantin' to sit out this war."

"I had to do what was best for my family and the farm." He looked over at Donegal. "The important thing is, I want you to come with me. I want you for my first lieutenant."

A shocked look came over Donegal's face. "Na did I hear you right? You're askin' me to be the first lieutenant?"

"You heard what I said. Someone in the company needs to understand proper military discipline and impart it to the men. I don't want us to look like a bunch of raw militia."

"Na, lad, you are lookin' at the wrong man for your lieutenant. I'll not do it."

"You are refusing to go with the company?" Wend searched for a way to convince him. "Simon, it's a way of taking revenge on the people who did all this to us." He waved his arm to take in the destruction of the farm. "And vengeance for what they did to Sally."

"Dunna be raising her name and trying to use it against me! You think, after putting her in the cold ground, I don't want to go after Welford and Northcutt and the rest of them?"

"Well, Simon, you must realize that the best way to do that is to go with the army."

"Na listen, Wend Eckert, I na'er said I wouldn't go with your company. I said would na go as a *lieutenant*."

Wend stared at the former corporal of the 77th Highlanders, puzzled at what he had said.

"You said you wanted somebody to train your men and discipline them like regular soldiers." He paused to gather his thoughts. "Well, I'm the man to do it. But as your company sergeant, not some fancy pants lieutenant who's na supposed to get his hands dirty or lay them on a private soldier. The man who is to make proper soldiers has to be one who has lived it every day and will be right among them and can kick them in the ass when the time comes. And of course, there's na better man in the county to do that than Simon Donegal."

Wend put his hand on his old comrade's shoulder. "We've been through a lot together. I'm glad you'll be along."

"Aye, we'll show them what a good company is like." He looked over at Wend. "But right now we got one problem: finding soldiers. The truth is, you've got to get started recruiting so I can have lads to train with my *tender* style."

Wend sighed. "Yes, I must get started. And it's not going to be as easy as Morgan had it. The best and most eager lads have already gone off in the rifle companies that went out last year."

"And don't forget, you got to think about officers and the other sergeants."

"Yes, I don't have a clue about that yet. I'll have to look over the militia rolls for likely candidates. I must have Rutledge supply that information."

"You know, as sergeants, it would be good to have someone with experience in the regulars—say, like in the old Virginia Regiment of the French War." He wrinkled his brow. "Someone like that farmer from Hardt's Store—Flannagan was his name. The one who was your sergeant in the raid on Wakatamico last year."

"Yes, he was a tough veteran. I'd give a lot to have him. But he lives out near the Ohio. And likely he's busy with his farm after the Shawnee burned it." Then Wend thought of something. "I know who would be good—Calvert, the corporal from Wood's company who led the squad that worked with me at Hardt's Store and the return trip from Wakatamica."

Donegal's face wrinkled up as he tried to recollect. "Aye, I remember him—he's a cobbler at Steffensburg. He had a good squad. Fought like the devil when the Shawnee war party ambushed you on the way back from Hardt's store. Maybe you should look him up."

"I just might do that. And having a cobbler in the company would be damned helpful."

Dusk was not far off when, at Colleen's direction, Charlie pulled the lead wagon into the open field beside the road. There were signs of many previous campfires, indicating that the spot was a frequent stopping place for travelers. When the horses were reined in, she sighed and slid to the ground, grateful for the opportunity to be on her feet after a long day of travel. Colleen looked toward the prosperous town, which spread out just to the east. She had been to Lancaster several times while working at the Proud Rooster, which was located on the western outskirts of York, and had always enjoyed her visits. After a moment she turned and watched as the other wagons of what she had come to call the Red Vixen Caravan pulled into the campsite.

Edna Farley joined her, and Colleen said, "We're on the very outskirts of the town. She waved toward a line of trees. "There's a small stream with adequate water right there. It's a good place to camp for the night. Then we'll leave early and roll through the town before the streets get busy."

Edna responded, "Now, Colleen, I've been thinking. We've made good time, very good time, since we left Fredericktown. But it's taken a lot out of the animals. And the people, too, if I might say. Maybe it's time to take a day of rest."

Colleen considered Edna's words. Then she nodded. "All right. I was mindful of pushing on for another day or two, but this is a comfortable campsite. We'll stay here for two nights. Tomorrow we'll let the people take in the town."

"Everyone will welcome that."

"Yes, let Lynch and the girls know about that. Meanwhile, have Charlie set up my tent and build my fire over by the tree line. That's the right place for everyone else to camp, right along the creek. We can find a private place for the girls to clean themselves up in the stream. We all need it after the last five days."

Edna turned and strode off, calling for the head teamster and Charlie as she walked.

An hour later the caravan's camp was set up, horses picketed, fires started, and the smell of cooking food wafted along the creek. Colleen lounged in a camp chair, enjoying the warmth of her fire against the chill evening air, and watching the flow of the creek water a short distance from her.

Her reverie was interrupted by a call from Edna Farley. "Soldiers coming! Cavalry coming from the west."

Colleen stood up and turned around to see a column of horsemen, two abreast, coming up the road. As they got closer, she counted a total of twenty-two, including two officers. They were smartly uniformed in short, gray jackets with green facings, tight-fitting white breeches, with brown leather boots extending up to just below the knees. Behind the troop was a wagon, driven by a black man with a woman of the same color beside him on the seat. Behind the wagon was a string of pack horses, led by another African.

Edna said, "Now they're a fine-looking body of men."

"Yes, and seem to be well fitted out. Wherever they come from, there was good money behind their establishment. Not like so many of the companies we've seen, without uniforms or proper arms."

"Look." Edna pointed to the column. "They're turning into the field. Perhaps they plan to camp here tonight."

"It would make sense," responded Colleen as she watched. "Darkness will soon be with us." She looked at the leader of the troop, who rode a tall, powerfully built hunter. "That's an elegant horse." She looked over the rider, commenting, "And an equally elegant officer. I wonder where they're from?"

Edna shrugged. "Well, if they're going to stop here overnight, we'll probably find out."

A thought struck Colleen. "We may have an opportunity for some profit here. Don't let the girls wander off."

Motioning with her hand toward the soldiers, Edna said, "Do you want me or Charlie to go over and find out about them?"

Colleen hesitated a moment. "No, if I know anything about men, they'll be over here soon enough once they discern there are women in our camp. Let's see what transpires."

She sat back down in her camp chair. "Meanwhile, I'm ready for supper."

Colleen's speculation proved right. The troop commenced setting up their bivouac with practiced speed. The horses were watered and placed on a picket line, then provided with grain. Tents went up in a row, supplies taken out of the wagon and from the horse packs that had been lined up on the ground. Soon campfires were sending flames skyward. The acrid smell of woodsmoke, from both the cavalry and the Red Vixen camp, permeated the entire site.

Colleen had been watching the cavalrymen while she ate her meal. As she was finishing, she observed a soldier with powerful shoulders walking over to the place where Lynch and Mrs. Farley were talking about some detail of camp business. The soldier discussed something with the two and after a few moments, turned and strode toward where she sat. Colleen finished the last bite of her supper, put the plate and utensils down by the fire, and leaned back in her chair.

The cavalryman arrived at the fire, took his helmet off, revealing a shock of red hair. Colleen noted that he was of average height, with powerful shoulders but rather small hips and thin legs. But her eyes were drawn to his head. The face was heavily scarred, presumably from smallpox. But the most singular thing was that the lower half of his left ear was missing, replaced with a nasty scar that had turned black with age.

The soldier gave her a slight bow. "Now good evenin', ma'am. My name is Quinn, Sergeant Quinn of the 1st Troop of the Palmetto Light Horse. Might you be Mrs. McGraw?"

"Good evening to yourself, sergeant. Indeed, I'm Colleen McGraw. Is there something I can do for you?"

"Now, ma'am, that depends. Your people say you are in the way of bein' a sutler for the army, carrying all sorts of goods in those great Conestoga wagons sittin' over yon. It happens we've been travelling for days without bein' able to procure provisions. We were thinkin' to buy them from merchants here in Lancaster, but if you were able to sell us what we need, that would be most providential and would save us time on our march to join the army."

"I'm confident we have what you would want. Flour, salt meat, sugar, tobacco, and much more."

Quinn cocked his head. "That would be good, ma'am. Now do you mind me askin', might you have a little spirits for sale in those wagons of yours?"

Colleen looked him directly in the eyes and smiled. "In prodigious amounts, sergeant. Some rum, which is rather hard to get these days, and plenty of whiskey."

A broad grin spread across the sergeant's face. "Ah, now, if I may say so, you're bein' here is like the Lord providin' an angel to help us in our time of need."

Colleen laughed. "You'll find I'm no angel. At least not the kind that inhabits heaven. I take hard coin only for my goods and nothing less. Don't expect me to provide anything on the basis of an army purchase voucher."

"No worry, ma'am, the good government of South Carolina provided us with hard money for our trip to join the army." He paused and looked over at the cavalry camp. "Now, if you don't mind, my lieutenant will come over an' make the bargain with you for what we need."

"That will be fine, Sergeant Quinn. And I might add, if your men have any money, they are quite welcome to come over and purchase personal items, liquor, sweets, and whatever else we have that might please them."

Quinn quickly glanced over at the fire where the five tavern girls were sitting and finishing up their suppers. They were laughing and giggling as they ate.

The cavalrymen returned his gaze to Colleen and responded, "I'm sure there would be some things the lads would be eager to be payin' for."

"I'm quite confident that we have *whatever* they have in mind."

Quinn made the slightest bow. "Thank ye, ma'am. Now I'll be makin' my way back to the lieutenant, and I'm sure he'll be waitin' on you presently."

"I'll be looking forward to that, sergeant."

With that, Quinn turned and hurried back toward the army camp.

Edna came over from the next fire. "Well?"

"We're going to do some trade here, Edna. Provisions for the troop itself and liquor to the men. And tell the girls to get themselves ready to earn their keep."

The older lady nodded. "We'll be ready." Without another word she headed to the fire where the tavern maids were gathered.

Colleen didn't have long to wait. In just a few minutes, an officer approached. She realized it was the man she had seen leading the troop. Looking him over, she decided her characterization of him as being elegant, even at some distance, had been accurate. He was blond-haired with blue eyes. The face was youthful, thin, and devilishly handsome, with fair skin bronzed by the sun and wind. But the young-looking face was somewhat belied by lines around his eyes and a hardness around both the eyes and mouth. Her eyes played over his body, and she decided he had not a discernible pound of excess weight on the lithe frame. His uniform had obviously been measured and sewn by a master tailor, for it fitted him exquisitely and spoke of money.

The officer arrived, took off his helmet and tucked it under his left arm, then bowed deeply to her, his right hand sweeping across his chest. "Good evening, ma'am. I am lieutenant Geoffrey Fairfield of the Palmetto Light Horse from South Carolina. If I am properly informed, you are Mrs. McGraw, the mistress of this establishment." He swept his right hand out to encompass all the wagons, tents, and campfires. He hesitated a moment and said, "Which I understand goes under the name of the Red Vixen Sutler Company."

"Well, Lieutenant, I am Colleen McGraw, and you are correctly advised about the name and nature of my business."

Fairfield grinned broadly. "I would assume that I am in the presence of the Red Vixen herself?"

"Lieutenant, many have presumed that to be the case."

"Be that as it may, Mrs. McGraw, Sergeant Quinn informed me you were a most attractive lady. If I may be so bold, having seen you myself, I realize he greatly understated your beauty. You would light up any room which you entered and immediately draw the gaze of every man therein."

Colleen cocked her head. "Lieutenant, do all the men of South Carolina employ such flowery language and exaggerated flattery as a matter of course?"

Fairfield smiled and bowed. "Why, Mrs. McGraw, I protest! Nothing I have said is in any way exaggerated." He smiled. "Perhaps we in the South speak with more chivalry than is the custom here in the northern colonies."

Colleen laughed and said, "Perhaps." Then she moved to change the subject. "Your sergeant—Quinn—had a singular appearance. Particularly in the matter of his left ear, most of which was missing. May I inquire what happened to the poor man?"

"Of course, ma'am. Quinn was formerly a member of one of His Majesty's dragoon regiments. The appearance of his ear is the result of a saber cut while in action against the French in the late war."

"How unfortunate."

"Well, Mrs. McGraw, the French cavalryman who inflicted the wound was even more unfortunate. Despite the pain he was suffering, Quinn promptly dispatched him with a ball from his pistol."

Colleen said, "Well, I had rather thought Quinn might have suffered his wound in a tavern knife fight." She thought a minute. "How fortunate for you that you have a sergeant with actual experience."

"Well, Mrs. McGraw, I am doubly fortunate, for I have another sergeant, named McCrae, who was also in a British dragoon regiment. The two men have certainly helped me train and equip my troop."

"Indeed, I see what you mean." There were a few moments of silence, and Colleen asked, "What about yourself, Mr. Fairfield? What part of South Carolina are you from? The only place I know the name of is Charleston, which I understand is the largest city."

"Well, of course we have a town house in the city, but our family plantation is in the low country north of Charleston."

Colleen was puzzled. "The low country? I'm not familiar with that term."

"The rough equivalent would be the term 'tidewater' in Virginia and Maryland. But we also have many swamps in the area."

"I see."

The lieutenant continued, "Fairfield Landing on Wando Creek is the formal name of our holdings. The creek is actually a small river, and the plantation is right at the head of navigation. My father founded it forty-five years ago." He shrugged. "It's rather modest, not like the grand places on the Ashley River." He smiled modestly. "But it does provide a rather comfortable income."

"So are you now the master of Fairfield Landing?"

"My father is still alive"—he smiled—"and in rather good health. So his oldest son took the opportunity to don the uniform and show our family's support for the patriot cause."

Colleen smiled. "Very interesting. I know so little of the South." Then she changed the subject to business. "Well, Mr. Fairfield, now that we've exchanged pleasantries, why don't we get down to particulars of what we can do for you?" She motioned to another camp chair and said, "Please sit down."

Fairfield took the seat, reached inside his jacket, and produced a piece of paper. He handed it to Colleen. "Here is a list of what we would desire to procure. Please tell me if you can meet those needs."

Colleen scanned the list, leaning over to let the flames of the fire illuminate the paper. Then she looked up at the lieutenant. "Mr. Fairfield, we'll have no problem supplying these items."

"In the quantity required?"

"Yes, we are well stocked." She paused and raised a finger. "That is, with the exception of one item. You have asked for a quantity of rum. I would suggest substituting whiskey. Since the British blockade, rum has been very hard to find, and when it is available, the price is quite dear. I can give you a very good price on the whiskey. We do have a small quantity of rum, but I must price it high and limit sales only to individuals."

Fairfield considered a moment and waved a hand. "Certainly the whiskey will do. I imagine the men will have to get used to it once we join the army."

Colleen called for Mrs. Farley, who walked over from her fire. She handed the older woman Fairfield's list.

"Edna, price these items out for me and compile a total amount for the gentleman."

Mrs. Farley nodded and hurried off. Colleen reached down and picked up a jug from the ground beside her. "This is whiskey from our stock. Perhaps we should share a drink, and you can confirm that it meets your requirements."

Fairfield smile. "Mrs. McGraw, nothing would please me more."

She poured him a cup and handed it to him, then filled one for herself. "Geoffrey, I believe it's time to become a little more informal. Why don't you call me Colleen?"

Fairfield bowed slightly and replied, "Of course, Colleen."

"Now, Geoffrey, I'll propose a toast. May fortune smile on us both in our endeavors with the army."

Fairfield nodded. "I will enthusiastically drink to that." He put his cup to his lips. After a moment he said enthusiastically, "Whiskey is not my preference, but this is very good."

"Thank you, Geoffrey. We pride ourselves at including only the best quality in all our stock and offering everything at a fair price."

Fairfield looked over at the girls, then back at Colleen. "My men were rather excited to see so many pretty young ladies in your camp."

Colleen looked directly at Fairfield and allowed herself a small smile. "They're not here by mere chance. I told you everything, whether goods or services, was offered at a fair price."

His eyes twinkled. "Ah yes, I quite understand."

Fairfield directed his gaze at Colleen, his eyes running over her, and she felt like he was imagining what her naked body would look like. It was a look in men's eyes she had seen many times before.

A knowing expression spread across Fairfield's face. "You said everything in this camp is on offer and priced at its value. May I be so bold as to ask if you meant that literally?"

Colleen gave him a coy look and took another sip from her cup. "Certainly, Geoffrey. But I would warn you that some things are of such value that the price is extremely dear and beyond the purse of most men."

The officer laughed and said, "Ah, yes, I *quite* take your meaning." He paused a second, then said, "It occurs to me, Colleen, that you are a most world-wise and practical woman."

"Indeed, I pride myself on that." She raised a finger. "And speaking of practical matters, I hope you would see your way toward allowing your men to leave their bivouac tonight and visit us for their personal needs. They will find many things they desire available, as I have said, at fair price."

Geoffrey shrugged. "I see no reason to preclude them from doing so."

Just then Edna Farley returned. She handed Colleen Fairfield's list, with each item priced and the total shown at the bottom. "Does that look right, Mrs. McGraw?"

Colleen quickly scanned the numbers, nodded her approval to Edna, and handed the paper to Fairfield. "Well, Lieutenant, does that price meet with your satisfaction?"

Fairfield looked at the paper for a long moment, then said, "Completely, Colleen."

"Excellent, Geoffrey. If it pleases you, we'll have all of that ready for you just after dawn, and upon payment, you can load it onto your packhorses or wagon."

Fairfield drained his cup and stood up. "That will be most satisfactory, Mrs. McGraw. I'll return to camp and let my quartermaster corporal know about the agreement." He bowed and said, "It has been my great pleasure to meet you and to do business with you. I am very hopeful that when we're with the army, we'll again be able to work together and perhaps share another cup of spirits."

"That would be my greatest pleasure, Geoffrey."

Fairfield bowed again, put his helmet back on his head, and strode off to the camp of his troop.

Edna said, "Now that's a well-mannered, handsome young officer."

Colleen said nothing for a while. Instead, she motioned Edna to take a seat. She sat down herself and picked up her long-stemmed pipe, which was already packed with tobacco, and lit it with a glowing stick from the fire.

When she had it going, she looked over at her associate and said, "Yes, he's handsome. Handsome and *very* smooth." She took a deep draw of the smoke, savored it for a moment, then exhaled. "But I get a feeling that he's not exactly what he claims. There's something more there than just the privileged son of a wealthy planter. I don't know why—perhaps it's the hardness in his eyes and mouth. But you know, I have an instinct in these things, and that sense is clanging like a fire bell right now."

"Well, Colleen, as long as he pays us like he's promised, it's no matter if he's the devil himself. That's not our worry."

Colleen shrugged. "You're right, of course. It's not worth worrying about Mr. Fairfield's pedigree." Then she thought a moment. "Once the cavalry get their supplies, we need to go into Lancaster and replenish the stock we've sold. We must arrive at the army with our wagons full."

"It may take some time to track everything down and get it delivered. More than one day."

"That's all right. We've just made a good profit off South Carolina. And it will be even better after those soldiers come over tonight. We'll stay as long as it takes to get what we need."

Wend sat under the canvas canopy, taking inventory of his personal tools, which had been saved from the fire, and meanwhile savoring the sunny, warm April day. The sound of hammers and sawing was ever present as work progressed on the new shop, and in the distance, more hammering could be heard where Specht and his men were finishing up the new hay barn. Wend watched as Andrew Horner directed the apprentices and carpenters in their work.

It was now well past the time when Horner and Billy had planned to leave for the army. But neither had brought up the plan since the raid and were concentrating on the work of rebuilding. Wend had been happy not to raise the subject, preferring to let sleeping dogs lie, but at the same time, he worried every day that Horner would suddenly come notify him that he was ready to leave.

Then Wend looked up from his work and was stunned to see his worst fears materialize. A one-horse cart, driven by Billy, was coming up the drive. Wend cursed to himself. It was obviously the cart and horse the two youths had acquired from the Widow Callow. He watched as Horner grinned broadly and left off from what he was doing to stride over to the drive. When the cart arrived at the shop, Billy pulled up the horse. Horner walked around the vehicle, inspecting it.

Wend heard him say to the driver, "Well, Billy, it's going to need some work, but there's nothing which can't be fixed in a few days. It's old but still sturdy."

Billy nodded vigorously. "I'll take it down and park it for now where they got the other wagons and turn the horse out to the pasture." He slapped the reins on the old horse's back and continued along the drive.

Wend came to his feet, then waited a few seconds until the dizziness passed. Meanwhile he felt a lump in his stomach. He realized it was time to confront Horner about his plans. He walked over to where Andrew stood beside the drive.

"Well, Andrew, I see that you and Billy still intend to travel to Washington's army."

"Of course, sir. I told Emily Crider I would find her, wherever she was. And Billy is determined to be a soldier."

"After all your years with us, I had hoped you would see that your duty was here, helping us recover from the raid, at least until things had gotten back to some semblance of normality." Wend looked into Horner's eyes. "You have been the force behind the rebuilding of the shop, and I have become entirely dependent on you. Hecht is still mourning the loss of his son, and the grief is affecting his work. I must soon start recruiting for the new company, so I will be unable to spend much time supervising the work of the apprentices." Wend took a deep breath. "I urge you to rethink your position."

"Sir, it is well beyond the time when I told you we would leave. I understand that you have supported me and taught me the secrets of our trade. And for that I am very grateful. I believe I have shown that in the days since the raid."

"But now you would leave at the very moment when I and the entire farm need you urgently?"

A look of distress came over Horner's eyes. "Mr. Eckert, you misjudge me! I still plan to go to the army. But things have changed. You are now going to the army yourself in a short time." He waved his hand toward the cart rolling along the drive. "Billy and I will go to the army, but we will go with you, when the company is ready and marches off."

A wave of relief rushed over Wend. He felt his body relax. He took a deep breath. "Andrew, you are correct. I *have* sadly misjudged you, and you have my apology and my gratitude."

There was a momentary and awkward moment of silence between the two men. Then Horner motioned toward the shop. "Well, sir, I need to get back to work, unless there's anything else to discuss right now."

"No, Andrew, everything we needed to talk about has been said."

That evening, with work completed at the shop, Wend entered the house and went right to the parlor. He was pouring himself a cup of whiskey when Peggy entered.

"Supper will be ready very soon, Wend." She went over and seated herself on the settee.

Wend grinned broadly at his wife. "My dear, you are looking lovely tonight." He held up the cup. "Would you like some whiskey?"

Peggy nodded, and he handed her the glass.

Wend poured himself a cup. He turned to his wife. "Well, it was a great day. Things are really moving along. The apprentices are making good progress with the shop, and Specht is doing wonders putting the farm back together." He took a sip of his liquor. "You know, I'm quite hungry tonight. I think I could eat a horse."

"I should like to see you attempt that."

"Well, I am quite hungry."

Peggy was looking at him sharply over her drink. She cocked her head and said in a puzzled voice, "You know, I haven't seen you this happy in weeks. You've been rather morose since the raid. You didn't even cheer up much when the committee said they'd pay for all the repairs." She took a sip of the whiskey. "What's happened to give you so much optimism?"

Wend walked over and kissed her on the forehead. "Well, my dear, I was the recipient of some very good news today."

"And that was?"

"Billy brought the horse cart over from Mrs. Callow's place. The one that he and Horner are planning to use to go north to join the army."

Peggy raised her eyebrows. "I'm puzzled. They're getting ready to leave for the army, and you are so overjoyed? I thought you dreaded losing Horner."

"I did indeed."

"So what has changed?"

"What has changed, my dear wife, is that both of them plan to stay here until the company is formed. In short, they will be coming with me! And will stay with the company. Billy will become a soldier, and Horner will work as a gunsmith to support us and the army itself." He smiled broadly. "What could be better?"

"That is good news. Particularly since it has apparently restored your humor."

"It has indeed!" Wend took a deep draft of the whiskey. "And now, Peggy, it is time that I start recruiting the company. I must begin immediately if we are to join the army in time for the summer campaigning season." He pondered a moment. "I'll go into Winchester tomorrow and get some handbills printed up. And I must start thinking about who will be my officers. I'll appoint them as soon as possible, then they can help with drumming up the men."

At that moment Wilma came to the parlor. "We be all ready for supper, Mrs. Eckert. And the children are at the table."

Wend drained his cup, put it down on the cabinet, walked over and offered his hand to Peggy, and said in a formal tone, "Well, Mrs. Eckert, shall we go partake of the meal?"

"Certainly, Mr. Eckert." Peggy took his hand and stood up. Then she looked over at the cook. "We're not happening to have horsemeat tonight, are we, Wilma?"

A look of astonishment came over the black woman's face. "Mrs. Eckert, *what* are you talking about? You know we would never serve *horsemeat* in this house! No, ma'am."

Peggy laughed heartily. "It's just a joke, Wilma." She looked over at Wend and took his arm. "Let's go join the children at the table and see how hungry you really are."

Chapter Seven

RECRUITMENT

Wend Eckert stood in the doorway of the Golden Buck, letting his eyes adjust after entering from the bright sunlight. Then he looked around the common room and saw David Rutledge sitting at a table in the back corner. Bush walked out of the kitchen, and Wend waved at him as he walked back. Wend took his seat across from the county lieutenant and gave the server who came to the table his order for a drink.

Rutledge's eyes ran over Wend, and he said, "Well, you're certainly looking better than the last time I saw you, at Eckert Ridge. How are you feeling?"

"Mostly I'm good. Still having spells of being unsteady on my feet, but they're getting less frequent. I'll be ready for service very soon. And at any rate, I'm ready to start recruiting men for the company."

Rutledge took a sip of his whiskey. "Well, that's good news."

Wend handed Rutledge one of the handbills he'd had printed. "I've a man out posting these all over town and particularly in the taverns and shops."

"Well, you won't have trouble. I've heard from a lot of men who are ready to volunteer." Rutledge quickly looked it over and furrowed his brow. "Wend, I'm a bit confused by this wording. It says you are looking for 'riflemen and other men willing to serve.'" He glanced up at Wend. "I was under the impression that we were recruiting an independent rifle company." He raised his eyebrows. "This implies you'll take men who aren't skilled with that weapon."

"That's right. If you remember, I insisted on the right to organize the company to my own ideas before I accepted the commission. Well, while recovering from my wounds, I've had lots of time to consider the structure of the company. Based on my experiences, I've come to the conclusion that it should be a company of light foot, not exclusively made up of riflemen. I plan to have half riflemen and half armed with muskets."

Rutledge straightened up in his chair. "Why, I've never heard of anything like that."

The server delivered Wend's whiskey, and he took a sip before answering. "Actually, David, there is some precedent for it. In the battalions of the Royal Americans during the French war and Pontiac's insurrection, it was customary for the light company to have a number of rifles as well as muskets. Usually the number was something like ten or fifteen rifles with the rest being muskets."

"Interesting, Eckert. I wasn't aware of that." He picked up his cup, looked at it for a moment, then said, "But you are talking about having half riflemen and half musket men. How did you determine those numbers?"

"Actually, I might have settled on a ratio similar to the Royal Americans, but the fact is I have, or will soon have, fifty muskets ready for service. So, with a company of one hundred men, the ratio would have to be fifty to fifty. There's no time to wait until I can build more muskets."

Rutledge stared at Wend. "I see. Well, that brings up the second question in my mind. I intended to ask where you planned to get the muskets." He raised a finger. "It was my understanding that those muskets have been intended for the 7th Virginia Regiment. Now you plan to appropriate them for your own company?"

"That's right, David. Actually, my contract with the colony simply says the firelocks are intended for use by the Virginia forces. It doesn't specify the 7th. We've just assumed that since it's the regiment which is organizing at the moment."

"Williamsburg might have considerable opposition to you using the muskets. They authorized us to organize a rifle company, expecting the weapons to be supplied by the men themselves."

"I've been in touch with the Rappahannock Forge, down at Fredericksburg, and I understand they have sped up their production of muskets. They can easily make up for our fifty firelocks. I plan to have James Wood correspond with Williamsburg and simply tell them we're going to use the muskets for a company that can be in the field by late May. I doubt they will object. And in any case, they may not have time to object, because we will have marched for Washington's army by then."

Rutledge's eyes registered skepticism. After a moment he said, "Let's be honest: you're essentially planning to abscond with the muskets. I realize we gave you wide latitude in organizing the company, but you should talk to the committee about your ideas. And you'll need to get Wood's cooperation in any case in regard to the muskets."

Wend simply nodded, then took a sip of whiskey and then changed the subject. "David, what I asked to meet with you about is the question of officers for the company. I'm looking for men with experience, men whom our privates will respect, and preferably unmarried men to reduce complications. I figured you could advise me on candidates who would be willing to accept commissions."

"Well, you rate three officers at least. Two lieutenants and an ensign." He put his hand to his chin and looked down at a paper on the table. "I've put together a list of likely men for the lieutenant positions." He looked back up at Wend. "The man at the top of the list—Reese Newkirk—is a good candidate for your first lieutenant."

Wend took a sip of his drink and thought a moment. "I remember him. He was second lieutenant in Wood's company in the Dunmore campaign. He did good work at that skirmish we had on the approach to Wakatamico, and then he led his half company in the advance when Crawford attacked Seekunk."

"That's right. He's a tough taskmaster, but his men like him," Rutledge continued. "He's a surveyor by trade, worked for Lord Fairfax. But that work has dried up because of the war and Fairfax having fled to England. And he's newly widowed. His young wife died in childbirth. All in all, he may jump at the chance to get away from memories here in Winchester and make a new start in the army. He's got a small cottage down at the south end of Washington Street."

Wend picked up the sheet of paper. "All right, I'll look him up."

Rutledge took a gulp of his whiskey. Then he made a crooked smile. "Now, Eckert, I have a suggestion for the ensign. Consider young Childers—the lad who's leading the half company guarding your farm."

"Because of my convalescence, I haven't seen him that much. Why are you recommending him? Does he have significant experience?"

Rutledge cleared his throat. "Frankly, most of his experience is at the College of William and Mary; he just graduated. It happens he's the second son of Langston Childers, master of Greenfields Plantation, ten miles south of Winchester."

Wend was puzzled. "Of course I've heard of the place. There's no larger plantation in the county." Wend took a drink from his cup. "And I once was introduced to Langston himself at Angus McDonald's spring fair at Glengarry." Wend sighed. "David, I asked you for experienced officers, and now you recommend a green-as-grass member of the gentry. What's this all about? The truth, please."

"All right. Frankly, since Childers's eldest son will inherit the plantation, he figures the army would be a good profession for young Edward. Want's him to make his own mark, as it were."

"So Childers has put you up to recommending him for my company?"

"I'll not deny it. But look here, Wend, the young lad volunteered to take the half company over to your place and stay as long as needed." He reached a hand toward Wend in supplication. "Why don't you keep an eye on him and see if he'll do for you?"

A sudden thought struck Wend. "Let me guess: Did the *esteemed* Langston Childers put a large amount of money up for the purchase of material needed to repair Eckert Ridge?"

"Lots of people did." Rutledge shrugged. "But yes, he put up a very substantial amount."

"And so now he's putting pressure on you to get Edward an officer's commission in the Continental Army. It's almost like purchasing a commission in the British Army. I thought we were trying to get away from all that."

The county lieutenant's face flushed. He took another quick drink of his whiskey. Finally, he said, "Wend, be reasonable. The influence of the wealthy will always be with us. All I ask is that you look the lad over, talk to him, and see if he'll do. He *is* a bright fellow. And after all, it's just an ensign's commission, and traditionally that's a learning position. It's not like I'm asking for him to be your first lieutenant."

Wend took a deep breath. "All right, Rutledge. I'll look him over and tell you what I think."

"Good, Wend. Here's the straight of it: we can't afford to anger Langston Childers."

After meeting with Rutledge, Wend left the Golden Buck to find that Billy, who had been putting up posters around town, was waiting for him with the chaise. It was pulled by Boots, the spirited bay horse with three white stockings. Wend had chosen to travel by chaise instead of horseback because of his spells of dizziness.

Wend climbed up into the conveyance and said, "All right, Billy, let's head for Steffensburg."

The lad touched Boots with the reins, and they were off heading along Market Street. Soon they turned onto the Great Wagon Road, heading south. Then, after the better part of an hour, they had the small town in sight and were soon amid a group of buildings. Wend pointed to a sign. "There's Calvert's Cobbler Shop. Pull up right in front."

He climbed down and said, "Drive around town and put up some of the posters where people can see them. And make sure you put one in the common room of every tavern."

Billy nodded and drove off.

Wend walked into Calvert's shop. He looked around and saw that the shoemaker was standing at a table, sorting through some pieces of cured leather. Two apprentices were working on uppers for footwear. Another was at a table cutting soles.

Calvert looked up from his work, initially puzzled at whom he was looking. Then recognition came into his eyes. "Lieutenant Eckert! Glad to see you again! It's been since late 1774, when we mustered out from Dunmore's War."

"Yes, good to see you again, Samuel."

"What brings you down here? As I recall, your place is way on the other side of Winchester."

Wend laid one of the recruiting bills on the table. "I'm taking a company to join Washington's army up north. Looking for good men who want to fight the king's injustice."

The cobbler picked up the bill and quickly scanned it. "There are plenty of such men in Steffensburg. I'll help you find those who are willing." He turned to one of the apprentices. "Here, Frank, take this and post it beside our door."

Wend grinned at Calvert. "There's one good man of this town I'd really like to have with me."

Calvert raised a hand. "Tell me who it is, and I'll speak to the lad for you."

Wend said nothing immediately, just stared into Calvert's eyes. "You'll not have to go far to find him. I'm talking about you, Corporal. I've a mind to make you the sergeant of one of my half companies."

"Well, now you flatter me, Eckert. And I liked serving with you last year." Calvert shook his head. "But I'm not going this time. It took me most of a year to recover my trade from five months with Angus McDonald's battalion in that Ohio war."

Frustrated, Wend appealed. "Samuel, we're trying to free ourselves from a tyrant king and parliament across the ocean. It's time for us to govern ourselves."

"Aye, that we are. But so were the Highlanders who followed Bonnie Prince Charles, these thirty years ago. And look what happened to them after Culloden. Many were rounded up and hung for their effort. The rest of them livin' under a rule harsher than they ever dreamed of before the revolt. That's why we have so many here who fled from Scotland." He waved a hand. "Look at Angus McDonald himself." He waved a finger in front of Wend. "Tell the truth, sir, I have no confidence we can beat the British Army. And once we lose, they'll treat the ones who took up arms against them the same way as they did those Scots." He shook his head again. "No, sir, I'm stayin' right here and tend to my business and keep my family out of it."

Wend, frustrated, stared at the former corporal, not sure what to say. Then he thought, *He's just expressing the same thing I felt until circumstances forced me to take up arms. I can't condemn him for that.*

Calvert broke the silence. "I'm sure you're disappointed with me, but I've got to put my wife and little ones first. And no man is going to change my mind."

Wend shook his head and put his hand on Calvert's shoulder. "Samuel, I'll not condemn you for thinking of your family first. And this won't change my mind about how indebted I am to you for all you did for me last year."

"Thank you for that, Eckert." Calvert raised a finger. "Now listen, I'll spread the word around town 'bout the company you are forming. And I'll make sure that they know what a fine officer you are and that they could do much worse than to serve with you."

"Thank you for that, Samuel. And if you are able to send me some lads, tell them to come up to the Wild Boar Tavern in Winchester on one of the days listed in the handbill, or they can just go right to Eckert Ridge Farm on Ashby Ferry Road south of the Battletown Inn. That's where we'll be mustering and drilling."

"Aye, Eckert, that I will do."

"Well, dear, here's Ensign Childers." Peggy showed the young officer into the parlor and waved him to a chair and then took her accustomed seat on the settee. "Won't you pour both of us something to drink?"

Wend looked over the young officer. He was dressed in a well-tailored example of the formal uniform of the Virginia militia, a blue coat and breeches of the same color. The coat had red facings and gold lacing. Underneath the coat he wore a red waistcoat. The lad himself was tall, golden-haired, with a lean, athletic physique. It struck Wend that the handsome young man reminded him of someone. Then he had it: *By God, a younger likeness of Geoffrey Caufield, the highwayman who had frequented Frederick County and Winchester the year before. Even the manners are the same.* Wend shook off the memory of the rogue and held up a cup. "Whiskey, Mr. Childers?"

"That would be my pleasure, Captain."

Peggy said, "That's a lovely, well-fitted uniform, Mr. Childers. Might I ask who made it for you?"

The young man beamed. "Why, I had it made by Hornsby in Williamsburg, Mrs. Eckert. They're the finest tailors in the capital. They had my measurements from when I was at William and Mary, and when I was commissioned into the militia, naturally I ordered it from them."

Wend couldn't resist. "Well, of course you did, Mr. Childers."

The ensign didn't notice Wend's sarcasm, but Peggy did. She shot him a glowering look and then hurriedly said, "Well, I asked because now that my husband is going to lead a company, he needs a proper uniform. He served through the recent war in the Ohio Country in regular clothes and his hunting shirt." She looked over at Wend again and continued, "I think he'll look very handsome in a formal uniform."

Wend cleared his throat. "That brings up a question, Mr. Childers: Do you happen to own a hunting shirt?"

Childers cocked his head. "*A hunting shirt?* Actually, no, sir. Never thought to need one. I've seen them on these backcountry riflemen and hunters, of course." He thought a second. "Is there a reason you think I should obtain one?"

"Might be a good idea if you are going to lead militia or army soldiers in the field. The men might respect you more. But even more important, there are many situations in border warfare against the tribal warriors, or even against the British, where you might not want to look like an officer."

Childers looked puzzled for a moment, then understanding came into his eyes. "Ah, yes. Yes, I see your point, sir. The scoundrels are not above targeting officers." He raised a finger. "I'll have our tailor in Winchester make one up."

Wend felt the urge to laugh out loud. Instead he took a sip of his drink to hide his mirth.

Peggy took pity on the lad. "Mr. Childers, you're going to be on the farm for a while longer. I suggest you have Alice Downy, Joshua Baird's wife, take your measurements and make you a shirt. I think it might look a little more authentic than something done by a tailor."

"Indeed, ma'am. I hadn't thought of that."

"Well, I'll talk to Alice tomorrow. I'm sure she'll oblige. She's made them for many of the men here on the farm."

Childers bowed slightly in the chair and said, "I'd be very grateful for that, Mrs. Eckert."

Just then Billy, in the formal serving clothes he wore when guests were present, came to the parlor door. "Supper is ready to be served, Mrs. Eckert."

Peggy said "Thank you, Billy. We'll be in shortly."

Billy bowed and departed.

Wend waved after the departing servant. "Well, Mr. Childers, that's Billy Wood. He is the first man to enlist in my company."

Childers's brow furrowed, and he stiffened in his chair. "Sir, are you saying you've enlisted an African slave? Lord Dunmore has caused an uproar for doing that in his forces."

"Of course not, Childers. We don't have slaves on Eckert Ridge. Billy and his whole family—father, mother, and sister—are free. In fact, that's why his last name is Wood. We bought them as slaves from an estate, and James Wood arranged their freedom through a bill in the Burgesses. They took his last name as a matter of gratitude. James felt quite honored."

"Ah yes, I see."

Peggy stood up, flashed the young officer her most flirtatious smile, and offered him her hand. "Will you see me into supper, Mr. Childers?"

Childers sprang to his feet and took her hand. "That would be my greatest pleasure, Mrs. Eckert."

Peggy looked over her shoulder at Wend. "Are you coming along, Mr. Eckert?"

After the meal the Eckerts and their guest had one final drink together in the parlor, and then Childers excused himself to return to the militia bivouac.

After seeing the officer off, Peggy came back into the parlor and took her seat. "Well, Wend, what do you think? Are you going to accept him as the ensign for your company?"

Wend threw up his hands. "Well, I don't see that I have much choice. It's important that I keep in Rutledge's good graces. I'll need him to help recruit and equip the company. And of course, there's young Edward's father and his influence. We don't want to get on the wrong side of him, either."

Peggy looked over her cup of whiskey and said, "You know, if we didn't have this pressure in favor of Childers, Horner would be a good choice. He's done so well in organizing the men and rebuilding of the shop. He's a natural at it."

"Yes, but Andrew would never accept a commission. He is totally averse to being in the army."

"I don't understand. He wants to go to the army as a gunsmith to find this Crider woman. Wouldn't it be even better to go as an officer?"

Wend shook his head. "He came to the colonies to avoid being conscripted into Frederick's army. His brother died of lung fever after being forced to stand sentinel duty in freezing weather when he was already sick and feverish. Andrew has vowed never to be a soldier."

A puzzled expression crossed Peggy's face. "Being a soldier is different here. But in any case, he fought and actually killed a Mingo warrior in Dunmore's campaign back in '74. And we know how well he fought against those raiders."

"He did all that because he had no choice. He understands that here in the backcountry, sometimes you have to fight. He'll do it when it means survival, but that's it." Wend shrugged. "And anyway, he'll serve a most-needed function with the army as a contract gunsmith."

Peggy stood up. "So you'll offer Childers the commission?"

"Yes, I'll go down to the camp and do it tomorrow."

"Well, if nothing else, we'll establish good relations with the Childers family. Only the Woods have more influence here in the county. And of course, Jean Wood is one of my best friends. Now I'll work hard to make acquaintance of Edward's mother."

"I see what's on your mind, *Lady Elizabeth*. We please the Childers's, and your conquest of Frederick County society is complete. Indeed, I can clearly visualize you sweeping into the ballroom at Greenfields Plantation in your most flattering and revealing pale-blue gown and catching the eyes of every gentleman present."

Peggy flashed her husband an irritated glance. "Wend! *When will you stop calling me Lady Elizabeth?* Some day you are going embarrass us both by doing that in public!" She turned and took a step toward the door. "Come along, it's late. Let's go to bed."

Wend quickly came up behind her and put his arms around her waist, arresting her movement. He whispered in her ear, "Yes, let's go to the bedroom, and you can show me how unladylike you can be."

Peggy laughed out loud. "Oh, yes. How ironic! You call me a *lady* during the day, but at night you want me to be the *harlot* from McCartie's Tavern in Sherman Mill."

"Well, I married both, and each gives me a different kind of pleasure."

Wend rode into Winchester on the first day of recruiting muster. The time specified was noon, at the Wild Boar Tavern, a favorite gathering place for tradesmen, hunters, teamsters, and the like. Wend was in Winchester a couple of hours early because he planned to see Reese Newkirk, the man Rutledge had recommended for first lieutenant. He turned onto Washington Street and asked a young lad which house was Newkirk's. The youth pointed to the next to the last house on the right. "That be it, sir."

Wend rode up to the house and dismounted. He knocked on the door and waited for a response. And waited. Finally he knocked again, more loudly, and there was still no response. Wend had turned to return to his horse when he heard the door open. He looked back to see Newkirk standing in the doorway.

But the person in the doorway was not the man that Wend remembered from the war. Newkirk was unshaven and disheveled. He leaned against the doorframe as if he needed support.

Wend said, "Good morning, Newkirk. My name is Wend Eckert."

"I remember you from the war. You were Angus McDonald's quartermaster and then an aide to the governor. And I've seen you shoot in contests over at McDonald's place." He wiped his hand across his face. "What can I do for you?"

"I'd like to talk with you about some business. May I come in?"

Newkirk pushed himself off the doorframe and shrugged. "You have business with me?" He shrugged and waved Wend into the house.

Wend walked past the man into the hall and smelled the overpowering odor of liquor on the man's breath.

"Let's go into the parlor, Eckert."

Wend took a seat, and Newkirk also sat down. There was a cup and small jug on the table beside the man's chair. The smell of the alcohol permeated the room.

Newkirk picked up his cup and drained it. "You want something to drink, Eckert? This is good stuff." He raised a finger. "Now that I think on it, I believe it's actually made out at your place, by that fellow Donegal."

Wend, embarrassed and shocked at the man's appearance, didn't immediately say anything, trying to find the right words.

Newkirk filled the void. "What, you think it's too early to be drinking?" A crooked smile spread across his lips. "Yes, I can see that's what is on your mind."

"Well, Newkirk, it *is* two hours before midday. And it looks like you started quite a bit earlier."

"Look, Eckert, I lost my wife. My wife and unborn first child! Not a month ago. I sit in this empty house, and they're on my mind constantly." He stared at Wend for a long moment. "You're damn right I drink. You'd drink too."

"I'm sorry about your loss. But becoming a drunkard and soaking yourself in self-pity won't bring them back. The living must get on with life."

"What do *you* know about it? Look, I know about you, Eckert. *You've* got a wife. A wife and children." He motioned at Wend with his cup. "And I know all about your wife. She's considered the beauty of the county. Men talk about her all the time in the taverns. I've seen her, running around in that little chaise, with her high-cheekboned face, her flashing eyes, and that shiny raven hair. No, you're in no position to lecture me on 'moving on.' You've never had to face up to losing your woman. The woman you've loved."

Wend felt himself getting hot, but he took a few moments to throttle the anger. Then he spoke slowly in a quiet voice. "Actually, Reese, you know very little about me. Because if you did, you'd be aware that I have had to live with the loss of two women I loved."

"You've had two wives die?"

"No, they weren't my wives, but they would have been had not tragedy taken them from me forever. And both times my heart was broken. My first love was a beautiful young girl from Philadelphia. Tall and stately, with flowing golden hair. Her name was Abigail Gibson. She was captured by the Mingo on Forbes Road and made the hostage wife of a war captain. Years later I was able to find her in an Ohio village, only to have her tell me she would rather stay with the tribe."

Newkirk was looking at him, surprise in his eyes.

Wend continued. "That's right, she told me she preferred life with the Indians. How do you think that made me feel?" Wend looked at the younger man, who still said nothing. Then he continued, "And then there was a marvelous Highland girl, a camp girl of the British Army. Mary Fraser. She was willowy with rich, gleaming auburn hair. She was smart as a whip and could be sweet as sugar or hard as steel, depending on what she was facing. I lost my heart to her, even more so than the first one. And I lost her by a foul trick of fate; I was told she was dead. So after a time, I married and then found out Mary was actually alive. I was crushed."

Now the younger man was staring at him. "I had no idea."

"Not many people know the whole story. But the point is, Newkirk, in both cases, I accepted the situation and got on with things. Devoted myself to my trade, built a farm, grew a family." Wend raised a finger. "And I'll give you another example. The man who distilled that whiskey—Simon Donegal—lost his wife in that loyalist raid on my farm last month. I assume you heard about that?'

"Everybody's heard of it."

"And just like yours, Donegal's wife was with child. The very first of his own. Yes, Donegal was crushed. But soon enough he got back to work and began to deal with his grief." Wend paused and shook his head. "Now listen to me. You're still young. You will always cherish the memory of your wife, but there will be other women and yes, children."

"For God's sake, Eckert, it's been less than a month. For me, it's too early to stop mourning. Give a man some peace and time." He gritted his teeth and stared into the distance. Then he turned back to Wend. "Why the hell did you come here anyway? What did you want to talk about? Tell me your business, and let's be done with it." He poured himself some more whiskey.

"I assume you're aware that I'm raising a company for service with Washington's army?"

"Everyone in town knows."

"Well, both Rutledge and James Wood recommend you as an officer in the company. I just talked to James before I came here, and he had nothing but superlatives about your service in his company during the Ohio campaign in '74. I myself saw you personally lead your half company up that slope under fire from the Shawnee just before we got to Wakatamica. And you led one of the columns in William Crawford's attack on Seekunk. You know how to train men and how to lead them in battle."

"That was in another world. Since then, I was married and lost my wife, all in a year. And the surveying business has dried up. I tell you I need time to sort things out." He sighed deeply and waved his arm around the house. "In fact, there are too many memories here in Winchester. I may well move southward or westward, anywhere for a fresh start."

"I was thinking of making you my first lieutenant. You want a fresh start, that could be it. A year in the army will give you time to think. You may have a different outlook when we come back." Wend looked at him directly. "Hell, Newkirk, it's a war. You may not have to worry about coming back. The enemy may solve all your problems permanently."

"You want me as *first lieutenant*? Are you a fool, Eckert? In my mental and physical state?"

"Yes. Like I've been saying, good hard work—training men, doing paperwork—would be the best thing for you. I'm willing to take the chance that you can deal with your grief and again become the officer you were in '74. That would be good for my company."

"I was right. You are a *fool*. I should tell Rutledge your lack of judgment ought to disqualify you from command."

"Regardless, I'm offering you the commission. Take a few days to think it over. I'll be recruiting again in four days at the Wild Boar. If you can come in, sober, and tell me you want the job, then you've got it. Or come to our camp at Eckert Ridge within that time. It's your choice: *drunkard* or *lieutenant* in the Continental Army."

Wend picked up his hat. "I'll let myself out. But if I were you, I'd throw that jug away, dry out, and start putting together my kit."

Without another word he left Newkirk sitting there, staring into the distance.

Wend left Newkirk's place and rode over to the Wild Boar on Loudoun Street. As he approached the tavern, he was encouraged to see that a sizable and rowdy crowd of men had gathered in front of the entrance. Many had rifles in hand. Wend recognized some of the riflemen from shooting contests; others were strangers to him. The keg of ale he had ordered was set up on a table near the front door, and tavern maids, with lots of bosom showing, were serving full mugs to all comers. He noted that one of Eckert Ridge's wagons was parked off to one side, where Andrew Horner stood talking to some young men. Baird and Donegal were amid the crowd enjoying the ale. Donegal wore his old red jacket from the 77th and his blue Highland bonnet. Joshua was dressed in hunting shirt and leggings.

Wend dismounted and tied his horse to the back of the wagon. All three of his compatriots joined him there.

Donegal said, "Wend, na the word got around the county, and we got a good turnout for our first recruitin'. Lots of possible, strappin' lads. Mostly good Ulster boys, but there are even some Germans."

Wend nodded. "Yes, I can see." He turned to Joshua. "What about the riflemen? Do you know them and their skill?"

"Aye, the better part. There be a few I've never seen before, and we'll have to see what they can do."

Wend turned to Horner. "You got the muster book ready?"

"Yes, sir. I've got it set up the way you said, with a place for me to write the names and for each man to sign beside his name."

Wend nodded and looked around. "All right, it's time for me to speak to the men." He walked up the steps to the small landing before the tavern's main door and raised an arm. Then he called out, "Your attention! Your attention!"

A few men turned to look, but most weren't distracted from the drinking and laughing and giggling maids. Wend felt a surge of frustration.

Joshua grinned and then took things in hand. He walked over to his horse, pulled out a pistol, and stepped up onto the porch beside Wend. Then he raised the pistol to the sky and fired. The hubbub stopped immediately, and every face turned toward the porch.

Wend said, "Now that we have your attention, let me introduce myself. For those who don't already know me, I am Wend Eckert. And the Committee of Safety has appointed me captain, with the authority to raise a company of foot for service with Washington's army. Now you are here because you saw the posters we have put up around town calling for volunteers."

A voice came out of the crowd. "And 'specially because of the free ale!" There was laughter throughout the crowd.

Wend grinned. "Yes, I was sure that would be an inducement." More laughter rippled through the ranks. Then he continued, "We want fifty riflemen, who will provide their own weapons, and the same number of men who will be armed with muskets. And the term of service will be one year."

A burly man with a rifle in one hand and a mug in the other shouted, "Hey, Cap'n, I thought we were forming a rifle company. A company like Morgan took up to the army last year. What do we want with damned musket men?"

Wend smiled. "You didn't read the poster very well. We're raising a company of light foot."

The man laughed. "Who said I can read? Ain't never wasted my time on that. But I damn well know how to shoot. Ain't that what's important?"

Wend was about to answer when Joshua called out, "Yeah, Jensen, I know you can shoot. But worse than you never learnin' to *read* is never learnin' to *listen*. Now shut that mouth of yours and hear what Cap'n Eckert has to say, and you'll find out the answer to what you're asking."

Jensen pushed his hat back on his head. "All right, I'm listening."

There was now general silence, and Wend began to speak. "All right, men, now hear me. We're forming a light company because it has more uses than a company with just rifles."

Another man called out, "I ain't never heard of mixing rifles and muskets in the same company."

Wend looked at the man. "I served with Bouquet at Bushy Run. He had mixed rifle-musket light companies, and it served him well. If you join this company, you'll soon learn the benefits of what I'm saying."

A rifleman standing just below Wend asked, "When's this company leaving for the army?"

Wend responded, "Good question. We plan to leave in about six weeks. We'll have a period of drilling and training in camp to get ready."

Jensen scowled. "Morgan and his men left four days after the muster list was filled out. What's this drilling all about?"

Wend had expected this question. He spoke out so all the men could hear. "Morgan's company left so soon because the army was already engaged with the British at Boston. It was urgent to get reinforcements there to affect the outcome. But right now the British are virtually all in Halifax, reorganizing after being forced out of Boston. They'll probably return in late spring or early summer to campaign, and the likely place is New York City. So we have time to organize, get fitted out, and learn our business before we have to march. If we do so, we'll be a sight more useful to Washington."

A young man in work clothes stepped forward. "I got a wife. Can she come along and get a ration?"

Wend said, "If she's willing to work for the company, as a washerwoman, a cook, a seamstress, or a nurse. And if she's fit enough to march like the men." He looked over the crowd. "But we can take only a limited number of family members, so I'll give favor to the wives of men who enlist the earliest." He looked at the questioner. "If you want your woman along, enlist today!"

Wend then pointed to a spot by the wagon. "All you men who fancy yourselves marksmen with the rifle, step over there. Joshua Baird will be the judge of whether you know your business."

There was a bustling movement as more than a score of men moved to where Joshua stood. When everyone had joined him, he waved his hand in the direction of old Fort Loudoun. "All right, let's take a little walk up the road here to where we can do some shootin'." He strode off, followed by the riflemen.

Wend looked at about thirty men, most of whom looked like town workers or were in from farms. "Now, which of you likely lads are ready to take up the musket to fight for our freedom from King George! Now's the time! Just step on over to the wagon and sign the muster book!"

There was a hush, everyone standing with no movement. Wend's heart sank. Was this recruitment going to be a bust?

Then a voice called out, "Hello there, Mr. Eckert!"

Wend looked through the crowd for the source, with no luck. But then he looked out into the street. Six men stood there in a group. Suddenly he recognized them—they were men from Calvert's old squad. A tall smiling man waved. "Hey there, sir! We just got here from Steffensburg. Took us longer than we expected. But we came to sign your muster book. We heard you was forming a company, and we all decided to come along together. We been thinkin' of joining a regiment. And if we're goin' to the army, there ain't no one we'd rather march with than you, sir!"

Wend remembered that the man speaking was named Sanders. "Sanders! Glad to see you." He motioned toward the others. "And glad to see all of you." He pointed to where Horner stood. "Step right over there and sign the book." Then he pointed to the keg. "And then take care of your thirst! If you came all the way from Steffensburg, you certainly worked one up!"

"Sure enough, Cap'n."

Sanders and the other five got in line where Horner stood ready with a quill and ink.

That started the others moving. The young man who had asked about women going along said to the man beside him, "Well, I'm going to make sure that Annie can come with me." He strode over to the wagon and got in line behind the Steffensburg men. There was a murmuring among the others, and most joined the line behind him.

Wend sighed in relief and stepped down from the porch. He watched as the line of men signed the muster book. Horner was instructing them that they had four days to get their affairs in order and report to Eckert Ridge, where they would go into camp to begin training.

As Wend watched, the young man who had asked about women traveling with the company finished signing and turned to go. Wend spoke to him. "Lad, what's your name?"

"Howell, sir. Ben Howell."

"Well, Ben, I appreciate you wanting to have your wife along."

"Cap'n, sir, she's the one who's wantin' to go. She says she wants to be close to me in case I get wounded or killed. Want's to have as much time as possible. We just got married a few weeks ago." He stopped and grinned. "And we're still livin' at my folks' place. Annie says she's ready to do whatever it takes to get out from under my ma's eyes."

Wend laughed heartily. "Well, Ben, that's understandable. But make sure she is aware of the conditions we'll be facing. She'll need to walk miles almost every day, work hard, sleep outside in rain and frigid weather, eat army rations, which for long periods will be mainly based on salt beef or pork." Wend looked closely at the lad. "Explain it all very carefully."

"Yes, Cap'n. I already said all that to her, sir. But she's determined. And when Annie puts her mind to something, ain't no stoppin' her."

"All right, Howell. Then we'll see you and Annie out at the camp on Eckert Ridge in four days."

Wend went into the tavern common room and found Jared Cole, the proprietor, behind the counter.

Cole spoke up, "Well, Cap'n Eckert, looks like you got a fine collection of men out there. You getting them to put their names on the muster roll?"

Wend nodded. "That we are, Jared. We'll get a good lot today." Wend pointed to one of his recruiting bills that were posted on the wall. "Now, as it says on there, get another keg of ale ready for Monday next. We'll be ready for another round of recruitment."

"You got it, Cap'n. And I'll have all my girls laid on to encourage the men."

"Yes, indeed, Cole. I'll vouch they're doing a good job out there."

"I always say, I got the prettiest maids in town. Bush's girls over at the Golden Buck don't hold a candle to them." Cole grinned, leaned over close to Wend, and whispered, "And I'll have the lasses talkin' up the men how much they'll admire them if they sign their name to fight against the king."

Wend grinned. "That's the stuff, Jared." He pointed to a jug behind the bar. "Now let me have a cup of that whiskey while I wait for Joshua to get back with his riflemen."

Perhaps a half hour later, Joshua walked into the common room, went to the bar and obtained a mug, and sat down beside Wend at a table in the rear. "Well, I checked out the riflemen. They can all shoot to our standards. And they seem a good lot."

Wend asked, "Do they all plan to enlist?"

Joshua took a pull on his cup. "Appears so. They were lining up to sign the muster when I came in here—all of them."

"Even that fellow Jensen? He seemed unsure he wanted to be part of a company that wasn't composed strictly of rifles."

"He was in line with the rest."

Wend frowned. "He could be a problem. Looks like he's loud and argumentative."

"He shot damn well. One of the top two or three." Joshua took another sip. "You know these hunters are independent cusses, always of a mind to say what they think. But it's sure he wants to kill redcoats."

"I guess you're right. But I'm going to be watching him. I need a disciplined company for the way I plan to train it."

Joshua waved a hand. "Don't think he'll be a problem." Then he gave Wend a sly grin. "But if he turns out to be a handful, I've no doubt Donegal can change his mind pretty fast."

Wend nodded. "Yes, Simon has plenty of experience at that. Well, in any case, we'll see soon enough."

As Wend entered the meeting room at the Golden Buck, he felt the eyes of nine men boring into him. With as much calm as he could muster, he said to the members of the Committee of Safety, "Good afternoon, gentlemen."

Several men responded in kind; others just nodded. It confirmed to him that he had something of a hostile audience.

James Wood motioned him to his seat at the end of the table.

Wend mustered a grin as he sat down. "Well, gentlemen, I received your urgent summons by rider last evening and made haste to be here promptly. Since your request was only two lines long and simply said that you wished to discuss the formation of the company, I would ask if you had a specific question or simply wanted me to brief you on our progress with recruitment?"

Wood looked around the table and then back at Wend. "Indeed, we would appreciate a report on that."

"We're doing well. We've enlisted over thirty riflemen, all good shots. And we signed on about twenty-five men to be armed with muskets at our first recruiting day at the Wild Boar." He paused and looked around the table. "And last night Ensign Childers said that nine of the men in the militia detachment guarding my farm have decided to enlist. Four of them are skilled riflemen, and the others will serve with the musket." He raised his hands and smiled again. "So I would say that we are about two-thirds of the way to finding our hundred men for our Frederick County Light Company, as I like to call it."

There was a long moment of silence around the table. Finally Wood cleared his throat and said, "Yes, that brings us to the *precise* subject we would like to talk to you about."

Wend displayed a puzzled expression and played obtuse. "Oh, and what would that be, *precisely*?"

"Wend, the members of the committee are rather concerned about the organization of the company you are forming."

Smith, the sheriff, added, "We volunteered to the government of Virginia to provide a rifle company. Instead, you have taken the liberty to organize a different type of formation, as you have just mentioned. We would like you to present your reasons for doing this and what you intend for its purpose."

There were nods and spoken "Ayes" around the table.

Wend sat for a moment looking at the committee. "Well, I rather guessed that was the purpose of this meeting." He stood up, preferring to speak from a position above the committee members.

"Gentlemen, as you will remember, I accepted this commission with the condition that I would have the authority to organize it to my own ideas. Well, after consideration, I believe that a true light company will be of more use to Washington's army than another rifle company. Rifles are extremely useful for sharpshooting. Rifles are also very useful in warfare against the tribes in the backcountry. But they have a more limited value on the formal tactical situation that we will encounter in fighting the British Army."

"We have reports," said Rutledge, "from the army that riflemen were very effective against British positions during the late siege of Boston. They took a heavy toll of sentinels and officers."

"Indeed, David, I'm sure they did. But that was a very static situation. Sharpshooters were able to fire at times of their own choosing from cover against fixed British positions. However, the war we are about to enter will be one of maneuver. Of advance and retreat, of charge and defense of field positions, often in open country."

Reverend Thruston raised his hand. "And you are saying that the rifle will not serve in that kind of warfare?"

"To a certain extent, yes. Of course, it can be used for long-range fire. And for skirmishers in preliminary actions before the main battle lines engage. But it has disadvantages, particularly considering how long it takes to load. Gentlemen, a trained soldier can fire three or four times faster with a musket. And rapidity of fire—volley fire, if you will—is a central advantage in the type of warfare we are likely to encounter." Wend looked around the room. "But rather than merely use words to explain, I am ready to provide you with a demonstration of the real value of having muskets in our company." He waved his hand. "I shall show you right here in this room."

Wend walked over to the door, opened it, and called out, "All right, come on in."

Immediately Donegal and Baird entered. Donegal was dressed in his jacket and bonnet from the 77th and carried a musket. He wore a leather belt with a cartridge case in front at his waist. He also carried a bayonet in a frog. Joshua carried his rifle and had a powder horn and bullet pouch on straps over his shoulders.

"We'll start with a comparison of loading." He pointed to the two men. "Both of their firelocks are unloaded." He turned to his companions. "Prepare to load your firelocks." He turned back to the committee. "I assume we can all agree that there are few men more familiar with their weapons than Joshua and Donegal."

Nods around the table.

Wend motioned toward his friends. "When I say, each of you load your firelock as rapidly as possible." He raised his hand, then quickly slapped it down. "Start!"

Donegal reached down, pulled a paper cartridge out of his leather case, raised it to his mouth, and bit off the ball. This opened the top of the cartridge, and he poured a small bit of powder into the musket's pan and snapped the batten shut. Immediately he grounded the butt of the firelock and dumped the rest of the powder down the barrel. Next he wadded up the empty paper and pushed it into the barrel. Then he leaned over and spit the ball in on top of the wad. Quickly he pulled out the ramrod and pushed home the ball and wad. He slid the ramrod back in place, raised the musket to his shoulder, and made as if he were pulling back the hammer.

Wend said, "Gentlemen, I think you will all agree Donegal took no more than fifteen seconds."

Everyone nodded, then looked over at Joshua to see his progress. He had measured out powder from his horn and poured it down the barrel. He had now put a patch and ball on top of his muzzle and was laboriously pounding it down against the resistance of the rifling. Finally he seated the ball, then raised his firelock and dashed out a bit of powder into the pan, closed it, and was finally ready to fire.

Wend said, "I think we can all agree that took near a minute. Donegal could have gotten off three, maybe four rounds in that time."

Rutledge said, "All right, you've made your point. But look, Wend, all of us had some sense that the rifle fired slower than a musket."

"David, that's only part of what I want to demonstrate." He motioned to Donegal. "Fix the bayonet."

Donegal pulled the blade out of the frog, slid the socket over the barrel, and twisted it until the slot in the metal engaged the lug on the barrel.

Wend said, "All right, let's demonstrate hand-to-hand engagement."

Joshua pulled out his knife and faced Donegal. "Now," said Wend, "you can see the problem a rifleman has. Donegal's bayonet, at the end of the musket, obviously has a longer reach than Joshua with knife in hand. Clearly the rifleman is at a disadvantage against a soldier trained in use of the bayonet. Now, when a rifleman fights warriors on the frontier, this is not a problem, because the Indians don't use the bayonet. Everyone is armed about the same way—firelock and knife and hatchet."

Wend looked up and down the table. "Now, I feel that with a mixed company, we will have several tactical advantages. First, we can operate in open order as skirmishers in front of a line of regular foot. Both rifles and muskets are valuable for that. In fact, British light companies normally are armed with the musket. The exception that I know about was Bouquet's placement of a few rifles in his light companies of the 60th and 77th."

He gathered his thoughts, then continued. "I found that a useful situation. When Joshua and I worked as scouts for Bouquet during his relief of Fort Pitt in 1763, there were several situations when the combination of muskets and rifles was very fortuitous. The riflemen performed sharpshooting duties, and the men with muskets provided rapid covering fire which distracted the Indians while the riflemen were reloading."

Wend looked around the room and saw that he had the men's attention. "Now, I believe that will be useful against the British. We'll use the musket men to protect our riflemen from British fire during skirmishing. But just as important, when our forces are facing a bayonet charge from the enemy—which is often the final phase of an engagement—we'll have the ability to have our musket men form line with fixed bayonets to counter the British advance and shield the riflemen."

Wend paused. "To summarize, based on my experience, I am convinced that the formation of a light company with mixed weapons will serve us far better, in more situations, than a purely rifle company."

Wend looked around the table. All the committee men were silent, considering what he had said.

After a moment Wood cleared his throat. "Donegal, you've seen as much fighting as anyone in this room. Both against Indians and French infantry. Do you think this makes sense?"

"Aye, Mr. Wood, it's as good an idea as I've heard. I've seen this mix of firelocks in battle, and I'm for it with my whole heart. You should take seriously the need for our company to be able to use the bayonet. I've ne'er been in battle when it didn't come into play sometime."

Wood looked at Joshua. "What about you, Baird? How do you feel about it?"

"Damn, James, the truth is, I'm here, and so is Wend, because of havin' muskets to cover me in battle. When Wend and I and Donegal and another Highlander named Kirkwood were scouting ahead of Bouquet's column on the way to Pitt, we was ambushed by a strong Mingo war party just as we was 'bout a mile from Fort Ligonier. We holed up in some rocks. Wend and I did the best we could pickin' off warriors with our rifles, but it was those two Highlanders who kept us alive. They kept up such a fast fire the Indians were busy just keepin' their heads down. We held out until a relief party from the fort reached us. I'm tellin' you, if we had just had rifles, our hair would be hangin' in a Mingo village right now."

There were murmurs around the table but no more questions. Finally Wood said, "All right, Wend, I believe we understand your idea." He looked around the table, then motioned toward the door. "We'll need to discuss this among ourselves. Wend, why don't the three of you have a drink in the common room, and we'll apprise you of our decision."

Wend felt a knot in his stomach, followed by a rising anger. *Thank you, Captain Eckert—you're dismissed while we discuss your fate.* It was like he had just been the subject of a tribunal. He rose and initially planned to simply stock out of the room. But he got hold of the anger and said, "Before going, I'd like to ask one question: If you decide we must form a company with only riflemen, what do we do with the other good men who have already signed the muster roll? They signed in good faith with the honest and patriotic intention of fighting for our freedom from a foreign monarch. Do we just send them home and say, 'Thanks, but we've changed our mind'? What effect do you think that will have on future recruiting in Frederick County?"

With that Wend nodded to the committee and followed his companions out of the room.

They found a table and ordered whiskey. Donegal said, "Ach, na, Wend, we told them the truth. We can do na more, lad."

Wend nodded and took the whiskey cup the maid handed him. He drank deeply. "I'm not sure we made any impression. Most of them have not done any fighting except against Indians. They have no idea what a charge of determined regulars looks like and that the bayonet is the only answer."

Donegal took some of his whiskey. "Aye, that's the truth. Or think if a company of riflemen was surprised by a force of redcoats out in the open or maybe in camp—they could be run over by a strong bayonet charge. The British would na have to fire a shot and a lot of good men would die."

Wend nodded in agreement. "That's the most dreaded outcome, and it could happen easy enough."

Joshua, having taken a gulp of his whiskey, put the cup down on the table. He looked over at Wend. "You goin' to resign if the committee tells you to go back to forming a rifle company?"

Wend sighed deeply. "I can't. We owe so much to the committee for all the materials and labor which they've given to us. I don't have much choice but to go along with what they decide." He looked toward the meeting room. "Even though they would be going back on their word to let me organize as I choose."

Their conversation was interrupted by some of Joshua's friends coming up to the table to talk with him. Wend sat brooding as Baird and Donegal exchanged gossip and jokes with the visitors. Time seemed to drag on, and Wend waved to the serving girl for another whiskey. A humorous thought came to him: *If the committee takes too long, I may have consumed enough liquor to tell them what I really think.* As soon as the idea occurred to him, he cautioned himself to limit his consumption.

After a half hour, James Wood came walking down the hall from the meeting room. Seeing the crowd around Wend's table, he waved him to an empty one in the far corner. The two men sat down across from each other.

"Well, Wend, there was quite an argument, with Rutledge leading the opposition. It seemed about an even split in opinion. But in the end, the vote was six to three."

"Six to three for what?"

"You get your light company."

Wend felt the tension that had permeated his body fade away. "I hope I had your support, James."

"Yes, I supported your decision. But the one you really want to thank is Angus McDonald. He swayed several members by siding with you on how important bayonets could be. He told a grim story about the Battle of Culloden and how the Highlanders charged with their great claymore swords, thinking they would make short work of the British. Then, when they got to the enemy's line, they found that muskets with bayonets far outreached their swords. The trained redcoats slaughtered the Scots. His description of how he saw many a friend go down to the soldiers made it very convincing."

"I'll speak to him."

"Indeed, you should. In any case, you can continue recruiting and we'll support you in keeping the fifty muskets." He grinned. "I'll send a letter to Williamsburg telling them that about the time you march off to the army. It will be what the French call a fait accompli."

Wend stood up. "All right, I'm glad that's settled. Now I can get back to work. I have more recruiting to do and much training."

Chapter Eight

THE CAMP
AT ECKERT RIDGE

It was the Monday evening after his second recruiting rendezvous, and Wend had just ridden Sonny back to Eckert Ridge. Now he stood beside Ensign Childers at the edge of the small field just west of the Bairds' house. Ten tents, in which the militia had been living, stood in a line along the south side of the open area. The ashes of several cook fires, each with a tripod over it, were in front of the tents. Those of Childers's militia who had not enlisted in the new company had departed. The others were sitting and joking around the furthest of the cooking tripods. One of the men was stoking up the fire beneath it.

Wend turned to Childers. "The men we recruited last week are being brought here from Winchester in wagons. They should arrive before dark. There will be around sixty."

"We really don't have enough room in these tents for all of them. Some will have to sleep outside."

"I'll send some canvas down from the farm. We still have a little which is unused. You can rig some kind of temporary shelter." Wend pointed to the tents. "Rutledge has more tents, and he's going to send them as soon as he can."

Childers looked at Wend. "How did your recruiting go today at the Wild Boar?"

"We signed most of the men we need. They'll be here by Friday. But we're still about ten short."

The ensign asked, "Are you going to hold another rendezvous at the tavern, sir?"

Wend frowned. "No, I don't think so. Anyone from town who was inclined to enlist has probably already signed the muster roll. I think I'm going to go to the German settlements out to the west and see if I can find some willing lads there."

"You don't mean the Mennonites at Opequan? I thought they were pacifists."

"No, there are some other German villages out there which are regular Lutheran. I think I may find some men who can be convinced to join the company."

A reflective look came over the young man. "I never thought of the Germans as soldiers. They mostly stay close to their trade or farms."

"Edward, *I* am a German."

A look of consternation came over the ensign's face, and he turned red in embarrassment. "Sir, I'm sorry to imply that Germans can't be good soldiers. It's just that I never thought of you as a German."

Wend laughed. "I suppose that's a compliment. But the fact is, my father's parents came over from the Province of Hesse. We were jaegers, or hunters, acting as gamekeepers for several generations. Later, my ancestors became gunsmiths. When I was young, we often spoke German in my family."

"I am sorry, sir."

"Think nothing of it, Mr. Childers. And in any case, the princes of the various German provinces maintain strong, well-trained armies. They are recognized as among the best disciplined in Europe." Wend thought of something. "Edward, certainly you have heard of the Royal Americans? The British 60th Foot?"

Childers's face wrinkled up in concentration. "I can't say that I have."

Wend thought, *Oh Lord, protect us from the ignorance of youth.* But he said, "Well, if you are going to be a soldier, you should be aware that the 60th was raised here in America in the aftermath of Braddock's defeat." Wend looked over at the youth. "That was just before you were born. In any case, it was and remains a regular British Army regiment, in fact the largest in the army, with four battalions. It was originally composed mostly of Americans, and the intent was to concentrate recruiting in the German areas of the colonies. It was believed that men of German origin were more amenable to discipline than your average colonial. And it was officered to a large extent by European officers, particularly German and Swiss."

"I had no idea, sir. But I take your point about Germans being good soldiers."

Wend was about to continue when the sound of a horse approaching interrupted him. He turned to see Joshua riding down from the drive into the campground.

Baird pulled up his horse. He took his hat off and ran his hand through his brown hair. "Well, Cap'n Eckert, your first recruits are about to arrive. They're rolling past the workshop right now."

Wend looked up at Baird. "Do me a favor, Joshua. Ride back up and find Jacob Specht. Tell him we've got to provide shelter for all these men, and have him get whatever canvas he can find down here so we can make improvised tents."

Joshua nodded. "You got it, Wend." He reined his horse around and headed back up the hill.

Wend turned to Childers. "They're here earlier than I expected. We need to have a talk before the men arrive."

"Yes, sir?"

"How long have you been an ensign?"

"Well, since I brought this half company over here." He waved his hand. "And before that, I was listed on the muster of the militia for a year. I drilled a couple of days."

"All right. That's about what I expected. Now listen carefully. Simon Donegal is the top sergeant of this company. In case you're not aware of it, he spent seven years in the 77th Highlanders and became a corporal. He fought in the Carolinas, the Forbes Campaign, participated in the capture of Ticonderoga, and marched with Colonel Bouquet in the relief of Fort Pitt during Pontiac's War." Wend looked his ensign in the eye. "I think we can agree your experience is dwarfed by his."

The young man flushed. "Yes."

"Now listen. We're going to spend about six weeks training these men to fight the British. I wish we had more time, but that will have to do."

"Well, sir, a goodly number of the men in my half company have had lots of experience fighting Indians out on the border." He smiled. "They've been telling me stories about the war last year with Dunmore."

"That's all good, Mr. Childers. But we'll be fighting a different kind of war against the British. European-style war. Now pay attention: to beat the redcoats, we're going to have to train like they do. We need to learn their kind of drill and tactics."

A puzzled look came over Childers's face. "But we're going as rifles and light infantry. We're scouts and skirmishers and sharpshooters."

"Yes, but believe me, Edward, there will be times when we have to stand in line and exchange volleys with the British. Or charge them in across an open field. That takes a different kind of discipline than fighting warriors on the border. Do you understand?"

Childers nodded but had a confused look in his eyes.

"So here's the main point I'm making: you are an officer, but you must listen to Donegal and learn from him. He's going to be instructing the men, and he's going to be instructing you at the same time. In the British Army, the sergeants and corporals train the company so the officers can use it in battle, and that is the way it will work here. Is that clear to you?"

"Yes, I think I understand."

"Donegal will teach you the proper orders to maneuver your men at drill and during skirmishing."

"I will try to learn as rapidly as possible."

Wend smiled. "Good. We can't ask any more than that."

The ensign pointed behind Wend. "Sir, here come the men."

Wend turned to see several wagons coming down the hill. They were full of men and their possessions. Others were walking alongside. Donegal, mounted, led the procession. When the wagons had reached the flat part of the camp, he pulled up, reined his horse around to face the men, and shouted, "All right, na this is your home for the present. Get all your things out of the wagons, and pile them up there." He pointed to a spot on the ground. Then he slipped down from his horse and walked over to where Wend and Childers stood.

Donegal grinned broadly. "And so na it begins! We're goin' to make soldiers out of these lads."

Wend laughed. "Well, Simon, you're the man to do it." Then a thought crossed his mind. "You didn't see anything of Newkirk, did you?"

Donegal shook his head. "You mean that surveyor you want to make first lieutenant? Nary a thing. Just the lads here showed up." He hesitated a second, then smiled crookedly. "Just these lads and a certain Mrs. Howell." He pointed to the last wagon in line.

Wend looked to see a willowy young girl with brown hair climbing down from the wagon bed, helped by two men. Wend recognized one of them as Ben Howell.

Donegal said, "Her first name be Annie."

"Yes, I talked about her with her husband. That incredibly young looking lad who's holding her hand."

"Now look at her closely, Wend, and half close your eyes. The lass is only sixteen. Now tell me who she reminds you of."

Wend looked hard at the girl and then felt a sharp tug at his heart. He took a deep breath. "Oh, good God, Simon! Except for the hair!"

"Aye. Thin as a rail, sparkling eyes, high cheekbones—'cept for the hair's brown, not auburn, glimpse at her quickly, and it's Mary Fraser. Takes me back fifteen years."

Childers looked bemused. "Mary Fraser? Who was that?"

Donegal put his hand on the ensign's shoulder. "Now lad, she was a bonnie wee lass who was an orphan of the 77th and the 42nd. Grew up in the army from the time she was four and as God is my witness, owned the hearts of all the young soldiers in two regiments. Good Lord, how that lassie could dance and sing." He shot a glance at Wend, then turned back to Childers. "But she had eyes only for a young scout from Pennsylvania."

The ensign stared at Annie. "So what happened to this Mary? Did she marry the scout?"

Donegal looked at Wend again, then shook his head. "No, lad. A sad thing happened. There was a trick of fate which separated them. And then the scout was told that Mary had died. So he went off and married another girl. Our Mary went back to Scotland after the war and became a governess to a rich family."

Childers said, "That is quite sad. I guess one can never guess what fate will bring."

Wend cleared his throat, then spoke to the ensign more sternly than he had planned. "Quite right, Mr. Childers. But back to *present* business. Make sure Mrs. Howell gets shelter and is afforded proper privacy." He looked over the men. "All right, you and Donegal get these men organized and rig what additional shelter you can with the canvas Specht will be bringing down. It's too late to do anything more today except get them a meal. Drilling will start in the morning." He turned to leave and said, "I'm going home for my own supper."

Wend walked up the hill past Baird's house. But as he walked, the memory of a certain auburn-haired vixen from the Highlands, and thoughts of things that might have been, were weighing heavily on his mind.

—m—

With supper complete Wend walked into the parlor and poured himself a whiskey. Then he stood looking out the front window, where he could see the workshop, which was now nearly rebuilt. The walls were up, and the roof was all but finished. Hecht had told him that morning that they could start moving back in in the next day or two. Wend reflected that once that was complete, they could use the canvas from the temporary shop for additional shelter down at the camp. A thought hit him: *My mind has become more preoccupied with the company than with my trade.* He sighed. *Well, there was no avoiding it for the next year.*

Peggy arrived and sat down on the settee. She cleared her throat and said, "Would you care to tell me what is hanging so heavy on your mind?"

Wend looked around. "What makes you think that I am preoccupied?"

"I'll tell you why: you were extremely quiet at supper, not bantering with the children like you usually do, and even more telling, you didn't eat well. You left meat on your plate. That's a sure signal something's bothering you."

Wend poured her a drink and handed it to her before he answered. "It's Reese Newkirk."

"Oh yes, the man who lost his wife and whom you offered the job of first lieutenant." She shrugged. "What's the problem?

"He was supposed to show up by today if he wanted the commission. I told him to report for duty by the time of the second recruiting.

I was looking for him at the Wild Boar today, and he didn't come, and then I thought perhaps he would ride directly to the farm." Wend took another sip. "Obviously he decided against it. I guess he was too far into the liquor to sober up."

"Or into his grief. Perhaps he simply can't get over losing his woman."

"It amounts to the same thing. He isn't here, and I need to look for another second-in-command."

"Didn't David Rutledge give you a list of possible officers? You'll just have to look into them."

Wend sighed. "Yes, but it will take time, and I could use an experienced officer *now*. Childers is eager, but he's a babe in the woods."

"Well, I'm sure you and Donegal will educate him soon enough."

Wend just nodded.

Peggy, after a sip on her drink, decided to change the subject. "Well, my dear, I have some news which may cheer you up."

"Go ahead, make your attempt."

"Well, while you were recruiting today, Alice and I took the chaise over to Glengarry to see Anna McDonald and some other women."

"That should cheer me up?"

"The rest of what I have to say will." She sat looking at him and smiling.

"Well, my dear, don't keep me in the dark."

"Jean Wood, Margaret Thruston, Abby Morgan, and several others, including *Elizabeth Childers*, were there."

"Ah yes, Elizabeth Childers; it looks like you are well into your campaign to bring our ensign's mother into your circle."

"I told you I'd be working on that. But that's not what I wanted to tell you. The fact is, it was a meeting about your company. We've decided to organize the women of Frederick County to make uniforms for your men."

Wend stared at his wife for a moment. "Good Lord, I hadn't even had time to think about that—I've been concentrating on recruiting. But you're right; we have to do something about uniforms." He put his hand to his chin. "What are you planning to make—the uniform of the Virginia militia?"

"No, that would be complex and take a lot of time. Anyway, I don't think there's enough blue and red cloth in the county. Alice and I talked to Joshua and Donegal about it. If you approve, *Captain*, we're going to make a uniform consisting of a hunting shirt, breeches, and leggings. Donegal thought that would be a good outfit for a light company."

Wend pondered that for a long moment. "Peggy, you are quite right. That would be entirely appropriate. And easier to make than a regular uniform. And there should be plenty of linen available for the shirts."

"Yes, all the ladies thought the same. Alice took a pattern for the shirt to the meeting, and Anna's going to get copies made for all the women to use."

Wend finished his drink. "Well, Mrs. Eckert, I'm quite grateful to you and the other ladies. We will look quite elegant when we march out for Washington's army."

Peggy beamed. "We shall do our part." Then a cloud came over her face. "But there's one thing we couldn't work out. *Hats* for the company. It's not something we can make, and we'll have to decide on the kind and then go beg for money from the committee. All that may be hard."

Wend considered for a moment. "Maybe the men will have to just wear their own hats."

Peggy made a face. "That would spoil the whole effect. No, we'll have to think of something."

Wend put his cup down. "Well, we can't solve that at this moment. I think I'll walk on down to the camp and see how things are coming this first night."

"Don't be too long. I plan to put the children to bed, then retire myself. It has been a long and busy day."

Wend gathered up his hat and headed out the door. The day had been warm and sunny, but now, in full dark with the moon up, the April air was quite chilly. Wend walked along the drive, looking at the lights from the houses. Soon he passed Baird's house and came to the point where the ridge started to slope down toward the field where the camp lay. There were now many fires, arranged in two lines, and he could make out several new, improvised canvas shelters in addition to the tents. Ranged around the fires were the newly minted soldiers, and he heard a buzz of conversation and laughing.

He was also surprised to see Donegal and Baird walking up the hill toward him. He stopped and waited for the pair to arrive.

Baird turned to Donegal and said in a jocular tone, "Well, like I told you, the good cap'n is here to make his rounds."

Donegal added, "Yes, we thought you couldn't resist coming down to take a look."

Wend said, "How are they doing? Are they fairly comfortable for their first night?"

"Aye," replied Donegal. "We've got everyone shelter, and the first meal went well enough. We issued out some of the pork and flour which was sent out from Winchester yesterday, and they made a meal of it. Na they've got full stomachs all around."

As he spoke, the sound of a song started with a few voices at one of the fires and quickly was taken up by many others.

Wend listened a moment. "I've heard that tune before; it was during Pontiac's War. The soldiers of the 60th used to sing it."

Donegal nodded. "Aye, it's called 'Yankee Doodle.'"

Wend was puzzled. "As I remember, its words mock colonials. And particularly our ability to soldier. Why are our men singing something which makes fun of them?"

Donegal replied, "The *British* words do. But it seems our lads up north in the army have new words for it and have turned it around now so they use it to mock the British. People were singing it at the Wild Boar this afternoon."

"Well, I'll be damned." Wend listened to the song for a few seconds. "It is quite catchy."

Baird said, "Indeed, particularly after you've had an ale or two."

Wend was about to make a joke about that when all three of them heard the sound of a horse coming toward them at the trot. They turned around to look, puzzled at who might be approaching at this time of night.

Baird said, "Why, it's someone in a militia uniform."

Donegal said, "Perhaps their lordships at the Committee of Safety have sent us some sort of dispatch. Maybe news from the north?"

Even with the moonlight, Wend could not immediately make out the man's face. But he was able to see that the horse had saddlebags and a canvas sack was hanging from the side of the animal. The man carried a long arm in the crook of his arm. He said to his companions, "That's funny, a courier would probably carry only pistols."

Then the man pulled up and dismounted. Taking the reins in one hand and his firelock in the other, he approached them leading the horse. In a moment he was close enough for the moonlight to illuminate his countenance.

The face was that of Reese Newkirk.

The officer approached the group, a serious look on his face. "Good evening, Captain Eckert. I regret my late arrival, but I had to settle several matters of personal business which took longer than expected. If you still want me as your lieutenant, I am ready to serve."

"As I said last week, your services are quite welcome." Wend looked at Joshua. "We need to get him shelter for the night. Do you have room in your place? When Rutledge gets the new tents here, he can start sleeping at the camp."

Baird shrugged. "We have room, and Alice won't object. She was used to having crowds of men in her place up in Carlisle, years ago. It will be just like old times."

Wend said to Newkirk, "Go ahead and turn your horse out in our pasture. Tomorrow come to my house after breakfast, and we'll begin planning the organization of our company and your duties."

"I'll be there, sir, ready to get started."

Wend said good night and started back toward his house, feeling better than he had for days. *Things were finally starting to come together.*

Wend stood before the stacked muskets in the rebuilt workshop. Gathered around him were Hecht, Horner, and the rest of the apprentices.

Hecht said, "Well, Wend, the lot of fifty are ready for issue, and the fact is, we've already got started on producing more."

Horner added, "Yes, and you can hardly tell the ones that were scorched during the fire. You can only see small places on the stocks where the scorch marks were too deep to completely eliminate. And that's only if you know where to look."

Wend smiled. "That doesn't matter. They're serviceable, and in any case, after a few weeks, they'll all show hard use."

As he was talking, there was the sound of a wagon approaching. Wend looked around to see it was driven by Sowers, with Donegal riding beside him. Behind the wagon a squad of soldiers followed on foot.

Sowers pulled the team up at the front door of the shop, and Donegal jumped down. He motioned toward the muskets. "Well na, we're ready to start carryin' the firelocks down to the camp. It's past time to start drillin' the lads."

Wend grinned. "*Well* past time, Sergeant!"

Donegal waved his men in, and with the assist of the apprentices, they began loading the muskets.

Wend and Donegal stood outside and watched the loading.

After a few moments, Donegal said, "I've got some business to settle with a group of the riflemen."

Wend looked over at the Scotsman. "Business? What do you mean?"

"Some of them are not taking kindly to discipline. They say they're signed on to be marksmen and skirmishers, not regular line soldiers. They don't think they should be taking turns at standing sentinel, drilling, and performing routine camp duties."

Wend said, "I'm not surprised. James Wood told me that they were having that problem with some of the riflemen up with the army in Boston. He learned about that down in Williamsburg. It seems that Washington wrote in dispatches they did good work as sharpshooters but were hard to control and were discipline problems in camp."

"Aye, that's what we're seeing here," responded Donegal. "Their leader is Jensen; the one who gave you some trouble at the first recruiting muster."

"I thought his mouth might be a problem. But Joshua said to take him on because he was one of the best shots. Well, *Sergeant*, what are you going to do about it? We must have all our men subject to the same rules of discipline and duty."

"That we shall. I'm planning to entertain Jensen down by the creek where there's a wee small grove of trees an' we can have some private words. I'm figurin' that once he comes to understand army discipline, the others of his group will fall into line." He shrugged. "Or I might have to have more little private talks down by the creek." He smiled at Wend. "But no worry, I'll have them understandin' their duty soon enough, one way or another."

Wend grinned at the big Highlander. "Yes, I'm sure you can handle that."

At that moment Horner called out, "Mr. Eckert, there's someone walking up the entrance drive." Then his voice took on an incredulous tone. "Sir, it's a *girl*. And she's carrying a sack over her shoulder."

Wend, accompanied by Donegal, stepped out into the drive and looked down the slope. Sure enough, he saw a young woman striding purposely toward them.

Donegal said, "Na that's no one I've ever seen. What could she want here?"

Wend shrugged. "We'll know soon enough."

In a few moments, the girl had arrived. She dropped the sack, looked around at the shop and the apprentices and soldiers, then boldly walked up to Wend. He noted she was indeed quite young, he guessed fifteen or sixteen, with dark brown hair and a somewhat plump body with wide hips. She was dressed in a blouse and skirt, with a shawl over her shoulders that was tied in front.

The girl looked up and down at Wend, as if sizing him up. "My name is Patricia McCray. And I'm lookin'," she said in a strong, defiant tone, "for a certain Cap'n Eckert. I'm told this is his farm and the men of the company he's forming are campin' here."

Wend, who was dressed in his working clothes covered by an apron, replied, "Well, you've found him. I'm Eckert." He pointed to Simon. "And this is Sergeant Donegal. Now, miss, how can I be of service to you?"

The girl again looked over Wend, examining his clothing, a look of doubt on her face. "*You're* the cap'n?"

"If you find that hard to believe, I have a piece of paper over in the house which says so, if you would like to see it."

Donegal put his hand over his mouth and chuckled.

The girl shook her head. "Well, I *guess* I'll take your word for it. Now, you got a boy here named Jed Carver?"

Wend looked at Simon, who nodded.

The Scotsman said, "Aye, we've got a soldier by that name."

"Good. I'm here to marry him on account he got me in a family way."

Wend smothered a laugh.

Donegal looked away, mirth written all over his face. But the girl saw his expression and said, "I ain't makin' no joke, *Mr. Sergeant*. Jed is sure enough the one who did it to me."

The apprentices were curiously looking over at the three. Wend said, "Miss McCray, I believe we should retire to my house, across the drive there, where we can discuss this matter with some privacy."

The girl looked around at all the men now staring at her. "Sounds like a good idea to me."

Wend turned to Donegal. "Get someone to go fetch the man in question to the house." Then an idea hit Wend. "And request that Ensign Childers accompany him."

Wend led the girl into the house and seated her in the parlor. A silence prevailed as she looked around curiously, her eyes widening in apparent awe.

Judging by her clothes and manner of speaking, Wend assumed she was used to rougher furnishings. He broke the quiet by asking, "Now, miss, where are you from?"

"My family has a farm north of the Battletown Crossroads. We got a log house, ain't nothing like this."

Wend was surprised. "And you walked all that way alone?"

"Course I did. How else would I have gotten here?"

"Yes, how else indeed." Then a thought hit Wend. "Do your parents know your condition? And where you've gone?"

"Course not! I packed up and left in the middle of last night. If my pa knew about me, he'd be here with my two older brothers to have a straight talk with Jed. And they'd be carryin' firelocks. That's why Jed better marry me afore they know."

Wend thought about the situation for a moment. Then he said, "Wait here, Miss McCray. I'll be right back."

He walked down the hall to Peggy's sewing room. His wife stood over a table cutting material for the hunting shirts.

"My dear, I have a situation, something we're both rather familiar with, and I need your help." He explained in a few words.

Peggy listened, chuckling as he talked. Then she said, "I think I should have a few minutes alone with the young lady."

Wend grinned. "Yes, I rather thought that would be a good idea."

Returning to the parlor, he motioned for Patricia to follow him. "I'd like you to meet Mrs. Eckert. She's back in her sewing room."

He left the girl with Peggy and went back to the parlor. Momentarily there was a knock on the front door. Wend opened it to find Childers accompanied by a tall, skinny, dark-haired youth of perhaps eighteen.

"Captain, Sergeant Donegal asked me to report to you and bring Private Carver."

"Yes indeed, Childers. Both of you come in." He waved toward chairs. "Have a seat. I need to talk to my wife."

Both men, looking puzzled, sat down. Wend walked back to the sewing room and knocked on the closed door.

Peggy opened it and stood in the door. She looked back at Patricia, who was just finishing fastening up her blouse. "Well, my husband, I should say *quite* pregnant—I think about two months and just beginning to show."

Wend raised his eyebrows.

Peggy continued, "She says there haven't been any other boys, and given her youth and seeming lack of guile, I rather believe it."

"Wait here; I'll call for you to bring her into the parlor in a few minutes."

Wend rejoined the two men and without saying anything else, walked over to the liquor cabinet. He filled three cups with Donegal's whiskey. He handed one to Childers and then gave one to Carver. Then he picked up his own.

He looked at the young private. "Carver, have you ever tasted whiskey before?"

The youth looked down at the cup, then shook his head. "No, sir. But I've had ale often enough."

"Well, this is strong stuff—far stronger than ale—so be careful to just take a sip." Wend raised his cup. "Now I'm going to propose a toast."

Childers looked bemused. "Sir, if I may, what are we toasting?"

"Why, we're toasting Private Carver's good fortune." Wend raised his cup toward the lad. "Congratulations, Private, this is your wedding day. And if I may say, she's a lovely lass."

Carver stood in shock with his cup raised, his mouth wide open. "Wedding day? Sir, I don't understand."

"Well, you *do* know a young lady named Patricia McCray, don't you?"

"Why, yes sir, I do. But...but..."

Wend interrupted, "And you've been sparking her for some time, haven't you?"

Carver's face reddened, and he looked over at Childers, then back at Wend. "Yes, that's true."

"Well, the girl happens to be here in this house, and my wife has verified that she's with child. And, Private, Miss McCray is quite insistent that it is yours, because she hasn't been in the hayloft, or down by the creek or over in the meadow or wherever you did it, with anyone but you."

Carver stood speechless.

Wend continued, "So now, lad, since you've had the *pleasure*, it's time to take the *responsibility* and do the right thing. It's your obligation to protect Miss McCray's reputation." Wend pointed to Carver's whiskey cup. "This probably would be a good time to take some of the liquor, as you consider your situation."

Carver took a gulp of the whiskey and then made a face, and then his body shook violently all over as the liquid burned its way down his throat.

Wend said, "Carver, remember, I told you to sip it."

Childers, who had taken a taste, said, "I'd heard that the whiskey you produced here was quite good, and I must say, sir, that it quite lives up to its reputation."

"Thank, you, Edward." Then Wend turned back to Carver. "Now, Private, in case you would think to argue about this, I believe you should know that Miss McCray's father and two brothers are not yet aware of her condition or whom she holds responsible. I would say that when they find all this out, you could expect them here to confront you with firelocks in hand. So the quicker you resolve the problem, the better."

Carver sighed deeply. "Yes, sir."

Wend smiled. "Excellent." Then he walked out into the hall and called out, "Peggy, bring in the young lady."

The two women shortly entered the parlor, and Patricia, upon seeing Carver, smiled broadly. "Oh, Jeddy, I missed you so. I just had to come!"

Carver looked around the room, an embarrassed expression on his face.

Wend said, "Now, Miss McCray, I'm glad to say that Private Carver would like nothing better than to take you as his wife, if that suits you."

"Of course it does!" Patricia ran over and threw her arms around the blushing soldier.

Wend gave her a minute to finish the embrace, then coughed discreetly and announced, "The wedding will take place this very day." He turned to Childers. "Now Edward, please go find Jacob Specht, and have him break you out a team and wagon and get a driver. Then you and the blessed couple will travel to Winchester, where you will prevail upon Reverend Thruston to do the honors. And also stand as witness to the happy nuptials."

The ensign nodded. "Yes, sir. I understand. I'm sure the reverend will be most willing."

Peggy grinned broadly. "Indeed, Thruston likes nothing better than a good wedding. You'll make his day."

Wend continued, "And Edward, when you come back, Donegal will have prepared a tent for the joyous couple to spend their wedding night in." He looked at Patricia. "And then in the morning, we will have a wagon take Mrs. Carver back to her parents' house, where she can reside while waiting for the child and for her husband's return after the company is mustered out next year."

A look of dismay came over Patricia's face. "Oh no, Captain! Please, I want to go to the army with Jeddy! I want him to see the baby. *Please* don't send me home. And anyway, Ma and Pa will be so angry when they find out! I want to stay here! I can be very helpful. I can sew, I can do laundry, I can cook! I'll do whatever it takes to stay! I brought all I need with me in that canvas sack."

Wend looked over at Peggy, who was showing exceeding amusement at the entire affair. She said, "Well, she *could* be very useful in helping make the uniforms."

Wend waved a hand in surrender and shrugged his shoulders. "All right, Patricia, you may stay and join the camp. But tomorrow you must sit down and send a letter to your parents explaining everything. Do I make myself clear?"

—m—

Joshua Baird raised the pistol into the air and pulled the trigger. The crack of the report resounded over the farm. Twelve horses, each tethered to a post of the pasture fence, whinnied and snorted in fear. After a few moments, they quieted down. No sooner had they done so than Joshua fired a second pistol. The results were the same, except that Sonny, the two-year-old, tried to buck but was held mostly down by the lead rope.

Jacob Specht walked among the horses, calming them, as Baird reloaded his firelocks. He called out, "That wasn't as bad as I expected. How long we got to do this?"

Joshua looked up from his loading. "We'll do this for a few days. Then when they get used to a single gun firing, we'll bring a squad of soldiers up from the camp and have them fire all their muskets in volleys. We'll just keep doin' that until the horses get used to it and steady out, including when someone is holding them by the reins or in their saddle."

Specht made a face. "I don't want to be the rider when you start doing that."

Baird grinned. "Hell, Jacob, you're the best man to be up there in the saddle. Ain't you the 'master of the horse'? You got to earn your pay."

"Shit, Joshua. I never expected to be doing anything like this."

Wend, who was leaning against the fence watching the work, said, "You didn't expect to be rebuilding Eckert Ridge after loyalists burned it down, but you are doing that and doing it well. At least working with horses is more in your line."

Joshua waved at the line of animals. "Well, they're doin' as well as you could expect, bein' we just started."

Wend pointed at Sonny. "Keep a close eye on him, and let me know if you have any trouble settling him down. I'm planning to ride him on the campaign, and I need a steady mount."

Specht looked doubtful. "He's pretty young and mighty spirited. Maybe you should take one of the older horses."

Wend stared at the young black horse for a moment. "No, the fact is I like his spirit and particularly his power. Given that we can calm him in the face of fire, that will be useful on the battlefield."

A new voice from behind the three men said, "He *is* a well-built animal. Look at those long legs."

The three turned around to see that Reese Newkirk and Donegal had approached.

Wend realized it had been Newkirk who had spoken.

The lieutenant continued, "That black definitely comes from good breeding stock." He quickly climbed over the fence and went over to Sonny, running his hands over the horse, then down each of the legs. "Yes, he's strong now, and when he matures, he's going to be a great racer and hunter." He looked over at Wend. "Are you sure you want to take him to war? I'd say he might be too valuable for that. A horse's chances for survival in conflict are not good. Actually, worse than a man's."

Wend considered his words for a few moments. "Yes, you're right about what happens to horses on campaign. But I need a horse which will give me all he has when the need arises. And since I bred him and know the stallion which sired him and particularly the mare who carried him, I'm sure he will give me his best effort when I call for it." He looked at Newkirk. "We take our chances in war, and so must the horses. And this one *will* go on campaign."

Reese nodded and changed the subject. "Well, sir, I could talk horses with you all afternoon, but we have some company business to discuss."

Wend motioned toward the new stable. "Let's go over there where we can talk away from the noise of pistol shots."

The three walked over and stood next to the stable.

Donegal pointed toward a paper in Newkirk's hand. "Na, it's time for us to make some corporals. We drew up a list."

Newkirk handed the paper to Wend. "We have six men, three for each half company. This list is based on what Donegal has observed over the first few days of drilling."

Wend looked over the paper. First on the list was Sanders, the leader of the men who had come from Steffensburg. Wend nodded. "Sanders is a good man; he was very stalwart during last year's war." Wend perused the rest of the list, the names on which were unfamiliar to him. Then he saw the last name on the list and looked up at Donegal in astonishment. "You want to make *Jensen* a corporal? After you just had to impose a sergeant's discipline on him down by the creek?" Wend pointed to a red mark on the Highlander's cheek. "And with you still bearing signs of his fist?"

"Na Wend, that big Lowlander and me came to an understanding down there by the stream. Sort of like after you whipped that drummer McKirdy of the 77th that night at Fort Ligonier back in '63. You and he got along well after that and fought alongside each other like brothers at Bushy Run."

"All right, I understand that. But making him a *corporal*?"

Donegal gave Wend a sly smile. "It's an old trick. Instead of letting him brood, we give him a bit of authority—which he likes—and then he's got reason to work for us instead of against us. And there's na denying a good many of the men look up to him."

Wend still wasn't sure about the idea. "What if he uses his rank to work against our authority? And sway his followers to his ideas?"

Donegal shrugged. "Then we break him back to private. He won't like losing authority or the shame of going back to the ranks."

Wend sighed. "All right, you're the regular army man. I'll take your word for it."

"Thank you, sir." Newkirk took the list back from Wend. "Now the next thing we need to do is appoint, or locate, two men suitable to be sergeants. One for each half company."

Wend took a deep breath. "I well aware of that, Reese. In fact, that's one of my biggest worries."

The lieutenant looked over at Donegal. "I've not seen anyone in the company with enough experience. However, perchance if we watch how these men"—he raised the list of corporals—"perform their jobs, we can promote two of them."

Wend frowned. "As far as I can see, none of them have any real experience, at least from the aspect of drilling or military discipline."

Newkirk raised a finger. "You're right, sir. And if I may be so bold, Captain, I know of a man who might serve our needs. He's Ulster and works as a surveyor's assistant. He has no real formal education, but he learns fast. And he served as a corporal with a ranger company during the last days of the French War and in Pontiac's War. He lives up north of Winchester."

Wend raised his eyebrows. "What makes you think he would enlist?"

"He's unmarried, and like I told you at my house, surveying is in the doldrums now. He could take a year away from it."

Wend looked over at Donegal. "What do you think, Simon?"

"It's worth a try, sir. I'm not eager to make anyone I've seen in the company a sergeant; they've na the experience for it. I'd have to be holding their hand for a long time tellin' them what to do every minute."

Wend thought a moment, then asked, "Reese, what's this fellow's name?"

"Thomas Wilder, Captain." Newkirk waved toward the horses. "I say let me take a day and ride up to his place and see if he's game. He and I have spent a lot of time together in the field, and I might be able to convince him."

"All right, Reese. Do that posthaste. We must get our sergeants in place as early as possible."

After the two had taken their leave, Wend walked back to the pasture fence line, just in time for Joshua to fire another shot. After the horses had calmed down, Wend waved to Specht to join him.

Specht walked over and put a hand on the top rail. "They're coming along well, sir."

Wend nodded. "Yes, Jacob, indeed they are. Now listen carefully. When I ride Sonny while I'm with the army, I'll need to take him over many obstacles. He needs to be a good jumper. Start training him to take fences immediately, for we have little time."

"Aye, Mr. Eckert, that I'll do. But I've little fear he'll be ready. I say he'll take to it as well as any horse I've known."

Wend, dressed in a new blue uniform with red facings and a tree-corned hat, all of which Peggy had had a tailor in Winchester make for him, rode his horse toward the white-frame Lutheran church that stood beside a cemetery and a white cottage-sized parsonage, at a crossroads about six miles west of Winchester. Another white building close to the church was obviously a schoolhouse. A village, consisting mostly of small houses, a blacksmith establishment, and a store, straddled the westward-leading road. All around Wend could see neat, well-maintained farmsteads. Suddenly it struck him that the area had the look of his old home on the outskirts of Lancaster. With that thought, he felt the rush of memories of his long-lost family. Then Wend gritted his teeth and shrugged the thoughts off and rode up to the parsonage, focusing on the business at hand. He dismounted and knocked on the front door.

A small, thinly built, brown-haired man opened the door. He wore spectacles and had a bushy beard.

Wend said, "I'm Captain Eckert of the Frederick County Light Foot. I'm looking for Reverend Scholz."

"*Ja, ja*, I'm Henry Scholz. And I have got the letter about you from the Reverend Thruston."

"Sir, I hope you were able to gather the other pastors for this meeting."

"*Ja*, there are four of us, all waiting for you this last hour."

"I appreciate your patience, Reverend. It took me a bit longer than expected; I'm not much used to traveling this far to the west of Winchester."

"Well, all is well now that you are here. Please come in, Captain."

Wend came in and took a seat in the chair that Scholz proffered.

Scholz said, "Now I will introduce you to the others." He pointed in turn to the other pastors. "Paul Kohler and Richard Bauman. And this is Ludwig Schreiber."

Scholz sat down, and all four men stared at Wend for a moment, then Bauman, a tall, lean man, spoke up. "Henry has read to us this letter from the reverend of the English church. We know why you are here. You want our boys for your army."

Wend cleared his throat and said, "Well, indeed I am here to recruit for the Frederick County Light Company. We need ten or fifteen additional men."

"And why," asked Schreiber, "do you come to us for these men? Aren't there enough English to fill your ranks?"

Bauman said, "*Ja*, this is a war between the English and the Ulster people against the king's men. Why should we join in?"

"*Ja*," said Schreiber, "Bauman is correct. We came to America to avoid all the wars made by the princes of Europe."

Schreiber was staring critically at Wend. Finally he said, "You have a German name and talk like you are one of us. But we know of you—you have an Ulster wife, and many people say you have become more Ulster than German." He waved his finger at Wend and then added, "It is not too bold to say that your children are like mongrel dogs." He stared at Wend brazenly. "You have diluted your German heritage. Why should we listen to your words as if you were one of us?"

Anger flamed up within Wend, and he almost sprang from his seat to physically confront the man. But then he realized that was what Schreiber wanted—he was baiting him. With difficulty he controlled himself. Taking a deep breath, he said, "Yes, my children have *mixed* blood. But, if I may say, it is my experience that mixed-breed dogs often have hardier characteristics and prove to be cleverer than those of one breed. They benefit from the combined characteristics of the parents." He looked defiantly at the four men. "To be sure, I have witnessed that in my own children."

He let them consider that for a moment. Then he continued, "And as to my heritage being diluted by marriage to an Ulster woman, I will take second to no German. My ancestors were jaegers of a great lord in the forests of Hesse for decades before they took up the trade of gunsmithing and came to America."

Wend paused and took a deep breath, and as he did so, a thought occurred to him. He looked into Schreiber's eyes and then into those of the others. "Gentlemen, we sit here today talking about our heritage, our German heritage. We are all proud of it. But so are those of English heritage, and those of Scot, or Welsh, or Swiss, and others who have come to these colonies. Wherever they came from, they all wanted the same things: the opportunity to live their lives in their own way free of the bonds and restraints of the old lands, to practice their own religion, to follow their own path to prosperity. And they have gathered together in communities of the same heritage. But that is breaking down. If you would look beyond your own villages, you would see that there are mixed marriages throughout our county and indeed throughout the Great Valley." He smiled at the four men. "And this rebellion, this war is going to lead to a mixing of peoples such as we have never seen before. If we win, I say there will be the beginnings of a new breed, a combination of all the different peoples in our colonies." He raised a finger. "Think of how we make iron. We put ore, lime, charcoal into a furnace. They are materials as different from each other as you can find. Then we combust them at high temperature, and what comes out? A single material far stronger than any of the ingredients."

Wend crossed his arms in front of him. "We may not see it come fully to fruition, but gentlemen, I believe that perhaps our children will come to live in a land where we are all one great people, like the iron from a furnace. Each of whom recalls and honors his own heritage but takes pride in being a people of a new nation, a nation of America."

The men stared at him for a moment. Wend could see that they were turning over what he had said in their minds. But then Schreiber scowled and spoke out strongly. "I pray that will never be the case. We must always take foremost pride in the heritage of our forefathers and live by it."

There was a long, tense silence in the room. Then Scholz sought to calm things. "I think my compatriots have spoken too sharply but with no intent to insult, Captain Eckert. Perhaps we should allow you to explain precisely why you think we should send our young men off to this war with you."

Wend sat silent for a moment. He thought, *The irony is that I'm a fine one to convince them, since I resisted joining this fight.* But he said, "Virginia and the Continental Congress are fighting to get rid of unjust laws and taxes made by the English king and parliament thousands of miles away. And beyond that, the fight is to ensure that we can govern ourselves forever. And here is why it is important to you: unless the German communities join in the conflict, it may be hard for you to have a say in the government of Virginia. We of German heritage must fight alongside the English and Scots settlers for the right to participate in the lawmaking in Williamsburg and in Philadelphia."

Scholz nodded. "I can see the point of your words, Captain. But there is another view. There is much doubt within our community that the colonists can prevail against the forces of the crown. If we join in with the rebellion, we may face severe consequences when the British triumph."

The other three nodded in agreement. Schreiber exclaimed, "Henry is quite correct! Better we stay out of this and be safe."

The four men looked at Wend. He let the silence of the moment stretch out, the most stone-hard expression on his face that he could muster. Finally he said slowly, "I thought German men of your learning and experience were more aware of the ways of the world than you are showing."

Scholz cocked his head and asked, "Herr Captain, what do you mean by that?"

They all looked at Wend curiously.

Wend allowed himself a tight smile. "Why, gentlemen, it is absurd, I repeat, *absurd*, to think that the British, if victorious, will treat you differently than anyone else. They will be of no mind to make an exception simply because you say you have been neutral. Only those who declare themselves loyalists and fight for the Crown will be favored." He looked around at the four. "Are you prepared to send your young men to fight for the king?"

Now the four sat silently staring at him. But he could see they were taking his words seriously.

He resumed talking. "Gentlemen, as I say, everyone but loyalists will feel harsh punishment and be subject to strict laws intended to exact obedience to the British government. And this will all be enforced by an army of occupation, made up of the British and their loyalists." He shrugged. "I dare say you will lose a great measure of the freedom for which you came to this country, even if you did nothing to advance the rebellion."

He paused again, then said, "I suggest you think that over. In my mind, it is better to bet on winning. And for you, I make this proposal: all I request from you is to mention at your next sabbath church service that we are looking for men for our company and that we will be at the store in this village on the Wednesday following to recruit. Let me repeat: I don't ask that you encourage your men to volunteer, just to make them aware of our need."

Wend smiled and sat back in his chair. "Well, that is all I have to say. It is your decision whether or not you honor my request."

Scholz looked around at his compatriots, then took a deep breath. "Captain, I will make the announcement under your terms." He looked at the others for their response. Bauman and Kohler looked at each other, then both nodded agreement. Schreiber stared straight ahead, his jaw set. Finally he said, "No, I will not make any such announcement. I am not for this war, and I will not see men of my flock sent off to fight for your congress."

Wend nodded his understanding. "Pastor Schreiber, I certainly accept your decision." He turned to the others. "And I thank you gentlemen for the measure of support to which you have agreed." He picked up his hat and stood to depart.

Schreiber cleared his throat. "There is something else I would tell you about, Herr Captain."

Wend looked at the pastor and asked, "Indeed, sir? And what would that be?"

"I have just received a letter from one of my relatives in the old country which contains news which might be of particular interest to you." He looked around at the others, then back at Wend, a sly smile on his face. "If seems the English king has reached out to the princes of our homeland and hired a goodly number of their soldiers as mercenaries."

Wend was puzzled. "You mean for service here in the colonies?"

"Yes, my dear captain, it means that thousands of German soldiers, I understand many from your very own province of Hesse, will be coming to America to fight for the king. You will certainly find yourself encountering them in battle. So, Captain Eckert, you may one day be fighting against men to whom you have some relation."

Wend was shocked by the news, but he put on his hardest facial expression. "Pastor, it matters *naught*. I will fight whoever the king sends against me, regardless of where they come from or whether they are British or a hireling. It is our cause which is important, and by taking the commission, I have vowed to support that with all my breath."

He looked around the room. "Good day, gentlemen."

CHAPTER NINE

DRILLING

Wend stood at the bar of the Golden Buck Inn, waiting to be served. After his meeting with the German pastors, he had ridden eastward into Winchester, where he had decided to rest his horse and take his midday meal before continuing on to Eckert Ridge. The common room was moderately full and servers were busy tending to the patrons. The barkeep, Georgie Boatwright, was a busy man, but after a few minutes, he came over to Wend.

"What can I get you, Captain Eckert?"

Wend grinned. "Some of my own whiskey, of course."

Boatwright promptly put a cup on the counter and measured out some of the whiskey. Wend dropped a coin and took his first satisfying sip as the liquor made its way to his stomach.

Boatwright took the coin and was about to move on to his next customer when he stopped and looked at Wend with a thoughtful expression on his face. "Say, Captain, there was a man in here asking after you a couple of hours ago. Wanted to know where your place was."

"You don't know the man?"

"Never saw him before, and he didn't give me his name. But it's a sure thing he's not familiar with the county, because when I told him where your place was, he asked me for directions on how to get there." Boatwright shook his head. "I had to explain to him how to go west to Battletown Crossroads and then take the road south to your farm."

"What did he look like?"

"Taller than average, burly shoulders, brown hair. Rough clothes like a farmer and hands of a working man. But very sure of himself."

The barman made a quick scowl. "Didn't buy anything to drink. Left right after talking to me."

Puzzled, Wend shrugged his shoulders. "Doesn't particularly ring a bell. Could be many men. Well, if he wanted to go to my place, I'll find out who he is and what he wants soon enough."

Wend took his drink to a table and waved to a maid to take his meal order. He was waiting for his food and going over the meeting with the German pastors in his mind when James Wood entered, looked around, and then walked over to Wend's table.

"Mind if I join you?"

Wend motioned toward a chair across the table. "Of course not, James."

Wood settled in and waved for a server. "Well, how's recruiting going?"

Wend replied, "Good. I've got almost ninety men. I just spent some time with several pastors from the German villages, asking for them to notify their young lads about the company."

"I'm told you already have some Germans in the ranks—mostly from the town and east of the wagon road."

"That's true—they're more secular than the communities out to the west. They've blended in well with other townspeople. But I'm not particularly optimistic about getting many lads from today's effort. The pastors weren't exactly enthusiastic."

Wood laughed. "No, I wouldn't expect they were. It was a little over a decade ago that some of the Ulster here in town had the habit of treating Germans coming in for supplies rather badly. There were fights in the streets and taverns. That was just before you arrived. There was quite a bit of ill will for a while, but it seems to have died down." He shrugged. "But the Germans have long memories."

"I experienced some of that when I was the only German living in an Ulster village, in Sherman Valley, Pennsylvania." Wend smiled. "But it ended when I married an Ulster girl."

"Knowing your wife, I can say you are a most fortunate man."

Wend smiled. "I could not but agree with you."

Then a frown passed over Wood's face. "Wend, however, I do have something to relate which will probably disturb you mightily. It's about Mrs. Eckert."

Wend went on alert. "Oh, something about Peggy which will disturb me?"

Wood nodded. "You know that that spy, Rhys, is to be executed tomorrow morning?"

"I had heard that, but it slipped my mind. I prefer not to think about him or his fate, except to be satisfied when he is gone."

"Indeed, Wend. But this morning Thruston and I went to see him in the jail at the square. Thruston wanted to offer him an opportunity for final reconciliation with the Lord, and I accompanied him just to check on arrangements for the execution."

"So how did my wife's name come up?"

"Rhys was in a vindictive mood, maybe a little crazy in the face of death. Instead of accepting Thruston's offer of prayer, he started talking about taking vengeance against you as the source of his downfall."

Wend was incredulous. "I rather thought I should be the one looking for retribution, seeing as Rhys is responsible for the destruction of my farm and the death of two people." Wend looked at Wood. "So how does Peggy figure in his vengeance?"

"He said she had been a prostitute."

Wend felt a shock run through his body. *The thing he feared most had materialized.* But with great willpower, he kept a straight face. "Peggy, a prostitute? Where would he get such an idea?"

"Rhys said he met a man, another peddler, from Pennsylvania. When passing through Winchester on a court day, he stopped to sell some of his wares and saw Peggy walk by and recognized her. He told Rhys over ale in a tavern that he knew her years ago and was certain she whored herself while working in her father's tavern in a small town called Sherman Mill."

Wend's mind was racing like the wind, and his heart seemed to be beating as rapidly as he desperately searched for the best way to respond. Finally, with a mighty effort to control his voice and speak calmly, he said, "It's no secret she was a server in the family establishment. But what father would be so despicable as to allow his daughter to sleep with the clientele? You could not possibly believe that story."

Wood waved his hand. "Well of *course* not! It was blatantly obvious, both to Thruston and myself, that Rhys had made the story up out of whole cloth in an attempt to besmirch you and your family as a last blow before he left this earth. He may have heard that you and your family came down from Pennsylvania and made things up from there." Wood pursed his lips. "Thruston was scandalized. I've never seen the man so angry. He berated Rhys in the kind of words I've never heard him use before, or *any* minister, for that matter. I tell you, Eckert, I wouldn't have expected Thruston to even *know* that language. At any rate, he told Rhys he was through with him, that he would have to make his final appeal to the Almighty by himself. And then he stocked out of the jail. I told Rhys if I had had a horsewhip in my hand, I would have used it and followed Thruston out of the building."

Wend said, "I thank you for telling me about this. It erases any regret I might possibly have felt about Rhys's end."

"Indeed, Wend. Imagine that rogue thinking *anyone* would credit such a story about a lovely, upright, churchgoing woman like Mrs. Eckert. I vow neither Thruston or myself will ever repeat it to anyone other than you."

—⁓—

Wend rode up the drive at Eckert Ridge and found Newkirk and Donegal in front of the shop, talking to Hecht. With them was a tall, lithe man Wend did not recognize. Wend pulled up and dismounted, securing the horse to the hitching rail in front of the house, then walked across the drive to join the group.

Newkirk motioned to the tall man. "Captain, this is Thomas Wilder, the man we spoke of earlier."

Wend nodded at Wilder. "Welcome to Eckert Ridge, Wilder. I assume if you are here, you are interested in serving with us. We need a sergeant for one of the half companies."

Wilder extended a hand. "Captain, there ain't no surveying work right now. If you'll take me, I'm your man. I'll sign the muster roll immediately."

Wend nodded. "Well, based on what Reese has said about you, that's done. You'll be sergeant of our rifles."

"Suits me fine, Cap'n."

Donegal said, "Now all we need is to find somebody to be sergeant of the musket men. I 'spect we'll have to take somebody from the ranks, but there ain't no logical candidate that I can see."

Wend smiled broadly. "Well, it happens that I have taken care of that. The sergeant of the muskets is coming up the drive right now."

The three other men turned to look down the grade toward Ashby Ferry Road.

Donegal stared for a moment. "Looks like a family of pilgrims."

Wend gave him a wry look. "They are, in a way. They've come all the way from the Ohio. I ran into them on the road from Winchester."

Newkirk shot a surprised look down the hill. He said incredulously, "You just engaged some traveling fellow with a family to be sergeant? On a whim?"

Wend laughed outright. "Certainly *not* on a whim, Reese. I did it with great pleasure. I would have made him sergeant of the company if Donegal weren't with us."

Donegal said, "You're playin' with us, Wend. You gonna stop it and tell us who be this man you were so anxious to sign on?"

Wend looked and saw that the wagon was close enough for faces to be recognized. "Look closely, Simon, and I'll not need to tell you anything. All will be clear."

Donegal took a step toward the approaching wagon and squinted hard, shading his eyes with his hand. After a moment he turned and looked at Wend. "I see it, but I dunna believe it. All is most certainly *not* clear. Did you conjure him up with some sort of spell? Are you a sorcerer all this time and me not knowing it?"

"It's not me, Simon. Let's just say the Lord works in strange ways."

Newkirk looked at Donegal, then back to Wend, exasperation written all over his face. "Are you going to let me in on what this is all about, or must I guess?"

Wend shook his head and grinned. "The man driving the wagon is Henry Flannagan. He was my sergeant when I was quartermaster of McDonald's battalion during Dunmore's campaign in '74. And more importantly, he was a sergeant in the Virginia Regiment during the French War. He was in from the beginning till the very end—Great Meadows, Forbes's campaign, the years patrolling the border. He's a fine soldier and just the man we need to get our musket men ready."

Donegal said, "I'm still puzzled what he's doin' here. His farm is out on the Ohio."

Newkirk remained bemused. "I certainly don't understand *anything*. Are you saying he came all this way, many days' journey, and with his family, to serve with you?"

Wend winked at Donegal, then said, "Of course, Reese. Men who have served with me are most anxious to renew their service." Then he broke out laughing. "No, Reese, I'm putting you on. The truth is, the Flannagans have had some trouble. And their misfortune is our good luck. But I'll let him tell you about it."

By now the wagon had arrived. Flannagan pulled up the team, slid down from his seat, then went around to help his wife down.

Wend made introductions. "Lieutenant Newkirk, this is Henry Flannagan. And the lovely lady is his wife, Martha."

Newkirk touched his hat to Mrs. Flannagan. "A pleasure to meet you, ma'am."

Wend motioned to the youngsters. "And these are the Flannagan children. Martha and the entire family will march with us as part of the camp."

Martha nodded. "We go where Henry goes. I made Mr. Eckert agree to that. I followed Henry when he was in Colonel Washington's regiment during the French War, when I was sixteen, just after we was married. An' I'll do it now, these eighteen years later."

Wend nodded. "Yes, of course you and all the children get rations. It was my pleasure, in order to secure the services of your husband."

Donegal said, "Now, damn it all, Henry, how about tellin' me and Lieutenant Newkirk how you happen to be here. The suspense is killin' us."

Flannagan frowned. "Our farm went bust. Couldn't get a good crop in after the war, because we had to spend so much time rebuilding after the Shawnee burned us out. And the worst was, the fire also burned most of our seed, and I didn't have money to buy enough for a good crop. So I finally left the farm and took the family to Pittsburgh to look for work."

Newkirk asked, "How did that lead to your coming here?"

"Well, in Pittsburgh I ran into Major William Crawford. You remember him from the war in 1774?"

Newkirk cocked his head. "Ah yes, indeed I do. My company served under him during the Seekunk raid right at the end of the war."

"Well, Crawford had a letter from Captain Wood about Mr. Eckert takin' a commission and forming a company." He looked over at his wife. "So Martha and I talked it over and decided to hurry here to join the company, hoping there was still room for us."

"That wasn't much of a gamble." Wend smiled. "Now, Donegal, take Sergeant Wilder and Sergeant Flannagan and his family all down to the camp and get them settled and ready to go to work in the morning."

When Wend and Newkirk were alone, Wend said, "Now that we've got our sergeants, we're ready to start some serious drilling."

Newkirk nodded. "Aye, Wend. I'll make plans for it." Then he asked, "How did your meeting with the German pastors go today?"

Wend sighed deeply. "It wasn't very encouraging." He waved his hand in resignation. "The pastors were lukewarm at best. One, named Schreiber, was downright hostile and refused to even announce our recruitment to his congregation. However, the others said they would announce it without comment."

"Well, we've actually got a useful number of men. We could march with those we have and be stronger than many companies."

Wend nodded agreement. "If we have to, but I'll still go to the muster in the German town and see if anyone shows up." He looked at Newkirk. "But now that we've got our sergeants, start drilling hard tomorrow. And after a few days, we'll start practicing skirmish order in the woods and in the fields."

"Aye, sir. It will be done. And it's high time." Newkirk put his hand to his chin. "Question, sir—have you thought about appointing a second lieutenant? It would be better if he were here to be part of the training."

Wend sighed. "Yes, we need one. Rutledge gave me a list of possible men, and I'll have to sit down and go over it. I'll do something about making a selection after the recruiting is finished."

After talking with Newkirk, Wend went into the shop with Hecht and looked over the progress on the manufacturing of muskets. Horner had the apprentices well in hand. A new batch of muskets was beginning to take shape. Then, feeling weary, he went over to the house, entered the parlor, and poured himself a whiskey. He sat down in his wing chair and tried to relax. However, the events of the day kept going through his mind, particularly the conversation with James Wood at the Golden Buck.

As he was thinking, Peggy bustled into the parlor. "I was working in the sewing room, and I thought I heard you come in. How did your meeting with the German pastors go?"

"It was all right."

Peggy gave him a sharp look. "Just all right? Well, you do seem rather discouraged. It must have actually been less than satisfactory."

"Peggy, my perturbation is not about the recruiting. The truth is, we've got some disquieting personal news which doesn't have anything to do with the Germans."

"Disquieting? Personal news? What do you mean?"

"On the way back from the German settlements, I stopped at the Golden Buck for refreshment, and James Wood joined me for a conversation."

"And he imparted bad news? Does it have something to do with the war?"

"No, like I said, it's about us. Or more precisely, it's about *you*." Wend paused and looked at Peggy. "He and Thruston had visited Rhys in jail, on the eve of his hanging. Thruston wanted to offer Rhys some solace on the eve of his execution, but the rogue was in a vindictive mood toward us."

"For God's sake, Wend. How could he hurt us? What kind of news could that despicable little man have about me?"

"He told them that he knew you had whored yourself. He said he got it from a traveling peddler passing through from Pennsylvania, who recognized you at a court day. The peddler described how you conducted business in your father's stable."

Shock spread over Peggy's face, and she was deadly silent. She walked over to the liquor cabinet and poured herself a drink, and Wend could see that her hand was shaking as she did so. Shaking enough that some of the liquid splashed out of the cup. She walked over to the settee, sat down, and took a deep gulp of the whiskey. She looked straight ahead and exclaimed, "Damn! Damn! Damn!" Then she turned to Wend. "Well, it seems that a person's past, particularly the mistakes, are always there, waiting to haunt her at some unexpected time and place." She put her head back, looking at the ceiling. "I suppose James asked you to explain the matter. How did you handle that?"

"No, my dear, actually he *didn't*. He condemned Rhys for spreading lies about you. He thought it was the most absurd thing he had ever heard, praised your virtue, and pledged he would tell no one about the story. And he said that Thruston had felt the same way and stormed out of the jail in disgust at what Rhys had said."

"Well, thank God for that." She sprang to her feet and began pacing the room, cup in hand. "But it won't end there. No, it won't. They'll tell their wives, sooner or later." She bit her lip. "Jean Wood and Esther Thruston will know about it. They may not say anything, but I'll undoubtedly see a certain look in their eyes. They'll always be wondering about me, wondering if it could be true."

Wend said quietly, "Peggy, you'll just have to be strong and live with that. And count on your friendship with the ladies of Winchester to keep the accusation from coming out in the open."

She stopped pacing for a moment and stood thinking. "Yes, it's a cross I will have to bear." Then she froze in place, staring into space for a long moment. "But this might not be the end of it. All it will take is another man, another traveling merchant who knows about me or slept with me, coming to Winchester and spreading the story. If that happens, people will put it all together, and we will be finished here—my reputation, your trade, our prosperity."

"Well, my dear, we have no choice but to hope that won't happen. And in any case, it's been over ten years since we came here, and this is the first time there's been a problem."

Peggy drained her cup. She looked down at Wend, and her chest heaved. "We thought we had put enough distance between ourselves and Sherman Valley. But we were wrong; we should have moved further south. Maybe all the way into Carolina."

"Well, in our current situation, there's nothing we can do. We certainly can't move on now. I'm obligated to lead the company, and we're deeply indebted to the people of Winchester for the reconstruction of our farm. And then there are all the people here who are supported by the farm. We'll just have to carry through and hope this doesn't happen again."

Peggy sat down and held up her cup to Wend. "I need another drink."

He got up and refilled the cup, then handed it to her.

She looked at the cup "This will help, Wend. But *not* enough. I shan't sleep well tonight." She thought a moment and sighed. "Nor a good many other nights in the future."

Wend, riding Sonny, pulled up to the yard of the Golden Buck in the late afternoon. He was on his way back from muster day at the German villages. Things had gone more successfully than he had expected, with nine men signing on to the company's rolls. Flannagan and Howard, one of the corporals, had been with him, and now they were riding directly back to Eckert Ridge in a wagon. Wend had had some business in Winchester and now, having completed it, intended to rest himself and the animal before riding back to the farm.

He handed Sonny off to the stable boy and was walking toward the inn's entrance when he heard the pounding hoofs of a horse being ridden at the gallop. He turned to see a man turn his animal into the yard and pull up. The stranger threw down from the mount and called to the boy for assistance. Wend noted he was tall and rangy, with jet-black hair. He was well tanned by the sun and of an indeterminate age. Wend thought he could be an old thirty or a young forty. He was well dressed for riding in a shell jacket, tight breaches, and shiny leather knee boots. There was a sword hanging from his side, a rather unusual sight for the backcountry.

Wend entered the common room, which was quite crowded. Waving to some acquaintances, he found a seat at one of the few open tables, which was located next to the counter. The stranger from the yard entered directly behind him, pistols in saddle holsters slung over his right shoulder and a set of saddlebags in his left hand. The man stood in the doorway for a long minute, his eyes sweeping around the room as if searching for someone. Then, apparently not seeing whom or what he was looking for, he strode up to the bar and inquired about accommodations for the night. Wend noted he had a distinctly Irish accent.

The server brought Wend's drink, and he took a grateful sip. Then he ordered his evening meal. He still intended to ride back to Eckert Ridge, but it would be a late trip in the darkness and he would arrive well after supper.

He had just taken another sip when the inn's front door swung rapidly open and banged loudly against the stop. Wend saw a young man, in gentleman's riding clothing, standing in the door. As had the Irishman, he scanned the room. Then his eyes settled on the traveler at the counter, and a satisfied smile came over his face. He reached down, unbuttoned his coat, and pulled a light dueling pistol from his belt. Wend noted that a second pistol was also tucked into the belt.

The youth shouted, "O'beirne, it's been a long chase, but I've caught you at last! Now turn around and face your reckoning!"

The man at the counter stood quietly for a long moment, not appearing to react to the newcomer's challenge. Then he shrugged his shoulders, reached out and picked up the cup in front of him, and drained it in one gulp. He looked down at the empty cup, then up at the barkeep, and said, "Sir, that's damned fine whiskey! I should not have expected to find such in a small border town!"

Then, in a flash of movement, he spun around to face the challenger, at the same time swiftly pulling his blade from its sheath so that it all seemed like one integrated movement. As he stood there confronting the young man, a demonic grin spread across his face. "Now, lad, you're right. This little pursuit has gone on far too long. It is indeed time to settle things."

People at nearby tables began get up and scurry away. They included a group of women who had been taking supper at the table next to Wend. Wend spoke up to the youth. "Sir, take care to let these ladies get clear." Then he looked up at the Irishman at the counter. "In any case, this is a poor place for the two of you to settle your differences. Why don't you take it to the yard?"

Sill looking straight at the boy, the Irishman raised an eyebrow. "That would do for me. I've no desire to spill the lad's blood here in the inn."

The young man bared his teeth in a fierce grimace. "Spill my blood? Not likely! In case you haven't noticed, I'm holding a pistol and you only have a sword in hand. O'beirne, right here and now, in this very room, you are going to finally answer for despoiling my sister and leaving her with child."

O'beirne grinned. "Now, my dear Harry, let me enlighten you. As concerns your sister, be assured that I didn't go any place that others hadn't been before me. And if you had taken the time to seriously discuss the matter with the beautiful and much-esteemed Miss Patricia Waterman, you would have found that her pregnancy is decidedly too far advanced for me to be the cause of it."

"Don't try to fool with me, O'beirne. And don't try to besmirch my sister's good name." The youth slightly lowered the pistol as he spoke. "Patricia told me in no uncertain terms—"

But he got no further than that, for with lightning speed, O'beirne lunged forward and in a deft sweep of the sword used the very tip of the blade to whip the pistol from the accuser's hand. The pistol flew several feet across the room, landing at the feet of the group of women, one of whom let out a small shriek as it landed.

The lad looked down at his hand in surprise to see it was dripping blood. Ignoring the bleeding, he reached down to his belt to pull the other pistol.

Wend had had quite enough of the drama. The lad was only a few feet from him, so he jumped to his feet and knocked the boy off balance. He fell on his side, the pistol still in the bloody hand. Wend kicked it out of his fingers, and it spun across the planking. Then he pressed his knee onto the lad's chest, pinning him to the floor, and slammed his right fist into the boy's face. Immediately he lay stunned and unresisting. Wend announced to the room in general, "We've had enough of this. Someone find Sheriff Smith or one of his men."

Phillip Bush shouted out from the counter, "Good work, Eckert. And I've already sent one of the kitchen boys running after him."

Wend nodded to Bush, then looked up at the Irishman. "That was an elegant move with the sword. It would seem you've had some experience."

"The sword is a very useful tool, if you are trained and practiced in its use." O'beirne slid the blade back into its sheath. "And thank you for dealing with the second pistol and the lad himself. Frankly, I didn't have any particular desire to harm him further. He's simply a bit naive and misguided about his sister's amorous inclinations and willingness to employ guile."

"So I gathered from your words."

"Yes, I'm afraid the young lady didn't have a clear idea whose child she was bearing so settled on me as a likely candidate."

Wend nodded. "One can find oneself in the wrong place at the right time."

O'beirne laughed. "Indeed, sir!"

Wend motioned to his table. "Why don't you take a seat while we're waiting for Sheriff Smith."

"My pleasure, sir, and I'll stand you a drink for your service." He sat down.

"My name's Wend Eckert. I have a farm a few miles east of here."

"A pleasure, Mr. Eckert. Shay O'beirne, of no particular place at the moment."

Wend grinned and said wryly, "I gathered as much."

Bush himself served the pair two whiskies. O'beirne tasted his and looked up at the innkeeper. "As I said before being interrupted, this is very fine stuff. Where do you get it?"

Bush grinned broadly, "Why, sir, from the very man you are sitting with."

The Irishman raised an eyebrow and said, "So you are a distiller by trade?"

Wend shook his head. "Not really. I'm the partner of a Scotsman who runs a distillery at my farm. I myself have no skill in producing liquor."

"And so, sir, I may assume you are a planter with significant acreage?"

"An incorrect assumption, sir. I have but two hundred acres which produces food for my family and animals. Actually, I'm a gunsmith by trade."

"Ah yes, how interesting. And how do you happen to be wearing that uniform? Are you an officer of the local militia?"

Bush interrupted. "He's the captain of a company of light foot the county is sending up to Washington's army."

O'beirne raised an eyebrow. "Ah, is that the case, now?"

Wend nodded. "Indeed, sir. In fact I'm just on my way back from a recruiting muster."

"And when is this company going north?"

"Just a few weeks. We want to do some training before we march. Probably will leave in late May, to be there for the summer campaign. We've heard that Washington may be bringing his army south to New York from Boston."

"Indeed, that's the expectation in Philadelphia, from whence I have just come."

At that moment Sheriff Smith and one of his men entered the common room. He looked down at the prostrate boy, who was showing signs of starting to awaken. Smith looked at Wend. "What's going on here, Eckert?"

Wend gave him a brief summary of the encounter and asked, "Why not put him in the jail for a couple of days, to allow Mr. O'beirne to continue his travel southward and for the lad to cool his ardor?"

"That can be arranged." Smith looked at O'beirne. "What's the boy's name?"

"Harold Waterman. His father's a rather substantial merchant in Philadelphia. My dear sheriff, I'll be on my way in the morning. I have no intention of proffering charges, and if you could have someone escort him northward, say to the fords on the Potomac, I'd be exceedingly grateful."

Smith motioned to his deputy. "Pick the lad up and take him to the cells." He looked back to O'beirne. "Don't worry, we'll disabuse him of following you. And now I'm going back to my good wife and my supper while it still has some warmth."

After Smith's departure Wend asked, "If you don't mind, Shay, what is your profession?"

"The practice of armed violence, offered at a certain price to any in need of my skill. I have done service for many princes in Europe. I've served the Dutch and in the armies of several German provinces. And assorted others."

"I should have guessed. And the promise of war has brought you to the colonies?"

"Precisely. I had it in mind to offer my services to your Continental Congress. However, just as I was in the process of introducing myself to various members, this bother with the Waterman family developed, and I was forced to take quick leave."

"How unfortunate. Why did you choose to ride south?"

"I heard stories of a town called Charleston in South Carolina, and it rather appealed to me. Their representative to the congress mentioned at one point that they were raising regiments and that a position of captain or major was not out of the question."

"So you have held the rank of captain in the past?"

O'beirne waved his hand dismissively. "Of course. My dear fellow, understand that I've been at this for a good while."

Wend took a sip of his drink and did some thinking. The silence pervaded the table.

O'beirne stared at Wend and finally said, "You look like you are turning something over in your mind."

"Yes, as a matter of fact, I was thinking of offering you a place in my company. There's a spot for a lieutenant available."

"A lieutenancy? You're thinking of offering me first lieutenant of your company?"

"Well, not first lieutenant, actually. That duty is filled by a very good man. But I'm in desperate need of a good second lieutenant." Wend looked carefully at the Irishman to see how he would react. It was much as he had expected.

"*Second lieutenant?*" O'beirne's face quickly formed a scowl. "My dear Wend, after my years of service, I cannot possibly consider such service. I'd not respect myself, and I think you wouldn't respect me if I accepted. No, I appreciate your thought, but it's out of the question."

Wend shrugged. "Well, it was just a passing idea. It occurred to me that you might consider it to avoid the long ride south without any certainty of employment. You know, a bird in hand and all that." He raised a finger. "And of course, our service is only for a year. It would get you into the army, where with your experience, you could probably arrange a transfer to service as a captain when the year was up."

"No, my friend, I'd rather take my chances in the South. So I'll be on my way in the morning."

"Well, then, shall we have supper together? I'm famished, and I have a long ride tonight back to my farm."

"Sounds like a capital idea, Captain Eckert." He looked around the crowded room. "It would seem this is a popular place. Do they have good fare here?"

"The best in town." He waved to Bush. "Show Mr. O'beirne what you're offering tonight."

—m—

The afternoon after the recruiting muster at the German village, Wend stood with Newkirk in a field near the company's camp. In the background the beating of a drum could be heard. Flannagan's oldest boy, thirteen-year-old Harvey, was training to become a company drummer. Listening to the sounds, Wend reflected that he had a way to go before he became competent.

In the field Donegal had the company broken into squads, each one drilling under a corporal. Flannagan and Wilder were moving around, supervising the activity.

Newkirk observed, "They're getting good. Much better than any militia I've seen."

Wend agreed. "Indeed they are. But they must get even better if we're to match the British. Donegal will teach them some moves our militia has never known."

Newkirk thought a moment and responded, "Well, we are running out of time. The company has to be ready to go north in just a few weeks, and we won't get the German recruits until tomorrow."

"You're right about that, Reese." Wend thought a moment. "It's time to start training the men in skirmish order. We'll put the nine new Germans at parade ground drill and have the rest in the field exercising open order starting tomorrow afternoon. The pattern for the company as a whole will be marching drill in the mornings, skirmish drill in the afternoons."

"Right, sir. I'll get with Donegal and Flannagan to make plans." Newkirk made a face. "I hate to bring this up again, sir, but is there any progress on naming the second lieutenant?"

Wend felt a brief flash of irritation at Newkirk's reminder, only a couple of days since he brought it up before. But it passed when he had to admit to himself that the lieutenant was right and it was the second in command's job to focus on the training of the company. "Yes, I've got to look at that list of men that Rutledge gave me and make a selection." He looked over at Newkirk. "I met the perfect man for the job yesterday at the Golden Buck, but he wasn't interested."

"Oh, would I know the man?"

"Decidedly not. He was a traveler passing through town. But he's a mercenary with considerable experience in Europe."

Newkirk frowned. "You offered the commission to a man you had just met?"

Wend laughed. "It was under rather unique circumstances that allowed the man to demonstrate his skills. But in any case, his knowledge would have been good for us."

A voice from behind Wend said, "Well, Captain Eckert, I would quite agree with you about that."

Wend spun around to see O'beirne standing a few feet away, reins of his horse in hand. After the shock of seeing the Irishman abated, he said, "Well, Mr. O'beirne, I hadn't expected to meet you here. I thought you'd be miles down the Great Wagon Road by now."

"Ah now, Captain, here's the truth of it: I spent a restless night thinkin' your offer over. And damned if the more I thought about it, the more sense it started to make. I said to myself, *Why ride hundreds of miles to the south for an uncertain chance to join the army when I can get there by taking up with these Virginia fellows?* The upshot of it was that by morning I had decided to accept your kind offer. That's why I'm here now, reporting for duty, if that offer is still open."

Wend looked at the sun, realizing how low it was in the sky. A thought struck him. "What took you so long to get here? It's only a few hours' ride from town. You could easily have been here by noon."

"Well, now, I took the liberty of seeing a tailor to have him measure me for one of those gallant blue and red uniforms like you are wearing. And then to get a few more items for my kit." He shrugged. "But if you've changed your mind, Captain, I can mount up, head back to town, tell the tailor to forget about it, and then take the road to the south."

Wend laughed. "The offer's still open." He pointed up the hill to the Baird house. "Go on up there and see Alice Baird. She'll arrange for you to have a place to sleep and keep your kit. Then in the morning, you can show me I made the right decision in asking you to join us."

O'beirne's lips formed into a crooked smile. "And how am I to do that?"

"You start helping us train these men. Particularly in open-field skirmishing and light-infantry tactics."

"That I can do, my captain. I've led light companies, and I've worked with jaegers. I know exactly what needs to be done. Give me a couple of weeks, and you'll have the best skirmishers in the colonies."

Newkirk shot O'beirne a skeptical glance. "That's a big boast, sir, for an unemployed mercenary. Perhaps a little modesty would be in order until you demonstrate that you can deliver what you promise."

A broad smile spread across the Irishman's face. "Mr. Newkirk, it seems I'm no longer unemployed. And if I may be so bold, mark this: if I said it, you can rest assured I will accomplish what I promise. Let's strike a bargain, Mr. Newkirk. You mind your business as first lieutenant, attending to the well-being of the men and the administration of the company, and I'll attend to the training of the men. Rest assured, if you watch me work and see the results, you'll have no complaint."

Newkirk's face reddened. He was about to retort when Wend raised a hand. "Reese, there's no doubt he's making some strong claims. But we owe him a chance to show what he can do."

O'beirne grinned. "Aye now, that's all I ask, and I thank you, captain." He turned to Newkirk. "Now, Mr. Newkirk, I think in a few days, we'll understand each other and become the best of friends."

Newkirk simply stared at the Irishman for a long moment, then said, "I sincerely hope I'm not disappointed in that." Then he turned and strode off toward where Donegal was standing.

Wend put a hand on O'beirne's arm. "Here, I'll go with you up to the Bairds' house and introduce you to Alice."

The two began walking up the hill. Wend said, "Let me make a point to you, Shay. I'm well aware that you have more experience in military service, particularly in European-style warfare, than either Newkirk or I. Our education, if you will, is in fighting Indian warriors in the forest and bush."

"Indeed, sir."

"And, Shay, it seems you are somewhat older than both of us."

O'beirne smiled. "It had occurred to me."

"Yes. Well, here's my point. I believe that Reese is worried that you might find it hard to become subordinate to him and offer the proper respect to him in his position as first lieutenant. That feeling could lead to untoward friction within the company. I'm asking you, as the older man, to make the effort to ensure that doesn't happen."

"I believe I understand, Captain."

"Be sure you do. Because if I think you aren't working well with Reese or are causing any disturbance within the company, you'll find yourself in need of another position immediately. Do I make myself clear?"

O'beirne reddened slightly but then flashed a wide Irish grin. "Perfectly, sir. And I *do* admire a man such as yourself who speaks plainly and likes to make himself understood at the very beginning."

Wend responded with his own grin. "Excellent. Now let me introduce you to Alice."

That last day of April brought an unusually warm evening, so that Wend and Peggy were sitting out on the front porch after supper. They had drinks in hand, watching the last of the sunset.

Peggy cleared her throat and said, "I met your new lieutenant, that O'beirne fellow, when he arrived today. He knocked on the door to ask directions to the company's camp."

"Oh yes, I was going to tell you about him. He's a professional soldier. Quite experienced."

"I'd say mercenary instead of professional. And yes, he had *experience* written all over him. Experience with war, experience with men, and considerable experience with women." She looked at Wend, gave him a knowing look, and said, "He damn well was undressing me with his eyes while I was talking to him."

"Well, my dear, I should expect that you are quite used to that."

"Of course I am. I was just pointing out to you that he was rather brazen in his gaze."

"I think that could be expected, given his background, as you so astutely pointed out."

Peggy took a sip of the whiskey. "I've been wondering why you were so impetuous as to give him the job immediately upon meeting him. Particularly when you have a list from Rutledge of men who are well-known in the county."

Wend told Peggy about the altercation in the Golden Buck and how well the Irishman had acquitted himself.

"So you were impressed with his military skills?"

"Yes, that was important. But the fact is, I gave him the job precisely because he wasn't on Rutledge's list."

Peggy's head snapped around to look at her husband. "Excuse me? Please explain that."

"My other two officers were essentially chosen by Rutledge. They forced young Childers on me for political reasons. And Newkirk was a favorite in Wood's company last year."

"So? I don't understand what you are getting at; it's a Frederick County company. Why wouldn't the officers be familiar to everyone?"

"That's not quite the point. The fact is, Newkirk and Childers actually owe their positions to people on the Committee of Safety, not me. I accepted them based on committee recommendations, not my independent choice."

"All right. How does that reflect on your choice of O'beirne?"

"He owes his job to me, not the committee."

"Ah yes—I think I'm beginning to see what motivated you. It is a question of loyalty?"

"Yes. Let me spell it out: if problems develop in the company— say, dissension among the men or dissatisfaction about decisions I make—Newkirk and Childers might report that back to Rutledge or Wood and this might lead to me having to explain myself to the committee."

"You mean they might, in essence, be spies for the committee?"

"In a sense, yes."

Peggy made a face. "I think you're being overly worried. You can't deny that the committee has shown great faith in you. And young Childers seems to hold you in much respect."

Wend shrugged. "Perhaps. But one thing is sure—O'beirne will have every reason to support me in a pinch."

Peggy took a drink, then said, "Well, in any case, the decision's been made about O'beirne. Send your wild Irishman up to see me tomorrow so I can take his measurements for the hunting shirt and breeches. I've got the ones made for you and the other two officers, and I should get his done as rapidly as possible. Time is dwindling before you march off."

Wend spent the next morning in the workshop, working on the pistols promised to Gerston's shop in Alexandria. It was a pleasure to be able to take his mind off the needs of the company for at least a short time and focus on the simplicity of the mechanics of a firelock mechanism. However, just before noon he was interrupted by Ensign Childers.

"Sir, Mr. Newkirk sends his respects and wanted me to tell you that the German recruits are here. All nine of them, sir. He thought you'd want to come down to the camp and look them over."

Wend looked up from his workbench. "Indeed I do, Edward." He stood up and took off his apron. "Let's walk on down to the camp."

When they arrived, the nine men were settling their belongings into tents under the supervision of Corporal Jensen. Newkirk and Donegal were standing together, watching what was going on.

Wend said to Newkirk, "Reese, let's get these men in line so I can talk to them."

The first lieutenant called out to Jensen, and shortly the men were in line. Wend looked at Donegal. "Are any of these men riflemen?"

Donegal nodded. "Aye, three of them. They brought their firelocks."

Wend said, "Have them fetch their rifles."

Wend moved along the other six men, asking their names and background while the other three got their rifles. When they came back, Wend inspected the weapons. Two were what he called "southern style," functional but with few carvings. Then he took the third in hand and was surprised.

"Where did you get this?"

"*Ja*, I bought it off a widow. Three years ago it was. I liked the grain of the wood and the carvings on the stock. Ans she was willing to sell it cheap. Sure, she needed money, I think."

"Do you know who made it?"

"No, sir, I can't say. There are some initials and a number scribed on the top of the barrel, just in front of the lock, but I don't know what they mean."

"They're WJE. And they stand for Wendelmar Johann Eckert."

"Well, sir, he sounds like a good German gunmaker. I can say the firelock shoots real well."

Newkirk was smiling and Donegal laughed outright. "Do you know who this is, Schreiber?"

"*Ja*, it's the captain. Captain Eckert."

Then a funny look came over the lad's face. He looked up at Wend. "Sir, did you make this firelock?"

"Sure enough, Private. About ten years ago. It was one of the first I made after I came to Frederick County from Pennsylvania." Then Wend thought of something. "Did I hear that your name is Schreiber?"

"*Ja*, Joseph Schreiber, my captain."

"Are you by chance related to Reverend Ludwig Schreiber?"

"*Ja*, indeed. He is my father."

Wend was stunned. Then he said, "I met your father a few days ago. He was not in favor of encouraging the men of his congregation to enlist for our cause. He declined to announce our recruiting muster. How is it that you have enlisted?"

The young man shrugged. "I have some different ideas than my father. He is from the old country. I was born here, and I like the idea that we make our own country. So when I heard from a friend that they were taking men for a new company, I decided to join. I am old enough to make my own decisions."

"I should think your father would not have been happy."

"It is not the first time my father and I have not been of the same mind. And I am a very good shot with the rifle. I think I can help Virginia become separate from England."

"That's a noble sentiment, Joseph." Then Wend thought of something. "Let's see how these three riflemen can shoot."

Newkirk raised his eyebrows. "Right now, sir?"

"Sure, why not?" He turned to Donegal. "Have someone set up a target. Let's say, one hundred paces." He looked at the three new men. "That's a reasonable distance for sharpshooting in battle."

Donegal had a man set up a piece of flat wood at that distance. Meanwhile the three men carefully loaded their firelocks.

Wend said, "You'll shoot while standing. No bracing or lying down."

The first man, Hoffman, shrugged and stepped up to the mark Wend had made in the dirt. He raised his rifle and fired almost immediately.

Donegal had a man run down and bring back the target. Hoffman had shot well; the ball had pierced the plank about six inches to the left and a little below the center.

The runner returned the target to its place down range, and the next man, Schact, carefully aimed and fired. His ball was about four inches directly above the center.

Schreiber stepped up to the line. Wend watched carefully. The lad exuded confidence as he checked out his lock, then reached up and wiped off the front sight. Just before putting the butt to his shoulder, he looked over at Wend and smiled. Then he raised the rifle, quickly sighted, and fired in one smooth motion.

Donegal motioned to the runner. "Na go fetch the mark, lad."

The runner brought the target back and handed it to Donegal, who looked at it, smiled, and handed it to Wend. Schreiber had placed his ball about one inch to the right of dead center. Wend held it up so all of the men could see it. "A very nice shot. Obviously Private Schreiber has practiced extensively."

Schreiber grinned broadly.

Then Hoffman said, "There is talk, Captain, that you are an expert marksman. My father told me that you were almost as good as Captain Daniel Morgan, who is the best in Frederick County." He waved into the distance. "Maybe you would show us how you shoot?"

Donegal raised his eyebrows and shot a quick look at Wend.

Newkirk quickly said, "That's not for you to ask, Hoffman. The captain's job is to lead, not shoot."

Wend stared at Hoffman for a long moment. Then he raised a hand. "It's all right, Reese. I'll take a shot at the target." He motioned to the runner. "Put the target back in the same place." He turned to Schreiber. "Here, let me use your rifle."

Schreiber grinned. "Yes, sir. I'll load it for you."

Wend shook his head. "No, Schreiber, I'll load it myself. Give me your horn and a ball and a patch."

Wend carefully measured out the powder and poured it down the barrel, then patched the ball and rammed it home. He smiled at Schreiber. "You've molded the ball well; it's a good, tight fit."

Then he primed the pan and turned toward the target. Within an instant he aimed and fired. Handing the rifle back to Schreiber, he had momentary doubt about the accuracy of his shot. He hadn't been practicing lately.

The runner retrieved the target, and Wend sighed in relief. His shot was a fraction of an inch to the left of Schreiber's, overlapping it slightly, so that there appeared to be a double-wide hole.

Newkirk exclaimed, "By God, dead center, sir!"

The nine recruits gathered around, nodding among themselves.

Donegal, in his best parade-ground voice, called out to Jensen. "Corporal, na we've spent enough time playin' with firelocks. Get these men busy starting drilling. Time's wasting, and they're behind the other men."

As Jensen shepherded his flock away, Wend turned to Newkirk. "How are the others doing in the skirmish training?"

"Very well, sir." Newkirk made a crooked smile. "I have to admit, O'beirne knows his business, at least in that regard. He and Wilder have been keeping them at it and showing them how it's done."

"Excellent, Reese." Wend looked around the camp and saw that Martha Flannagan and the other women were busy at kettles, preparing stew. The aroma aroused Wend's hunger. He looked at the sun. "Time for me to go up to the house for my dinner. I'll come by later in the day to watch some of the drilling."

Shay O'beirne lounged at the counter in the Golden Buck, a cup of whiskey at hand, in the late afternoon. The whiskey was incidental to his presence. He was primarily concerned with talking up a youthful and very pretty tavern maid named Jenny Croft, and his goal was a night of intimate pleasure with the young lady.

O'beirne was doing very well with buxom, blond-haired Jenny when he saw Newkirk enter the common room from outside and stand by the door, surveying the interior. Both men had come into town for business. Newkirk was ordering supplies for the company. Shay had pleaded the need to visit a tailor to complete his wardrobe since he had left Philadelphia on short notice. Shay thought, *Hopefully he'll see some friend and go talk with him, allowing me to be alone with Jenny.* However, his wish was dashed when Newkirk came over to the bar beside him and ordered a glass of ale.

The first lieutenant said, "Well, it took some searching, but I found the right kind of paper for cartridges."

O'beirne nodded. "Well, then we can have the lads start making them up tomorrow in the evening after drill is over."

Newkirk nodded. "My thought exactly." He took lifted his cup and took a sip.

There was a pause in conversation. Shay was thinking how he could arrange to be alone with Jenny again when a stranger entered and came up to the counter on the other side of Newkirk. He pointed to Reese's ale and called out to Jenny, "I'll have some of that, if you please."

The man looked at the two uniforms and said, "Well now, do we have officers of the local militia? Was there a muster today?"

Shay looked the man over. He was of somewhat underaverage height, overweight, and dressed in the rough clothes of a traveling man of some type. Without explaining their uniforms, he asked, "What business are you in, sir?"

Jenny delivered the ale, and the traveler said, "I'm a dealer of leather goods. Here for court day tomorrow. You come by the square, you'll see me selling out of my cart, with tables set up for display of my goods."

Newkirk said, "Are you new to Winchester? I know most of the regular vendors, and I don't recall seeing you."

"Ah now, sir, you are *very* observant. *Very* observant indeed. I've only been here once before, a couple of months ago. Actually, that was when I was working my way south along the Great Wagon Road. I've been selling my goods down in lower Virginia and North Carolina. Now I'm on my way back to my home in Wills Creek, Fort Cumberland, if you will."

"I hope you find profitable sales tomorrow."

The peddler took a gulp of his ale. "I expect to; this was a memorable place when I was here last." He smiled to himself. "The sales were indeed good." He sat quietly thinking for a moment, then he turned to the other two with a conspiratorial leer on his face. "And I found the answer to a mystery. A mystery of many years."

O'beirne said, "A mystery, friend? Now everyone likes to hear about a good mystery. Do you care to share it with us?" He leaned forward to look past Newkirk and asked, "Incidentally, might we know your name?"

"Howard McColley, sir. But of course, everyone just calls me Howie. Howie the leather man."

"Ah yes, easy to remember. Now, Howie, what about this mystery you resolved here in Winchester?"

"Well, on that day two months ago, just at the end of sales, a raven-haired woman came to the wagon of a man next to me—an ironmonger named Rhys—and looked over his wares." McColley took another gulp of his drink. "And I was startled to recognize the woman. She was originally from my own home village of Sherman Mill, north of Carlisle in Pennsylvania."

Newkirk said, "Well, I assume you had a fond reunion with the woman?"

McColley snorted. "Not likely! The woman was no friend of mine. As a young girl, she had been a server at her father's tavern. And more than that, she had tarted herself. In plain fact, she was a favorite whore of traveling men from all over the Allegheny Valley, who paid handsomely for bein' entertained in the hay of her father's stable."

O'beirne said, "Ah yes, I see. But what made her presence here a mystery?"

"Well, she had a young man of the valley, a wagoner who she was keepin' company with and a great friend of mine."

Newkirk raised an eyebrow. "You mean when she wasn't in the stable with paying gentlemen?"

"That's it. They had an understanding that they'd be married and they'd use the money she'd earned to help move out of the valley to a larger town. But then, like any whore, she crossed him. She got engaged to a German gunsmith who had come to the valley after his parents had been massacred by the Mingo on Forbes Road. Well, my friend didn't like it much."

O'beirne said, "I can imagine. And what happened?"

"I'll tell you what happened: Soon enough, the two men got into a fight in her father's tavern. The gunsmith smashed my friend's head against the fireplace hearth with a log, and he ain't been right in the head since." He looked at the two officers in turn. "And then the gunsmith and the harlot got married and left the valley right after the wedding. They just disappeared. Everyone wondered where they went." He shrugged. "And so I was surprised to see the woman, Peggy McCartie, here in Winchester. Of course, her married name is Eckert." He shook his head. "There she was, dressed all fine-lookin' in a pretty gown, for all anyone would know, acting like a middling lady with money behind her. And as she was shopping, other finely dressed ladies came by and was talkin' to her like she was somebody important."

Newkirk and O'beirne exchanged looks. Reese asked McColley, "Did you mention this Mrs. Eckert's background to anyone in town?"

The leather monger took a deep pull on his cup. "Just to Rhys. He and I went out to a tavern later, and I told him all about her, but then I went to my rooms and didn't see anyone before I pulled out in the morning." He grinned. "But I aim to spread the word about the high-and-mighty Mrs. Eckert this time. I'll fix that woman and her Dutch gunsmith." He pointed to them. "That's why I'm lettin' you know the truth about her."

O'beirne replied, "And you're right, Howie, it is an intriguing story indeed. Imagine a harlot masquerading as a decent lady. It's no more than justice to expose her and set things right."

"Damn right, Lieutenant. I'll get back at her—and that Wend Eckert—for playing foul on my friend."

Shay nodded. "Indeed, McColley. They deserve nothing better." He put on a thoughtful face. "But all that aside, I'm glad we met, for I might have some business for you."

"Business? How do you mean, sir?"

"Yes, I need a good set of saddle holsters for my pistols. Might you have some in your stock?"

Howie McColley's face lit up. "Indeed I do; in fact, I have several examples. You come by tomorrow, and I'll show them to you."

O'beirne frowned. "Tomorrow? I'm afraid that won't do. I must be back to my company camp tomorrow morning early. Could you possibly show me them tonight?"

"Well, they're in my cart. We could go out and take a look, if you're serious, sir."

"I'm very serious about doing some business with you out there." He looked at Newkirk. "You coming along, Reese?"

The lieutenant nodded and said, "Yes, Shay, I'm with you on this." The three walked out to the yard, where McColley's cart was parked.

The peddler pointed to a one-horse cart parked in the corner of the yard and said, "We have to hurry. The evening light is fading."

O'beirne looked over at Newkirk and smiled at him. Then he reached up and grabbed McColley by the collar, spun him around, and hit him full force in the face. The leather dealer buckled at the knees, and Shay quickly pulled him, half walking, half dragging along, into the stable.

The stable boy, who was graining horses in their stalls, looked over and asked, "What's happening, Mr. O'beirne?"

"Mr. McColley is not feeling well," explained the Irishman. "He wants to head back to his home tonight instead of staying for market day tomorrow. Be a good lad and hitch up his horse and cart."

The boy looked at the obviously distressed peddler. "Sir, I don't understand. Why would he want to leave if he's sick?"

Newkirk said, "We understand he wants to see his own doctor and be under the care of his good wife."

Shay said, "That's quite right." He reached into his pocket and pulled out a coin. "This should help you understand, lad."

The young man looked at the coin and then at McColley. "Yes, sir. I see what you mean. He definitely needs to get home." Then he went to a stall and led out a horse into the courtyard.

O'beirne said to Newkirk, "While he gets the cart hitched up, get our horses out and saddled."

Newkirk nodded and headed for the stalls.

Meanwhile, McColley was starting to regain his strength. O'beirne grabbed him by his shirt and slammed him against the side of a stall. Then he pulled a knife from inside his coat and put it to the man's throat. "Mr. McColley, it happens that the two of us are not going to let you besmirch Mrs. Eckert or Eckert himself. Now, do you feel the fine edge of that blade against your neck?"

McColley nodded vigorously. Then Shay continued, "Good. Now we all know that a single slice across the throat is the quickest and most efficient way to send a man to eternity. At this moment you have to make up your mind about how you are going to depart Winchester. You can leave driving your cart, or we can send you to your Maker right now, throw your earthly remains into the cart, and transport you several miles to the north and into a grove along the road, where you and the wrecked cart will be found some weeks in the future, after the varmints have gobbled up most of your body." He paused and gave Howie a demonic grin. "Nod your head right now if you'd prefer to drive out, or the next thing you'll be seeing is your Maker or the devil himself."

McColley nodded rapidly.

O'beirne pricked the man's neck with the point of the knife, and blood trickled down onto his collar. "Howie, my dear man, remember how that felt, because if you try anything, you'll feel the rest of the blade."

Shay grabbed McColley by his coat and escorted him out to the yard, where the stable boy was just finishing hitching the horse. Meanwhile, Newkirk had their horses ready. Shay put the point of his knife in McColley's side. "Now get up into the seat and take the reins."

The peddler, who was now shaking uncontrollably, did as he was told.

Shay called out, "Newkirk! Get mounted and lead our friend out to the road!" Then he looked up at McColley. "You follow the lieutenant. And don't be foolish about anything. We have pistols and won't hesitate."

McColley slapped the reins on the horse's back and drove out of the yard behind Newkirk.

O'beirne handed another coin to the stable boy. "Now, what did you see here tonight?"

"Nothing to remark on, Mr. O'beirne. A traveling man name McColley came out with you, told me he was not feeling well and wanted to begin traveling for his home. He definitely had the chills; he was shaking horrible-like. He left, and you kind gentlemen left with him, to make sure he got a good safe start on the road in the dark."

"Aye, my good lad! That's exactly right. I can see you have a bright future ahead of you!"

And with that, Shay mounted his horse and followed after the cart.

The better part of an hour later, and about three miles northward on the Great Wagon Road, they came to a deep creek with a bridge over it. Shay rode up from his position behind the cart and called to McColley to rein in his horse. Once he had done so, the Irishman looked down at the peddler. "Now, my fine fellow, we are going to leave you to make your own progress. Listen sharp and heed my words: if I ever see or hear about you being in Winchester again, I'll hunt you down and finish this night's work by sending you to your rewards. Do you have any doubt to my sincerity?"

McColley looked up, a look of pure hatred on his face. "No, you bastard, I don't."

Newkirk, who had come up on the other side of the wagon, held up the peddler's heavy horse pistol and then tossed it high in the air so that it dropped into the middle of the stream and sank into the deep water.

Shay waved northward. "Now off you go, McColley. And mind you heed my words."

Without saying another word, the peddler slapped the reins on his horse and moved out. The two lieutenants sat watching him as he crossed the bridge and continued along the wagon track.

Newkirk looked over at the Irishman. "Do you think there's any truth about that story he told about Mrs. Eckert?"

O'beirne eyed his companion. "I'm confident *every* word of it is true. That oaf is not clever enough to make up a tale like that."

A look of shock came over Newkirk's face. "But Peggy Eckert, a harlot? How can you believe that?"

"Think on it, Reese. Think of tavern girls you've known. There are many temptations and easy money. A young backcountry girl might jump at the chance for hard money."

"But in her own father's tavern? Never would I have thought of such a thing. Look at what a refined woman she has become."

"Reese, have you ever been to Europe?"

"You know I haven't."

"Well, in London and Paris, and other large cities, there are places called Women's Social Associations, or some such title." Shay paused and grinned at his comrade. "A noble title, but in fact they are elegant brothels where ladies of elevated status have banded together to practice the oldest profession. They are women of good birth who have fallen on hard times and wish to live in the style to which they are accustomed, at any personal cost. And their clientele are men of the same class who desire the company of lovely and well-mannered ladies."

Newkirk commented, "I assume you have frequented such places?"

The Irishman grinned broadly. "Indeed, when my purse permitted. My personal favorite was one called the New Female Coterie, in London." He was quiet for a long moment, then said, "But the point I wish to make is that on more than a few occasions, ladies of these associations have been able to marry well and live a respectable life with an understanding husband and society affording a blind eye to their past transgressions."

Newkirk said, "I think I see where you are headed."

"Yes, we need to consider the idea of *redemption*. Peggy Eckert was accepted by a good man, has raised a fine family of children, and has become a pillar of Winchester's society. It would be a shame to let youthful indiscretion bring her down now."

Newkirk added, "Not to mention she has used her good offices to organize the women of the county to provide the company with uniforms."

Shay looked over at the first lieutenant. "I propose we both vow that what we have learned tonight will never be passed on." He paused, looked at the cart, which was about to disappear around a bend in the road. "For I venture to say that we both have a debt to Wend Eckert. He pulled you away from a bad situation after the death of your wife, and he provided me employment when I was on the run and unsure from whence my next farthing would come."

Newkirk offered O'beirne his hand. "That's an easy vow to make and an easy one to keep."

The Irishman accepted his hand. Then they turned their horses southward.

Reese looked at the darkening evening sky. "It's going to be a fairly long ride back to Eckert Ridge. We'll have to push it."

The Irishman grinned. "*You* ride back to camp. "I've got some very important unfinished business back at the Golden Buck. I'll be back in camp before noon tomorrow."

CHAPTER TEN
MAY MANEUVERS

Lord Dunmore sat in his chair, mildly uncomfortable as he braced himself against the movement of his flagship as it rolled to its anchor cable in the choppy waves of the Elizabeth River. He turned to his senior aide. "Harbridge, this blasted wind, kicking up the river, is a bother. We need some real spring weather."

"Yes, my lord, a calm would be quite welcome. But when Hammond arrives, we may have news which will get us out of the river and allow us to return to terra firma."

The secretary, youthful Dudley Fellows, spoke up. "Can't be soon enough for me. I look forward to being able to write without having to hold myself and everything on my desk steady against the ship's movement."

At that moment there was a knock on the door and Steward Howser swung it open. He turned and announced, "Governor, Captain Hammond is here."

"Well, have him come in immediately!"

Howser stepped back, and the captain strode in, followed by Captain Price Coleman of HMS *Otter*.

Dunmore boomed out. "Well, Hammond, I hope you have some good news for me!"

The captain made a tight smile. "I think you will be happy with our report, Your Lordship." He motioned to Coleman. "I believe the *Otter*'s exploration has found the most advantageous site for our base of operations."

"Indeed, sir, and would you care to inform me?"

Hammond smiled and nodded. "It's an island in the bay, just over thirty miles from where we lie now. It is close to our preferred area of campaigning and will provide us with all the natural features we require." He motioned to the *Otter*'s captain. "Price will explain completely."

Coleman nodded to the governor. "Yes, my lord. The name of the place is Gwynn's Island. It is about three square miles in size and located near the mouth of the Piankatank River." He walked to the table and unrolled a chart he had been carrying. "We drew this ourselves on board the *Otter*, so it is a bit crude and hardly to accurate scale. But I believe, sir, it is adequate to show all the major features."

They gathered around the table.

Coleman pointed to the island. "As you can see, it is located just south of the mouth of the river. It is triangular in shape with its longest side toward the mainland shore to the east. It is separated from the mainland by a narrow channel called Milford Haven. There are two good anchorages for our ships. A large one just between the mouth of the Piankatank and the northwest coast of the island which could take most of our ships. There is also room for several ships to anchor in Milford Haven itself."

Dunmore nodded as he looked over the map. He pointed to a square marking on the island itself. "What does that signify?"

Coleman said, "Sir, there's a large plantation on the island. That represents the location of the main house, farm buildings, and slave quarters."

Harbridge asked, "Do you know who owns the plantation?"

"Of course, sir. We spoke with him. It's a certain John Randolph Grymes."

Dunmore exclaimed, "Why, I am acquainted with the man! Met him several times in Williamsburg." He looked around the table. "Is he loyal to the Crown?"

Coleman nodded. "Aye, that he is, sir. He professed his loyalty and said he would welcome your presence and our forces on the island."

The governor smiled. "Excellent."

Harbridge looked up from the chart. "What about water? Is it adequate to our needs?"

The *Otter*'s captain nodded. "We didn't search out all the sources ourselves, but Grymes said there were several springs. He thought there was enough for our force. In any case, sir, there are numerous places nearby on the mainland where we could fill our casks."

There were nods around the room.

Harbridge asked, "What about room for a smallpox hospital? Is there sufficient open space that we can set up a facility which can be isolated from our main camps? I needn't tell you how pressing the need is. More than twenty bodies were deposited in the river last night, and that's not unusual."

"There is certainly adequate land for that. In fact, I have in mind a place in a pine grove just inland from the shore on the southern side of the island which will serve admirably for that purpose. Actually, I marked it on the chart." He pointed to the spot.

There was a silence around the table as all present reflected on the situation.

Then Hammond cleared his throat and said, "The island is rather well located for our operational needs. The mouths of several rivers and bays are nearby, within an easy sail of a day or less, specifically the Rappahannock and the Potomac to the north, and to the south, we have Mobjack Bay with its numerous tributaries. These water features will allow us to move expeditions inland by boat when we are ready to take the offensive."

Coleman added, "Also important is that near the island are many smaller bays and creeks, which will facilitate the easy landing and recovery of parties to forage for provisions at nearby farms, plantations, and villages."

Hammond pointed to Milford Haven. "And this is important: the channel will provide a significant obstacle for any rebel attacking force, particularly if we emplace some gun batteries to cover the waters."

Dunmore nodded. "Yes, I quite agree."

Hammond continued, "Accordingly, I would say that Gwynn's is a most favorable location for our base. I submit we should make plans to move our fleet there and occupy it as soon as practicable."

The governor looked over at Harbridge and raised an eyebrow in query for his opinion.

Harbridge moved closer to the chart, took some time running his eyes over it and the surrounding territory, then said, "I second Captain Hammond's recommendation. We should sail as soon as all the ships can be made ready."

Hammond looked around the room. "With favorable winds, it is a day's sail, no more." He raised a finger. "However, I suggest that when we leave, we make a feint. I propose we sail south as long as we are visible from the Norfolk area, as if we were abandoning the Chesapeake and Virginia itself, then once out of sight, head eastward across the Bay and then circle northwest to Gwynn's."

Harbridge shrugged. "Is that of any real value? It seems an unnecessary complication. The rebels will soon discover our presence on the island. There's no hiding a fleet of a hundred vessels."

Hammond stared at Harbridge for a moment. "You are quite right, sir. Inevitably the enemy will find where we have gone, but if we can temporarily delude them that we have sailed away from the Chesapeake, it will give us time to establish ourselves on the island without interference. I intend to start building fortifications on the landward side as soon as we arrive. In any case, the time given to us by a tactical surprise cannot but help us."

Dunmore waved a hand. "Yes, yes, it makes sense. We'll do as the captain recommends." He looked around the room. "Now all of you must do your part to get the fleet ready to sail." He motioned toward Hammond. "I am aware that because of the way we hurriedly abandoned Norfolk, some of the merchant ships are undermanned. You must make sure they have adequate seamen for the voyage."

Hammond nodded. "We will temporarily draft navy seamen to them for the movement."

Harbridge said, "We must get as many provisions and other supplies as are available here, to provide for us until we can develop sources at Gwynn's." He turned to Fellows. "You should begin immediately composing the necessary orders for the fleet's preparations."

The captain nodded. "Yes, my lord."

Then Dunmore smiled broadly at Hammond. "And one more thing: please send a tender out to bring Colonel Northcutt to this ship immediately. I have instructions for him. And HMS *Raven* must be readied for an ocean voyage."

Hammond looked puzzled. "My lord, I fear I don't understand."

"I'm sending Northcutt to Halifax to brief General Howe on our situation here and our plans for the future and to plead our case for reinforcement. Northcutt and the *Raven* will leave as soon as possible."

Hammond stared at the governor for a long moment. "Well, my lord, the *Raven* is a significant asset to my squadron, and I regret her loss, even temporarily. But things shall be done as you wish."

Dunmore beamed. "Well, gentlemen, you all know what must be effected. Let us get moving and start the process, which will surely be successful and ultimately result in the return of Virginia to its rightful place under the rule of king and parliament."

"Now, Colly, I've never seen you look more handsome." Edna Farley was looking over Colleen McGraw as she stood just outside her tent in the early evening light. "That light-green dress really brings out the color of your auburn hair." She moved around to see Colleen's other side. "Yes, all is quite elegant. You're going to have that young lieutenant panting like a dog."

Colleen laughed out loud. "Frankly, I could be dressed in rags, and he'd have the same reaction. He seems endowed with an excess of carnal desire." She smiled tightly. "Well, in that respect, he's going to be quite frustrated."

"In any case, he will be here soon. Do you really believe he's going to have a carriage, like he said?"

Amusement spread over Colleen's face. "In the city of New York right now, with the army encamped throughout the town and all around us? And with many of the senior officers renting houses and bringing their wives? More likely he'll be in a small wagon with a nondescript team. But I won't embarrass him by calling attention to the matter."

"Well, Colleen, he does seem rather well off. I mean, the son of a wealthy planter?"

"I hear most of those southern planters put on a good show when in reality they're heavily in debt."

"What does it matter, if you can benefit from their show?"

Colleen grinned. "A very good point, Edna. And I do intend to enjoy Lieutenant Fairfield's largess tonight. It will be a treat to dine under an actual roof, in the warmth of a fireplace instead of a canvas fly and the draft of spring winds."

At that moment Edna's son, Charlie, came over and said, "That lieutenant from South Carolina is coming up the road."

Colleen grinned and asked, "What kind of conveyance does he have? A farm wagon?"

"Farm wagon? No, ma'am! He's got a carriage with a matched team of blacks. And a driver and two dragoons as outriders."

Colleen and Edna hurried to look down the road toward where Manhattan lay. Colleen saw that Charlie had made no mistake. Geoffrey Fairfield was lounging in the rear seat of an open carriage, its top down. She exclaimed, "Well, I'll be damned."

Edna laughed and said, "Given the line of work we're in, that's certainly true. But at least for tonight, you are blessed with traveling in elegance."

Colleen smiled broadly. "Well, if I'm to face damnation in eternity, at least I should enjoy as much luxury as I can in this life."

The carriage arrived and the driver pulled up the team. Fairfield stepped down, swept his hat off, and bowed to Colleen. "Good evening, Mrs. McGraw. Are you ready for our evening in Manhattan?"

Colleen gave the officer her broadest smile. "Indeed, Lieutenant Fairfield." Then she turned to Charlie. "Could you please fetch my cape?"

"Yes, ma'am. I'd be glad to."

Colleen turned back to Fairfield. "And what time should my people expect me back at the encampment tonight?"

Fairfield raised his eyebrows. "Rather late, I should say. We southerners believe in enjoying a meal in leisurely style."

Charlie arrived with the wrap, and Fairfield took it from him and with the skill of a man who has done the chore often, carefully draped it over Colleen's shoulders. As he did so, he motioned toward the carriage and said, "I would have preferred an enclosed coach, but regretfully such was not available in the town."

Colleen winked at Edna and then turned back to the officer and said, "Yes, that would have been so much *more* comfortable in this chill weather, but we will just have to make do, Mr. Fairfield, won't we?"

He nodded. "Quite." He offered her his hand. "Now, if you are ready, it is time for us to depart if we are to make it to the room I have reserved at the appointed hour."

He handed Colleen up into the carriage, then touched his hat to Edna and hurried around to take his place on the seat beside her.

As the driver turned the carriage around and started off toward the city, Colleen turned to her escort. "Geoffrey, did you say we'd be dining in a private room?"

"Of course, Colleen. We're going to a place called Fraunces' Tavern. It's owned by a man named Samuel Fraunce, but he's turned proprietorship over to his son-in-law, a chap named Charles Robinson. I've made it my business to become friendly with him, even if he does seem to have some blatant loyalist tendencies. The establishment is considered one of the best in town, and the food is quite good. But because it's popular, the common room is always filled with rowdy officers, and it's rather normal for ladies to be dined in quiet privacy."

She laughed. "Geoffrey, hasn't it occurred to you that I grew up in rowdy common rooms?"

Fairfield looked over and smiled. "Then all the more reason for you to be able to enjoy the pleasure of our companionship tonight in elegant and peaceful surroundings."

They rode along, engaged in conversation, for at least a half hour, going from the rural area of the campsite down into the built-up section of Manhattan. Finally they came to a large brick building located at the corner of two streets, and the driver pulled up.

Geoffrey said, "Well, Mrs. McGraw, we have arrived at Mr. Campbell's establishment."

Colleen looked up at the building. "Very impressive, sir. I've never seen a tavern or inn with four stories, if you count the attic where the gables are." She laughed. "But then, I've spent most of my time in small towns."

Fairfield laughed. "Well, I'm told it was originally built as a residence. Which is why it has so many private rooms."

He escorted her into the hall. On one side was a long, spacious common room. The entire place was filled with officers, virtually all holding cups of libation and engaged in raucous conversation. Colleen was aware that many turned to stare at her. Fairfield gave his name to a server, who said, "Ah, yes, sir. Your room is ready. Please follow me."

He led them up a flight of stairs, then down a hall, finally ushering them into a room brightly lighted with many candles and featuring windows looking onto the street below. He pulled out a chair and helped Colleen into her seat. Geoffrey took his own and the server said, "I'll tell the waiter for this room that you are here, and he will arrive momentarily."

Once they were alone, Fairfield smiled at Colleen and said, "I apologize for the brazen stares which you received as we passed through the first floor. These officers have been in the field for a long time, and I don't think they've seen many attractive women at close quarters."

Colleen leaned back in her chair and laughed heartily. "Geoffrey, your southern gallantry is misguided in my case. Brazen stares were the least I had to put up with as a tavern maid and the mistress of a tavern. They faze me not at all."

"Well, Colleen, tonight the men down below saw a beautiful woman, tastefully dressed, who could hold her own with any lady of the gentry in the low country. I doubt they could have resisted looking at you. As for myself, I can picture you looking quite proper in a ballroom or on the veranda of our mansion or of that of any around Charleston."

"Nonsense! Your mother would be scandalized if she had the slightest sense of my history. She would chase me off your property with her riding quirt."

Fairfield was grinning and about to answer when there was a knock on the door. He said, "Ah, that would be our server."

The door opened, and in marched not a server but three officers in well-tailored uniforms. Colleen saw that all were quite young. Two were in their early or midtwenties. The third, who she noticed had a rather swarthy complexion, seemed even younger, probably in his late teens. All were bright-eyed and sported mischievous grins on their faces, undoubtedly fueled by drink.

Fairfield stood up. "Gentlemen, can't you see I've chosen to entertain this lady in private? What has prompted you to be so rude as to interrupt us?"

The oldest of the officers, still grinning, replied, "Come now, Fairfield. You are being quite selfish. And we're all part of Washington's official military family. It is totally impolite for you to keep such a lovely lady to yourself."

The second officer added, "The least you could do is invite us in to share a drink."

"I shall decidedly *not*. And you are quite aware that I am not actually considered part of Washington's military family. My troop is simply under his direct command for field service."

The oldest officer grinned and said, "Well, Geoffrey, you may not be part of the *immediate* family, but we all consider you at least a *cousin*." He bowed and swept his hand in Colleen's direction. "And to be polite, you must as a minimum introduce us to the lady."

Fairfield sighed. "I doubt if the general would feel the same way about my relationship to the staff. However, if it is the only way to get rid of you, I shall make introductions."

Fairfield turned to Colleen. "Mrs. McGraw, may I introduce you to these—*ahem*—gentlemen. We have Captain George Baylor and Captain Caleb Gibbs, aides-de-camp to His Honor Lieutenant General George Washington, commander in chief of the Continental Army." He looked at the youngest officer and said, "And I am afraid I am not familiar with this gentleman, who I do not believe is actually on the staff."

Baylor said, "He's not. This is our good friend Captain Alexander Hamilton. He is late of King's College, here in New York City, but has just taken up duties as commander of an artillery company, the guns of which are emplaced to defend the harbor when the British arrive."

The young, swarthy officer bowed deeply, then said formally, "My pleasure, Mrs. McGraw."

All three officers had displayed looks of concern when they heard the title "Mrs." connected with Colleen's name. Now young Hamilton, in an earnest tone, asked, "Mrs. McGraw, is Lieutenant Fairfield entertaining you because your husband is engaged in business away from the city?"

Colleen made a demure smile. "I'm afraid my husband is far beyond business matters or any earthly activity. He has been in a much better place for several years."

The broad smiles returned to all three officers. Baylor said, "We are indeed sorry for your loss, Mrs. McGraw. Can we take it that *you* reside here in the city?"

Fairfield, whose voice now betrayed considerable irritation, said, "Mrs. McGraw is actually from Fredericktown, Maryland. She is here on mercantile business connected with the army."

Colleen smiled as engagingly as she could at the officers. "Let me be more precise than Geoffrey, gentlemen. I am actually engaged in providing sutler services. My establishment is equipped to move with the army and is currently encamped to the north, in a meadow just at the edge of Manhattan. It is called the Red Vixen Sutler Company, and I hope you'll come patronize us for your needs of various kinds."

Gibbs exclaimed, "You can count on that, Mrs. McGraw."

Colleen thought of a question. "Well, Captain Baylor, since you are on the staff, perhaps I can take this opportunity to ask you the question which is on everyone's lips: Do you really expect the British to come here? And when do you think that will be?"

Baylor looked over at Gibbs, then back at Colleen. "Well, we know that General Howe took his army and the fleet and sailed to Halifax to lick his wounds from the Boston campaign. And recently one of our privateers captured a British transport with soldiers on board—Highlanders. We learned from them that they are sailing for Halifax and that Howe is waiting for more reinforcements from England before he moves. We have word from British sources that his objective will indeed be this city. Howe covets New York to be his headquarters. It has the best harbor in the colonies for the fleet and for supply ships, and the city itself has perfect facilities for housing the headquarters itself. So we are in the process of setting up works to provide for the defense."

Gibbs spoke up. "And Washington is doing everything he can to build his army. Many of the men who were with us at Boston have gone home at the expiration of their one-year enlistment. We're asking for new regiments from all the colonies and for them to send all the militia they can spare."

Colleen frowned and then asked in a thoughtful tone, "So many of your men are new to the army? And largely untrained?"

Baylor nodded. "Regretfully, you are correct." Then he added, "As for the when, Mrs. McGraw, we can't know for sure, but the expectation is that the British will come in early summer."

Colleen responded, "So it is likely that our army actually has some time to get ready for the invasion?"

It was Hamilton who spoke up. "Yes, that's true. But you must understand that the New York area is going to be hard to defend. It is broken up into so many land masses, divided by the harbor and rivers. I fear the British may well be able to find undefended places to land where we won't have been able to place troops."

"That's not very encouraging," responded Colleen.

Baylor answered, "The simple truth is we can't recruit and organize enough troops to defend everywhere. Washington shall have to fortify the key positions and be ready to move men rapidly to where the British come ashore."

Gibbs answered, "That's why we need as many men as we can get. The British will have tens of thousands of men, and we will be lucky to have twenty thousand fit for service."

Colleen had more questions, but at that moment, the waiter entered. He looked around the room and said, "I was told this would be a meal for a couple. Has there been some change in plans?"

Fairfield said in an authoritative voice, "There has most definitely been *no* such change in plans. These *gentlemen* are just leaving." He motioned to Baylor. "Isn't that so, George?"

A grinning Baylor looked at his compatriots, then to Colleen. He made a small bow. "Mrs. McGraw, it has indeed been a pleasure meeting you. We shall now withdraw and leave you to your intimate supper." He smiled knowingly at Fairfield.

Caleb Gibbs said, "And as for myself, I vow to accept the invitation to visit your establishment, Mrs. McGraw." He winked at Fairfield. "Very soon."

Baylor agreed. "I'll be there myself, when duties permit."

The serious young Hamilton said, "It has indeed been a pleasure meeting you, Mrs. McGraw."

With that, all three left the room, and the waiter shut the door behind them. Colleen heard laughter as they walked down the hallway.

The waiter said, "Shall we start with something to drink before supper?"

After ordering drinks, the waiter brought them a bill of fare, and they ordered roasted beef in a sauce.

While waiting for their food, Colleen said, "You didn't tell me you were serving directly under Washington. How did that come about?"

"Well, actually the general was very happy to see us arrive. The army has a desperate shortage of cavalry."

Colleen was puzzled. "Why is that? We have many good horsemen and no lack of animals here in the colonies."

"It's not the men or the horses. It's the proper equipment and training. You have no idea how difficult it is to get a dragoon properly kitted for service."

"Well, South Carolina has managed to do it."

"Yes, but only for a few troops so far. That's why we were able to send only one northward at this time. Think on it. You must have proper saddle and accouterments for the horse, all of which have to be of standardized design. Each cavalryman needs a sword, a pair of horse pistols, and a carbine. There also must be proper leather equipage for him to carry them—slings for the carbines, holsters for the pistols, pouches for his ammunition. It all takes time and money, for those things are not readily available here in the colonies. And then the horses must be trained to perform as a unit, just like soldiers drilling. Beyond that are the uniforms and helmets. Leather or metal helmets must be specially manufactured, which takes time. I assure you, it is quite complex."

Colleen nodded. "I'm beginning to understand."

"The biggest problem we had was procuring enough pistols and carbines. Pistols have to be made to the same standard. And there was an almost total dearth of short-barreled carbines in Carolina. We had to engage several gunsmiths to make enough for the troop, and I can tell you, that took goodly time."

Colleen went silent for a long moment and stared off into the distance at the mention of gunsmiths.

Fairfield caught the look on her countenance. "You seem suddenly bemused. Did something I say cause that?"

She shrugged. "Not really, but your mentioning of gunsmiths caused me to think of a problem I'm facing."

Fairfield picked up his drink and smiled. "Would you care to share that with me? I can be very sympathetic."

Colleen laughed. "You can be as sympathetic as possible, but it won't relieve my worry." She sighed. "I fear I'm about to lose my best girl. Her name is Emily Crider. She's a willowy blonde, not yet twenty, who has a sweet personality and sings like a bird. The men find her very attractive. But she's fallen in love with a young tradesman and wants to marry him."

Her companion's face wrinkled up. "It's not clear to me how my remarks reminded you of your problem."

"Because the man is a gunsmith's apprentice. And he has vowed to come to the army to find her."

"Well, there are many things in time of war which could keep him from making the journey."

"Yes, that had been my hope, but Emily got a letter today which has her exultant. That's why she is so much on my mind. It seems the boy's master has been commissioned captain of a company of foot, and once they recruit all their men, they're coming to join the army. The apprentice, whose name is Andrew Horner, is ready to become a journeyman and will come with the company as a civilian to tend firelocks for soldiers."

"Where are they coming from? At least it may take them a while to get here."

"They're from a town called Winchester in Virginia. Are you familiar with it?"

Fairfield's eyes opened wide for a moment, but then he shrugged and waved his hand dismissively. "Yes, I've heard the name in passing. I believe it's in the Great Valley of Virginia. That will take them many days of travel before they arrive."

"Yes, that's correct. And it happens that I am quite familiar with the man he works for, the captain. He's a German gunsmith I met when I was a tavern maid in York, Pennsylvania." She took a drink and looked at Fairfield playfully. "Actually, I'll admit that as a young girl, I was romantically involved with him. He's from Pennsylvania himself. His name is Wend Eckert."

Fairfield choked on the liquor he had just swallowed. He coughed some out of his lips and quickly put his napkin to his mouth. After a few seconds, he said, "I'm terribly sorry—that went down the wrong way."

Colleen stared at Geoffrey for a long moment. He seemed extremely disturbed. But she simply said, "Well, that happens. I've done that myself."

Then the door opened, and the waiter entered bearing their food on covered plates.

"Well," said Fairfield, "my dear Colleen, shall we forget at least for a while the problems of our lives and enjoy the meal?"

Colleen smiled. "Indeed, let's do so."

—⁂—

After delivering Colleen back to her camp near midnight and heading back toward Manhattan, Fairfield signaled the driver to stop. He called out to Sergeant Quinn, he of the mutilated ear, who was riding as one of the outriders, to join him in the carriage.

"Quinn, you scoundrel, tie your horse to the rear of the carriage and join me here on the seat."

The sergeant complied, and Fairfield signaled the driver to resume their travel. Quinn asked, "Well, Caufield, did you have a successful evening with the young lady?"

A scowl passed over the lieutenant's face. "Damn it, Quinn, watch yourself. That's the second time in the last few days you've called me Caufield instead of Fairfield! Someday you're going to say it in front of somebody who is important and raise questions about me."

"Look, Geoffrey, *Fairfield* is too close to *Caufield*. You should have chosen a name more different from the last one you used."

"I thought it would be easier for you to remember. But obviously I erred." He shrugged. "However, it's too late to change it. So just be more careful."

Quinn looked over at his lieutenant. "What the hell is your real name, anyway? You've used at least four since we've been together."

"That, my dear Quinn, is something you shall never know. Not one soul west of London has ever heard that name, and none shall."

Quinn made a face, then asked, "So how did your night with the lady go? Everything you expected?"

"Of course. I'm well on my way to her bed. It's just a matter of time."

Quinn put his head back and laughed. "That's what you thought with that gunsmith's wife in Winchester. Peggy Eckert was her name. You were confident she was a sure thing, but she was actually leading you on. Then she pulled the bloody rug out from under you in that inn. Fooled you proper, she did. You never got under her skirts. And the witch left you sitting totally nude and cold in a bed chamber with your clothing and pistols lying outside on the ground as your comeuppance. I had to go fetch them for you before anyone found the stuff."

"I could have gone all night without you reminding me of that embarrassment." He looked over at the sergeant. "But it is funny that you bring up Eckert's name, because there is actually some news about him."

"News about that gunsmith? Now how the hell would you have news of him?"

"Prepare yourself, Quinn, for a bit of a shock. It turns out that Mrs. McGraw knows Eckert."

"What? How in the devil's name?"

"Have you noticed they are of about the same age? Well, she allowed as how they were romantically involved in their youth, when she was a tavern maid."

"But just how did it happen that she brought Eckert's name, of all things, up in the first place?"

"One of her tarts is in love with Eckert's apprentice. A youth named Horner. Horner is coming to the army to try to find the girl and marry her. Colleen is upset about losing the tart."

"So what is the actual news about Eckert?"

"He's coming to the army too. As captain of a company from Winchester. That could be bad news for us, given what he knows about our background."

"Damn it! I knew you should have let that merchant Grenough kill him. We could have waited until Grenough did the honors on Eckert and then taken care of Grenough. It would all have been very neat. Instead you decided to step in and save Eckert, as some sort of romantic gesture toward his wife. Even though she played you for the fool."

"That wasn't exactly how it happened."

"Close enough. The point is you saved his bloody life for no good reason. And I say you are still carrying the torch for that raven-haired wife of his, despite what she did to you and despite what you say."

Fairfield's face turned red. He said angrily, "Leave it, Quinn! Do you understand?" He stared at the sergeant for a moment, then continued, "What I find discouraging is that every time I find a wench who I really fancy, Eckert has already been there." He shook his head. "But this time, by God, I will bed the woman. Mrs. Colleen Alison McGraw will succumb soon enough."

Quinn laughed heartily. "I don't know, Fairfield. She's as hard a one as I've seen. And that's saying something. I think the only thing she loves is cold hard gold or silver." He looked over at his companion. "You had a good thing going with that planter's wife in Charleston. She was young, pretty, and willing. And her family relations got you the lieutenant's commission. It's a shame you can't be happy with the ones who swoon for you. You always want to go after the wench who is a challenge."

"Of course. Don't you see? It's the sport of it all."

"Some sport."

They rode for a while in silence. Then Fairfield changed the subject. "When are we supposed to get this conveyance back to its rightful owner's carriage house?"

"We're already late. The stableman I bribed wanted it back by midnight. But you taking your leisure time at supper has put us well behind."

"You said the owner was out of town and not due back anytime soon."

"Yes, Geoffrey, we are late but not in trouble. The stableman may be a little upset, but let's just get back as soon as possible and I'll deal with him."

Colleen was taking her breakfast in front of her tent. She sat beside a crackling fire, which took some of the edge off the morning chill.

She was just finishing up when Edna arrived and dropped into the other chair. Colleen greeted her, then asked, "How was business last night?"

"Very good. The word is getting out around the army about us. Lots of men came looking for liquor, and the girls were quite busy. The busiest since we arrived."

"That's excellent news. Make sure the girls get a good rest so they're ready for work tonight."

Edna replied, "Yes, I told them to sleep in this morning." Then she continued, "Well now, Colly, you look like you are none the worse for wear at the hands of your southern gentleman. How was the fare at supper?"

Colleen grinned. "Actually, things went quite well. The food was fine. But it wasn't the food which made the evening successful."

"Pray tell, what happened?"

"We had just been seated in our dining room when three young officers, feeling their drink, imposed themselves on us."

"You consider that fortunate?"

"Absolutely, Edna. It turned out that two of the officers were aides on Washington's staff."

"You mean the commanding general?"

"Do you know any other General Washington with the army? Anyway, don't you see how useful that will be, to have connections on the staff?"

Edna nodded. "Yes, I see what you're thinkin'. Knowing what they are planning and is likely to happen could be extraordinarily helpful."

"Exactly! I intend to cultivate them very carefully. I invited them to come out to our camp, and if they do come, we will treat them very well indeed."

"Well, what if they are not enticed by your offer?"

"Then I'll find some way to stay close to them. I'll not let this opportunity slip away."

"You said there was a third officer. Who was he?"

"Oh, yes. His name was Hamilton, and he was quite young. An artillery officer, apparently known well by the other two. But he was a strange bird indeed. Quite dark-complexioned and with very serious, penetrating eyes." She shook her head. "He sort of gave me the shivers. Looked like he was staring right into my soul."

Edna put her head back and laughed heartily. "He may never get over what he saw there!"

"My impression was that he rather liked what he was seeing."

"How did Lieutenant Fairfield take the imposition of these three officers?"

Colly laughed. "Not well at all. He seethed and ushered them out as soon as possible."

"So, has Mr. Fairfield now served his purpose? You droppin' him once you ingratiate yourself with those staff officers?"

Colleen raised a finger. "By no means, Edna. I found out something about him while talking with the others. His troop has been attached to headquarters, at least for a while. That's why the staff men were so close to him."

"Now that's a stroke of luck. Having as many friends there as possible can't hurt. And in any case, he's lustin' to bed you. You can make good use of that." Edna raised her eyebrows. "Is it in your mind to let him?"

Colly sat silent for a long moment, a calculating look on her face. "Not unless I must to keep him interested. And there's much I can do to keep him excited before I go to that extreme." She looked into the distance for a moment, then her face lit up as she remembered something. "Edna, the strangest thing happened last night. As conversation developed, I mentioned the problem that we are having with Emily Crider. And I mentioned that her lover Horner worked for a gunsmith in Winchester, and then, in passing, I mentioned Wend Eckert. The moment I spoke his name, Geoffrey gagged on his drink and had to wipe his face."

"Did he mention why that happened?"

"No, he just excused himself, saying the liquid had gone down wrong." She shook her head. "But I couldn't shake the feeling that it all happened because I mentioned Wend's name."

"Are you saying he knows Eckert? Or something about him?"

Colleen raised her hands. "How could he? How would the two have possibly met?"

"It does seem strange, Fairfield being from way down in the South."

Colleen said, in a quiet voice, "Edna, I'll admit I'm puzzled by him. He acts very gallant and gentlemanly, never is at a loss for words in any situation. He's the very ideal of a well-mannered man. But I can't get rid of the feeling that he's not what he seems or claims to be. It's driving me to distraction."

"Well, since you intend to keep him dangling on the line, perhaps time will tell the story."

Colleen nodded slowly. "Yes, I think you are right. Sooner or later the truth will expose itself."

The small boat approached the *Raven* and bounced wildly in the choppy water as it rode alongside, banging rhythmically against the hull. A Jacobs ladder was quickly lowered, and Northcutt, bracing himself to keep from falling, could see several heads looking down from the deck, including the captain, Lieutenant Proctor.

The boat cox'n said, "Careful, now, sir. Watch the waves—you've got to time it carefully gettin' onto that ladder, or you'll find yourself in the water."

Northcutt felt panic rising and a lump forming in his stomach. "You needn't tell me that. I can damn well see it with my own eyes!" He took a deep breath, and then as the boat was lifted high by a large wave, he grabbed the highest rung he could on the ladder. The boat dropped out from below him, and he hung momentarily by his hands, flailing wildly with his feet to get a footing. Finally he got his right foot onto a rung and with a great sense of relief, started pulling himself upward. After he had gone up a couple of steps, hands reached down and grabbed him under his shoulders. Then he was unceremoniously hauled over the rail and deposited onto the schooner's deck by two brawny seamen.

Proctor stood nearby, hands clamped behind his back, looking at him with a mischievous smile. "Sorry you were so roughly handled, Colonel Northcutt, but we wanted no accident in getting you aboard."

Northcutt, relieved at feeling solid wooden planking under his feet, sighed deeply. "No need to apologize, Lieutenant Proctor. Given our circumstances over the last few months, I've had to make many of these small boat transfers, but I've never developed any facility for them. I'm particularly grateful for the assistance in this case, with such a nasty chop in the river today."

"Ah yes, I quite understand, sir." Proctor put his hand on Northcutt's arm and gently steered him aside. Then he said in a quiet tone, "Now Colonel, we have a peculiar custom in the navy, and that is to call the commanding officer of a ship, whatever his actual rank, by the title *captain*. I'd be much obliged if you could refer to me by that while onboard."

Feeling embarrassed, Northcutt responded, "Of course, of course, *Captain*. I regret the improper form of address."

"Not at all, Colonel. Now, once the men have hoisted all your bags aboard, we'll get you settled in your quarters. We've arranged for you to have the ship's best quarters, aside from my own cabin, of course. You'll sleep in the master's stateroom."

Northcutt smiled. "I am *most* grateful for that, sir. I appreciate your thoughtfulness."

The mischievous smile returned to Proctor's face. "Before you thank me so profusely, Colonel, I must inform you that the cabin is about the size of a large closet in a house ashore. And given your height, you'll find that you have to crouch over to move around below; there are only about five feet between decks. The *Raven* is built for speed, not comfort, sir."

Northcutt said in a resigned tone, "Yes, I quite understand." Then he asked, "How soon will you be able to sail?"

"Immediately, sir. That wind which is causing so much chop in the river is coming in a very favorable direction for us to leave the anchorage and stand out of the roads. We'll be passing the Virginia capes in a few hours and entering the Atlantic." He looked over to where seamen were working to unload the boat. "We'll sail as soon as your baggage is aboard."

Northcutt found the *Raven*'s voyage to Halifax as physically sickening as the one across the Atlantic from England years ago. There was nowhere that he could make himself comfortable. When in the miniature cabin, he found the air stale and he was physically sick. The swinging bed, designed to make sleeping easier, seemed to make things worse for him. Moreover, the little schooner often heeled over so much that the bed banged against the side of the cabin. He found things were marginally better on deck, where at least the air was fresh, but just looking at the waves made him nauseous. Northcutt resigned himself that the only way out of his discomfort was the completion of the *Raven*'s voyage and arrival in Halifax.

To his credit, Proctor was doing his best to speed that result. The *Raven*, under full sail as often as conditions permitted, was rushing northward. The weather and winds cooperated—until the third day after leaving the Chesapeake. On that morning, high winds and seas, accompanied by rain squalls, buffeted the little schooner. Given the inclement weather, Northcutt at first attempted to remain below decks in the tiny wardroom, but the vessel was buffeted around, often tossing him against bulkheads. He was thankful that he had had nothing to eat, for he continuously felt like retching.

In desperation he went up to the main deck, determined to stay there regardless of the wind and rain. When he got topside, he found crewmen moving about rapidly amid the pelting rain, furling the fore and aft sails. Others were up in the rigging, working on the square sails. Then he saw Proctor standing beside the rail. The captain was dressed like a common seaman, with a short coat, canvas breaches, and a stocking cap. Northcutt made his way to the young officer's side.

Proctor, speaking loudly above the gusting wind, pointed toward the masts and said, "Well, I carried my mains as long as possible, but we've just dropped them. The men are busy furling them for now." He motioned aloft. "I'm carrying just my topsails and a staysail on the bowsprit, and I've had to take a reef in the topsails. That's as much canvas as I dare." He looked over at Northcutt with that mischievous smile again showing. "But with the shortened sail, she'll ride a little better for now."

"I am most grateful."

"Well, with luck this blow won't last too long, and we'll be able to crack on more sail. I'm under orders from Hammond to get you to Halifax as fast as possible, and I'll drive her to the maximum which conditions permit."

Northcutt, feeling sick, could only nod.

The *Raven* had a low quarterdeck, raised only by about a foot above the main decking but separated by a railing. Proctor motioned to the rail. "If you're determined to remain up here in the weather, I suggest you stay near the railing and be ready to hang on. And keep your feet planted wide. Even under shortened canvas, we're still going to take some nasty rolls!"

Northcutt took a deep breath and nodded to signify his understanding.

— ∞ —

Wend Eckert, with young Ensign Childers at his side, stood at the edge of the open field, watching as Newkirk, O'beirne, and Donegal exercised the company as skirmishers. The half company of riflemen was in a loose line in front, working in pairs, as if sharpshooting at an advancing enemy force. The musket-armed men were behind, acting as a line of support. Then, on Newkirk's order, the riflemen turned and retreated through the musket line. O'beirne, leading the musket men, had them advance several steps, form a line with the men about two feet apart, kneel, and simulate firing a volley, as if a strong enemy line were approaching. Then he ordered them to stand and fix bayonets, as if getting ready to repel the enemy in close fighting. Once they had their bayonets ready, he gave the order, "Charge your bayonets." The men leveled their muskets at waist level and shouted a loud "Ha!"

O'beirne called out, "Now forward, march!" The men started forward, and Flannagan, sergeant of the half company, called out, "Damn your asses! Keep the line dressed! You *must* keep the line straight, and mind keep your interval with the men on either side. A charge with the bayonet works only if you keep the line straight and tight!"

After the half company had advanced a few steps toward the imaginary enemy, O'beirne halted the men and called for them to gather around. They formed a half circle around him and Flannagan.

"All right, lads, that was not bad considering we've only been doing this for a couple of days. Now when you charge, mind what your good sergeant just told you: keep your line straight, and don't let the interval between men open up." O'beirne looked around with a twinkle in his eyes. "Now let me tell you something important. The reason we've got half the company carryin' the musket instead of the rifle is to defend the riflemen. It happens I've been engaged all over Europe with different kings' armies, and I'm here to tell you that the best defense is an offense." He grinned at the men around him, who were looking at him askance.

"I can tell by the looks in your eyes that you're askin', What do I mean by that?" There were nods around the group of men. "So here's the truth of it: when an enemy is chargin' at you with his bayonets fixed, you can't just stand there with your own bayonets fixed waitin' for him. You do that, he'll sweep you away every time. You'll never stop them! No, the only answer is a countercharge. You fire a volley at the enemy as he closes you, to thin his ranks out and maybe even make his line falter, and then you charge at him. You got to sweep the enemy back. They've got to be made to run."

Now the men were nodding their understanding. The Irishman said, "So we'll be practicing this maneuver over and over again till you are the best men with the bayonet in His Lordship General Washington's army." O'beirne's mouth wrinkled into a crooked, scornful smile. "Such as it is."

After a few more repetitions of the drill, the men were dismissed for the evening meal. Wend waved for the officers and sergeants to join him. After complimenting them on the progress that had been made, Wend said, "Now we're going to discuss a new tactic that Donegal, Baird, and I have been thinking about. Something based on the experiences we have had in warfare on the border."

Newkirk furrowed his brow. "Sir, I'm a bit confused. We've been teaching the men to fight after the manner of British regulars. Line formation drills and skirmish tactics like light companies of their foot regiments. Now suddenly you say you want to do something more like fighting in the Ohio Country. In any case, many of these men, particularly our riflemen, have experience doing that."

Wend grinned. "You're spot-on, Reese. But I never said we'd *only* fight like the regulars in open-field combat. I said we had to learn to do that, in situations for which it is appropriate and the only way to counter them." He looked around at his leaders. "And we've got a good start on that—Shay is right, we're probably already better than most of the companies in the Continental Army." He looked around at the group. "You've all been doing a good job with the men."

There were smiles and nods from the officers and sergeants.

O'beirne asked, "So, my good captain, what's this new thing we're going to teach the men?"

Wend said, "All right. Here's what I want you to do. Listen close: The three sergeants, who know the men best, will form eight groups of ten men each. Each group will consist of six musket men and four riflemen."

O'beirne looked puzzled. "You're going to combine rifles and muskets in small groups? Now that I don't understand."

Wend grinned. "Patience, my good Irishman. That's exactly what we're going to do—and for a good reason."

Newkirk had been doing some quick calculating. "That leaves us with eighteen riflemen unassigned."

Wend nodded. "Yes. Split them into two groups of nine each."

O'beirne said, "I admit you've now got me totally confused. What is this all about?"

The others, except for Donegal, all nodded in agreement.

Wend turned to the Highlander. "Simon, tell them what we intend."

Donegal started to speak, but suddenly Newkirk held up a finger, a look of concentration on his face. "Wait a second, I think I'm beginning to see what you are planning."

Wend and Donegal looked at each other. Wend motioned toward the first lieutenant. "All right, Reese. You've led troops on the border. Have a go at it."

Newkirk said, "Aye, I'll do that. First, these small groups would be useful for patrolling and scouting. And undoubtedly picket or camp-guard duty." He stopped and thought a moment. "And in each group, you have the riflemen for long-range sharpshooting, while the musket men provide for rapid firing if the group is attacked by an enemy force. A smaller version of what we've been doing here." He looked at Wend. "How am I doing?"

Donegal nodded. "Aye, Mr. Newkirk, you've got a good part of it there. But there's a bit more to it." He looked around at all the faces. "Na, the captain and I figured there may be times when we are out in advance of the main force, scouting or as vanguard. If a larger enemy formation is seen to be advancing toward our force, we may find it necessary to amuse them until reinforcements can arrive."

O'beirne put his hand to his mouth, concentration in his eyes. "And just how do these little mixed groups help us do that? It seems you would want to form a line and try to mass your fire."

Wend said, "Yes, but if we're severely outnumbered, we would be quickly overlapped and flanked. What I have in mind is what I call an interrupted line."

O'beirne responded, "A what?"

"You heard me, Shay. An *interrupted* line means our little field squads—that's what I intend to call them—would be spaced out at a distance from each other. Maybe twenty yards, maybe thirty yards apart. I'm not sure yet what the proper interval would be. But it would be so that they could support each other with their rifle and musket fire. It would give us a width almost as wide as a battalion in line of battle. There's no doubt we couldn't make a long stand, but I believe it might enable us to delay the advance of an enemy force." He thought a second. "It would be particularly effective in wooded or partially wooded ground, where our field squads could be under cover and the enemy would not know our strength. All he would know is that fire was coming from a wide front, and he would have to stop his advance and send out skirmishers to feel us out."

O'beirne said, "Yes, I am beginning to grasp your idea." Then his face lit up. "And from their cover, the riflemen could take down some of the opponent's officers and sergeants."

Donegal smiled broadly. "Aye, sir, now you're beginning to see it. The truth is, we're going to mix line tactics with backcountry fighting."

Wend said, "A long time ago, Donegal and Baird and I marched with Bouquet on the relief of Fort Pitt and the Battle of Bushy Run. And then Joshua scouted for him the next year on the expedition into the Ohio Country. The good colonel modified European tactics to take on the Indians. Now we are going to modify frontier fighting to confound the British." He paused to let that sink in. Then he said, "The three sergeants will spend the next day or so organizing the field squads. You know the men pretty well now, so make sure that you allocate the talent as evenly as you can among the eight groups, each led by a corporal. We'll start exercising the squads the day after tomorrow."

With that said, Wend said good evening and headed back to the house for evening meal. Donegal and the other two sergeants stood talking about how to set up the squads, while Newkirk, O'beirne, and Childers walked toward the Baird house.

Childers looked at his companions. "What do you think of this idea—these field squads the captain wants to organize. I never heard of anything like it."

O'beirne laughed. "Well, lad, there's much you haven't heard of. But I'll admit I'm a little skeptical. With the company so spread out, it means the corporals who lead the squads will often have to make many decisions on their own. The officers and sergeants can't be in close contact everywhere along a broken line like Eckert was talking about."

Newkirk responded, "Shay, I think Eckert is on to something. You're used to fighting in Europe. Close line formations of men under the direct control of officers every minute. Fightin' the tribes, we're used to being spread out under cover. And the corporals and sergeants always have to take a lot of responsibility. Both in fighting and in scouting. Don't forget that our corporals are all men who have experience, mostly in Dunmore's campaign in '74 out in the Ohio Country. I think it can work."

The Irishman said, "Well, we're going to find out in the next few days. I'll hold my opinion until I see it in the field."

Reese grinned at O'beirne. "Don't bet against Wend Eckert. You get a chance, talk with Corporal Sanders. He was with him during Dunmore's War. He said Eckert got him and his men out of some tight spots by doing things nobody thought would work. Like a ten-man squad fixing bayonets and charging a big war party. Everybody thought it was insane, but things were hopeless anyway, so they followed him, and damned if it didn't work."

O'beirne shrugged. "I didn't say I was against this idea, just that I hadn't ever seen anything like it and I'll not judge it till I see it in action." He grinned broadly, then laughed out loud. "I will say one thing: that damned pistol ball which grazed his head didn't seem to hurt his brains any. From what I've seen since I met him, he does seem to make good use of them."

An impish look came over Childers's face. "Maybe that ball shook up his brains and made him think even better."

O'beirne and Newkirk looked at each other and then broke out into loud laughter. The Irishman put his hand on Childers's shoulder and said, "Young lad, I'm sayin' right here there's hope for you yet."

Wend stood at the edge of the patch of land at the far western edge of Eckert Ridge Farm. The area was partly wooded, partly scrub bush, partly grasses. He was watching as four of the new field squads, controlled by Newkirk and Donegal, were practicing skirmishing. Donegal was moving between squads, advising the leaders and men to make the best use of the bush for concealment and where to position each man within the squad formation as they advanced. It was the second day of training the new squads, the other four having practiced on the preceding day.

Suddenly Wend became aware of a horse approaching at the gallop. He turned to see the horse and rider and soon recognized Tom Shields, one of Sheriff Smith's men. Shields pulled up right beside Wend and threw down off his mount.

Wend said, "Tom, what's Smith so excited about that he's got you pushing that animal so hard?"

"I'm carrying dispatches! Military dispatches for you from Wood and Rutledge." He handed a leather case to Eckert.

As he took the case, Wend asked, "You know what's in them?"

"Sure enough, some of it at least. A courier came in from Williamsburg, riding relays to get here fast."

"So what's the excitement about?"

"It's Dunmore! Dunmore and his men and all his ships left Norfolk a few days ago. And now they've landed at an island in the Chesapeake not far from a town called Gloucester, if that means anything to you."

"I've heard of it. It's down some distance to the southeast of Fredericksburg."

"Well, wherever it is, they want you to march for this island as soon as possible."

Wend sighed and exclaimed, "Damn!" Then he turned back to the drilling troops and called out loudly for Newkirk and Donegal. They ordered the men to rest and came striding toward where he stood.

Meanwhile, Wend began reading the dispatches.

Then he was interrupted by Newkirk's voice. "What's going on, sir?"

Wend looked up. "News from Williamsburg. Dunmore's occupied an island off the coast of the Bay near Gloucester with his full force and is fortifying it. It is believed he intends to begin operations in that area. Meaning raids and possible occupation of parts of the Tidewater."

"How does that affect us? We're for the main army at New York."

Wend looked at his two subordinates. "Not any more, Reese. We're ordered to march as soon as possible for Gwynn's Island to join the force forming to oppose Dunmore. After he's dealt with, they expect to send us north."

"My God," exclaimed the lieutenant, "we still have a lot of preparations to make. Supplies and provisions for the march, uniforms for the men. The women are still making hunting shirts, and the hats we ordered from Carlson's in Winchester haven't arrived. All in all, it will take days."

Wend responded as he tapped the letter he was holding, "This is from Rutledge. It says he needs to send a courier off tomorrow to tell Williamsburg when we will leave and how long it will be until we can arrive at Gwynn's Island." He shook his head. "So I've got to send an answer back to Rutledge by this rider."

Donegal asked, "How far is this damned island?"

Newkirk spoke up. "I've been to Gloucester, a few years ago. I'd say we could make it in ten days from when we leave, maybe eight if we force the march."

Wend said, "Rutledge says they'll rush getting us provisions ready and arrange wagons to carry them. We've got most of what else we need here now; it's been arriving steadily over the last couple of weeks. And we can leave without all the uniforms. We fought an entire war in the Ohio Country without uniforms."

Newkirk said, "I was talking with Alice the other day, and she says many of the hunting shirts have been coming in. We might be able to get the rest if we send riders to the women still working."

Wend scowled. "In any case, they can be sent to us later." He looked at Donegal. "So considering all that, when can you have the men ready to march?"

The sergeant looked at the sky for a moment, then back at Wend. "Three days, if Rutledge comes through with the provisions. The men will na like it; they didn't expect to leave for a fortnight. But we can do it."

Wend took a deep breath. "All right, we'll try for three days from now." He looked up at Shields. "Come up to the house with me, and I'll write out a dispatch for you to take back to Rutledge and Wood."

He turned back to Newkirk. "Drilling is over. Get the men back to camp, and start making preparations. Come hell or high water, we march in three days."

PART III
THE TIDEWATER

CHAPTER ELEVEN
MARCHES AND MEETINGS

Wend walked out on the front porch at dawn and studied the sky as it brightened. He was satisfied there were absolutely no clouds, and with little wind, it was unlikely they would see any as they traveled. They would have a sunlit, warm day to begin their march. Around him the farm was already alive. He saw Specht and some hands bringing in the horses for morning feed. He also heard the noise of men shouting down at the company encampment and realized Donegal already had them at work breaking camp. There had been a final planning meeting of the officers and sergeants the night before, and it was agreed that the company would leave at noon.

Behind him the house was also full of activity. Peggy and the servants, who had all been up for hours, were moving around, preparing for guests. Wend expected the gentlemen of the Committee of Safety to arrive early in the morning, and Peggy had gotten word that many of their wives would accompany them or come in later in the morning by carriage.

As he was musing, Peggy joined him on the porch. "Wend, you better get into uniform before things start to get busy. I've got it laid out on the bed for you." She took his arm. "Anyway, I'm looking forward to seeing you in that officer's uniform I had the tailor make for you. I think you'll look marvelous in the blue and red."

"I'd rather be wearing the hunting shirt you made for me. Much more comfortable."

Peggy responded, "It will look good for all the officers to be dressed in the formal uniform for the Committee of Safety. You can change into the hunting shirt in camp the first night." She smiled broadly. "I can't wait to see all the men in their hunting shirts, breeches, and black hats as the company marches off."

Wend turned and quickly kissed his wife on the cheek. "I'm still amazed and proud at how you women rallied over the last three days to finish up the uniforms for the men."

When Wend had told Peggy about the change in orders and the need to leave as soon as possible, Peggy had immediately sent off a rider to alert the other women of her uniform committee. And that had set off a flurry of activity in Winchester and throughout the county. The ladies had banded together to ensure the appearance of the Frederick County Light Foot would make them proud. And with Rutledge's assistance in arranging transport, on the previous evening, a wagon had come up the drive at Eckert Ridge carrying a heavy load of shirts, breeches, and black hats for the company. Along with those made by Peggy, Alice, and the women of the camp, there was enough to outfit every man in the company.

As he was thinking, he saw a brief scowl come over Peggy's face. He asked, "What's making you unhappy?"

"I was thinking that it's a damn shame you and the company are departing directly from the farm to go down and cross the Shenandoah at Ashby's Ferry. You won't get a send-off in Winchester like when Morgan's rifle company left last year."

Wend laughed. "Frankly, I'm rather glad to miss all the fancy speeches and ceremony."

She looked at him sternly. "Well, think of all the women who made the uniforms. They deserve to see all the men of the company dressed out in their handiwork."

"Well, I hadn't thought of that."

Peggy gave Wend a gentle, playful shove. "Men never think about matters like that. Now go on upstairs, and put on the uniform. And you still have some of your things to pack up. Donegal is sending a man with a wagon, and he will be here soon so you can load in your kit."

By the time Wend had finished and come back downstairs an hour later, the wagon was out front with Billy and another man waiting. The wagon was already loaded with the baggage of the other officers and camp items, and it took a few minutes to arrange things to accommodate Wend's belongings.

They had just finished when James Wood, Angus McDonald, and David Rutledge came riding up the drive. Wend also saw several wagons with people standing around them near the intersection of the drive and the Ashby Ferry Road.

The soldiers took the wagon back down to the camp to finish loading it and Wend greeted the three committeemen. They swung down off their horses and shook hands with him.

Wend pointed down to the wagons at the bottom of the drive. "Who's in those wagons?"

Angus answered, "It's some families of your soldiers. Came to watch as you depart, lad."

Rutledge said, "You may see more arrive. There are a number of people in town who were planning to come on out."

Wend was surprised. "They'd have to have left early in the morning to get here by noon."

Wood smiled. "Indeed they would. But apparently they think it's worth the effort." He patted Wend on the shoulder. "Let's go into the house, if we may. I've got a map of the area you are going to and one which shows the route I recommend you take. I've gained some familiarity with roads while traveling to Williamsburg and back all these years. I've also had occasion to go through Gloucester."

Angus added, "As have I, though long ago."

Wend led them into the dining room, where the maps could be spread out on the table. Wood motioned with his finger. "You'll start by going down to Fredericksburg. After crossing the river at Ashby's Ferry, take the road that goes through Red Store. I believe you've been there before."

"Yes, I'm sure of that. We crossed that road last year on the way up to Alexandria on that hunt for John Connolly. But it's after Fredericksburg that I have no knowledge of the roads, nor do I have knowledge of the exact location of Gloucester and this Gwynn's Island."

Wood answered, "There's a pretty good road that generally follows the west bank of the Rappahannock. That road goes all the way down to the shores of the Bay, but you'll have to watch for a road, about here"—he pointed to where the Rappahannock widened—"that takes you southwest to Gloucester. You'll need to send guides out to make sure you're going right."

Wend said, "I'm taking Baird along for just that purpose. He's got the knack for finding his way in strange territory."

McDonald laughed. "I knew Joshua would find a way to go along."

Wend smiled. "Yes, he insisted. Said Alice would put him to work once we left. In any case, he'll come on home after we join up with the other forces down there."

Rutledge spoke up. "You'll be working with the 7th Virginia. It's still recruiting and forming up in that area. The colonel is a man named Daingerfield, William Dangerfield. You'll report to him for duty. A dispatch I got from Williamsburg indicates they are trying to round up additional forces, including artillery, to reinforce the 7th. Of course, your company is part of that reinforcement."

Wood said, "We also got word that the convention has, for the first time, appointed some generals for our Virginia forces. The new commander overall is Andrew Lewis." He looked at Wend. "I believe you met him last year when you were on Dunmore's staff in the Ohio Country."

"Oh, I met him all right. It was when Dunmore assigned me to make sure Lewis and his brigade turned around and went home after the treaty with the tribes was signed. Lewis was not happy about that and not happy with me at all. After the Indians attacked them at Point Pleasant, they were after revenge." Then Wend had another thought. "What happened to Patrick Henry, Colonel of the 1st Virginia? They didn't make him a general?"

"No, but it doesn't much matter, because it is expected that he will be elected governor. Probably in the next meeting of the convention, while you are in the Tidewater." James shrugged. "So you may have to deal with both of them sometime while you are down there."

Wend rolled his eyes and said, "I can hardly wait."

Wood grinned. "Wend, I know you'll be very tactful, realizing you represent Winchester and Frederick County."

"I'll try."

Wood raised a finger. "As a matter of fact, I'm leaving today for Williamsburg, for the upcoming session. Unless you object, I'll ride with you, at least for the first couple of days."

"Of course you're welcome, James."

At that moment Peggy came in and greeted the three men. Then she said, "The rest of the committee is arriving." She motioned to the door. "And the company officers are here."

Newkirk, O'beirne, and Childers entered the room. Wend said, "Gentlemen, I think you all are quite familiar with Lieutenant Newkirk and Ensign Childers. And this is Shay O'beirne, my second lieutenant." Wend described O'beirne's background to the committee men.

Shay smiled broadly and made a small bow. "It is my great pleasure to meet you gentlemen. I look forward to serving Frederick County and Winchester."

Wood looked over O'beirne as if sizing him up. "Well, Mr. O'beirne, we certainly welcome a man of your experience to our company."

Wend said, "He has indeed provided a great deal of perspective to our training and organization, James."

Rutledge said, "Shall we go in and join the rest of the committee? We have some important business to transact before you leave, Wend, not the least of which is consuming some of your whiskey."

Wend said dryly, "Yes, we had anticipated that need."

Wood laughed and said, "David, they know you too well here at Eckert Ridge."

The social affair in the Eckert house spread over the parlor, central hall, and dining room and went on for well over an hour, as the wives of the committee and virtually all of the Eckerts' neighbors, including Abby Morgan and Widow Callow, arrived. Peggy floated around the room, looking extraordinarily elegant. She was dressed in her favorite medium-blue gown, which complemented her blue eyes and raven hair. Her hair was tied with ribbon that matched the gown.

Also present were young Ensign Childers's parents, come to see their son march off to war. Wend noted that Peggy made sure to spend time with them.

Finally, as the noon hour approached, James Wood, accompanied by Rutledge, took a place before the hearth. He called for the assemblage to gather together. "Your attention! Your attention, please!" he called out. "We have some important business to attend to!"

Wend saw that Rutledge was holding a long thin item wrapped in a cloth. He wondered what was about to happen.

Wood made a short speech about the mission of the company, how it had been recruited for service with the main army in the north but would now start out by campaigning against Dunmore.

Then he called for Wend to join him and Rutledge. Wend made his way to stand beside them.

Wood looked over at Rutledge. "David, time to uncover what you are holding."

Rutledge unwrapped the object and held it up for all to see. It was a sheathed sword, with a leather belt attached to the sheath. The county lieutenant pulled the blade from the black scabbard and held it up for all to see its gleaming steel. Then he said, "When we of the committee commissioned Wend Eckert to be captain of our company, we soon realized that he had no sword, which of course is a prerequisite for the commander of a company of foot. So we set about procuring one for him, and our great friend Isaac Zane agreed to forge and shape the steel for the blade. Other craftsmen of the county cut and fitted the leather to cover the grip and made the sheath. So this weapon"—he held it high and swung it in an arc—"is truly the product of our great county and fit for the fine leader of our soldiers."

The assemblage broke into applause. The politician stood smiling, one hand holding the grip and the other carefully supporting the end of the blade. After the clapping ceased, he said, "Before we present this to our captain, I would like to note that engraved on the blade, just below the hilt, is the following inscription. There are two lines. On top, *Frederick County, Virginia.* And on the bottom, *W. Eckert, Captain.*"

Wood proffered the sword to Wend, with the grip toward Eckert.

Wend felt his face flushing and the sea of faces looking at him expectantly. He was at a loss for words, but he knew he had to say something. Finally he was able to mutter, "I vow to use this to the best of my ability in the service of Frederick County and Virginia!"

There was applause and Wend took the sword from Wood. Then he took the sheath from Rutledge and slid the blade into it. He was about to buckle the sword around his waist when he heard Peggy's voice call out, "Not yet, my husband. I have something for you."

Wend looked up to see his wife making her way through the crowd. To his complete surprise, she was carrying a long scarlet sash in the exact same shade as the facings of his uniform. She came up to him and wound the material around his waist and tied it on one side. Then she assisted him in buckling the sword belt.

As she assisted him, she leaned close and whispered in his ear, "I wanted to send you off with something besides your memories of last night's passion." Then she kissed him on his cheek, to a round of cheers from the party.

Rutledge grinned and said, "I should like to have heard what Mrs. Eckert said to her husband."

Peggy looked at him with a gleam in her eye and said, "And *that*, David, is something you shall *never* know."

There was an uproar of laughter in the room.

At that moment Shay O'beirne, who had been watching from out in the center hall, called out, "Ladies and gentlemen! Listen! Sergeant Donegal is bringing up the company."

The room quieted, and then everyone heard it—the sound of drums beating the marching cadence. Wood waved toward the door. "Let us all go out and greet the men of Frederick County's company of light foot!"

In a rush, the people flooded out onto the porch and the ground in front of it. Wend walked down the steps and stood waiting with his three officers in line side by side behind him.

The company was just coming out from behind the Baird house, with Donegal in front, the fifer and two drummers behind him. Just then Newkirk said to Wend, "Captain, did you happen to look down the drive?"

Wend turned to look and felt a shock. There was a huge crowd lining the drive. There were scores of wagons, saddled horses, and hundreds of people gathered on both sides. The assemblage extended from just beyond the gun shop down to where the drive met Ashby Ferry Road.

Wend exclaimed, "Good God!"

Newkirk answered, "We may not have been able to go to Winchester for a farewell, but the town seems to have come to us."

Wend heard James Wood's voice from behind; he stood on the steps. "I heard that people were talking about coming out to see the company leave, but never expected anything like this!"

Rutledge, standing beside Wood, said, "They would have had to leave in the early hours of the day to get here by now."

Then O'beirne, standing behind Wend, tapped him on the shoulder. "Now my darling captain, beggin' your pardon, but since you aren't familiar with carrying the sword, I might suggest that when Donegal and the men get here, you might want to pull it out and hold it straight up in front of you. That's the normal drill for an officer in command when his troops are present."

Wend whispered back, without turning around, "Thank you, O'beirne. I'll have to learn how to handle the damn thing."

"My pleasure, Captain. And when we get some time, it will be my honor to show you all the moves you are supposed to make with the sword when on parade."

While they were talking, the company had approached and was now in full view. Donegal had the men marching by the half companies in a column of threes. Donegal was out front, with Wilder leading the rifles and Flannagan ahead of the muskets.

There was a hubbub as everyone remarked on their uniforms. Each man wore a natural-colored linen hunting shirt with a rain flap over the shoulders. They wore dark-brown breeches with lighter-colored leggings reaching up to the knees. On their head were black hats with brims around the front and sides, while the rear brim was turned up. All except for Donegal, that was, who wore his old blue 77th bonnet.

As they approached, Wend took pride in the precise, even steps each man took, the correct slope of every shouldered firelock, and the rigid posture of every soldier.

From the stairs he heard Rutledge say, in admiring terms, "Damn, look at them! By God, they march like regulars!"

Wood responded, "Undoubtedly we owe that to Donegal."

Without turning around, Wend said, "Yes, James, and to the tender mercies of Wilder and Flannagan. They've been drilling them without mercy."

Wood said, "Well, they've done their job magnificently. Wait till Lewis sees them; he won't believe his eyes."

Wend's eyes went to the rear of the company formation. Walking behind, in a tight group, were all the women and children. And after them was a caravan of conveyances. There were two farm wagons driven by soldiers, carrying baggage, tents, and provisions. Next came Horner with his horse cart, loaded with tools and his personal belongings. Finally, there were two Conestogas, hired from Abby Morgan and driven by Jake Cather and Elijah McCartney, both men very familiar to Wend. These carried barrels of salt meat, a number of muskets that had been finished for the Virginia forces, and a significant amount of gunpowder that Frederick County was sending to Lewis. As he watched, Joshua Baird stepped out from beside the stable, rifle slung over his shoulder and leading his tall hunter, Beau, saddled with pistols in holsters and saddlebags behind. The scout fell in behind the Conestogas.

When the company came into sight of the watchers along the drive, cheers and clapping erupted. Meanwhile, Donegal brought the company to a halt directly in front of the porch steps. Then he ordered a left turn, so that the men were facing the house. It was executed by the members of the company in unison.

Moving with the posture and precision of step only gained by years of training, Simon left what had been the head of the column and marched back until he was directly in front of Wend and the officers. Then in a voice that undoubtedly was heard all the way back in Winchester, he ordered the company, "Present arms!"

The men raised their firelocks to the salute. Donegal called out, "Company all present and correct, sir!"

Wend suddenly heard O'beirne's whispered words. "Captain, it would be a good idea for you to raise your sword up until the grip is right in front of your eyes, then lower it back down rapidly, so as to return the salute."

Wend did so.

Once Wend had finished, Simon called out, "Order, arms!" and when that had been executed, he then directed the men to ground their arms.

Wend knew what was to come next. In as stern and official-sounding a voice as he could muster, he called out, "The Committee of Safety will present the company standard."

Donegal ordered, "Private Wood, advance to the front."

Billy, suppressing the urge to grin, marched forward to take his place beside Donegal. Then he carefully slung his musket over his left shoulder.

Rutledge, carrying a wooden staff with a small, square-shaped, blue flag, came forward. He raised the staff up high, while James Wood held out the flag itself so that everyone could see. In the center was the now-familiar rattlesnake in thirteen segments, colored white against the blue background. Above the snake was the word *Liberty* in large letters. Below the snake were the words *Frederick County Virginia*.

Wood said in a loud voice, "Men of the Frederick County Light Company, carry your standard with pride. We of the county and of Winchester know you will serve in a manner which will honor the people who are sending you forth."

Cheers erupted from the people on the porch and those along the drive.

When the cheers had died out, Wend said, "Men of the company, it is time to march!" He paused for effect, then ordered, "Officers, take your posts!"

His three officers marched to their positions. Then Wend called out, "Lieutenant Newkirk, take charge!"

Newkirk saluted, then ordered the company, "Shoulder your firelocks." The long arms were raised in unison to the left shoulders of the men. Then he ordered, "Company, left turn!" And in unison the men faced left. Newkirk, Donegal, and Billy, flag in hand, proceeded to the head of the column.

Newkirk drew his sword and held it straight up in front of himself. "Company, at the quick step, forward, march!"

The entire column moved off down the slope of the drive, the sound of renewed cheering coming from all the watchers. Once the last of the wagons had passed by, Wend turned to Wood and Rutledge. "I must say goodbye to Peggy and my children."

Wood laughed. "Don't take too long. The horses will get restless. They'll want to be with their herd mates with the company!"

Wend said, "I shan't be long" and bounded up the steps to where his wife stood. He took her arm, escorted her into the house and back through the hall to the privacy of her sewing room. There he took her into his embrace. After a long moment, he said, "You are as responsible for the success of today as anyone in the company or on the Committee of Safety. You were brilliant in getting the women to work together on the uniforms, and you have virtually taken over the management of the farm while I attended to the company. He smiled, kissed her again, and said, "No man could ever ask for a better wife."

Then Wend looked into her eyes and saw tears forming. He laughed. "Why the tears? You're the one who so staunchly wanted to see me march off at the head of a company! Now you've got your wish!"

"Oh, stop it, Wend! Of course I'm crying. I may never see you again, and I'll worry about you every day until you come home." She took a deep breath, then continued, "And I'll also be proud of you every day you are gone for what you are doing for Virginia." She pushed his chest gently with one hand. "And now it's time for you to join your company. James is waiting out there."

Wend kissed her again, then took her arm, and together they walked to the porch.

The children were all gathered near the door and Wend hugged and said a few words to each of them.

Then he went down the steps to where Wood was already mounted and Specht was holding the reins to Sonny. Specht said, "Good fortune, sir" and handed over the reins. Wend said to the lead hand, "Jacob, I'm counting on you to hold the farm together and make it prosper."

"I'll not let you down, sir!"

Wend quickly mounted, looked one more time at his wife and children on the porch, then kicked the young stallion in the flanks, and the two men were off to catch up with the column.

As they galloped down the drive, the remnants of the crowd, now starting to break up to head back to their homes, gave the two riders a ragged cheer. Wood, ever the politician, took hat in hand and waved it profusely at the people standing by the drive.

Soon they reached the Ashby Ferry Road and turned southward to overtake the marching column.

—〰—

Northcutt stood beside Proctor as the *Raven*, running close-hauled with all her sails set in a strong wind, raced through the coastal waters off Halifax. He could see the buildings of the town rising above the harbor. Between the schooner and the actual harbor was a massive fleet of ships riding to their anchors. Numerous small boats were plying the waters between the ships and landings ashore. A goodly number of the anchored vessels were warships ranging from ships of the line to little sloops of war and schooners like the *Raven*. But it was clear even to Northcutt's inexperienced eyes that the overwhelming number were merchant transports.

Proctor said, "Clearly several troop convoys have arrived since I left for Virginia." His face lit up, and he pointed toward a large warship. "By God, there's the old *Prefect*. I started out on her as a midshipman years ago. My mates in the gunroom called me Prefect Proctor. She's been laid up in ordinary for quite a while." A thoughtful look came over his face. "But obviously they recommissioned her for war service, and it appears she has escorted a convoy across the Atlantic."

Northcutt, looking for an appropriate response, commented, "She is very powerful looking."

Proctor shot Northcutt his mischievous smile. "Looks that way, but she's actually rated as only fifty guns. The navy now considers ships of her class too small to stand in line of battle. The lordships of the admiralty prefer that the minimum for new ships of the line to be sixty-four guns."

"So why have they sent her over here?"

"Economy, my dear colonel. *Economy*. The rebels don't have any ships of the line. But given her size, the *Prefect* makes a good flagship for a squadron of smaller ships. And her crew is less than a sixty-four or seventy-four gun ship. The navy is planning to establish several squadrons of small ships to blockade the rebel coast, and a fifty-gun ship has spacious quarters for carrying a commodore and his staff to manage their operations. I've no doubt that's why the *Prefect* is here."

Suddenly the *Raven*'s sailing master, Flowers, called out, "Captain, flagship's in sight, and she's got the query flag up."

"Right, Flowers, make our number."

The master called out to a master's mate, who quickly hoisted a series of signal flags.

In a few minutes, another signal went up on the flagship, and the master's mate called out to Proctor, "Sir, we've been directed to anchor close aboard the flagship."

Proctor said, "Very well." Then he turned to Northcutt. "Now's when we start having some fun. We'll have to do some precise maneuvering through moored ships to get close alongside the flag."

The young captain stepped to the quarterdeck rail and called out to the master, "Mr. Flowers, we've been invited to anchor beside the flagship. I'll have lines and ground tackle handled smartly—*most* smartly, if you please!"

"Aye, and you'll not have any reason to complain, Captain."

Proctor turned to the helmsman. "Ease your rudder to larboard— make for the gap between those two vessels." Then to Flowers, he called out, "We're coming to larboard; haul the mains as close to the wind as she'll take. We need the best speed we can make."

Meanwhile Flowers was positioning men about the deck and others were scrambling up the ratlines in preparation for handling the square topsails. Another group was busy preparing the anchor to be let go.

The *Raven* was now moving even faster. She swept through the gap between the two anchored vessels and then carefully steered between two more before approaching the great flagship with an admiral's flag flying at the peak. Northcutt looked over at Proctor and saw he had a look of intense concentration on his face.

Suddenly the captain called out, "Flowers, I'll have the mains down, if you please!"

The master screamed out some commands, and the gaffs on the large fore and aft sails on the two masts immediately dropped, with men rushing to keep the canvas from flapping in the wind.

Proctor called to a man standing at the very bow, "Bosun, prepare to let go the anchor!"

The ship's bosun called back, "Ready sir!"

Proctor looked at Flowers and shouted, "Take in the main topsail and back the fore topsail!"

The master responded by shouting orders to the men up on the yards of the topsails. Immediately the topmen released the sheets of the topsail on the mainmast and others on the spar began to quickly furl the canvas. Simultaneously Northcutt saw that crewmen were hauling the fore topsail spar around so the wind now pushed the sail back against the mast, slowing the ship dramatically. Proctor quickly walked over to the side and looked down at the water, watching for the ship to come to a stop. In just a few seconds, he called out, "Let go the anchor!"

A man sitting with one leg over the rail swung an ax, cutting a small line that secured the anchor, and it immediately dropped into the water with a great splash.

Proctor was still watching the water, and Northcutt looked down himself and saw that the ship was now making sternway. This went on for a few minutes, and then the ship's motion abruptly stopped and the captain called out, "Anchor is dug in! Take in the fore topsail!"

As the topmen were performing that task, Proctor called down to Flowers, "All right, Mr. Flowers—snug the ship down, set the in-port watches, and get a party busy swaying out a boat. And make sure the boat crew is properly dressed out in the ship's livery!"

The captain turned to Northcutt. "Well, Colonel, we'll shortly get you ashore for your mission to army headquarters, and I'll go pay my call on the admiral. I have dispatches for him from Hammond." He grinned. "And I have no doubt he'll want to hear all the news from the Chesapeake."

An hour later Northcutt, thankfully, stepped onto the firm ground at the fleet landing. Strangely, he suddenly felt unsteady on his feet, as if the earth itself were moving below him. Then he realized that the problem was internal to him; after days at sea, he was unaccustomed to still ground, and his body and mind were still trying to compensate for the constant movement of the ship.

As he was contemplating this, Proctor called up to him from the *Raven*'s boat. "Colonel, we're going over to the flagship, and then back to the *Raven*. When you are ready to come back after your meetings, take one of the fleet boats which ply back and forth through the anchorage. If that's not available, have the officer in charge of the landing signal us to send a boat for you." Proctor pointed to a tall mast with a crosstree and halyards. "They'll send our number by flag, and we can send a boat in for you."

"Thank you, Proctor!" Northcutt said. Then he tucked the leather dispatch case under his arm and stepped up to a midshipman who was in charge of the landing and inquired where army headquarters might be. Having received directions, he tucked the leather dispatch case under his arm and set off on foot.

Soon enough Northcutt arrived at the large house that had been taken over to serve as army headquarters. There were numerous officers standing around in front of the building and a pair of sentinels in front of the doors. He walked into the building to find aides moving about, many with papers in hand. He questioned one, a young captain, about where the adjutant general might be and was directed down the central hall to where another captain sat at a writing table, in front of a door, with a sentinel standing beside him. "You'll want to see Captain Gardiner. He's the secretary to the adjutant general and the general."

He approached the captain, who was busy looking at documents, and said, "Excuse me, sir."

Gardiner looked up and ran his eyes appraisingly over Northcutt. Then he dropped his eyes back down to the papers on the table and said, "Yes, sir. And what might your business be?"

"I'm Lieutenant Colonel Northcutt, commandant of the King's Loyal Virginia Legion. Here with dispatches from Governor Lord Dunmore."

The captain looked up again and examined Northcutt more carefully. "You say you're here from *Virginia*?"

"That is correct, Captain. I have just arrived on a vessel and have dispatches to deliver and important business with General Howe. I have been charged with a direct verbal communication from Lord Dunmore himself."

The captain made a face. "*Everyone* in this building has important business with the general." The young aide stared off into the distance. "*However*, Colonel, seeing as you have come in from Virginia, let me talk to Colonel Paterson, the adjutant general, and see what he would do." He rose from the table and went through the door into the room behind him.

Northcutt felt frustration rising. He had expected that there would be priority given to communications from the governor of a colony, but now, looking around the headquarters and reflecting on the number of senior officers standing around, he realized that presumption had been somewhat naive.

Gardiner was back in a few minutes. "All right, sir. Colonel Paterson will see you. Please follow me." The captain led Northcutt into a large room, with a desk to one side. There were several officers in chairs at the other side of the room, presumably waiting to see General Howe.

The colonel at the desk stood up and extended his hand. "Colonel Northcutt, welcome to Halifax. I understand you are carrying dispatches from Lord Dunmore."

"That's correct, sir. I'm carrying written correspondence and have been directed by the governor to personally brief the general. There are some matters of critical importance regarding our campaign in Virginia of which the general should be made aware."

Paterson sat back down. "Yes, I'm quite interested in what's been happening in your colony." He reached up and said, "Please give me the dispatches."

"Lord Dunmore specifically ordered me to deliver them personally to the general."

Paterson dropped his hand to the desk and looked sternly at Northcutt. "Colonel, when you hand *me* those dispatches, they are considered delivered to the general. I will make a preliminary review of their contents."

"Sir, events in Virginia have become strategically quite serious. It is important and urgent that I personally brief the general. Today if at all possible."

Paterson was looking perturbed now. "Look, Colonel, please pass those dispatches to me." He reached out again to Northcutt. "You, sir, have *my word* that I will arrange for you to see the general."

Northcutt held on to the case tightly. "When will I be able to see the general? I would greatly appreciate it if he could receive me now."

Paterson's face flushed. He responded with a sharp edge to his words. "Colonel Northcutt, the general is sitting down with the senior officers of the last troop convoy, which has recently arrived. And when *that* interview is concluded, he is scheduled to meet with the gentlemen seated over there. *They* have been waiting with great patience." He pointed to the waiting officers. "And after that he will be going to his quarters to prepare for a social engagement this evening. Let me repeat, I will get you in to see the general as soon as possible." He looked sternly at Northcutt. "Now, *sir*, if I may have those dispatches?"

Northcutt hesitated briefly and reflected he could not press his case again without further angering Paterson, which just would not do. He reached out and passed him the dispatches.

Paterson said, "Thank you, sir. Now if you will impart to me where you are staying, I'll get in touch with you after I have digested the contents of these communications and am ready to take you in to meet the general."

"Colonel, I just arrived on the dispatch vessel *Raven* and have not found quarters ashore." Northcutt decided he should try to establish a better relationship with the chief aide. He smiled and said, "My room aboard the vessel is about the size of a closet. Perhaps you could recommend a reputable establishment where I could take a room?"

Paterson looked over at Gardiner, who was still standing beside Northcutt, and the two broke into laughter.

Northcutt looked at the two officers, then asked, "Excuse me, gentlemen, did I say something amusing without realizing it?"

Gardiner responded, "Colonel, that is *exactly* the case. We have thousands of men billeted around the town and over four thousand loyalist refugees from Boston living in every conceivable abode, some of them not meant for humans. You are lucky to have living quarters aboard ship."

Paterson nodded. "Indeed, sir. I'm sympathetic to your situation, but there is little choice but to remain where you are, inconvenient as it might be."

"I see, gentlemen. Then I will retire to HMS *Raven* and await your summons."

Northcutt, feeling a wave of disappointment, turned to go.

Paterson interrupted him in a more friendly tone. "Ah, Northcutt, hold on a second. It happens there is a social planned for this evening. A reception and entertainment. It's to welcome the officers of the latest two troop convoys which have arrived. Things begin at eight. We should be delighted if you could attend, and I submit you will find it a pleasant diversion after your voyage."

Northcutt responded, "That would be my pleasure, Colonel."

"Excellent, Northcutt." Paterson motioned toward the captain. "Gardiner will give you the details and directions to get to the hall." Then a thoughtful look came over Paterson's face. "Sir, just a minute. The senior major in the 23rd Foot, General Howe's regiment, is named Northcutt. Is he by chance related to you?"

"By the chance of birth, Colonel. He is my elder brother. His full name is Gerald Penfold Northcutt."

"Yes, I know him well. Then here's good news for you. He will be at the reception tonight. You will be reunited with him in a matter of hours."

Gardiner coughed into his hand. "Ah, Colonel Paterson, may I remind you that Major Northcutt is escorting Mrs. Loring tonight?"

A sly grin came over the adjutant general's face. "Ah, yes, it had slipped my mind." He turned to Barrett and drew quite close to him and spoke in a low tone. "I should alert you to a particular matter. Your brother has a specific duty tonight. He will be escorting a very young and lovely lady." He looked around the room and said very softly and at the same time gave Northcutt a meaningful glance, "Who, shall we say, has a special relationship with the general."

Northcutt stood puzzled for a moment, then it hit him. "Oh yes. I quite understand, Paterson. Thank you for advising me of the matter."

Paterson, still very close, said, "I know you will be very discreet."

"Of course, Colonel. It happens that before the governor's family arrived in Virginia, we had a similar situation with a young lady in Williamsburg which required delicate management." He cleared his throat. "The problem resolved itself when Lady Dunmore and the children arrived, as such things usually do."

A smile crossed Paterson's face. "Then we understand each other."

"Completely, sir, and thank you for mentioning it, Colonel. That was very thoughtful."

"Not at all, Northcutt. My pleasure."

Northcutt was about to follow Gardiner out of the room when the door to the general's room opened and several officers came out. Out of curiosity, Northcutt glanced at them. He noted that they were clearly officers of Highland regiments, dressed in short coats and wearing bonnets. Then he stared in surprise at one of the men. He smiled and called out, "Thomas! Thomas Stirling!"

The officer looked over at Northcutt. He also grinned. "By God, Barrett Northcutt! What in the devil are you doing here?" He looked more closely at him and said, "And in uniform, of all things!"

Northcutt smiled. "Well, it is a bit of a story, Thomas."

Stirling looked over at the officer standing beside him. "Charles, this is Barrett Penfold Northcutt. He and I spent many memorable hours at the card table back when I was in New York with the regiment, prior to our return to Britain." He turned back to Northcutt. "Barrett, this is my senior major in the 42nd, Charles McDonald."

Barrett shook McDonald's hand, then said, "So you've got command of the 42nd, Thomas? Congratulations!"

"Yes, actually I've had the battalion for several years now. We were garrisoned in Ireland, and then when the insurrection broke out, we moved to Glasgow to recruit up to strength. We just arrived in convoy two days ago. The 71st Highland was also in the convoy."

"I hope you had a pleasant crossing."

Stirling rolled his eyes. "I wish I could say so, Barrett. But the fact is we had a stormy trip. One blow after another. And two ships of the convoy, one carrying a company of our battalion and the other a company of the 71st, disappeared. We have no word of them as of now."

McDonald said, "There were some of those rebel privateers hovering around the convoy. The fear is the two ships, having been blown away from the convoy, were captured."

Stirling shook his head. "Yes, I'm quite worried." Then his face brightened. "But tell us, Barrett, how do you come to be here and in uniform?"

"As I said, it's a long story. As you are aware, when we were together in New York City, I was pursuing land acquisition for speculation and development. When Lord Dunmore arrived in '71 to assume the governorship of New York, I was referred to him by friends to assist in some of his personal land purchases. A friendship blossomed, and he invited me to join his staff as an adviser on colonial land matters and the general political situation. Then, when he was ordered to Virginia to take that governorship, I went along."

McDonald motioned toward Northcutt. "We've heard about the governor's efforts to hold the colony for the Crown. I assume you've taken the uniform in that cause."

Barrett said, "Indeed, Major. The governor appointed me lieutenant colonel commandant of a battalion. I was charged with raising and commanding the King's Loyal Virginia Legion."

Stirling said, "Well, congratulations. But what are you doing here in Halifax?"

"I'm here to deliver dispatches and plead our case for a battalion of regulars to add some backbone to our loyalist forces."

"Ah yes, I see."

At that moment Paterson looked up from his desk. "Gentlemen, I'm most happy that you are enjoying this opportunity to renew your acquaintance. But since *we* are still at work here, perhaps I could convince you to take your fellowship out into the hall?"

Stirling looked over at the adjutant general. "My dear Paterson, I am sorry we're disturbing you. But it was simply the joy of encountering an old friend. We shall leave immediately. But we look forward to seeing you tonight at the entertainment."

Paterson waved his hand. "Yes, Thomas, we shall see you there. Now begone so that I can finish up in time."

Stirling grinned broadly to Northcutt and McDonald. "Let us go so poor old Paterson can keep his nose to the grindstone."

Once they were walking in the hall, Stirling said, "Northcutt, are you aware of the reception taking place tonight?"

"Yes, Paterson told me and invited me to attend."

"Well, if he hadn't, we'd have invited you." He thought a second. "Here's an idea: Why don't you come with us to supper? The general recommended an inn which he said had excellent fare, so we'll have a good meal, imbibe some cheery libations, and then stroll on over to the great warehouse which they have turned into a hall for the evening."

"I'd be delighted, Thomas. After a week aboard a small dispatch vessel, I'll welcome some fresh meat and vegetables."

McDonald said, "As will we after a wretched crossing aboard the old *Prefect*."

Stirling grinned. "Shall we go? I want to have supper and get to the hall a little early. Our pipes and drums are providing some of the entertainment, and I want to make sure everything is ready."

Barrett replied, "By all means, Thomas! Let us depart."

Wend and James Wood sat in camp chairs before the fire, which was well on its way to burning down to embers. Wend, feeling the night chill, rose from his chair, went over to a pile of wood, and threw a couple of pieces into the flames, which responded by flaring upward. Wend looked upward and could see that the black sky was clear of clouds, with stars visible from horizon to horizon. Around them were many more fires and the sounds of a military camp—laughing, shouts, men and women talking, metal cooking implements clanking. In the distance Wend could hear the occasional neighing of a horse on the picket line.

The company was spending the first night of its march encamped in the woods near Ashby's Ferry with the intention of crossing early in the morning. Wend was a little spooked by the location, for it was the spot where he had ambushed and killed Richard Grenough and where Welford and his men had assembled before attacking Eckert Ridge. It was getting late, and the officers and sergeants had just left to make their pre-lights-out rounds of the camp. Wend, still on his feet, went to a small table, picked up a jug of whiskey, and offered Wood a refill. The politician readily accepted.

After Wend sat back down, Wood looked over and said, "Wend, one of the reasons I decided to ride with you is because I wanted to brief you on some of the political machinations going on down in Williamsburg. They might affect you directly or impinge on the course of the campaign against Dunmore."

"You know I always welcome your advice, James."

"The first thing is the matter of making generals; it's been an intense process in the legislature. You're well aware that initially Henry was considered a candidate. But his handling of the 1st Virginia quickly revealed that his military skills were quite limited. So he was soon dropped, and the committee dealing with military matters put together a list of more experienced men. Your old friend Andrew Lewis soon became the safe choice as commander of Virginia's forces. He's getting a bit long in the tooth, but he has led ranger and rifle companies on the border since the days of Braddock. And of course he led a brigade during the Ohio campaign in '74."

Wend said, "Henry can't have been happy about being shunted aside."

"No, and when the list of generals was published, he took it as an affront and immediately resigned from military service. But that was what we expected, and despite Henry's histrionics, nobody, not even him, was really *that* upset about the outcome. His forte is really political manipulation."

Wend interjected, "As far as I'm concerned, his forte is manipulation of any kind."

Wood smiled. "You could be correct. However, as you may be aware, the Virginia Convention is in the process of writing a constitution. A committee, chaired by Reginald Cary, has been hashing it over for some time. My understanding is that two lawyers named George Mason and James Madison, are primarily responsible for the structure of the document. But Henry is also on the committee. The reason I'm going to Williamsburg is to participate in the final deliberations and the approval vote in the general convention. But the important thing for you to know is that, given his public popularity and political clout, Henry is the most likely choice to be the first governor of the state."

All that was a bit of a shock to Wend. "I hadn't paid much attention to the news out of the capital."

"Well, one thing can be said about Henry: he is much better at political maneuvering than the military variety."

Wend looked down at his cup. "He certainly maneuvered me the way he wanted in the case of Connolly and the tribal uprising last year."

"Yes, but in the end, you came out of that looking like a rose, and Henry was quite happy about the job you did. He's got you on his favorable list."

Wend said, "I wish I wasn't on any of his lists at all."

Woods grinned. "Well, he isn't likely to cause you any trouble. At least in the near term. He's got two things on his mind: the governorship and marriage."

"Marriage? He isn't married already?"

"He was." Wood looked around. "The truth is his first wife went insane. Almost four years ago. Totally out of her mind. Henry secluded her in the cellar of his house under the constant care of servants. However, she died last year. There are rumors of suicide."

"Kept her in the cellar? That sounds cruel."

"No, Wend, it showed great concern for her well-being. The mental asylum in Williamsburg is a hell-hole. She had a far better life in Henry's basement."

Wend thought that over for a moment, then cocked his head and looked conspiratorially at Wood. "So now Henry is ready to remarry. Knowing him, I would expect he has some wealthy widow in prospect."

Wood laughed. "Well, that wouldn't be a bad guess. But in this case, you would be at least partially wrong."

Wend raised his eyebrows. "Oh? Not wealthy or not a widow?"

"Not wealthy but in line for eventual wealth. Most importantly, not a widow. Actually a very young—and rather beautiful—lady."

"Who is the *lucky* maiden?"

"Her name is Dorothea Spotswood Dandridge, and she is nineteen. Her family lives on a rather grand plantation in northern Hanover County."

Wend thought a moment. "Wasn't Spotswood the name of a royal governor some years ago?"

"Yes, and if you had spent any time in the capital, you would recognize the name Dandridge." He looked at Wend. "A very wealthy and influential family. The former Martha Dandridge is married to a certain George Washington."

Wend raised his eyebrows. "So Henry and Washington are going to be related by marriage?"

"Yes, and there is not much love lost between the two men. Sparks can fly when they rub elbows."

Wend looked into the fire. "Henry is pushing forty and taking a bride of less than half his age."

James shrugged. "You know, those types of marriage can work out. Look at Angus McDonald and his wife. The age difference is about the same."

Wend contemplated that a moment. Then he remarked, "At that age, she's going to have a lot to learn playing the governor's wife."

Wood nodded. "Indeed, but I've met the lady, and she is intelligent, spirited and strong-willed. I suspect she will quickly grow into the role." He grinned at Wend. "In appearance, she is fair-complexioned and slim-figured, with raven hair. As a matter of fact, she could be your wife's younger sister."

"Well, if that's true, I can vouch that Henry is going to have his hands full. How did he happen to settle upon this vixen?"

Wood winked at Wend. "Interesting you should ask that. It is a bit of an arranged marriage, resulting from an intriguing story. It happens Miss Dandridge was being courted by a certain Scots sea captain, a handsome devil but rather rough around the edges and, I am told, with something of a shadowy background. Never met him, but I hear his name was—let me think—oh, yes. The name was John Paul Jones. And in truth, she had rather a hankering for him. Well, as you might suspect, her father considered the affair unsuitable and was having none of it."

"You mean, he forbade her from seeing the sailor?"

"Exactly, my dear Eckert. He had his sights on what he considered better things for his daughter. And he communicated in no uncertain terms to this fellow Jones that he was not to see the lovely Miss Dandridge again." Wood took a pull on his whiskey. "Then he lost no time in spiriting her down to Williamsburg and thrusting her into the society of the capital, where, given her looks, sooner rather than later, she caught the eye of eligible gentlemen, including, of course, Henry. And things developed from there. The betrothal was announced recently."

"Well, interesting story, James. But you said there were political currents you thought I ought to know about."

"Well, this new constitution for our dominion which Cary and Mason are drafting appears to have lots of interesting ideas: a two-chamber legislature, among other things. But I am told by insiders that, knowing that Henry is likely to be the first governor and knowing his manipulative nature, they intend to make the executive relatively weak and limit his term to one year. Henry, on the other hand, would like to make the governorship more powerful and of longer term. And he does have his popular supporters in the convention. So there will be considerable debate and dealing once the draft is presented to the assembled representatives."

Wood stopped talking for a moment, looking into the flames. Then he said, "But the really important decision to be made about Virginia and its constitution is how we will stand in regard to England. Do we declare independence or maintain a distant relationship with the mother country?"

"So, James, where does Henry stand?"

"Henry is most strongly behind independence, and he has a lot of supporters. However, there is a significant party which wants us to set up our own government but still call the king our sovereign."

Wend cocked his head and looked at Wood. "And James, if I may ask, where do you stand on that?"

A puzzled look came over Wood's face. "Why would you doubt my position? I am for an independent Virginia."

Wend shrugged. "I simply couldn't recall you saying where precisely you stood."

"Well, now you know. And it is the most important vote we will take in Williamsburg this session. For we must not only decide our position, we must also communicate that decision to our representatives at the Continental Congress, for the same question is being debated in Philadelphia and there will soon be a vote on whether all of the colonies will band together to seek their independence."

Wend said, "Grave matters, indeed."

Wood turned to look directly at Wend. "The reason I've gone over all this with you is there may be some impact on the administration of Virginia's army and particularly how it is used. I believe the vote will be for independence and that the convention will throw all the resources it can muster into the early and final defeat of Dunmore and his loyalists. You can look toward a climactic battle which will attempt to force him out of Virginia, and it is my belief that your company, because of the discipline and training you have imparted to your men, will be in the center of it all."

CHAPTER TWELVE

MATTERS OF IMPORTANCE

Wend was in his tent, inspecting and reloading his rifle and pistols, when there was a tapping on the front post and the flap was pulled open to show Shay O'beirne standing there, a crooked smile on his face. He asked the Irishman, "Yes, Shay, what is it?"

O'beirne pulled the flap fully back and stepped into the tent. Then he said in a conspiratorial tone, "Now my darling captain, there's been a rumor floating 'round the camp ever since the Honorable James Wood rode off for Williamsburg this very morning." He grinned and said, "The rumor of a little private expedition on the part of the captain and some members of the company. Members whose homes just happen to be at Eckert Ridge."

Wend stared at O'beirne for a long moment. "We have some private business to conduct. There's no way it concerns you or any other member of the company. You, like the others, can enjoy a couple days' rest after five days' hard marches to get us here to Fredericksburg."

"You're right, Captain, it doesn't *concern* me, but it does *interest* me. An Irishman is always interested in the concept of vengeance." He grinned. "Especially against Englishmen. And you *are* planning to make a visit to a certain English planter, aren't you? A planter with loyalist sympathies?" He motioned down at the bed where Wend's weapons lay. "I suspect you would find another brace of well-handled horse pistols and a trained sword of some use to you."

"Let me get this straight: You're volunteering to ride with us into danger and possible trouble with the law, even though the attack on

Eckert Ridge in no way affected you? Everyone who is going—me, Donegal, Baird, Horner, and Billy—lost family, friends, or property on that day."

O'beirne grinned. "The idea of sitting around in camp bores me. And anyway, you didn't have any call to help me on the night we met in the Golden Buck. Let's just say it's a return of the favor. And it won't hurt you to have another man along who—how shall I phrase it—has had a close relationship with the business of killing and won't hesitate when the time comes to pull the trigger."

Wend thought a long moment. *Six would definitely be better than five.* "All right, Shay, but one caution: no *killing* unless they fire first."

"How discouraging. But then, it is your party."

"Get your weapons and horse ready. We leave within the hour."

—ᴍ—

After their supper, accompanied by ample libations and good cigars provided by Northcutt to Stirling and McDonald, the three officers, feeling quite mellow, strolled along the waterfront until they came to the warehouse that was to serve as the hall for the evening's ball.

As Stirling had requested, they had arrived early, and the place was essentially empty, except for servers finishing preparations and members of an orchestra.

Stirling pointed to a corner of the warehouse, near a set of double doors designed to allow large objects to be brought in and out on wagons. "There are our people."

Northcutt saw men in Highland uniform, some with pipes and others with drums.

McDonald said, "Let's go over and see how Lieutenant Campbell and Sergeant Tavish are doing."

They walked over to the group of soldiers. McDonald introduced Northcutt to Campbell, who was the 42nd adjutant, then asked, "Everything ready?"

Campbell motioned to the soldiers. "Aye, sir, as far as the pipers and dancers. They've run through the routine. Tavish has everything worked out well." He shook his head. "But Miss Fraser and her navy accompanists haven't arrived yet. They were coming over in a later boat. She said she wanted to practice a little before the ball starts to test out how music sounds here in the building."

A female voice said, "We're here, and we'll be ready to practice in a moment."

Barrett looked around in the direction of the voice and was stunned by the sight of the most attractive redhead he had ever seen. Then in a moment, he changed his mind. She was the most attractive *auburn-haired* woman he had ever encountered, for her hair was actually a rich, copper color with a natural gleam that the room's candle lighting played off. A pale-green gown accentuated her hair and showed off a spare figure and waist that could have belonged to a street waif in London. Northcutt looked at her face; it was high-cheekboned, with skin that had been darkened by exposure to the sun. That was unusual, for most women treasured pale skin and powdered their faces to enhance that effect. But in this girl, the tanned skin perfectly complemented her hair and highlighted her beauty. Then he saw her eyes. They were green and doe-shaped. But no deer's eyes had ever exuded such warmth and intelligence. Northcutt estimated she was in her late twenties.

Charles McDonald turned to Northcutt. "Barrett, let me present Miss Mary Fraser, the matron of our hospital." Then he said, "Mary, this is Colonel Barrett Northcutt, of the King's Loyal Virginia Legion."

Mary extended her hand, and Barrett took it as he made a bow. "Miss Fraser, it is my great honor to meet you." As he spoke, he looked up and noted that she had one of the most beguiling smiles he had ever encountered.

"It is my pleasure, Colonel."

Northcutt wanted to say something to impress her, but for one of the few times in his life, he found himself tongue-tied, having no idea how to start a conversation with the girl. He simply stared at her.

Meanwhile, McDonald said, "Mary, guests will soon be arriving, so if you want to rehearse, you had best do it immediately."

"Indeed, Charles." She turned to two sailors standing behind her who were dressed in the ship's livery of the *Prefect* and motioned them to follow her.

Barrett noticed one carried a violin and the other a flute.

Mary called out to one of the pipers, "Tavish, come join us; we're going to run through our piece quickly so I can get the feel of the sound in this room."

As the musicians got ready, Barrett turned to McDonald. "My God, what a marvelous-looking young lady!"

MacDonald laughed. "Northcutt, your reaction is typical of men when they first see Mary."

"I can completely understand that. How is it that she is with your regiment? Is she the wife of one of the officers?"

"It may seem hard to believe, but she is an orphan who grew up in Highland regiments, first the 77th and then the 42nd. I recruited her father into the 77th, over twenty years ago. As a sergeant, he was killed leading a rearguard action at Fort Duquesne at the forks of the Ohio in 1758. Her mother and stepfather died of fever in the West Indies. She grew up in the care of chaplains and surgeons and, with great determination, essentially educated herself to the level of a middling woman. She spent the last eight years as the governess of an estate in Scotland and returned to the regiment just before we sailed."

Northcutt asked, "What does the matron of the hospital do?"

"She's the head nurse. Trains the others, assists the surgeon, and takes care of paperwork." McDonald paused a minute. "Mary learned her nursing from her mother and has often treated men on the battle-field. This is indelicate for me to say, but the fact is she was seriously wounded in battle, taking a ball in her side." He looked at Northcutt. "And don't tell the surgeon that I said this, but my impression is that she has nearly the practical skills of a physician."

Barrett stared at Mary. "What an extraordinary woman."

McDonald laughed. "The subalterns in the mess would enthu-siastically agree with you." Then McDonald looked over to where the violinist and the flutist were warming up. "Wait till you hear her sing. I'll wager you will vow you've never heard a more lovely voice."

The two watched as the three accompanists—violin, flute, and piper—took their positions behind Mary. She nodded, and the violin and flute played an introduction. Then Mary began to sing. And in a few seconds, Northcutt knew McDonald was not exaggerating. She sang with a sweet, lilting voice in perfect key with the instruments. Then she paused, and the bagpipe took up the melody in company with the other two instruments. After a few moments, the pipes stopped and Mary picked up the vocal. She sang for a short time and then with violin, flute, and pipes again playing together, finished the piece.

Stirling, McDonald, and Northcutt broke into enthusiastic applause, and Mary responded with a curtsy.

Stirling said, "Mary, you and your accompanists sound marvelous. I vow you will be the hit of the ball and a credit to the regiment."

Mary smiled. "Well, I think it did go very well, considering the short time we've had to practice together. Thank goodness we rehearsed several times on the voyage coming across." A worried look crossed her face. "Hopefully we'll be as good when we perform for the assemblage."

An hour later the hall was filled with people. Besides military officers of all ranks, there were many of the loyalist men and women who had been carried with the army from Boston. All were dressed in their best finery, and it made for a bright crowd, all seeming very happy and intent on enjoying themselves. Captain Gardiner, the adjutant general's secretary, came by, and Northcutt engaged him in conversation, remarking on the apparent happiness of the assemblage.

"Indeed," said the captain. "This is the first opportunity they've had to get out and forget their worries. After all, they've lost their homes, possessions, and livelihoods. Their future is uncertain. But tonight they can put all that aside for a few hours and show a brave front." He smiled. "Every person here hopes that after a brief campaign, they will be able to return to their familiar surroundings and rebuild their lives and fortunes."

Northcutt was about to agree, but at that moment, he saw his brother entering the ballroom. On his arm was a pretty, slim-waisted, elegantly dressed, well-coiffed blond woman whom Northcutt estimated to be in her midtwenties. He said, "Well, William, here is Gregory and the young lady."

Gardiner turned and looked at the couple. "Yes, that is Elizabeth Loring." He called out, "Major Northcutt! Gregory! Please join us—I have a surprise for you!"

The major looked over, and then pleasure registered on his face as he recognized his sibling. He turned to the lady and said something, at which point she stared momentarily at Barrett, then turned back to her escort and laughed. Gregory steered her toward the two officers.

After an affectionate greeting, Gregory said, "Well, something I never thought I'd see: my younger brother in uniform, and that of a lieutenant colonel at that!"

Barrett shrugged. "It's the sign of the times, Gregory. I don't pretend to be a professional like you and have no intention of remaining in uniform a day longer than necessary."

Gregory laughed. "Pray it won't be much longer. Once we get to New York and give the colonists a hard knock or two, things will end quickly." Then he asked, "But what are you doing up here?"

Barrett said, "I'll explain soon enough, but first you must introduce me to the young lady."

"Ah yes! My neglect in the excitement of seeing you after all these years." He motioned toward her and said, "Barrett, may I present Mrs. Elizabeth Loring. Her husband, Joshua, has just been appointed to the duty of commissary general."

Elizabeth gave her hand to Barrett, who made a slight bow and said, "My pleasure to meet you, Mrs. Loring."

"And mine to meet you, Colonel Northcutt. I am very much indebted to your brother, who was so good as to escort me tonight as my husband is busy attending to his new duties."

Barrett smiled and said, "Yes, it would have been a shame if such a lovely lady had been unable to attend this ball. It looks to be a marvelous evening."

Gregory looked at his brother. "Barrett, would you be so good as to entertain Mrs. Loring while I get her some refreshment?"

"That would be my pleasure."

Gardiner also took his leave. "Colonel, I have duties to attend to with regard to some of the performances."

Barrett said, "All the better for me to visit with Mrs. Loring."

After they were alone, Mrs. Loring said, "Barrett, please call me Betsy. Everyone does."

"Of course, Betsy."

Northcutt looked around and saw that people had continued to flow in and the hall had now become quite crowded. The orchestra had been playing, and dancing had begun. At that moment a door opened and a party of officers entered the room, greeting people along the way. Many turned to look at the new arrivals, and a round of polite clapping began. Northcutt noticed that among them was Paterson, the adjutant general. He was walking behind an officer in general's uniform. Northcutt turned to Mrs. Loring. "I've never seen General Howe. Is that he?"

Betsy looked at the man leading the group of officers and then smiled at Northcutt. "Indeed it is, Barrett. He is quite distinguished looking, don't you agree?"

"Certainly, ma'am." Barrett quickly looked him over: Slightly above average height, Howe had maintained a lean figure, which showed off well in his well-tailored uniform. He had active eyes which darted around the room, and now and then he waved at individuals.

Northcutt turned to comment to Mrs. Loring and noticed she had a look of some distress on her face, and he saw a bead of perspiration on her forehead. "Are you all right, Betsy? You look uncomfortable."

She shrugged and made a tight smile. "It is nothing. I'm having some slight discomfort. Undoubtedly something I ate earlier in the day. Assuredly it will pass when I have some libation."

As if on cue, Gregory arrived with drinks for the three of them. "I've got rum for you, Barrett, and some wine for Betsy."

They toasted the king and then took their first sip. Meanwhile, the orchestra stopped playing and a sergeant struck the floor with the staff of a halberd for attention. Captain Gardiner, standing next to him, raised his arms and called for quiet in the hall.

"Ladies and gentlemen, General Howe hopes that you all are enjoying the evening. We have all been busy for many days making our preparations to return to the rebellious colonies, so it is quite appropriate to pause for a few hours to relax and refresh ourselves. But beyond that we take this occasion to welcome the latest additions to His Majesty's forces here in America. I refer, of course, to the newly arrived 42nd and 71st Highlanders." Gardiner motioned to where both Stirling and Lieutenant Colonel Fraser, commandant of the 71st, stood together. Cheers and clapping erupted from the crowd.

After it subsided, Gardiner announced, "And to mark their arrival, the two regiments have prepared a selection of Highland music and dancing for our enjoyment. Please welcome the pipes of the 42nd and dancers of the 71st." Gardiner waved toward a door leading from the outside, and as he did, the audience heard the groaning sound of bagpipes being inflated, accompanied by a drum cadence. Momentarily, the pipers and drummers appeared marching into the open area in front of the orchestra. Clapping erupted from the assemblage. When they reached position in front of the orchestra, they wheeled toward the audience and halted. Then they played two tunes on the pipes.

Upon their completion, to the beat of the drums, eight kilted Highlanders, each bearing a broadsword, marched in through the doors to center stage in front of the pipes. They placed crossed swords on the floor, and then to the sound of pipes played at a fast pace, the men danced around and over the swords, to the increasing applause of the spectators.

Presently the dancers finished, picked up their swords, and to a resurgence of clapping, marched back out of the doors.

Hardly had they left when Mary, followed by her accompanists, entered through the same doors. The girl walked with smooth, confident steps, her head held high, to the center before the pipe band, and the two sailors stood behind her. The same piper who had played with her before marched out to join the two sailors.

Mary nodded to her compatriots, and they began the musical introduction. Then Mary began her song.

As she sang, Northcutt looked around the room. The assemblage was dead silent, visibly mesmerized by her voice. Barrett was convinced Mary's performance was better even than at the rehearsal.

Gregory said, "What a stunning woman. I wonder how she happens to be with the 42nd?"

Betsy nodded. "Yes, she sings marvelously. And she is lovely for a redhead."

Barrett responded, "It happens I've met her." He explained Mary's background to them and what her role was with the regiment.

Betsy smiled. "I wonder how it is she is not married?"

Barrett laughed. "I'm told she is being pursued en masse by the junior officers of the 42nd. However, she seems to be resisting all advances."

Betsy shook her head. "Foolish girl. If she's come up from being a camp girl, what a coup it would be for her to marry into money and society."

"Well," said Gregory, "we shall not resolve her problem here." Then he suggested, "Shall we sample the refreshment tables? I saw some alluring plates when I went for drinks."

Betsy said, "Yes, let's! And I need another libation. And *this* time, Gregory, I need something stronger than this wine."

Gregory gave her his hand and looked over at Northcutt. "Will you come with us?"

Barrett replied, "I have some people I wish to visit with. Let me rejoin you later."

After the couple had left, Barrett made his way toward where Stirling and McDonald were standing. Fortunately, they were talking with Mary Fraser, and he felt an urgent need to make up for his earlier inability to converse intelligently with her.

As he joined them, McDonald asked, "Well, Northcutt, what did you think of the performance of our men and of course, Mary?"

"Most entertaining. I had never seen Highland dancing before." Then he smiled at Mary. "And Miss Fraser's performance was most excellent. You have a gift, Mary. Where did you receive your training?"

"I picked up my singing as a way to entertain myself and my friends on campaign. The chaplain of the 77th taught me a bit, but after that it seemed to come to me naturally."

"Well," said Barrett, "then I was right—it is a gift."

Stirling looked over. "Indeed, a gift, but those of us who have known her since her youth know how hard she works at everything she sets her mind to. She makes the most of the gifts the Lord has given her."

Mary blushed slightly and was getting ready to reply, but just then a handsome lieutenant arrived. He nodded toward Stirling. "Beg your pardon, Colonel, but Mary has promised me the first dance after her performance, and I am here to collect on it."

Mary smiled. "Dougal is quite correct, Colonel. With your permission I'll honor that promise."

"Of course. Please enjoy yourselves."

The two left for the area reserved as a dance floor.

Barrett, frustrated at losing the opportunity to spend time with the girl, looked over at McDonald. "Charles, there is a great mystery here: How is it that such a beautiful and gifted woman of Mary's age remains a spinster? Give me the truth."

McDonald laughed, then took a sip of his drink. "Now you've asked an interesting question. The truth, Barrett, although you'll never get *her* to admit it, is that she bears a torch for a former lover."

"Someone back in Scotland?"

"Not Scotland. The man lives in Virginia."

"Virginia? That seems tragic."

"Indeed, Barrett. But I believe she can't bring herself to settle on another man. That's the real tragedy. My fondest hope is that with all these fine young officers in the regiment, she will finally become romantically involved."

Barrett took a deep breath and was about to comment when an ensign in the uniform of the 23rd approached them.

"Sir, are you Colonel Northcutt?"

"Indeed I am."

"Sir, I'm to tell you that your brother, Major Northcutt, request you join him. An urgent matter has arisen."

Puzzled, Northcutt excused himself to Stirling and McDonald and followed the ensign. They pushed through the crowd to a corner of the room, where he could see Betsy Loring sitting in a chair with her right hand to her forehead. Gregory stood beside her.

Gregory dismissed the ensign and when he had departed, said in a quiet tone, "Mrs. Loring is experiencing serious discomfort. I need to get her back to her apartment. Please stay with her until I can get her carriage."

Barrett said, "Wait, before you do that, what about locating a doctor? Surely there are numerous battalion surgeons here in the hall."

Betsy quickly looked up at him and shook her head. "No military surgeon." She bit her lip. "Excuse me if I am indelicate, but this is a female indisposition."

Then she put her hands to her waist and leaned forward, obviously in pain.

She said quietly, "A midwife would be more appropriate."

An idea immediately hit Barrett. "I believe I can help you." He looked up at Gregory and said, "Wait here! I will be back instantly."

Without waiting for an answer, Northcutt pushed his way rapidly through the crowd until he saw Mary Fraser at the center of several young Highland officers. He walked right up to the group and said in his best military voice, "Gentlemen, I must talk privately with Miss Fraser. It is a serious, urgent matter."

He looked around at the subalterns, all of whom were registering displeasure, even anger, in their eyes.

Mary looked up at Northcutt, then turned to her admirers. "Please, gentlemen, I'm sure the colonel would not speak so peremptorily unless he had good reason. Please give us some distance."

The young men retreated, and Mary said with raised eyebrows, "You *were* rather abrupt, Colonel."

"Miss Fraser, I have very good reason. There is a young woman here who is having severe medical problems, and I'm counting on your good offices to assist her."

Puzzlement spread over Mary's face. "Surely there are many physicians in the ballroom. I am merely a nurse."

"The lady has intimated to me that her problem is of the female variety and she strongly prefers that she be administered to by another woman. Actually, she asked for a midwife, but I'm sure there are none in this room or readily available. Am I right in guessing that you have attended to women experiencing this type of problem?"

Mary nodded. "I have performed numerous births and attended other kinds of similar situations." A look of great concern came over her face. "However, I am not sure I would have the authority to perform medical treatment when there are so many surgeons available. I could face discipline if I exceeded my authority."

Northcutt put his hand gently on her arm. "Mary, now listen close: This woman has a special relationship with General Howe. *Very special.* Do you understand?"

Mary raised her eyebrows and stared at Barrett for a long moment, then slowly nodded. "Yes, I'm not naive, Colonel."

"Good. I can assure you that you will have the full protection of the commander in chief under these circumstances. Now let us hurry, for the woman is in obvious pain."

—⟋⟍—

In the early morning dusk, the six horsemen rode up the drive to River View Plantation, home of loyalist Dalton Crosswell. All was quiet. They pulled up directly in front of the manor house, an imposing white structure three levels high with a portico supported by six columns. Beyond the mansion flowed the broad Rappahannock, an impressive outlook even in the dim light.

Wend motioned to Horner and Billy. "All right, find the tobacco barn and fire it. Then hit the other outbuildings. Once they are alight, go to the slave quarters and make sure they stay in their huts. We'll watch for any house servants coming up from the quarters for early chores. And remember, no shooting except in self-defense. Brandishing your firelocks should keep the Africans and overseer at bay. And when I make the signal, ride back here without delay."

Horner nodded. "We won't take long, Mr. Eckert."

Wend said, "We'll wait here while you build the fires and will take no action until we see the flames of the barn."

It was about twenty minutes later that Wend saw fire licking up the side of a building about 150 yards away, partially obscured from view by pines. He nodded to Joshua and Shay. "All right, there goes the tobacco; take your positions at either end of the portico."

The two dismounted and ran to their places. Wend looked at Donegal and nodded. "Go ahead and do the honors."

Donegal slid out of the saddle and, horse pistol in hand, walked up to the front door. He reversed the firelock so that he was holding it by the barrel and started loudly banging the butt against the door.

It took long minutes, but presently the door was cracked open and a face stared out. Donegal quickly moved back to the ground before the portico. Then the door opened about halfway, and a tall, middle-aged man stood looking out at Donegal and Wend, who was still mounted on Sonny.

The man swung back the door fully and stepped out onto the porch. He was dressed in a blue housecoat and had a stocking cap on his head. Wend asked, "Are you Mr. Dalton Crosswell?"

"I am he, and who might you be? And what do you want at this hour?"

"I am Wend Eckert, gunsmith of Frederick County and captain of the Frederick County Light Foot."

The expression on Crosswell's face was pure astonishment and something to behold. He stared at Wend, his mouth open wide.

Wend said, "I expect you heard I was dead. A certain Major Welford would have told you I was shot in the head." He grinned. "Crosswell, here's what you need to know: over time, many men have found, often to their dismay, that I am not easy to kill." Wend paused, and a smile crossed his face. "And Welford is simply the last who has been unsuccessful in trying to do so."

Crosswell stood in shock, unable to speak.

Wend was about to resume speaking when suddenly O'beirne called out. "Freeze, Crosswell! Put your hands where I can see them."

Then, pistol aimed at Crosswell, Shay slowly walked along the portico until he was beside the planter. He reached behind the man and came out with a light dueling pistol in his hand. He blew the priming out of the pan and threw it on the ground. "The rascal was holding this behind himself. Now you can continue, Captain." Then he retreated to his station.

Wend said, "Crosswell, before I tell you exactly why we are here, I want you to call your wife."

"My wife? Why on earth do you wish to see her?"

"I want her to hear what happened to her son, Lindsey Crosswell. I want her to know how he died. And to have that memory for the rest of her life."

"Sir, what kind of a man are you, to so cruelly distress a mother?"

"What kind of man? I am German by birth, Ulster-Scot by marriage, Highlander by the brotherhood of battle, and Virginian by the order of a Pennsylvania sheriff. And undoubtedly as hard a man as you are likely to ever encounter."

There was a flurry of activity behind Dalton, and a handsome woman in her forties, dressed in a night coat and cap, pushed past him. "I am Lillian Crosswell. You know something about Lindsey?"

"We know how exactly he died." Wend pointed to Baird, standing, pistol in hand, at the end of the portico. "Tell them, Joshua."

Baird stood staring at the Crosswells for a long, dramatic moment. Finally he spoke. "Aye, I was with him when he took his last breath. He was shot trying to burn down the main house at Eckert Ridge."

Wend interjected, "He was shot in the chest by my wife, who is the Ulster-Scot part of me. She was raised in the backcountry, has fought Indians, birthed three children, and is a damn fair shot with a pistol."

Lillian Crosswell sobbed. "Is that what killed him?"

Joshua said, "Not directly, Mrs. Crosswell. He didn't have it that easy. He was being brought back here in a wagon by that spy Rhys, the ironmonger. But I caught up with Rhys the next evening, and he tried to get away but upset his wagon during the chase. Now listen close. Your son was smashed up in the crash. All the iron pans and pots broke loose and pounded into him as the wagon rolled over. A lot of his bones were broken, and he had a big gash in his head. But he didn't die right away. That would have been easiest for him. No, he suffered in agony most of the night and mercifully for him, finally died just as the sun was comin' up the next mornin'."

Lillian Crosswell gasped, then her eyes welled up in tears and she turned and buried her head in her husband's side.

Crosswell exploded in anger. He shouted at Baird, "Sir, how can you be so cruel as to describe in such coarse language a son's death to his mother? No woman should be subjected to such horror."

Wend stood up in his stirrups and shouted, "You speak of horror, Crosswell?" He pointed to Donegal. "I'll tell you about horror. That man suffered the *horror* of watching his young wife shot by a loyalist while she was standing right beside him. He was sprayed with her blood and then watched her live only long enough to realize she was dying." Wend gritted his teeth. "And Crosswell, that young wife was bearing in her womb a child who died with her." He shook his head, "That is *horror*! And there was also the *horror* of a mother holding her eight-year-old boy in her arms as he died, shot by one of the men who raided our farm. Maybe by your son!"

Wend swept his arm around to take in the entire plantation. "We know that raid was launched from this very place, with your enthusiastic support. We know you and your son recruited most of the men who rode in the attack." He looked directly at Crosswell. "Know this: The only people killed in the raid, aside from some of the attackers, were the woman and the young boy. And Eckert Ridge Farm has been rebuilt better than ever, and muskets are again being made for the soldiers of Virginia. So innocent people died, not for some great triumph in the name of the king but for nothing!"

There was a long silence, broken only by the sobbing of the woman. Finally Dalton Crosswell asked, "What do you intend to do to us? Do you intend to take our lives?"

Wend said nothing. Instead he raised his pistol, first pointing it in the general direction of the couple on the portico. Then he raised it straight into the air and fired. He shook his head and replied, "No, Crosswell, I'm not taking any lives. But I am taking your livelihood and your shelter." He waved the pistol in the direction of the tobacco barn. "Look there!"

Crosswell looked and for the first time saw the flames. "Oh my God! You've fired the tobacco! Our entire crop will burn!"

"Yes, and my men have by now also fired every other farm building. Your stables, sheds, and your carriage house. All are at this very moment being consumed by flames. Only the slave quarters are spared."

Lillian pulled away from her husband and stared at the fires. "Dalton, everything will be destroyed! That crop is our fortune."

"More than that is about to be destroyed!" Wend signaled to Donegal, who gave Crosswell a shove. "Get down off the portico—you and your wife. Do it now." He pointed the pistol at Crosswell.

The plantation owner took his wife's arm and escorted her away from the porch.

As he finished speaking, Horner and Billy came riding up, carrying torches. Horner waved behind them. "Everything is fired, Mr. Eckert. And the Africans didn't try to interfere in any way."

Wend thought of something. "What about a white overseer?"

Horner shook his head. "Didn't see any. If he figured out what was going on, he must have decided it wasn't his business to stop it."

Wend nodded. "Good. Now fire the house!"

Crosswell shouted, "You bastards!"

Horner and Billy ran into the house. Soon flames were visible in the windows. In a few minutes, they returned and mounted their horses.

Lillian shrieked, "Oh God above! How shall we live? What will we do?"

Wend answered the question. "You have only one choice! What you did has been reported to the convention in Williamsburg. In due course, men will come for you. You must flee this very day. And the only place you can go is Gwynn's Island, which Dunmore and his loyalist forces have occupied. Certainly you have boats at your landing. I suggest you gather some food and sail to the island."

"Oh, in God's heaven, we shall have nothing," wailed Lillian.

Wend said, "You will have your lives and shelter when you get to the island." He paused a moment and then continued, "And when you get there, tell the governor, and, more importantly, his henchmen Northcutt and Welford, that Eckert lives and is coming for them. I'm coming for them with one hundred of Virginia's finest men at my back. Sooner or later, in some manner, they will pay their debt to me, and I shall not treat them as kindly as I have you."

Wend signaled to the others to mount and then waved at them to depart. They rode off down the drive, while Wend sat Sonny in front of the burning house and watched the Crosswells. When everyone had gone, he said to the couple as they stood observing the flames consume their mansion, "Remember what I told you to say to the governor and his minions." He took his hat off and swept it in front of him in mocking salute to them. "And now I bid you good day and a safe journey."

Wend turned Sonny and spurred him forward at the gallop to join the others, taking care not to look back as he rode.

Soon he assumed his place at the head of the small troop. They traveled in silence for several minutes, and then Shay O'beirne brought his horse alongside Wend's.

"Now, my darling captain, if you'll permit me to say, that was a lovely piece of revenge, ruining a man like that. Indeed, most excellently executed. Only one thing would have made it more satisfying, and that would be if we could just have had a little blood flowing. Say, Master Crosswell wounded with a pistol ball or perhaps horsewhipped, lying in the lovely Lillian's arms? Aye, now that would have been a fine sight."

Wend looked sternly at the Irishman. "Shay, you are indeed a cruel and cynical bastard."

The lieutenant grinned. "I always appreciate compliments, my dear captain. I plead guilty to being a cruel cynic indeed. And about the bastard part, in truth my sainted mother was never quite sure about precisely who my father might be. She had several choices and could not decide between them and finally decided on the most handsome of the lot. When I look in the mirror, I'm thinkin' she made the right choice."

Wend made a tight smile. "Shay, I think it is the devil himself who is your father. But just keep this in mind: when I do catch up with Welford and Northcutt, there *will* be blood—as much as even *you* could desire."

CHAPTER THIRTEEN

THE ISLAND

Five men stood around the table in front of General Lewis's tent, which was located in a grove of pines close to the road from Gloucester. The grove was about a hundred yards from the narrow channel, known as Milford Haven, which separated the mainland from Gwynn's Island. A couple of companies of the 7th Virginia were bivouacked nearby, from which point a steady buzz of camp noises emanated.

Both the *Dunmore* and HMS *Roebuck* were anchored in the channel and lay in plain sight of the tent's location, open gunports showing their cannons. To the north of the island over one hundred additional ships were visible where the main body of Dunmore's fleet lay in Hills Bay at the mouth of the Piankatank River.

Three of the men at the table were officers of the 7th Virginia, specifically its colonel, William Daingerfield, Lieutenant Colonel Alexander McClannahan, and the senior captain, Thomas Posey. The other two were General Andrew Lewis himself, commander of Virginia's forces, and his chief aide de camp, Captain Seth Coulter, both of whom had arrived that morning, having made the arduous two-day journey from Williamsburg to assess for themselves the situation at Gwynn's.

Posey was performing the briefing and was referring to a map laid out on the table. "From what we can see, Dunmore's landed most of his troops on the island, including the 14th Foot, the Queen's Loyal Virginia Regiment, the King's Loyal Virginia Legion, and the Ethiopians. We believe most of the marines have remained on board ships with the Royal Navy Squadron." The captain moved his finger to the northern point of the island, where the channel was at its most narrow. "They've built a significant fortification here, with heavy naval guns emplaced, to control the narrows. Clearly they believe that is where we would be most likely to try a boat attack." Then he slid his finger down to the southern end of the channel. "There's a smaller battery of guns emplaced here." He looked up at the general. "Between the two and the ships in the channel, they can easily cannonade our positions across from the island, making any attempt by us to cross nearly impossible."

Lewis nodded. "I understand. Now what about these raids you said they've made along the coast?"

Daingerfield spoke up. "So far there have been three of which we are aware. The latest was the day before yesterday. They land men of the loyalist regiments from boats, with marines and armed sailors to back them up. They sweep through the countryside, hitting plantations, gathering provisions and sometimes Africans who run off with them. The local militia units can't muster and catch up with them before they're back to their boats."

Posey added, "We can't be ready for them because we never know where or when they will strike. Their boats and small sailing tenders give them great mobility. And we don't have enough men from the 7th here to keep detachments in logical places for raids and still man our fortifications along the channel."

Daingerfield looked at Lewis. "I'll remind you we have only half the regiment here. The rest are down near Williamsburg, still organizing. We'll not really be able to accomplish anything until we have more forces on the scene."

Lewis said, "Yes, yes, I damn well know the disposition of our forces! And give me credit for understanding your problem. I gave orders for the rest of your regiment to march up here as soon as possible. But there was a question of finishing recruiting and gathering enough rations for the march. They'll be on the road as soon as that is resolved."

At that moment Captain Coulter said, "Gentlemen, look out on the road. There's a rider there, about one hundred yards away, apparently looking us over." He looked at Daingerfield. "Do you know who he might be?"

They all turned to look and saw a lean, rangy mounted man in a hunting shirt, with a broad floppy hat with the brim turned up on one side to hold a buck's tail. He was sitting on a long-legged, powerfully built hunter. A rifle was slung over his left shoulder, the butt by his head. The spirited horse was prancing around, unhappy to have been pulled up.

Dangerfield shrugged and said, "I have no idea. He could be a courier from Williamsburg or from one of our militia outposts, warning us of a boat movement by the British."

Lewis had been staring at the rider. He laughed heartily. "Shit, gentlemen, that ain't no courier, and it ain't no damned tidewater militiaman. Only one man sits a horse like that. As I live and die, that's Joshua Baird! Known him since Braddock's expedition, these twenty years gone by now. He's the best scout in Pennsylvania—or Virginia for that matter"—he looked around at the officers and with a broad grin said—"except possibly me."

Daingerfield said, "Well, General, the question is, what is he doing here?"

"Nowadays he's livin' near Winchester, in the Valley. And if he's down here, I'll wager that means he's scouting for the light company Frederick County is sendin' down. We sent them orders to come work with your regiment. Likely they're not far away."

The general walked out into the middle of the wagon track and waved his arm. Then he shouted, "Yo, Joshua! Joshua Baird! Get your sorry self over here!"

Baird pulled on his reins to quiet the horse and stared in the direction of the tent. Then he reined the horse's head around and spurred toward them at the cantor.

Joshua pulled up the horse beside Lewis and, looking down, grinned broadly. "Now, Andrew, don't you look fancy in that pretty blue uniform with all the gold braid?"

"Seemed appropriate to wear it since they made me a general. I allow how it ain't near as comfortable as a hunting shirt and leggings."

Joshua threw down from the saddle. "Andy, I got to say I ain't ever seen no land like this tidewater. All the way down from Fredericksburg it just kept gettin' flatter and flatter the farther we come. Most of the way it's been like ridin' across a table, 'cept it's got a mess of scrubby

315

little pine trees where they ain't been cleared away for fields." He waved at the two ships lying out in the channel. "If'n they fired one of their big cannons I swear the ball would fly halfway to Fredericksburg cause there ain't nothin' to stop it."

Lewis grinned, "Well, you ain't far wrong about that, Joshua." He motioned back up the road. "Where's that company from Winchester you are scoutin' for?"

Joshua responded, "They'll be along presently. Can't be but a little behind me."

"Good. We can use them—there's only five companies of troops here right now, plus the county militia. I'm going to have some additional troops come up from Williamsburg, but that will take some time." He motioned to the table "Come on over and have a drink."

Lewis introduced Baird to the others. Then he said, "Let's finish what we were talkin' about, gentlemen."

Daingerfield said, "The real question is how we drive the British off Gwynn's. Rifles and muskets against naval cannon won't do the trick. We can bring in as many battalions of foot as you can muster, but a boat assault across the channel would be suicide against the guns of the *Dunmore* and the *Roebuck*. The truth is, General, we need cannon, *heavy* cannon, to drive off the ships and silence their batteries on land, or we're playing a losing game."

Lewis sighed. "Daingerfield, you ain't tellin' me anything I don't already know. I got people looking for guns down in Norfolk. All we got are light field guns, and they're going to come up with the new troops. We can use them to amuse the British a little, but they won't do much good against those eighteen-pounders on the frigate out there. I was hoping to get some naval guns off of ships in Norfolk harbor, but Dunmore and his followers scooped most of them up when they left the city. And if we do find some useful guns, they got to be transported up here, and the roads aren't much to speak of. And any way you come, you got to cross two deep rivers. Then, any kind of heavy rain is going to make it even worse. Wagons carrying those heavy guns will sink right down into the mud."

Daingerfield said, "Well, we wish you luck, sir. Until then, we'll do the best we can, trying to contain the enemy. And we'll try to think of a way to stop these naval raids."

Just then Posey pointed to the road. "Men coming!"

They all looked, and seven men, dressed in hunting shirts and black hats, had rounded a bend and emerged from behind a grove of pines. They walked in loose formation with their firelocks at the ready.

Joshua said, "Yep, that'll be the company's advance guard. Sergeant Flannagan is in charge." He walked out and waved to the sergeant and then shouted, "This be the headquarters, Flannagan!"

The sergeant said something to one of the men, who turned and ran back up the road. Then he called the men into formation and marched them down, halting on the road in front of the tent. Leaving them standing at attention, he marched up to the where the officers and Joshua stood, presented arms, and said to Daingerfield, "Sergeant Flannagan leading advance of the Frederick County Light Foot, sir! The company is ordered to report to the colonel commandant of the 7th Virginia Regiment."

Daingerfield returned the salute and said, "This is the headquarters of the 7th. You and your men can stand easy until the company arrives."

Flannagan replied, "Yes, sir" and marched back to where his guard stood, not dismissing them but standing to in formation.

Lewis raised an eyebrow. "That sergeant knows what he is about."

Joshua grinned. "You bet, Andy. He spent the French War in Washington's Virginia Regiment."

Lewis looked back at Flannagan. "It shows."

As he spoke, the faint sound of drums became audible. They all heard it at the same time, and Joshua said, rather unnecessarily, "That'll be the company."

Lewis went out to the road near where Flannagan's guard stood, and the others followed. Soldiers of the encampment also walked out to the road to see the newcomers arrive.

Momentarily they saw Eckert come into view on horseback, followed by Newkirk, Donegal, and Billy, carrying the standard, marching side by side. Behind them the drummers beat out the cadence, followed by O'beirne leading the rifles in column of threes.

There arose a buzz as the soldiers of the 7th, few of whom wore anything resembling a uniform, remarked on the appearance of the Frederick County men. Then the musket half company marched into view, led by Childers. Behind them came the women and children, the company wagons, and then the Conestogas.

Wend halted the company in front of the general and Daingerfield. He doffed his cap in salute, then said, "General Lewis, the Frederick County Light Foot, reporting for service with your forces, sir."

"Welcome, sir." Lewis turned to Daingerfield. "Where do you want them to camp?"

Daingerfield waved across the road. "Right over there, in that grove of pines. There's room for the tents and wagons."

Wend told Newkirk to take charge and move the company into the encampment.

Lewis called out, "All right, Eckert, swing down from your saddle and come over to my tent. Let's have a talk." He motioned for Daingerfield and Posey to join the meeting.

The general sat down in a camp chair and pointed to a jug. "Whiskey, Eckert? You probably could use some after marching in this hot sun."

Wend filled a cup and sat down.

Lewis was staring at him. Finally he said, "So, Eckert, you've decided to throw in with the patriot cause?" Before Wend could answer, Lewis looked over at the two 7th Virginia officers and said, "Let me tell you a little story: Back in '74, Eckert here was a lieutenant on Dunmore's staff. After fighting off the damned Indians at Point Pleasant, where they ambushed us, I led my brigade across the Ohio and we moved fast for the Shawnee villages on the Sciotto. We intended to pay them back for all our friends and kin who died at that battle. My brother was one of the men we left in the ground at Point Pleasant. We was nearly there, in fact we had just had a skirmish with a party of Shawnee and our blood was up, when Dunmore and some of his staff—including Eckert here—come riding out of the forest and made us stop. And not only stop—Dunmore told us a peace treaty had been signed and we were to turn around and go home." Lewis stared into the distance, breathing heavily, and continued, "Just like that, leave it and go home with the Indians safe and comfortable sittin' in their towns, protected by a treaty we didn't have no say in makin'. Meanwhile, there were scores of wives and children in Virginia who would never see their husbands and fathers again, all because of the dastardly attack of Cornstalk and his bloody warriors. And the Shawnee were safe because Dunmore wanted to curry their favor cause he could see the rebellion coming and he wanted them as allies."

Lewis took a deep drink from his cup. "And Dunmore left Eckert with us, to be our governess—our damned nursemaid, if you will—to make sure we went back across the Ohio with our tails between our legs."

Wend had had enough. He leaned forward in his chair. "Damn it, Lewis, I don't know why you want to go through all this in front of these men, but give it a rest! I was serving the lawful governor, not because I wanted to be on his staff but because it was duty. Just like you were working for him as a colonel of brigade in the militia. You've no cause to bear a grudge against me for doing my duty, same as you." Wend paused and then pulled the hair back from the left side of his head. "Look there, Lewis! You see that scar? One of Dunmore's men shot me there. Shot me during an attack on my farm, just a few months ago, because I wouldn't take a commission in his army and because I was making muskets for the Virginia forces."

Daingerfield looked closely at Wend. "You're a gunsmith?"

"Indeed, Colonel. In fact, I was making muskets intended for this very regiment."

Daingerfield sat up in his chair. "So where are those muskets? I was promised them some months ago. My men are armed with an assortment of rifles, fowling pieces, and a very few muskets."

"My men are armed with those muskets. We used them to equip half the company."

Now anger spread across the colonel's face, and he looked like he was about to speak. But Wend held up his hand. "But we made more. In one of the Conestogas that came in with us are fifty stand of muskets, complete with bayonets and cartridge cases."

Posey burst out, "By God, that will equip at least one of our companies!"

Daingerfield nodded. "Yes, Eckert, our recruiting hasn't been as successful as yours. Our average company is fifty to sixty men."

Wend said, "And the other Conestoga is loaded with kegs of gunpowder. Donated by the merchants of Frederick County to help with the defeat of Dunmore."

Posey grinned. "That is most welcome! It seems you've come bearing gifts."

Daingerfield, now more restrained, nodded and said, "Yes, that will be most welcome."

Lewis was staring at Wend, still nursing his resentment—Wend could see it in the general's eyes. He said, "Look, General, let me be straight. I didn't want to go to that war against the Shawnee or be an officer on Dunmore's staff, but they forced me by threatening to cancel a contract I had to renovate the colony's old muskets. That was my main source of income." Wend raised a finger. "And to tell you the truth, I didn't want to take this commission, to lead Frederick's company. I turned down the Committee of Safety's request. But then Dunmore's men attacked my farm and burned out my gun shop. They killed a woman and a child who lived on the farm, as well as destroying many of the buildings." He reached up to the scar on his head. "Not to mention this. So give it a rest, General. I've got as much reason to hate Dunmore and his henchmen as you do."

There was a silence at the table, the officers frankly embarrassed by the contretemps between Lewis and Wend. Wend stared at the general, fully expecting him to lash out, calling him insubordinate.

Coulter, the aide, bit his lip and looked around, clearly searching for a way to ease the tension. Then he said, "Why don't we continue the briefing we were conducting before Captain Eckert's company arrived."

Lewis nodded and said grudgingly, "We will talk no more of past events."

Coulter motioned to Posey. "Please give Eckert a quick summary of what you told us, then move on to what you know about the enemy's disposition on the island."

Posey realized what Coulter was doing and quickly launched into a review of the British raids and artillery positions. The strategy seemed to work, for the general diverted his attention to the map and Wend could feel the tension draining out of the atmosphere.

The Northcutt brothers and aide de camp Gardiner were cooling their heels in Betsy Loring's parlor, which was part of an apartment on the second floor of a building in the central part of Halifax. It had been some time since they had arrived at the residence, and cigar smoke was heavy in the air. Betsy, Mary Fraser, and Mrs. Loring's maid were secluded in a bedroom.

Suddenly the bedroom door opened and the maid came out and headed for the cook room. Gardiner sprang up from his chair and asked her, "What is toward?"

The maid, fussing around the stove, said, "Miss Fraser wants hot water, boiled cloths, and a bucket." She looked around. "We need more coal. There's a bin downstairs at the back of the building. Could one of you gentlemen fetch me some?"

Gardiner shrugged. "I'll go."

The maid handed him a bucket and a short-handled scoop. "Here. You'll need these."

Gardiner left, and the woman busied herself stoking up the coals in the stove. Northcutt, cigar in hand, strolled over to stand beside her. "I don't suppose you could intimate to me what the lady's problem is, could you?"

Without looking at Northcutt, the maid said, "You suppose right. I ain't sayin' nothing. You'll have to ask Miss Fraser or Mrs. Loring, if they want to tell you." She put a large pot of water on the stove, then went off to a closet to find suitable cloths.

Gardiner came back with the coal and fed a couple of scoops into the fire. He looked up at the other two men and said, "Before we left, I was able to get a message to Colonel Paterson about the trouble, so that he could inform the general. I shouldn't be surprised if the general didn't arrive after he's put in as short an appearance at the ball as he can diplomatically manage."

Barrett asked, "Shouldn't we try to get some word to *Mr.* Loring?"

Gardiner cleared his throat and shot Barrett a knowing glance. "Loring is very busy with his new duties. Regrettably, he hasn't been able to keep company with his wife since shortly after we arrived in Halifax. Naturally, we'll inform him in due course."

Barrett raised an eyebrow. "Ah yes, I quite understand. One's duties can consume an overwhelming amount of time." He thought to himself, *Now this is a damned strange arrangement indeed. The husband knowingly ceding his wife's favors to another man, even if he is the commanding general.*

The bedroom door opened, and Mary came out. She was wearing an apron and had pushed up the sleeves of her gown. She strode over to the cook room. "How are you coming with the water and cloths?"

The maid answered, "The cloths are ready." She pulled them out of a pot with tongs and laid them on a large piece of material. "We can carry them in on this."

Mary nodded her approval. "Good. Take them in. I'll bring the pot of hot water."

The maid headed for the bedroom door, and Mary reached out to pick up the pot. Gardiner had walked over beside her, and now he stopped her. "I'll carry that for you. But before we go, I'll ask you to give me a brief idea of what Mrs. Loring's problem is."

Mary's face furrowed up, and she answered, "I'm not sure I should…"

But before she could finish, Gardiner said, "The general will be here shortly. I should be able to give him at least an idea of what is happening."

Mary looked over at the Northcutts and bit her lip. "What about them?"

"It's all right, Miss Fraser," Gardiner motioned to the other men. "These gentlemen will be on their honor not to let what you say get beyond this room."

Gregory spoke up. "That's quite right, Miss Fraser. We shall not repeat anything you say."

Mary looked around the room, then shrugged. "Mrs. Loring is a few weeks pregnant. But she's losing the baby. It's called a miscarriage."

Gardiner, a look of alarm on his face, said, "My God! How serious is this? Shouldn't we call a surgeon?"

Mary shook her head. "No surgeon. I've attended to this before, more than once. Actually, I did it in an army camp in the middle of the Ohio Country bush when I was fifteen. And once she has expelled the tissue, she should recover rapidly."

Gardiner considered what she had said for a moment. "All right, but don't hesitate to call on us if you need to get the assistance of a physician."

"I *shan't* need help." She looked at the other men. "In any case, I assume the fewer who know about this, the better. Now if I might get back to work?" And without waiting for an answer, and before Gardiner could react, she picked up the pot herself and hurried into the bedroom.

Gregory Northcutt watched her go. After the door was shut, he said, "A red-haired spitfire if I ever saw one."

Barrett, still looking at the bedroom door, grinned broadly. "I should say a sassy red vixen, beautiful but with claws at the ready." He took a long draw on his cigar. "And beyond that, quite a lady."

A few minutes later, they heard steps coming up the stairway, then a tap at the door, which immediately swung open. In walked General William Howe.

He looked around the room and nodded to Gardiner and Gregory. Then he looked at Barrett. "And who, sir, are you?"

Gregory Northcutt answered. "General, he is my brother, Lieutenant Colonel Barrett Northcutt of the King's Loyal Virginia Legion."

Howe looked over Barrett, then said, "I wondered about that uniform. Never saw one like that before. Can I assume you are with Dunmore's forces?"

"Yes, General. I just arrived in Halifax. I'm here with dispatches and a personal message from the governor."

Gardiner said, "Colonel Paterson has the dispatches, sir. He's going to arrange an appointed for Colonel Northcutt with you as soon as practicable."

"I quite understand. But what is your role in this business tonight?"

Gardiner spoke again. "We were fortunate that he was aware of a nurse in the 42nd who is experienced with the type of malady affecting Mrs. Loring."

Barrett said, "She is a very experienced nurse, General; in fact they call her the matron of the hospital. Colonel Stirling acceded to her treating Mrs. Loring but asked me to come along to ensure her safe return to her quarters when done."

Howe nodded. "Ah yes. And thank you for your assistance in the matter of obtaining her services." He turned back to Gardiner. "And just what is Betsy's medical problem?"

Gardiner motioned Howe aside and whispered into his ear. A look of distress immediately spread across his face. "Good Lord!" he exclaimed.

Earlier Northcutt had located some rum in a cabinet. Now he held up the bottle and said, "General, we may have a long wait. Perhaps you would like a libation?" He held up a cup. And then he pulled a cigar out of his coat. "And a cigar made of excellent Virginia tobacco?"

Howe looked around the room, sighed deeply, and sat down in a comfortable chair. "Yes, a drink and cigar would be most welcome."

—m—

The officers of the Frederick County Light Foot were seated around a table under a canvas fly in front of Wend's tent, enjoying their first meal since arriving. The meal had been cooked by Mrs. Flannagan and was being served by Billy Wood. Both received compensation out of the officer's mess for their labor.

Wend was relating what he had learned earlier in the briefing of Lewis by Daingerfield and Posey. He had told them about Lewis's plans to bring more troops and artillery to the island as soon as possible. He finished by saying, "Lewis and his aide will head back to Williamsburg tomorrow. He thinks it will be several weeks before the reinforcements can be gathered and march here."

Newkirk looked up from his plate. "So what do we do in the meantime? Just sit here and wait?"

Wend said, "Glad you asked, Reese. They want us to send some riflemen up to positions they've prepared along the channel and amuse the British on the ships with aimed fire. Make it inconvenient to move around the upper decks and rigging." He hesitated a moment, then continued, "Daingerfield said they don't have marksmen to compare with our backcountry boys."

Newkirk thought a moment, then said, "All right, sending eight or ten men each day ought to make it hot for the British."

Wend responded, "Yes that should do it." Then he looked around the table. "But the immediate problem facing Daingerfield is stopping the raids by the British along the coastline. They come ashore from boats to forage. He says just two days ago, they hit farms to the north, taking away great amounts of food and about a dozen slaves who threw in with the British."

O'beirne saw it right away. "So the real problem is there's no way to figure out in advance where they're going to strike."

Wend nodded. "You're right about that, Shay. Daingerfield wants to protect the coastal farms, but he's quite frustrated."

Young Childers shrugged. "Why not station some small militia pickets along the coast to warn of where the British are headed or where they land?"

O'beirne rolled his eyes. "Now, my dear young fellow, you are absolutely right about that. And then your fine picket, having sighted a British landing party, sends a mounted courier to warn the local militia captain, and by the time they get the word out and muster and march to where the lobsterbacks have landed, the scoundrels have done their robbery and taken the loot back to their boats. And we have a couple of farms that have been ravaged and a company of militia which have marched hard for hours just so that they can go back home. Aye, lad, that's a fine plan."

Childers blushed and looked down at his plate.

Newkirk, who had been sitting quietly, hand to his chin, spoke up. "The only way to stop them would be to know in advance where they were planning to strike." He shrugged. "But that would mean having someone on the island—a spy, if you will—in a position where they could be aware of their plans and also somehow able to notify us in time." He spread his hands wide. "But that's a virtual impossibility."

Wend sighed. "Yes, that *would* be the answer, but as you said, it's not practical." Then he changed the subject. "Let's give the men a day of rest after the march, and then we'll start drilling and practicing with our field squads after that." Then another thing occurred to him. "The Conestogas will be unloaded soon, and then they'll head back to Winchester. Notify your men that if anyone wants to send back mail or lighten their load of personal belongings, Jake Cather will take it with them."

Newkirk seconded Wend's words. "That's a good thought. Some of the men have loaded themselves up with too much stuff. We're going to have to be much lighter in the field once we get to Washington's army. They might as well get rid of it now. I'll have Donegal check things out and encourage those with too much to discard some of their kit."

———ɯ———

Early in the morning, Wend stood near the shore, on a low knoll known as Cricket Hill, looking out over Milford Haven. O'beirne and Corporal Jensen, with a squad of ten riflemen, were selecting advantageous positions for firing harassing shots at the ships.

Jensen, in his usual blustering way, was exhorting his men. "All right, here's your first chance to get at them redcoats! We're gonna make them scared to run around the decks of those big ships out there!"

Young Howie Cole, while looking down to check the lock on his rifle, asked, "Now, Corporal, you said we're goin' to be shootin' at sailors. Can we still call them redcoats?" He looked up and grinned at Jensen. "Maybe we should call them 'red jack tars' instead."

Jensen shot the young rifleman an angry stare. "Damn it, Cole, I don't care what you call them. You can call them anything you want, as long as you put a ball in the right place!"

"Oh, I'll do that all right, Corporal. Just wanted to know what type of Britisher we was goin' to call them."

There were giggles around the squad.

Wend smiled at the exchange. At the same time, he used a small telescope to look over the ships. When he was young, his father had taken him along from Lancaster to Philadelphia to pick up gunsmithing supplies ordered from Germany and England. Wend had seen merchant ships in the port, but nothing like the *Roebuck*, which easily qualified as the biggest vessel he had ever seen. And he had never laid eyes on a naval ship before. The line of gunports, sixteen from bow to stern, with the black muzzles of cannons projecting from them, was sobering. And there were more guns on the frigate's open decks. The *Dunmore*, almost as large, had ports for six guns per side. Wend thought about the damage all those cannons could achieve.

As he was doing so, Billy Wood, who had come along as messenger, cleared his throat and asked, "Mr. Eckert, can we talk, just us two, for a minute?"

Wend nodded, then led Billy a short distance away. "What's on your mind?"

"Sir, I heard you gentlemens talking at supper last night. You was speakin' about how to stop the British from raidin' along the coast." He looked over at the island. "About how there would have to be someone over there to find out where they were going."

"Yes, Billy, that's what it would take. But you must have heard that there's no good way to get someone on the island without being discovered."

"Well, sir, I think there's a way to get someone on the island." He hesitated for a second, then said, "I could go, sir."

"You? For God's sake, Billy, how would you get on the island?"

"Sir, you forgettin' that I can swim?"

"Well, I know you learned how in the creek and the river, but the Bay is another matter." He waved over toward Gwynn's. "And I'm told there's a strong current in that channel."

"Well, maybe a boat could get me over to the other side of the island, where there ain't no current and probably ain't nobody watching."

Wend stared at Billy. "Well, you've obviously been thinking about this."

"Yes, sir. After hearing what you said at supper, I couldn't get to sleep last night thinkin' about it. So long as I was awake, I planned it out a little bit."

"Well, even if we could get you over there, they'd probably catch you in short order. You'd be a strange man on a small island."

Billy grinned broadly. "Well, that might be a problem if I were *white*. But Mr. Eckert, I heard people sayin' they got all those Africans over there bein' soldiers for Governor Dunmore. And there must be a passel of young ones, and women also, who've come in from the plantations with the men. I figure they wouldn't notice one more black walking around. And they wouldn't have no idea about a black man spyin' on them. They think all of them over there is on the island cause they're escapin' from their masters." Billy straightened up to his full height and patted his chest. "They wouldn't know I was a man with no master who was fightin' for Virginia!"

Wend said, "What if they saw you swimming in and caught you right on the beach?"

Billy grinned broadly. "Then I just tell them I escaped from a plantation and I'm aiming to join with the British!" He thought a moment. "Afore I go, one of the officer's from around here needs to give me the name of a plantation, so what I tell the British will sound real."

Wend stared at Billy for a moment, thinking, *By God, he's made some good points. And it just—just might work.* Then a thought hit him. "But how would you get word back about a raid coming?"

Billy smiled broadly. "I figured that out too. You send a boat out to look for a light on the far side of the island at a certain time each night. If they see my light, that means I got some word on a raid. Then they come close to shore, and I swim out to the boat and get brought back here so I can tell you what I know about what they're planning."

Wend's mind was working. "All right, let's think about this. We can get you on Gwynn's, and you probably can stay undiscovered, and we might be able to get you back. But it does no good if you don't have a way to find out their plans. And they aren't just going to tap you on the shoulder and tell you."

"No sir, Mr. Eckert, they ain't. But there's bound to be evidence of what's happening. Gettin' boats together, soldiers makin' ready. I figure word will get out on the island about what is goin' to happen and where. They don't figure anyone from our side is among them, so they might talk pretty freely." He shrugged. "It ain't perfect, but the way I see it, it's got a chance of workin' out."

Wend stood in deep thought for a long moment. "All right, it sounds possible. But I can't make the decision. I'll talk to Daingerfield tonight and see how he feels about it. Then I'll let you know."

Billy smiled broadly. "Mr. Eckert, I *know* it can work. And I'm the only one of the soldiers here who can do the job. You tell the colonel I'm ready to go when he gives the word!"

Conversation had long ago tapered off as General Howe and the other three officers waited in Betsy Loring's parlor, each lost in his own thoughts. Barrett had just looked at his pocket watch to see that it was approaching 2:00 a.m. when the door to the bedroom opened and Mary came out carrying a bucket with a cloth covering the top. He thought he could see weariness in her face and a touch of sadness in her eyes.

She looked around and said, "Can I ask one of you to dispose of what is in this bucket?"

Gardiner jumped up from his chair. "Excuse me, miss, how should it be disposed of?"

Mary handed him the bucket. "Wherever they normally empty the night soil for this building will be quite adequate."

Howe stood up. "Miss Fraser, what is Mrs. Loring's condition, and when may I see her?"

"Mrs. Loring is feeling much better. She just needs to stay in bed for a while and get some rest. And she should have good, nutritious food when she wakes up." She waved at the bedroom door. "You can go in now, if you desire. In fact, please do; she could use encouragement and support. But don't stay too long. She's very weary, and she must get some sleep."

The general headed for the bedroom.

Mary called out, "Oh, General Howe. Mrs. Loring has been calling for a drink of the alcoholic kind. Please don't give in to her desire. I shouldn't let her have any until at least the evening tomorrow."

The general turned around and looked at Mary. "Ah yes, I understand." Then he started for the door again but stopped almost immediately and turned back to Mary. "Miss Fraser, please allow me to express my appreciation for your services tonight. It was most fortunate that you were available to assist Mrs. Loring. You have my gratitude, and I shall remember your excellent care of her."

Mary smiled. "I'm just glad that I could be of service in her hour of need."

Howe nodded, and then went into the bedroom and pulled the door shut behind him.

Barrett asked, "Mary, is it necessary that you remain to check on Mrs. Loring's progress?"

Mary shook her head and sighed deeply. She took her apron off and then started to pull her sleeves down before she answered. "No, nothing more is required. I should get to the landing. There's supposed to be a boat from HMS *Prefect* which was to wait for me, and I don't want to keep the sailors waiting any longer than necessary."

Barrett said, "Yes, and I promised Major McDonald I would ensure you got there safely. Let me help you with your cloak, and then I'll escort you to the landing."

Mary gave him one of her beautiful smiles and said, "I should greatly appreciate that, Colonel."

Soon they were walking along the waterfront, passing warehouses on one side and moored merchant ships on the other. They went in silence for a while, then Northcutt asked, "Major McDonald told me you were brought up in the regiment as an orphan. Have you been with the army all your life?"

"No, Colonel, although the army feels like my home. I left the regiment in 1767, when it came back from the colonies and was garrisoned in Ireland. I was lucky enough to obtain service as a governess on a large estate in the Highlands, where I remained until just a few months ago. I returned to the regiment when it was ordered for service in this insurrection." She paused, a look of deep reflection on her face. "I thought my experience as a nurse in a marching battalion would be of service to the men."

Barrett said, "How very gallant of you, Mary. I understand that's a word normally associated with soldiers, but it occurs to me you are a soldier in your own right. After all, you will be facing the same dangers as the men."

Mary laughed. "Yes, I've learned that first hand, at a place called Bushy Run in 1763."

Barrett was intrigued. "You must have been no more than sixteen at that time. If I may be so intrusive, what happened?"

"Actually, I was still fifteen." She looked over at him. "I was treating a young scout's hand wound when a nearly spent ball hit me in the side."

Now Northcutt felt a shock. "Did you say a *scout*?"

"Yes, he was a German boy, actually a gunsmith, only a few years older than I, who was helping our chief scout."

My God, thought Barrett, *that could only have been Eckert*. After he regained his composure, he said, "Well, thank God you recovered from the wound."

She flashed him the marvelous smile and replied, "Yes, just barely. But at one point, I thought I would be joining my parents in heaven." She looked at him again and said, "I think God spared me for some reason. I choose to think it was to help children and soldiers. So I have dedicated my life that kind of work."

"Indeed, that is quite admirable of you."

Mary didn't answer. Instead she pointed to a boat moored at the landing, a sailor sitting on a bollard on the pier beside it. "That's my boat."

The sailor called down to the boat, and the crew, which had been sleeping onboard, shook themselves awake.

Northcutt saw a young midshipman—he could not have been more than twelve or thirteen—jump up to the pier, still rubbing the sleep out of his eyes.

"Hello, Miss Mary! We were a bit worried about you."

"Everything's fine, Mr. Blandford. But I'm very tired, so I'm most glad you are here for me."

The youth grinned from ear to ear. "Our pleasure, ma'am. The first lieutenant said we weren't to come back unless we had you on board."

Mary turned to Northcutt. "Well, Colonel, thank you so much for escorting me. I shan't hold you any longer from your quarters. You must be as weary as I am."

Barrett made a small bow. "Actually, my quarters, like yours, are aboard one of His Majesty's ships—the dispatch schooner *Raven*, anchored out beside the fleet flagship."

She exclaimed, "Oh, I didn't realize" and turned to the midshipman. "Mr. Blandford, can we take the colonel out to his ship?"

Blandford nodded. "Of course, ma'am. That will be no problem." The lad gave Mary his hand. "Let me help you into the boat."

Northcutt watched as Mary, with great agility, stepped down into the boat and was seated. Then Blandford motioned for him to take a place beside her.

Shortly they were underway, with four rowers doing their work and the midshipman at the tiller.

Mary looked back at Blandford. "The flagship is close in. We can drop Colonel Northcutt off on our way to the *Prefect*, which is farther out."

The youngster at Mary sternly. "Ma'am, I'll remind you that I am the *senior naval officer* in the boat, so it's my decision. And I'm taking you right out to the *Prefect* so you can get your rest. Then we'll take the colonel to his ship. We're the duty boat tonight and have to be up anyway, so we might as well be working."

Northcutt quickly agreed. "Yes, Mary, that's the proper thing to do. You're the one who has been laboring hard."

It was a calm evening, with the sea almost like a mirror. With a clear sky, the moon provided a modicum of light. The oarsmen pulled the boat swiftly through the water, and soon they were approaching the *Prefect*. A voice called out from the ship, "Ahoy, the boat!"

Blandford called back, "Lady!" and then he stood up to better see as he took the boat alongside. In a moment he called, "Toss oars!" and the rowers brought their oars up out of the water and then stowed them in preparation for tying up alongside.

Once they were moored, there was the bustle of voices up on the ship's deck, and Northcutt looked up to see a chair being lowered on a sling.

Mary looked at him. "This is the fun part for me. And a graceful way to get aboard in a gown."

"Indeed, I see," he responded.

She said, "Well, Colonel, good night. And thank you for all your help tonight."

"It is I who should thank you, for your willingness to tend the lady. In any case, I hope we shall meet again."

"As do I, Colonel. As they say, the army is a small world. I wish you good fortune in your business here in Halifax."

With the assistance of a seaman, she rose and made her way to the chair. Blandford carefully buckled her in, then turned to the men and ordered, "Eyes down!" He called up to the deck for them to hoist away. Immediately the chair rose swiftly until it was above the ship's bulwark, then was carefully swayed inboard.

Meanwhile, Blandford had the sailors cast the boat off, and they began the trip to the *Raven*.

Barrett was sitting just in front of Blandford, and he said, by way of making conversation, "She is a beautiful and interesting young woman."

Blandford turned to Northcutt, his face wrinkling into a broad smile with a gleam in his eyes. "Indeed, sir. And *most* intelligent. She has been teaching the midshipmen French on the trip over. I assure you, the classes have never been so well attended and the students so eager to learn. She's made the chaplain, our usual schoolmaster, jealous."

"I imagine so. I cannot fathom why such a handsome and talented woman remains a spinster."

"Well, it's not for lack of men trying to win her favor. All the young officers of the 42nd are eager to spend time with her."

"Yes, I saw that at the ball last night. She always had quite a crowd around her."

"And the ship's lieutenants and older midshipmen have been trying to gain her interest. She lives with us in a room off the gunroom mess, but the wardroom is always inviting her up for meals." Blandford was silent, lost in thought for a moment. "Confidentially, sir, there's a story circulating among the officers on the ship, based on something Major McDonald was overheard saying to our captain, that she's carrying a flame for an old lover that she lost by a twist of fate. A young scout she met and fell in love with during Pontiac's War in the American frontier, back in the early sixties. A German backcountry tradesman of some kind."

Northcutt felt a knot form in his stomach. *That confirms it. She was Eckert's lover. And now he's dead.* Then another thought hit him. *I will never be the one who tells her of his death.*

He looked up to see they were coming close aboard the *Raven*. Just then the watch called out, "Ahoy the boat!"

Blandford shouted back "Aye, aye!"

There was a bustling aboard the schooner as the duty men prepared to receive the boat. Northcutt turned to Blandford and asked, "What does it mean when you shout, 'Aye, aye'?"

Blandford grinned. "It tells them there is an officer on the boat intending to board the ship. So they can make preparations. That's also why we called out, 'Lady' when we made the *Prefect*."

"Ah, I see. It will take me a while to get used to all these nautical customs."

The midshipman brought the boat alongside the *Raven*, right where the iron rungs in the side made a ladder to deck. The youth laughed. "Sorry, Colonel, no *chair* for you."

"I expect I can navigate the ladder without too much difficulty, Mr. Blandford. Good night, and thank you."

Being very careful to judge the movement of the boat, Northcutt seized a rung, got his feet on a lower one, and then climbed upward, reaching the entry port without any serious awkwardness. He turned around to see that the boat was already away from the side and heading for the *Prefect*.

He was surprised to see Lieutenant Proctor, dressed in his informal coat, emerge from the companionway leading from his cabin and stride toward the entry port. He called out, in a joking manner, "Well, our errant passenger has finally returned aboard."

Barrett said, "Sorry for the inconvenience. I certainly didn't expect you to be awake, Captain."

"Well, I ordered the watch to notify me when you returned. To be honest, we were getting a little worried about you. After all, it is near eight bells of the midwatch—close to four in the morning."

"I expected to be back in the early evening, but there was a ball last night and I went with some friends."

"Yes, we heard that the army was having some sort of affair. Must have been quite exciting to go so late."

Northcutt shook his head. "It didn't, but by chance I was drawn into a medical situation, Proctor. I won't go into details, but the mistress of an important officer developed a problem of the feminine kind and I was in a position to assist by recruiting a nurse to assist her. It took several hours to resolve, and then I escorted the nurse back to her ship."

"Indeed, sir." Proctor raised his eyebrows. "Would I happen to know of the officer?"

"You would, but I'm sworn to secrecy as to his identity and that of the distressed woman." He gave Proctor a sly look. "You are, of course, free to speculate."

"Oh, I assure you I will." He laughed, then said, "I was told you came back in a boat from the *Prefect*. Can you tell me how that happened, or is that part of the secret?"

"The nurse is a young woman attached to the hospital of the 42nd Foot—the Black Watch. They came over on the *Prefect* with a convoy."

"Ah yes, I see. Fortunate that someone knowledgeable was available to assist this woman."

"Yes, quite fortunate." Barrett looked up at the bright moon, now low in the western sky. He put his hand on the bulwark. "It happens the nurse is *most* attractive and *quite* accomplished, in *many* ways."

Proctor raised an eyebrow and stared at Northcutt. "Colonel, if I may be so forward, the words you used and the tone in your voice when you described the woman bespeak a rather significant level of admiration."

Northcutt didn't directly answer. Instead he queried, "Well, Captain, let me ask: Are you married?"

"No, frankly my naval duties have limited my opportunities to have lengthy interactions with what one would consider eligible ladies."

"Well, then we are in similar circumstances. I'm going to be forty in a couple of years, and I have been so focused on accumulating both land and financial resources, and lately serving as adviser to Dunmore, that I've not had any sustained involvements with females. Casual, short-lived liaisons, but nothing serious. And to be honest, I have not had any yearning for the binding entanglements of marriage."

"Colonel, are you going to tell me that the charms of this young Scotswoman now have you regretting your bachelorhood?"

Northcutt stood looking at the harbor waters for a long moment. "Proctor, I confess this girl has enchanted me. She has the face of an angel, a smile which makes your heart jump, sings with the voice of a siren, and is endowed with uncommon intelligence. And in answer to your question, indeed I am for the first time infatuated with the idea of matrimony, were it to be with Miss Mary Fraser." He took a deep breath. "However, given the geographic circumstances, there seems little prospect that fate will ever bring me into her presence again, at least long enough to allow time for me to pursue her favors. I fear she will persist only as a lovely memory in the recesses of my mind."

Proctor looked over at the *Prefect*, barely visible in the distance. "Well now, sir, I wouldn't be so pessimistic. In time of war, things change rapidly. Who knows where chance may take you—or the lady. Stranger things have happened."

"I pray providence may prove you right."

PART IV
A KIND
OF FREEDOM

Chapter Fourteen

THE CALM BEFORE

The fishing boat, pulled by four rowers, thrust its way through the Bay waters a half mile to the east of Gwynn's Island. Shay O'beirne, crouching in the bow, telescope to his eye, peered through the blackness of the night as he surveyed the low shoreline. The night was perfect for what they were about. He looked up at the sky, blessing the solid cloud cover that blanked out the moon and stars, ensuring maximum darkness.

Beside him, stripped down to just a pair of drawers, sat Billy Wood.

They had left an inlet several miles to the south of their camp just at dusk, moving by sail until they were a couple of miles south of Gwynn's. Then Jack Cowell, the waterman whose boat they were in, had dropped his sails to make the boat less visible and his crew had taken up their oars for the final approach.

Shay said to Billy, "There are three sets of lights visible. A group of them at the northern end, possibly some kind of encampment. They look like campfires burned low to the embers. Down to the south, there's a single point of light. Might be where that small battery is at the lower end of the channel."

He was quiet for a moment, peering through his glass. "And then, in the center, well inland of the beach, there are several lights close together." He looked over at Billy. "I think it might be at the site of the main plantation buildings in the center of the island."

Billy nodded.

Then O'beirne pointed past the northern end of the island. "Of course, there are the riding lights of all the ships up in Hills Bay."

Billy pointed directly ahead of the boat. "Mr. O'beirne, put me ashore right in the middle of those two lights along the beach. It's all dark, and chances are ain't nothin' there."

"Yes, my thought exactly." He turned back to Cowell. "Steer for between the two lights. Right in the middle of the island."

"All right." He stood up to see better. "We'll be close to shore shortly." He scanned the shoreline. "I've fished this area often enough. There's good water for this boat inshore, so the African won't have to swim far afore he can put his feet down and just walk on in."

Billy grinned. "That suits me jus' fine, Mr. O'beirne. The less swimmin' I have to do, the better."

Time passed, marked by the relentless movement of the oars. The shoreline drew closer and closer; the lights to the north and south became brighter.

Finally Cowell said, "All right, we'll close another hundred yards or so, then you'll be about twice that distance from the beach. I say you'll have to swim fifty yards, and then you'll be able to touch the bottom with your feet."

Billy reached down and picked up the oiled bag, in which were his clothing, a knife, and within a smaller sack, a pack of candles and a flint and striker. A cloth strap had been tied around the bag, and now Billy slipped the loop over his head. "I'm ready to go, Mr. O'beirne."

Suddenly Cowell called out to the oarsmen, "Vast rowing." And then he said to O'beirne, "Now's the time for him to go."

The Irishman put his hand on Billy's shoulder. "All right, lad, in you go, and remember, we'll be off the shore at this spot every night just after midnight. Show the light, and we'll stay until you get out to the boat. You can count on that. And now, best of luck to you!"

Billy nodded, then stood up, slipped his legs over the side, and splashed into the water. O'beirne watched as he began paddling to the shore. After a few minutes, he was lost to view. Shay turned back to the captain. "Let's get out of here."

Cowell said, "Aye, and none too soon for me. I'm worried about runnin' into one of those small tenders the British use." He called to the oarsmen, "All together now, give way!"

The oarsmen picked up the beat, while Cowell put the rudder over and turned the boat southward. "Just a little rowing, men, to put the island some distance behind, and we'll hoist the canvas."

O'beirne had been watching the shoreline and now thought he saw some movement right at the water's edge. *Or maybe*, he thought, *it's just my wishing it so.* He turned to face the stern. "Cowell, I think he's ashore."

"Aye, he should be on the beach by now." The captain stared at the shoreline. "But I have to tell you, with all the British on that island, I'm thinkin' that's the last we'll ever see of him."

Northcutt, finishing his briefing, pointed to the map on General Howe's conference table and said, "So, gentlemen, to sum things up, Lord Dunmore, here at Gwynn's Island, has placed his force in a location which is both highly defensible and advantageous as a starting point for an offensive campaign. All we need is a modicum of support from the main army in the form of a strong battalion of foot. The governor urges dispatch of such a unit posthaste, and he can assure you that we will go on the offensive and Virginia can be held for the Crown."

Sitting around the table were Howe, Lieutenant General the Earl Cornwallis, Major General James Grant, and Colonel Paterson. At a separate writing table was Captain Gardiner, making notes of what was said.

Grant spoke up. "Correct me if I am wrong, Northcutt, but don't you already have the 14th Foot?"

Barrett looked at Grant. The man was quite corpulent and had a smug, self-satisfied look on his face. Howe had asked him to attend the briefing because, having fought in the French War, he was considered to be something of an "American expert." Northcutt responded, "We have three understrength companies of the 14th, sir. At present, they amount to just over one hundred and twenty men." He thought a moment, then added, "Moreover, the regiment has been in the West Indies for many years and is quite worn down. Captain Samuel Leslie, the senior officer of our detachment, is of the opinion that it will shortly be ordered back to England to be rerecruited and reorganized."

Paterson, who had been staring down at the map, said in a matter-of-fact tone, "That is quite correct. I'm preparing plans now for their eventual return. Quite frankly, in their present strength, they would be of little use to us except as a battalion of detachments for guard duty and other such work."

Cornwallis asked, "Northcutt, I would appreciate a summary of Lord Dunmore's current strength. I don't recall hearing that information in your brief."

Northcutt had studiously avoided stating that number, for he felt it was the weakest part of their position. But now he had little choice. "Well, of course, for regulars there is the detachment of the 14th, of which we just spoke, and the marines from the Royal Navy squadron, which amount to perhaps another 100 available for use ashore. We have formed two provincial regiments, the Queen's Loyal Virginians and my own King's Loyal Virginia Legion, each with something over 100 men. Then we have the Ethiopian Regiment, which ostensibly has nearly 500 men, but unfortunately, the Africans have proved highly susceptible to the smallpox and other contagions, so their available field strength is rarely above a couple of hundred. Thus our effective strength in the field, from all sources, rarely exceeds 600 men." Barrett moved to capitalize on the matter. "So you can see that a full-strength battalion of regulars would push our effective strength to well over 1,500 men, or the size of a strong brigade. It is important to consider that while the colonials have authorized several battalions, they are still recruiting and their training is abysmal. Clearly, they would not be a match for a force of regulars such as we are discussing."

Grant's fleshy face wrinkled into a puzzled expression. "I am rather disappointed by the low number of men you have actually recruited for your two loyalist regiments. I would have thought there would be more men ready to come to your colors. My appreciation is that there is significant loyalist sentiment in the middle colonies and even more as you go further south." He raised a finger. "And in '74 Dunmore fought a rather effective campaign against the Ohio tribes. I would have expected that would have earned considerable support for him among the people of the border country."

Cornwallis nodded. "Yes, I *also* would have thought that to be the case." He looked over at Howe and then back at Northcutt. "But then there is this matter of the Africans. My understanding is that late last year Dunmore, on his own authority, issued a proclamation extending freedom to slaves who came to your colors. Was that not a significant overreach in policy by a governor? Shouldn't a decision like that necessarily have had to come from London?" He paused briefly, looking around the table. "I suggest that that action has hurt your recruitment more than it has helped, because of the negative sentiment it has caused among plantation owners and whites in general. The thought of arms in the hands of the blacks is an overriding fear among many, particularly after the well-known slave uprisings earlier in the century."

There was a heavy silence around the table, with the eyes of all the officers on Northcutt. He knew he had to respond with an effective answer. He took a deep breath and began speaking. "I admit that it could have some influence on recruitment and the support of the people in general. But I believe an even more telling factor is that our supporters live intermingled with those who support the insurrection and are afraid to show support for the Crown for fear of losing their property and even their lives to the mob."

Grant straightened. "Come, Northcutt, do you have any evidence to support that?"

Barrett stared at Grant and smiled. "As a matter of fact, I do, sir. With respect, I would call your attention to the raid we recently conducted on a musket manufactory in Frederick County, near Winchester."

For the first time, Howe spoke up. "Indeed, Colonel Northcutt, I read the description of that in Lord Dunmore's dispatches. I must say, a rather bold stroke over a long distance."

Grant asked, "It may have been bold, but I don't understand how that bespeaks of loyalist support."

Northcutt thought, *Well, Grant, you've walked into this one.* He said, "General, it speaks volumes about supporters who are afraid to be open about their loyalty to the Crown but are willing to help if their assistance can remain clandestine or will be supported by Crown forces." He looked around the table. "Most of the men who conducted that raid were loyalists living in the Fredericksburg area who came together in secret to join with a very small band of men from my regiment. In other words, they were ready to act when they knew they would be protected."

Northcutt paused for effect, then continued, "And I say to you all, if we had a full battalion of regulars campaigning with us, showing the support of the government and mastery over the Virginia forces, we would have a great number of subjects rising up in favor of the king and parliament."

Barrett saw that his words had had some effect. Grant's face flushed, and he looked down at the table. Cornwallis was nodding slightly. Howe was staring straight ahead, hand to his chin, obviously reflecting on what he had heard.

Finally Paterson broke the silence. "When we relieved General Gage, I recollect being briefed about a plan which Dunmore had put in progress to raise the Ohio Indians in our support. The idea was to have them join with backcountry loyalists and conduct large-scale raids on the Virginia and Pennsylvania border settlements, to force a diversion of rebel forces. A man named Connor, or some such, who reputedly had influence with the tribes, was to be sent to convince the tribes to act in our favor. What ever became of that?"

Northcutt said, "The agent was Colonel Connolly, John Connolly, sir. And you have described the plan correctly. In addition, Gage authorized his regular forces manning the forts on the northern border to take to the field and march with the column of border settlers and Indian warriors." He paused and then said, "Unfortunately, Connolly was apprehended by militia in Maryland and a party of men assisting him were ambushed and killed by the rebels."

Howe sat back in his chair. "Yes, I read about that plan. In general concept, I thought it a good idea. While it didn't work out in this case because of the discovery of Dunmore's agent, the concept remains valid—quite valid, I believe. Were for some reason this insurrection to last longer than I expect, we most certainly would find occasion to use the tribes as allies."

There were nods around the table. In a moment Howe raised his hand. "Colonel Northcutt, between reading Lord Dunmore's dispatches, which are quite detailed, and listening to your excellent brief, I feel most familiar with the situation."

Northcutt realized that the general was about to make a decision. "Thank you, sir. I hope that you will see your way clear to support our request for reinforcement."

Howe got up, went to his desk, and picked out a cigar from a wooden box. Then he walked over to the hearth, took a taper from a holder, set it alight, and used it to ignite the tobacco. All the men at the table sat in respectful silence, and Northcutt took his seat.

The general took a further moment to pull on his cigar and make sure it was drawing properly. Then he turned back to face the table. "Northcutt, let me repeat, I was impressed by the content of the dispatches. And your briefing was succinct and informative. I wish you to express my personal appreciation and admiration to Lord Dunmore for the work he is doing in Virginia. He is the only governor who has put up an effective resistance to this damnable rebellion."

"Thank you, General. I shall make certain to convey your sentiments."

"Yes, I would appreciate that. Now let us discuss the specific points you have made." Howe walked over to the wall, where a map of the colonies was posted. "First, you have stated that holding Virginia with a strong force would split the colonies and make it difficult, if not impossible, for the rebels to send forces up from the Carolinas and Georgia." He looked at the officers at the table. "Your assertion is quite correct, and as a matter of fact, we have strongly considered that idea in this very room. However, Northcutt, we have selected another option to deal with the southern rebels." He pointed to South Carolina. "You may not be aware of this, but even as we speak, my second-in-command, General Clinton, supported by a navy squadron under Commodore Parker, is approaching the city of Charleston by sea with a very strong force. Their objective is to take the city and then extend our power throughout Georgia and the Carolinas." He turned and looked at Barrett. "That, in large measure, will snuff out the worry of troops and supplies coming up from the south."

Grant, with a self-satisfied smirk on his face, interjected, "*Our* information is that there is strong and widespread loyalist sympathy in the Carolinas. *Certainly more than you seem to have found in Virginia.*

We are confident that many men will come to our colors and we will be able to form a significant number of provincial regiments, thus augmenting our regular forces."

Northrup suppressed the urge to snap a sarcastic reply back at Grant. Instead he nodded and said, "I repeat that we have many allies among the people of Virginia. And don't forget, General Grant, that we have a hundred ships in our fleet filled with loyal subjects of the king."

Paterson, seeking to smooth things, quickly said, "Yes, Northcutt, we certainly appreciate that. However, you must see General Howe's point. It is simply better to cut off the potential rebel reinforcements at the source than try to stop them once on the way."

Northcutt nodded. "I understand your point, James."

Howe nodded his agreement, then began to speak again. "Now our main effort will be against New York. We will use the forces here at Halifax, more still coming from England, and a large quantity of soldiers from the German principalities which have been contracted to assist in our efforts. We are told they are currently en route across the Atlantic." He motioned toward Philadelphia on the wall map. "I'll remind you, Northcutt, that I and my brother, Admiral Howe, are empowered by the king as peace emissaries. When we arrive at New York, I intend to enter into negotiations with members of the so-called Continental Congress and this Washington fellow. I am convinced there is a strong chance that once the leaders of the rebellion see our overwhelming strength, they will accept the reasonably lenient terms which will be extended. Or, if they do not, a short campaign which demonstrates our superiority over their ill-disciplined, untrained, and poorly equipped troops will acquaint them with reality and force them to acknowledge the error of their ways." He looked around the table and then directly at Barrett. "In either case, peace and the reestablishment of the king's authority will shortly be achieved throughout the colonies. When that occurs, Lord Dunmore will return to his legitimate control of Virginia, without the need for an extensive military campaign. I suspect he will be back in his Williamsburg residence by the new year." He shrugged. "Thus, I don't see the need for reinforcement of his forces at present." He shrugged. "Of course, in the unlikely event that our strategy fails"—Howe looked at his generals with a smile on his face—"we can revisit the situation in Virginia."

Grant said, "A most unlikely eventuality. The colonials must come to their senses once they see the size of our army and understand our determination."

Cornwallis merely said, "Indeed it would seem so."

Howe motioned toward Northcutt. "Colonel, I will of course provide a dispatch confirming what has transpired here and my written instructions for Lord Dunmore."

Northcutt nodded and said, "I understand, sir."

"My instructions will be, in view of the pending negotiations, that the governor maintain his base on that island and keep his force intact, so as to be a potential threat to the insurrectionists." Howe pointed to Virginia on the map. "By doing that, he will be most useful to us by keeping most of Virginia's battalions tied down in the colony for defensive purposes. Our information is that there are very few Virginia units with Washington's army for that very reason. And I caution him against attempting an offensive operation, for that could have a negative influence on our negotiations with Washington and their congress."

Barrett replied, "I will relay that sentiment to Lord Dunmore."

Paterson said, "We will have dispatches for the governor ready for you tomorrow, Northcutt, and you can plan to sail immediately afterward for Virginia."

Howe waved at the officers at the table. "I believe we have finished here, gentlemen. Let us all return to our duties." He grinned broadly. "Or our pleasures, as may be the case!"

There were laughs around the room, and they all rose and strode out of the office, leaving Howe to his cigar and his own thoughts.

—m—

Wend stood at the edge of an open field about a quarter mile to the west of the Chesapeake shoreline, watching O'beirne and Donegal exercising three of the field squads in a skirmish line. Wend was feeling increasingly confident that the idea of combined rifle and muskets squads was valid. But, he reflected, the only real test would be in action against an enemy formation. Just then he heard the sound of hoofs rapidly approaching and turned around to see Newkirk and Captain Posey of the 7th gallop up.

Newkirk called out, "Captain, we need to talk."

Wend walked over to where the two men sat their horses. "What has got you so excited?"

Posey said, "You and Donegal need to come back with us and to meet with Colonel Daingerfield."

"Me and *Donegal*? Why Donegal specifically?"

Newkirk and Posey looked at each other and laughed.

Wend, getting a little irritated, asked, "What is so *damned* funny? And please explain why in the world Daingerfield would want to see Donegal."

Posey stopped laughing and said, "A courier has just come in from Williamsburg carrying a dispatch which says General Lewis wants Donegal at his headquarters posthaste."

Wend was stunned into momentary silence. Then he exclaimed, "Lewis wants *Donegal*? Donegal *specifically*?"

Newkirk explained, "Wend, it seems that a ship loaded with Highlanders from the 42nd and 71st regiments has come into port near Norfolk and has been taken into custody by our forces. Lewis wants Donegal to help with negotiations. He thinks some of them might know Donegal and trust him more than anyone from the government."

"What kind of negotiations? And why would Lewis think of Donegal? He's never met him."

Posey shook his head. "Daingerfield didn't say. You and Donegal better just come up to camp and let the colonel explain as much as he can."

Wend sighed and turned back to the field. He shouted for Simon to come and join him.

Donegal strode over, somewhat frustrated. "Na, listen, Wend, we just got these squads doing the advance proper like. Now is a hell of a time for a talk."

Wend grinned. "It appears your fieldwork for the day is over, Simon. Turn it over to O'beirne and come along. You can ride double with me—we're only going to Dangerfield's headquarters."

Donegal made a face. "Aye, now? This *very* minute? What the hell is this all about?"

"You're going to love it, Simon." Wend swung up onto Sonny and reached down to help the Highlander up behind the saddle. "I'll tell you what I know on the way."

After the short ride, all four men dismounted at Dangerfield's tent. The colonel was sitting at a table placed under a fly, looking over paperwork in the shade it provided.

Wend asked without preamble, "May I ask what the devil this is all about, Colonel?"

Daingerfield said nothing. Instead he held up a piece of paper and handed it to Wend. Then he said, "Easiest for you to read it yourself."

Wend scanned the words. Then he looked over at Donegal. "I might have known. James Wood is actually the one who is behind this."

A puzzled look spread over Donegal's face. "*Wood?*"

Wend explained, "This says that James talked with Lewis and our old friend Patrick Henry. They want to try to convince these Highlanders, about two hundred men—that's one company from the 42nd and one from the 71st—to join our cause. He thinks they might prefer that to spending the war as prisoners. Wood got the idea that you may know some of these men from back in the French War."

Donegal considered a moment, then said, "Aye, it's possible. They'd be mostly sergeants by now."

"Well, he thinks it might influence them if they saw that a former compatriot was serving with our forces. At the very least, they might listen to you more than some Virginia politician."

Donegal rolled his eyes and pursed his lips. "This is a fool's mission. I'm thinkin' there's no way they'll change their coats. Ain't like a Highlander, and in any case, they probably expect the redcoats will make short work of our army. They'll be remembering Culloden and what happened to the rebels after that uprising."

Wend looked over at Daingerfield. "He's right, Colonel. The British punished the rebels in that war very harshly. There were many executions and long imprisonments."

Daingerfield shrugged and said, "I don't doubt your word on that. But it makes no difference." He pointed to the dispatch. "That's an order for Donegal to proceed to Williamsburg, and I intend to see that it happens."

Wend thought a moment. "Colonel, I have a suggestion. Let's send Joshua Baird along with Donegal. Given all the scouting work he did for the British, he may know as many men in those companies as Donegal. And Lewis knows Joshua and will accept what he tells him about dealing with those Highlanders."

Daingerfield signaled his agreement with a wave of his hand. "I'll not object to that." He looked over at Donegal. "Get what you need together, and come back here with Baird in an hour. I'll have a horse ready for you, and the two of you can accompany the courier back to Williamsburg."

Donegal grinned at the colonel and then at Wend. "I'll be ready. And I've a mind Joshua is going to love this."

Wend said, "Why do you say that?"

"Na that's simple enough—it will keep him from having to go home with the Conestogas!" He grinned. "And I'm sure they have some fine, jolly taverns in Williamsburg; such places seem to be quite lacking around here."

Wend shrugged. "I can't fault your thinking on that."

Donegal took his leave to get his kit together, and Newkirk went with him. Wend picked up the reins to Sonny and was about to lead him back to the company camp when Daingerfield called out to him. "Eckert, hold a bit."

Wend turned around. "Yes, Colonel?"

Daingerfield said, "I'm worried about that spy we put on Gwynn's. This is the fourth day since he went ashore. Cowell's had his boat out there off the island every night, but there's been no signal."

Wend's brows furrowed. "I think we must give it time. Billy may be finding it hard to get useful information. And if he finds its useless, I'm sure he'll signal to be taken off. All we can do is wait and keep watching for his light."

HMS *Raven*, a day out of Halifax, was sailing southward in a fresh breeze and relatively calm waters. Northcutt leaned on the schooner's bulwark, watching some gulls as they soared above the sea in the gentle wind and occasionally swooped down to the surface. For a change, his stomach was relatively quiescent. He wondered whether his body was getting accustomed to the ship's motion or it was simply because of the relatively mild weather.

Standing there, Barrett could not avoid contemplating the difficult duty of explaining to Dunmore the failure of his mission. This was the first time he had ever been unsuccessful in his service to the governor, and he knew that His Lordship would not take Howe's denial of his request in good humor. Moreover, beyond denying the request for troops, Howe had in essence ordered Dunmore to remain on the defensive rather than launch action against the rebels. So in actuality his mission had resulted in restrictions on their ability to act.

Meanwhile, Proctor and Flowers were fussing with the sails, trimming their settings to get the most speed possible out of the ship. The young captain walked over and said, "Well, Colonel, if this breeze holds and the seas remain quiet, we may make a fast passage down to the Virginia Capes."

"Captain, you'll never get a complaint about this kind of weather from me." He shook his head and continued, "However, I'm not in any hurry to give His Lordship the general's decision. He will not take it well."

"Yes, Colonel, it's never pleasant to be the bearer of bad news. I've often had to do that in this role."

Northcutt was about to respond when there was a shout from the lookout in the ship's foremast. "Sail ho! Sail ho! Topsail in sight off the starboard bow."

Proctor said, "Excuse me, Colonel!" and rushed to take a telescope from a bracket on the quarterdeck rail. He snapped it out to its full length and aimed it at the newly sighted sail, which was now just visible above the horizon.

Interested, Barrett walked over and stood beside the young captain. Proctor was studying the vessel intently. He muttered quietly. "A single mast. It's a large sloop."

"Is that unusual?"

Proctor looked over at him. "Yes, this far out. You see a lot of sloop rigs in the coastal trade." He took another look through the glass. "Northcutt, while on the flagship, I received a briefing on the activities of the rebel navy. It's not large, but they have been active."

Barrett, surprised, raised his eyebrows. "I wasn't even aware they had formed a navy."

"Aye, they have one, such as it is: formed from converted merchant ships, and there is even a corps of marines." He turned to Northcutt. "I just learned that, back in March, a small squadron landed a party of marines on New Providence Island in the Bahamas and raided a fort at a place called Nassau. Took it totally by surprise and captured both the fort and the town. They seized a large amount of military stores and particularly a great supply of powder."

"I suspect taking the powder was their major objective; we are aware that they have a shortage of that."

"Indeed, sir. But more to our present situation, they informed me that there is one of their warships, named *Providence*, attacking merchant vessels in these very waters. It has captured several already. The captain is a man named Jones. A certain John Paul Jones."

"Rather bold of him, raiding in this area so near to our fleet headquarters."

"Yes, and I bring the subject up because his ship is sloop rigged— that's why I'm studying this one so carefully."

"If it turns out that's the *Providence*, are you going to fight?"

Proctor lowered the glass. There was a gleam in his eyes. "Colonel, I would like nothing better." He motioned toward the guns along the deck. "And we are probably more heavily armed and have a larger crew than the rebel." Then he sighed. "But there will be no fight unless he presses the point."

"Why, sir?"

"My overriding duty, Colonel, is to ensure you and your dispatches reach Gwynn's Island safely. I can not subject this vessel and you to even the chance of capture. Thus I must avoid combat if within my power."

Meanwhile Flowers joined them at the rail. He said, "I believe that fellow has adjusted his course to intercept us, sir."

Proctor put the glass to his eye again. "Indeed, sir, it appears you are correct." He looked over at Northcutt. "Well, Colonel, you may get to witness a sea fight if he chooses to engage." Then he turned back to the master. "Flowers, I'll have the bos'n pipe the crew to quarters. Clear for action, sir!"

Flowers signaled the watch bos'n mate, who picked up his pipe and began whistling. Immediately hands began to emerge from below deck, running to the guns, others climbing the shrouds up the fore and main masts. Soon powder monkeys began bringing gunpowder bags and round balls up for the cannons, and Northcutt saw that a squad of musket-armed seamen was assembling on the quarterdeck. Other men carrying small arms made their way up to the fighting tops on the masts.

Proctor saw Barrett watching the armed men, and said, "Since we're too small for a marine detachment; some seamen serve as musket men and sharpshooters in the tops." Then he snapped his glass up to his eye again. "That's definitely an armed sloop; I can see the gunports. He's better armed than I thought. And he's damn well trying to close us."

Northcutt, who could see the intruder fairly well now, said, "He seems to be moving quite fast."

"Aye, he's got the windward gauge. He can approach or retreat as he desires." Then he called out to the main deck, "Cast the guns loose and run them out as soon as you are ready! I want our friend to see the *Raven*'s strength!"

Northcutt watched as the crews of the six guns on the starboard side heaved on the tackle and in near unison the cannons rolled into firing position, their barrels extending well out of the ports.

Proctor stood, hands clasped behind his back, surveying the ship's readiness. "I doubt that Jones, if that is he, will want to contest with a ship of twelve four-pounders. His job, in a tiny vessel such as that sloop, is to snap up merchant prizes, not fight."

Northcutt looked back up at the intruder, who was now fully visible and rapidly descending on the *Raven*. "I am not much acquainted with nautical matters, but it is a *very* small craft, is it not?"

"I should say not more than sixty or sixty-five feet in length, probably little more than one hundred tons in burden." Proctor put the glass back to his eye. "Well, he's not flying any kind of ensign." A puzzled look came over the captain's face. "Actually, I don't believe the rebel congress has actually designated a proper flag for their cause.

What one sees most often is that damned snake flag, or they sometimes show one with a pine tree on it."

"That's what we see in Virginia also, Captain."

"I'm of the sentiment that we should designate their ships as pirate vessels and be done with it. Hang them out of hand when captured."

"I'm sure there is considerable agreement with that idea, sir."

Proctor waved toward the American sloop. "He's close enough to see our black beauties with their snouts outboard and ready for him. We should get a reaction soon enough. Will he choose to dance with us or run?"

※

Colonel Daingerfield sat at the table in front of his tent, and Wend could see a look of intense concentration on his face. Also at the table were Captain Posey and the regimental adjutant, Lieutenant Greer.

Daingerfield said, "It's now been five days since we put your man ashore on Gwynn's, and we've heard nothing. And it has been a week since the last boat raid by the British." He looked around at the others. "The British have tended to conduct these incursions about a week apart. So we are due for a visit by them any day now."

Posey said, "Since they tend to sail at night and come ashore at dawn, they could be raiding at this very moment, and there would not have been time for a messenger to get to us."

"Quite correct," said Daingerfield. He looked around the table. "So we are likely to have another visit by the British, conducted with impunity."

Posey raised his hands. "It seems the only remedy will be when we get Lewis's reinforcements and drive the British away."

Wend sighed. "Well, gentlemen, I have thought about this at some length. There is one possible course of action which would at least give us a better chance of intercepting the British on one of their raids."

Daingerfield cocked his head. "Indeed? Perhaps you would share your idea with us, Captain Eckert."

"Well, sir, the problem is that it takes so much time for troops to get to the area where the British raid that it's all over by the time they arrive."

The colonel threw up his hands. "Tell me something I don't know, Eckert."

"Well, Colonel, it seems to me that we could position forces closer to their landing site and thus be ready to intercept them shortly after they land."

"Brilliant, sir. Of course, there's only one problem. How do we know where they're going to land? That's what your African friend was supposed to find out for us."

Wend paused long enough to ensure irritation didn't enter his voice. "Sir, obviously the British will either land somewhere to the north of the island beyond the mouth of the Piankatank, most likely along the Rappahannock, where there are a lot of plantations. Or they will go south along the coast to the many little bays or inlets which provide access to just as many plantations and farms." He showed the southern areas on the map that lay on the table. "I propose that we soon as possible send a company northward to position itself closer to a landing along the lower Rappahannock and another here to the south." He pointed to an area on the map that was centrally located between several large plantations. "These might well be their targets."

Posey nodded. "Yes, I see what you're getting at. We should also call out groups of militia to act as coast lookouts who could inform the troops."

Wend nodded. "My thought exactly, Captain." He looked up at Daingerfield. "It's not perfect, but it gives us more of a chance of stopping the British than if we sit here in camp. And actually, nothing of consequence will happen here until Lewis arrives with artillery. Since we are overdue for a raid, I propose that two companies march for those positions as soon as possible. And that riders be sent out immediately to alert the militia to establish lookout posts."

Daingerfield looked down at the map and drummed his fingers on the table, mulling the proposition over. After a few moments, he looked up and said, "All right, we shall give it a try. The only other option seems to be sitting here impotently, and as Eckert has pointed out, we have nothing to lose."

Posey looked at his colonel. "So who will you send, and where?"

Daingerfield said, "Eckert's company, since he made the proposal and, to be honest, his men are the best equipped." He looked over at Posey. "And your company, insofar as you are senior in the regiment."

Wend asked, "Who goes north, and who south?"

Posey said, a smile on his face, "The last two raids have been to the north. I say the next will most likely be to the south. So that is the position of honor." He looked at Daingerfield. "Which of us will march south?"

The colonel stared ahead for a moment. Wend thought, *The man is torn. Posey is his senior captain and thinks he should have the assignment. But I'm the one who proposed the plan. And quite frankly, I've got the better-trained company.*

Daingerfield grimaced. Then he turned to the adjutant, Greer, and said, "Paper and ink, please."

Greer brought them immediately, and Daingerfield tore two slips of paper. He quickly wrote a word on each, then shuffled them in his hand and gave them to Greer facedown. "Put one in front of each captain, Greer."

The adjutant did so. Then Dangerfield said, "All right, gentlemen, turn your paper over."

Wend did so, and was gratified to see the word "South." He held it up so all could see.

Daingerfield grinned. "Well, as they say, *the luck of the draw.*" He sat for a moment, lost in thought. Then he stood up and said, "Gentlemen, you will march as soon as possible. Light order, so you can move fast. No baggage, no tents, no women and children, no wagons. Only what your men can carry on their backs. And ammunition for a fight."

Then he turned to Greer. "Lieutenant, get couriers on their way to the local militias. We need lookouts in place posthaste."

"Good Lord. This place is even bigger than Alexandria!" Joshua Baird sat his horse, looking in astonishment at the town of Williamsburg.

Donegal said, "Na, Joshua, if you think this is big, you'd probably fall right off that tall horse of yours if you laid eyes on Philadelphia. Now, me lad, there's a big town!"

Joshua shook his head. "This town is big enough for me. Damned if I want to be in a place like Philadelphia, where there ain't no proper trees to mention and everything is all bricks and stone."

Lieutenant Daniel Collins, the courier who had accompanied them down from Gwynn's Island, added, "Well, Norfolk was a big place, that is, before Dunmore bombarded it and it was set afire. It's just ruins now. Burned out buildings and rubble." He kicked his horse. "But we can't waste time jawing. Come along, gentlemen, let me take you to General Lewis."

Joshua laughed. "Now, Collins, we been in the saddle for two days. Two long, *dry* days. Just makes sense we get some refreshing libation before we see the general. Like in a tavern. I'm wagerin' you know a good one close by his headquarters."

Donegal smiled. "I think that's a bonny idea. And we can clean some of the dust off our clothes while we're wetting our dry throats."

Collins thought for a long moment. "All right, that makes some sense. And in any case, Lewis may be engaged in some way. I'll see you to an inn, a place where you can also get a room, and then go find out the best time for you to see him."

"Na, since it was the general who invited us down to this fair town," said Donegal, "while you're seein' him, could you get him to pay for the room? It's na fair we should have to take this out of our own purse!"

Collins nodded. "Yes, I'll see about that. Now let's ride for the inn and get you settled. Then I'll check with the general's staff and see when you are to meet with him."

As it turned out, the audience with the general occurred that very afternoon. Donegal and Joshua had just finished their first drink and ordered a second when Collins returned. He entered the common room, looked around, and seeing the pair, strode right over to where they sat. "All right, Donegal, the general considers this urgent. He wants me to take you to him right away."

Joshua responded, "Well, it happens we have another round coming, Daniel. Why don't you join us, and then we'll go 'round to see what old Andy has in mind."

"Baird, the next set of drinks can wait. General Lewis wants you to get to the camp of the Highlanders as soon as possible."

Just then the tavern girl arrived with the drinks on a tray. Collins raised his hand. "Sorry, miss, take those back. These gentlemen have an appointment for which they must leave instantly."

Disgust on his face, Joshua rose from his chair and grabbed his hat. "Come on, Donegal, let's go see Lewis."

Simon sighed, drained his whiskey cup, and rose also. "All right, Collins, let's be gone."

They walked a short distance to a large brick building. Collins said, "This is the capital. It's where the Burgesses used to meet and where the convention has been meeting since last year. There are also some offices, and right now Lewis is using one."

They entered the building and walked along a short hall to where a young officer was sitting at a desk before a closed door.

The young lieutenant asked, "Collins, are these the two to see the general?"

"Aye, Sergeant Donegal and Mr. Baird."

The lieutenant entered the office but was back instantly. "General Lewis says come right in."

The two entered to see that three men were in the office. Lewis sat behind his desk, pulling on a pipe. Patrick Henry sat in a chair drawn up to one side of the desk, and James Wood stood leaning against the wall on the other side of it.

It was Henry who spoke first. "Well, my old friends Donegal and Baird. Last seen up at my headquarters in Culpeper last fall."

The two men nodded to Henry. "Aye, that's the way I remember it, Colonel Henry," said Joshua. "Just afore you sent us off on that chase all over the countryside in search of John Connolly and his crew."

"Indeed, and I have no regrets. You and Captain Eckert dealt with Connolly and his conspirators as well as I could have wished." Then a frown came over his face, and he raised a finger. "But I do have a question: Whatever happened to the men I sent with you, Captain Ballantyne and his squad? They never returned to the regiment."

Simon and Joshua exchanged quick looks. Then Joshua said, "Well, that sergeant, name of Seidal, he was killed in a fight we had with Connolly's henchman Dick Munger and his men. And as for Ballantyne and them Carlin brothers, all I know is when we left to come back to Winchester, they was sittin' next to a cheery campfire, plannin' their journey."

Donegal nodded. "Aye, that's the truth of it. They was figurin' the best way to get back. If they didn't ever get to your battalion, Mr. Henry, they must have had some accident along the way."

Henry made a tight smile, with a twinkle in his eyes. "Yes, I rather thought you would say it was something like that." He shrugged. "In any case, everything worked out as I could have wished."

James Wood waved at Joshua. "I'm glad Captain Eckert sent Baird along. I should have thought of that; he probably knows as many of these Highlanders as Donegal."

Joshua grinned. "Aye, he sent me along to watch out for Donegal and keep him out of trouble."

Donegal looked sideways at the scout. "Na that's funny—Wend told me to watch out for you. Said you needed mindin' with so many taverns here in town."

The two men looked at each other and laughed.

Meanwhile, Lewis raised a hand, signaling quiet. "Let's get to the business at hand, gentlemen."

Donegal and Baird said, "Yes, sir" almost in unison.

Lewis put his pipe down and leaned back in his chair. "Now, we've got near two hundred Highlanders, a company each of the 42nd and the 71st, in a guarded camp not a mile from here. They were on ships blown away from their convoy by a storm. Sailing alone, they were then taken by a privateer. After capturing the two ships, the privateer took all the officers onto his ship and consolidated all the soldiers and their families onto one ship. He was escorting the two prizes back to port when they were separated by another storm. During the storm the Highlanders took advantage of the bad weather and overcame the prize crew and restored the regular crew to control."

Donegal said, "But why did they come here to the Chesapeake? Why didn't they sail up to Halifax?"

"The stormy weather had blown them well south, and they were getting short on water and provisions because of being overloaded with double the number of passengers. They also were worried about being recaptured by privateers on the way north. They knew Dunmore was attempting to hold the colony, so they thought they could join up with him."

Joshua said, "They would have been a hell of a reinforcement for Dunmore."

Wood interjected, "That's exactly right, Joshua. It would have made it much harder for us to deal with him. But luckily, we were able to capture them by use of a ruse."

"A ruse?" asked Donegal.

"Yes, the ship made Norfolk and lay off the port, and they talked to some men on a fishing boat, asking where Dunmore could be found."

Henry said, "Thinking quickly, the fishing boat captain said he was a loyalist and glad to see the Highland soldiers. He offered to lead their ship to Dunmore." Henry smiled. "Instead, he led the ship up the York River and had them anchor off Yorktown. There, some of our small vessels were able to surround them and convince them to surrender."

"Damn!" said Donegal. "To think Highlanders would have been so easily fooled."

Lewis leaned forward. "The fisherman was very convincing, and once the ship was at anchor, and surrounded by both boats and under the guns of batteries ashore, they had little choice. Particularly with wives and children aboard."

"Aye, now, General, I see how that could have happened."

Lewis said, "It was a good piece of work by our people. But now the job is to convince these Highlanders to join our side. Think of how a battalion of them could help Virginia's cause."

Henry added, "They should find it in their interest to switch sides. It was only thirty years ago they were revolting against the king themselves, fighting for their own independence."

Lewis nodded. "Yes, and particularly with the inducements we are willing to provide."

Puzzlement spread over Joshua's face. "Inducements? What the devil is an inducement? Na'er heard the word."

Wood said, "We're going to give them something of value to join us." He looked over a Henry. "Most especially land of their own."

Henry said, "Yes, we'll grant each man who joins us a substantial amount of land on the border, all in one area, so they'll have their own community. That will be more property than they could ever dream of having in Scotland."

A sly look came over Joshua's face. "And it wouldn't hurt the government of Virginia to have a bunch of trained soldiers living along the border, right where they can face the Ohio tribes."

The three leaders exchanged glances. Henry coughed, stared down at his hands, and said, "Well, yes, that idea *had* occurred to us."

Donegal nodded and looked over at Joshua. "Aye, I'm sure that it did."

Wood cleared his throat. "That brings us to why we arranged to have you come to Williamsburg. Our thought is that these soldiers would be more amenable to an offer presented by someone they know and can respect. A Highlander like yourself, Donegal. They're likely to trust someone they've marched with, rather than a group of political men like ourselves."

Lewis reached down to his desk and picked up a piece of paper. "Here is a list of their sergeants and corporals. Look over it, and see if you personally know any of these men."

Simon took the paper and looked at it. Immediately he broke into a grin and looked over at Joshua. "Na look at that very first name. Sergeant Daniel McNabb. Company sergeant of the 71st."

Baird raised his eyebrows. "Daniel McNabb. Sounds familiar. Big hulking man? Used to be in Robertson's company of the 77th?"

"That's the one. He was a private back in '63 but must be the same fellow."

Lewis asked in an eager tone, "So you're saying you know him?"

"If it's the same man, aye, sir. Won't know for sure until I lay eyes on him. Be a wee bit older now."

Henry beamed. "Excellent. It seems highly likely you know one of the leaders of the group, and we've told you we're prepared to grant them significant amounts of land. And we would be amenable to other things, such as implements needed for farming and supplies to start them off. So you have something to offer in negotiations."

Lewis said, "We consider this urgent. So we'll have Collins escort you to their camp. We have them encamped just over a mile from here, out toward the river." He stood up. "You can leave immediately."

Donegal held up his hand. "Beggin' your pardon, now, General. But there's somethin' very important we need before we go. It's as important as anything else you spoke about."

Puzzled, Lewis asked, "Yes, and what would that be?"

"Several jugs of whiskey or rum."

Joshua said, "Dickerin' always goes better if tongues are loosened by liquor."

Henry and Wood looked at each other. Henry grinned. "Yes, I learned that long ago. We'll get you the jugs posthaste."

Lewis called in Collins. "Get these men several jugs of whiskey as fast as possible."

A totally puzzled Collins asked, "Whiskey, sir?"

"Damn it, Lieutenant, you heard me!" He pointed at Donegal and Baird. "And take these men with you."

Henry added, "And then you must be off without delay, so you can speak with those Highlanders this evening."

Chapter Fifteen

THE RAID

Wend sat on the ground, staring at the crude map of the area south of the Piankatank and Gwynn's Island. They had gone into camp in a wooded meadow after a march of ten miles over rough wagon roads. The three other officers of the company also sat with him contemplating the map, while around them were the squad fires of the company and the noises of an active army camp as the men went about cooking their rations.

Newkirk looked up from the map. "This whole coast is cut up with bays, inlets, and small rivers emptying into the sea. No matter where the British land, we're going to have trouble getting to them. Every way you turn, there's some body of water we have to march around."

Wend said, "That's why I picked this spot to camp. We're three miles inland, so that we can march in any direction if they hit the shoreline anywhere from here in the north to the mouth of Horn Harbor Bay to the south."

Shay pointed to a place below Horn Bay, which extended miles inland. "But look how far inland this bay goes. If they land south of there, it could take half a day or longer for us to get around the headwaters and into position to attack their landing party. We'd be as useless as if we were in our camp up at Gwynn's."

Newkirk said, "Wend, he's right. And the map shows several plantations down there. The British can also land from two directions: from the Chesapeake itself, to the east, or they could enter Mobjack Bay to the south and come ashore from there. Maybe we should move down to the south now."

Wend gritted his teeth. It was indeed an intractable problem. "Yes, but there's also a goodly number of plantations and farms around us here. They'd be as good a target as down below Horn Bay." He looked around at the faces. "And remember, one of the reasons we're at this particular spot is because Cowell docks his boat in a small cove due east of us. It's the easiest place for him to bring Billy to us if by chance he picks him up tonight at the island or if he himself sights a British flotilla moving in this direction."

O'beirne sighed. "Now, lads, I hate to bring this up, but I truly think Billy is a lost cause. I'm of the mind they caught him or he's been forced into hiding on the island and is afraid to move. No, I wager we'll not hear from him. If we get any warning, it will be from Cowell or the militia pickets Daingerfield ordered to be posted along the shoreline."

A grim look came over Wend's face. "Shay, I'm not ready to give up on Billy. He may be making sure of any information he's got. Also, it's just possible the British aren't ready for their next raid yet."

There was a period of silence, everyone looking down at the map.

Then Childers spoke up. "Captain Eckert, I have a thought. Why don't we send half the company south of Horn Bay. Then they'd be in position to counter a raid there, while the other half remains here."

Shay laughed. "Now, me college lad, I'm going to tell you something those black-robed, high-foreheaded professors of yours at William and Mary would not have taught you."

"Yes, sir? And what would that be?"

"In the military arts, as it were, it is considered bad form to split your force, particularly in the face of an equal or stronger enemy. And, lad, we are told that the British landing parties have most often been more than one hundred men. Sometimes a great deal more than that."

Childers flushed. "Well, I was just thinking about it."

Wend raised a hand. "Let's *do* think about it. Unlikely as it might be, our ensign may have stumbled onto something."

Newkirk raised an eyebrow. "You mean you're actually *considering* splitting the company?"

Wend sighed. "Regrettably, while it's usually the wrong move, it may be the only answer in this case." He pointed to a spot south of the horn. "If we positioned a portion of the company here, they could respond to a raid over this wide area, whether the British come from the Chesapeake itself or Mobjack Bay. And the rest of the company could remain here, ready to deal with a raid on the north side of Horn Harbor Bay."

O'beirne said, "But each half company would undoubtedly be greatly outnumbered."

"Indeed," responded Wend. "But it might not be *that* bad a situation. The British probably have gotten complacent. Based on past experience, they won't be expecting a counterattack. According to reports on prior raids, they'll probably be broken up into detachments to hit various plantations and gather provisions. A half-company-sized force, skillfully handled, and with the advantage of surprise, might be able to fall on isolated British parties. Meanwhile, the other half company, notified by messenger about where the British have actually landed, or even alerted by the sound of firing, would rapidly march to support the engaged company." He threw up his hands and sighed deeply. "It's not *ideal*. Damn, it's not even *good*, but I think it is all we have."

The four officers stared at the map for long seconds. Then Newkirk asked, "So is that what you want to do? Is that your decision?"

Wend looked around at the three men who were now staring at him. "Yes, that's it." He worked some calculations in his mind quickly. "Newkirk, you'll take four of the field squads and march around the headwaters of the Horn and find a favorable location to wait." Wend pointed to a spot on the map. "Probably about here. Meanwhile, I'll keep the other four field squads, and the two rifle squads, with me."

He looked up at the sky. "Reese, there's a good three hours of evening light left. Select your squads, get them to finish their meal rapidly, then march as soon as possible. You'll have some light for the first part of your march. And take that guide Daingerfield gave us, Jared Brown; he should be able to find the way in the moonlight." He pointed to a spot on the map. "You've got to push it so that you are at this point, south of the Horn Bay and just west of the three largest plantations, by dawn."

In less than an hour, Newkirk and his four squads marched out of the camp, taking a wagon track that Brown said led around the head of Horn Bay. As he watched them go, Wend felt a knot of uncertainty in his stomach. *Had he made the right decision by splitting the company? Or had he played the fool? He realized only the arrival of the British, and their choice of landing site, would determine the outcome.*

—⟋m⟍—

Northcutt and Proctor stood on the *Raven*'s quarterdeck, watching the sloop approach.

"Well," said Proctor, "he's within a mile now. We'll know his intentions very soon."

"He doesn't seem to be very hesitant about approaching us. Do you suppose he hasn't seen our battery?"

The young captain considered for a long moment. "Not unless he's blind. Perhaps he wants to taunt us since with the wind in his favor, he can turn and run quite easily."

They waited in silence for several minutes as the sloop continued steadily on course. Soon it was just a few hundred yards—Northcutt thought less than a quarter mile—distant, and directly on Raven's beam. Suddenly there was a flurry of activity on the small vessel's deck and in her spars, and her rudder was put over, for she turned to starboard and paralleled Raven's course. Then a flag was run up at the rear of her great mainsail.

Proctor looked through the telescope. "Yes, there's that damn rattlesnake ensign fluttering from her gaff." He snapped the telescope shut. "And my dear colonel, he's run out his guns. I saw five black snouts."

"That would be one less than we have in our broadside."

The captain grinned broadly. "Quite correct. However, we don't know what weight of ball they throw. But both Jones, if that is he, and I know that we still have the advantage. We're larger, with a bigger crew and two masts." Proctor pointed toward the sloop. "If we do engage, I shall endeavor to rain balls about his spars, and that tall single mast. If we disable a spar or two, let alone take down that mast, he's finished. Undoubtedly the rebel is as aware of his deficiencies as we are."

Proctor stared at the sloop for a long moment. Then he turned and walked to the quarterdeck rail. "Mr. Anson!" he called out. "Mr. Anson, come to me if you please." He turned back to Barrett. "I believe

I will provide a compelling inducement for the rebel to make a choice about his course of action."

Northcutt knew Anson was the ship's warrant gunner, having sat with him at the wardroom table often enough.

Soon the gunner arrived and put a finger to his forehead in salute to the captain. "Aye, sir, and what do you have in mind?"

Proctor grinned. "I have in mind a little fun with the rebel." He pointed to the sloop. "I should say he's now just three or four hundred yards away."

Anson turned and stared at the vessel. "Nearer three hundred, I'd say, sir."

"Yes, I dare say he's looking us over. Well, Mr. Anson, do you suppose you could put a shot near or through his rigging, just as a small reminder that we know our business?"

"Indeed, sir, it might be done with little trouble."

"Then do so at your will, Mr. Anson. I desire one shot only, carefully placed."

Anson touched his hat. "I will lay the gun myself, Cap'n."

Proctor nodded, and the gunner strode down to the main deck. He stood contemplating the six guns in the battery, then walked up to the second from the bow and began sighting along the gun. He gave directions to the men at the tackle, having them adjust the muzzle back and forth. Then he picked up a burning-slow match and timing for the upward roll of the ship, touched off the gun. A loud bang resulted, and smoke and flame erupted from the muzzle.

Proctor and Northcutt watched the arc of the ball as it flew toward the Rebel vessel. It passed over the sloop, just feet above the fore and aft mainsail and just abaft the square topsail.

Anson strode back to stand in front of the quarterdeck and called out to Proctor, "Now, Captain, did that suite your desire?"

Proctor grinned. "Nicely done, sir. My compliments to yourself and the gun crew."

Northcutt had kept his eyes on the sloop. Suddenly he called out, "Proctor, he's turning!"

Proctor walked over to the rail, his eyes riveted on the rebel. "Yes indeed, sir. We have drawn him out and forced him to make a decision." He clasped his arms behind his back. "I should say he has decided it is convenient to look for more likely prey." The captain turned and called down to the master, "Mr. Flowers, secure from quarters. Set the regular watch!"

Barrett said, "Well now, that is something to remember about this voyage. I regret my being the cause of you not being able to fight that Captain Jones, or whoever the rebel might be."

"No need for an apology, Colonel. That was an amusing piece of distraction." Proctor stared after the departing *Providence*. Then he said, in something of a whimsical tone, "In a few years, I shall be posted to command of a larger ship, perhaps a twenty-gun ship or a frigate, with a much more numerous crew and several lieutenants to assist me. A ship whose proper business is exchanging broadsides with an enemy." He sighed. "But I shall always fondly remember my time here on the *Raven*. She is a sweet little vessel, and I will miss the freedom of sailing independently instead of as part of a squadron or fleet, under the steely eyes of a more senior officer."

Northcutt nodded his understanding. "Yes, I can understand that. It seems in much of life, the more senior or higher in rank you get, you actually have less freedom of action than when young. There are more constraints on your behavior, imposed by both the people you work for or the strictures of society."

"There's much truth in what you say, Colonel. I often contemplate that very notion when alone in my cabin." He looked over at Northcutt. "And that must be a consideration for you now as you prepare to explain General Howe's decision to your governor, who despite his high position, has now been restrained by someone of even greater rank."

Northcutt sighed deeply. "Indeed, Captain, you are quite correct."

"Well, a few days will see us to the Virginia Capes. Then we shall see how His Lordship takes the news."

Lord Dunmore leaned back, relaxing in his chair behind the wide desk in his office. The office had been set up in a large bedroom of the house belonging to John Randolph Grymes, the largest landowner on Gwynn's Island. The governor was enjoying a cigar and a cup of rum and at the same time, taking in the grand view of the Chesapeake that was visible through the wide, tall windows to the east. Another set of windows on the north side of the room also afforded an excellent view of the scores of ships of the Floating Colony in Hills Bay.

Dunmore reflected that he had many reasons to be satisfied with the state of affairs. In the month since they had arrived, comfortable camps had been established for all three of the loyalist regiments and the 14th Foot. Fortifications, well armed with artillery, had been set up along Milford Haven to secure the island from any attempt to cross by the rebel rabble. Frequent raids on local plantations and farms had kept provisions flowing in, with the result that his troops and loyalist supporters were far better fed than they had been during the time at Norfolk. The raids had also resulted in the desertion of Africans from plantations, most of whom had chosen to become soldiers in the Ethiopian Regiment.

There were, as always, a few flies in the ointment. It turned out that the navy's assessment that the island could provide enough fresh water for all the loyalists had been in error. In fact, there were few sources on Gwynn's. However, they had been able to make up the difference by filling casks during the raids ashore. But the most serious problem was that smallpox was as rampant among the Africans as it had ever been. They had set up an isolation hospital on the southern end of the island, near the beach, where all the cases could be treated. The medical personnel had also established a program of inoculations for the former slaves, but it was still too early to see if it was having a significant effect. The fact was, they were still suffering a high number of deaths every day. The governor took a long pull on his rum, then drew heavily on his cigar. He thought, *The damned pox situation seems intractable.*

At that moment there was a tap on the door and the secretary, Dudley Fellows stepped in. "My lord, there are some people here to see you. They are a couple, the Crosswells, whose plantation is near Fredericksburg."

Dunmore thought a moment. "Ah yes, *Dalton* Crosswell. Former member of Burgesses and the man who played such a crucial role in the raid on Eckert's firelock manufactory."

"Yes, sir, the very same."

"But what are they doing here?"

Fellows answered, "He and his wife just arrived by small boat. In fact, they are refugees and requesting that we shelter them. And I'm afraid they bear some rather disturbing news."

"Disturbing news? Pray tell, what is it?"

"Sir, they're waiting outside with Mr. Harbridge. He recommends you see them immediately and allow them to relate their story directly to you."

Dunmore crushed out his cigar and quickly downed the rest of his drink. "Very well, show them in, Dudley."

Fellows opened the door, and Harbridge ushered in the Crosswells. Dunmore was momentarily stunned by their appearance. He sat staring at the couple. The clothing of both were soiled and torn, and Lillian's hair was askance. Their faces were haggard by weariness, their eyes seeming to have sunken into their sockets. Their cheeks and foreheads were both dirty and burned by exposure to the sun.

Harbridge helped Mrs. Crosswell into a wing chair near the windows, where she sagged down in obvious exhaustion.

After a moment Dunmore remembered himself and, rising from his chair, hurried around the desk and extended a hand to Crosswell. "My dear Dalton, it is good to see you again. And we are most thankful that you have arrived safely to Gwynn's Island." Then he went to Lillian and bowed deeply to her. "Mrs. Crosswell, we will immediately provide for your well-being."

Dunmore turned to Fellows. "Dudley, please arrange for one of Mrs. Grymes's maids to come and provide personal assistance to the lady." Fellows nodded and hurried from the room. Then the governor turned back to Crosswell. "My God, sir, please relate to us what has happened to you and why you are here."

Crosswell ran his hand through his hair and sighed deeply. "You're damned right I'll tell you. Our plantation was burned by a gang of rebels. Everything was destroyed but the slave quarters. And we were told that their so-called government in Williamsburg, that damnable 'convention,' as they call it, would be sending agents to apprehend us." He grimaced. "All in reprisal for that raid in Frederick County."

Dunmore asked, "My God, have you any idea who these men were?"

Crosswell looked around and said, "Their leader said he was Wend Eckert. Wend Eckert, the man who Major Welford told us was dead."

For the second time in a few minutes, Dunmore was stunned speechless. Then he exclaimed, "For God's sake, man, what are you saying? Welford personally told me he shot Eckert in the head with his own hand at close range and that there was no chance he survived."

"My lord, would you tell me why anyone would ride to my house and assume the identity of a dead man? This person seethed anger and was obviously out for revenge." Crosswell looked over at his wife. "And after announcing who he was, he and his men horrified my wife by telling her in excruciating detail how her son had suffered and died in the retreat from the raid. I tell you, she still has not recovered from the shock."

Harbridge coached, "Tell him the rest of what they said."

Crosswell nodded. "Oh yes, Eckert specifically demanded that I tell you that he was coming to exact revenge, particularly from Colonel Northcutt and Major Welford. And that he was coming with a company of one hundred men at his back."

Harbridge said, "My lord, I have little doubt this is all true. For some reason beyond all logic, Eckert survived. In reality, it is quite possible that he is here among the rebel forces besieging the island."

The muscles in Dunmore's face tightened. Then he asked the planter, "How did you get here? It must have been a most dangerous journey. Did you steal your way through the rebel lines?"

Lillian Crosswell answered. "That would have been impossible. We feared rebel troops or militia stopping us and asking questions if we traveled by road. We came by small, open boat, sailing down the Rappahannock and then southward down the Bay to this place." She quivered. "Sailing by day and sleeping on the shore at night, hiding like animals in the bush." She raised her hands, both formed into fists, and broke into tears of anger. "Like *animals*, do you understand? Fearful that rebel militia would stop us and take us prisoner. We had only some cold food we were able to take before we left." She sobbed. "God, Your Lordship, how could things like this come to pass?" She shook for a moment, then said, "We have lost everything! Everything we have worked for over the years, building River View Manor into a fine estate. What shall we do? Where shall we go?"

Dunmore approached her and took her hand in both of his. Then he said in a soothing tone, "My dear Mrs. Crosswell, please do not despair. I urge you to keep faith with your king and your governor. We are preparing to take the colony back from these deplorable insurrectionists. I have a strong force here on the island and in the fleet you see anchored nearby. Moreover, I am expecting reinforcements from General Howe's army which is now in Halifax preparing their return to the conflict. When that occurs, we shall go on the offense and in good time return proper order to Virginia. Rest assured, you will soon find yourself restored to your estate and your wealth. And then we shall ensure you get recompense from the assets of those who have harmed you and your property."

There was a knock on the door, and then it swung open. Ethel Grymes rushed into the room, followed by an African maid and Fellows. She exclaimed, "Lillian Crosswell! It's been two years since we met at that ball in Williamsburg. Do you remember me? My God, what has happened to you?"

Lillian nodded. "Yes, I remember—we sat across from each other at supper."

Dunmore assisted Lillian to her feet and spoke to Ethel. "They have been turned out of their plantation by a mob of these despicable rebels. I would be most grateful if you could assist her with nourishment and clothing."

"Of course we will! Please, my dear, come with us, and we will have you feeling better in short time."

While they were talking, John Grymes had quietly entered the room. As the ladies left, he stepped forward and extended his hand to Crosswell. "Hello, Dalton. It's been a while since we were together at the card table down in the capital."

"Yes, John, it's been a while. And those were certainly better times."

Grymes nodded. "Indeed they were." He looked over at Dunmore. "But we must trust in Lord Dunmore and General Howe to restore the colony to its proper governance. In the meantime, I insist you accept my hospitality."

Crosswell sighed. "Regrettably I seem to have no choice for the time being but to impose on you."

"Think nothing of it, Dalton." Grymes put his hand on Crosswell's arm and motioned toward the door. "Come with me, and we shall afford you the opportunity to clean up and don some proper clothing. And then we shall have a libation to restore your spirits."

"My God, John, that sounds marvelous after the last few days."

After they had left, Harbridge closed the door behind them.

Dunmore strode over to the sidebar and poured a cup of rum. He quickly downed the entire cup, then he turned to Harbridge and Fellows. Anger was evident in his expression. "Damn it! Get me Welford! Immediately! I must understand how it is possible that this dead man Eckert is once again causing me problems! How could Reginald have been so wrong?" He looked around at his aides. "Or does this devil Eckert have some supernatural power of reincarnation?"

Fellows looked over at Harbridge and then said, "Your Lordship, I'm afraid that Major Welford is aboard HMS *Otter*. He and his regiment are performing tomorrow's raid. They are in the process of sailing as we speak."

Dunmore glared out the window at the fleet in Hills Bay, his face reddening. Then he turned back and, between gritted teeth, said, "I will see him upon his return. Immediately upon his return!"

Harbridge said, "It will be done, sir."

At dusk Donegal, Baird, and Lieutenant Collins rode along Yorktown Landing Road from Williamsburg, soon arriving at the camp of the captured Highlanders. Collins pointed out that there were actually two camps, one for the Highlanders and the other for the Virginia soldiers charged with guard duty.

Donegal could see that the Highland camp was set up in strict military fashion, with rows of tents and squad fires. Sentries of Virginians ringed the camp. Highland soldiers, wives, and children moved around, stood in groups conversing, or were sitting by the fires.

Collins led them to a tent where the officer of the guard was seated behind a field desk, with a sergeant also present. He said, "This is the entrance to the Highland camp. I'll clear you to go in with the officer of the guard." All three swung down from their horses, and Collins walked over to the tent and talked briefly with the officer. Then he turned back and shouted, "You're clear to enter. I'll stay here with the guard."

Taking the jugs of whiskey with which they had been provided, Donegal and Baird walked into the camp. They were immediately confronted by a burly Highland private of the 71st. He held up a hand to stop them. "Ach, now, where might you two be plannin' to go?"

Donegal looked over at Joshua. "Seems like they've got their own guards set up."

The Highlander said, "Aye, that we do. As in any military camp. And as I asked, what's your business?"

Simon said, "Na, we understand your leader is a sergeant named Daniel McNabb. Would that be the way of it?"

The Highlander raised an eyebrow. "Aye, McNabb is his name. What is that to you?"

"Well na, my good lad, would you happen to know if this sergeant of yours was formerly in the 77th during the late troubles with the French here in the colonies?"

The man gave Donegal a sharp look. Then he nodded slowly and said, "Aye, he was indeed. He's always telling us stories no end about those days and the fights with the red Indians during the Pontiac War that happened after that."

Donegal looked at Baird and grinned. "Aye, that would be Daniel!"

Joshua nodded vigorously. "McNabb always did have a way of tellin' stories."

Donegal nodded. "And the more he had to drink, the more excitin' they got." Then he told the Highland guard, "Now, my good lad, it happens we've been sent by the government of Virginia to discuss certain matters with McNabb. Would you be kind enough to take us to him?"

The guard turned to a very young soldier who had been standing by. "All right, lad, take them to McNabb's tent. But keep a sharp eye on them while you go. We've had enough of Yankee tricks."

Donegal pointed to his bonnet. "Now, laddie, do you think a soldier of the 77th would be aimin' to trick a fellow Highlander from the old country?"

The guard said, "You've chosen to live with the Yankees. No tellin' what you'd be about." Then he waved them into the camp.

The private led them along the central camp street. They had not gone far when a corporal, sitting by a campfire, called out to Joshua, "Hey, na I've seen you before! You're that scout used to work for Colonel Bouquet, back in '58, when we marched with General Forbes. Your name is Bird or something like that."

Joshua turned. "Aye, I worked with Bouquet. And my name is *Baird*, Joshua Baird."

The corporal nodded. "Aye, that be it. I saw you often enough. I was a private in Captain McIntyre's company of the 77th."

Donegal looked over and said, "Now I think on it, I recognize you. Wouldn't you be Donald McBayne?"

McBayne squinted at Donegal. "Aye, and I recognize you too! You was mates with Bob Kirkwood, the one who was so good at stealing chickens and hogs."

"You're right about that. And that's why we ate well in McDonald's company."

They kept moving, and several other veterans greeted them along the way. Finally they came to the last fire on the central street and saw a burly man sitting on a log beside it.

Simon looked over at Joshua. "Sure enough that's Daniel. Older looking, but that's him."

"Well hell, Simon, we all got near thirteen years on us since the 77th was sent home."

McNabb stood up, a look of surprise on his face. "Na the Lord preserve me, if it isn't Simon Donegal and Joshua Baird. What in the devil are you doing here of all places?"

Donegal said, "We came to have a little talk and remember old times." He held up his jug of whiskey. "And we brought this along to loosen our tongues and help freshen the memories of the old days."

McNabb laughed a deep, hearty laugh. "Yes, those were good times. It was recalling them that brought me back into the army." Then he became serious. "But before we get to that, tell me why you are really here. You didn't come just to have a jolly night with us."

Donegal looked over at Baird, then said, "Well, as a matter of fact, the general of all the Virginia forces, a man called Andrew Lewis, and men who are leading the government, did ask us to have a wee little talk with you about matters related to the present unpleasantness between the colony and His Majesty's army."

McNabb threw up his hands. "Aye, I see it. They're wantin' you to get us to join the rebels."

"That was the general idea."

"Well na, we've already gone through that. There were some men down here from that 'convention' tryin' to convince us to fight the British." He shrugged. "We had a meetin' of all the sergeants and corporals and decided there was no way we'd be doin' that."

Donegal grinned. "Well, they thought havin' another Highlander talk to you might change your mind about throwin' in with Virginia."

"Ach now, do you think we canna remember what happened after Culloden? How the British hung many men simply for fighting against them? And we remember very well all the harshness which was visited on the people of the Highlands. We're no ready to face that again when the British put down this rebellion, as they're sure to do."

"Well, the Virginia government is ready to reward you for changing sides."

"Oh, now they are offering to bribe us? To treat us like mercenaries fighting for money?"

Joshua laughed. "Well, they don't call it a bribe. They call it an *inducement*."

McNabb looked puzzled. "So what does that mean?"

Joshua grinned. "It's a special word I just learned. Truth is, it's a fancy word that means a *bribe*."

All three men laughed.

McNabb threw up his hands. "And what would this great *inducement* be?"

Donegal said, "Each man who fought for Virginia would get a large grant of land in the western part of the state. Their own place and the necessary tools to farm it."

"There are lots of us who aren't farmers and don't want to take up the plow."

Simon said, "The land would be yours to do with what you want. You could sell it for the money and then go where you want. There are many people willing to buy western land. It would be worth good money, Daniel."

Joshua added, "It's a fine offer, McNabb."

"I told you, we already had a meeting. And here's the truth of it: a grant of land from Virginia won't be worth a farthing when the British defeat that mob under the command of this Washington fellow and retake all the colonies. As they surely will. If you could see how many battalions are being sent to Howe, you'd be wasting no time joining us." He waved his arm around the camp. "There's not a man here who doesn't know that's exactly what is going to happen." He pointed toward them. "*You* are the fools, trying to stand up to the king's army. You'll soon be running and hiding like hares with the dogs baying behind. And these leaders in Williamsburg will be facing His Majesty's justice. I say, soon enough they're to be served with the noose."

Donegal smiled at his old friend. "All right, Daniel, I told them I'd make the offer, and na I've done that." He pulled the cork from his jug and said, "If ye can put your hand on some cups, we'll sit here by your fire and remember the days when we were all young."

The three veterans sat before the fire and reminisced for an hour, becoming progressively more mellow. After an unknown number of cups and Donegal filling McNabb's cup once more, the sergeant stopped and then lowered it. He looked thoughtfully at Simon and Joshua and raised a finger. "I just remembered: you were both friendly with Lizzie Fraser, and her daughter, little Mary, weren't you?"

Donegal said, "Of course we were." He looked over at Baird. "It weren't much of a secret that Joshua was real sweet on Lizzie. Like as not he'd have married her if he hadn't been away on a long scout when Corporal Fraser was killed during Grant's battle at Fort Duquesne. Instead she had to marry Sergeant Iverson, 'cause she needed a ration for herself and little Mary."

Baird reddened and replied, "Simon, damn your loose mouth."

Donegal laughed. "For God's sake, it's the truth. And fifteen years later, what does it matter?"

McNabb looked at Joshua. "Well now, that's interesting, 'cause I never knew that. But what I was going to say is that Mary is back with the 42nd."

Simon and Joshua, astonished, looked at each other. Then Donegal said, "I dunna understand how that can be. I got a letter from Mary, a few years ago, sayin' she was the governess at a grand manor in the Highlands."

Joshua interjected, "I thought sure she would be married by now, a beautiful lass like that."

Donegal asked in a thoughtful tone, "Is that it? She's married to someone in the battalion? That's the only way I ken she could be with them."

McNabb grinned, enjoying their puzzlement. "She's still a spinster, and she is indeed with the regiment, up in Halifax by now."

Donegal retorted. "Damn it, McNabb! Stop leading us on. Tell us how she can be with the regiment if she's na married to a soldier."

The sergeant took a sip from his cup. "It's quite irregular, and there is a wee bit of mystery about it all. Yes, a *mystery*." He paused, looking first at Donegal and then Baird. "Now keep that gaping mouth of yours closed for a while, Donegal, and I'll tell you about it."

McNabb topped off his cup again, took a deep draught, then said, "Right after my company had been recruited in a town just north of Perth, we marched down to join the regiment at Glasgow, where both the 42nd and the 71st were drilling and preparing to sail for the colonies. While travelin' we stopped at a wee village along the Glasgow road to get water and have a rest, when out of a tavern walks none other than Bob Kirkwood, all dressed in the fine clothes of a man of business."

Donegal asked, "Kirkwood? What would he be doing there? He's living south of Edinburgh, last I heard, making barrels."

"Well, he told me he was up there trying to sell barrels from his works. But that's not what was curious about it. There was a person dressed in man's clothing who was with him."

Donegal raised his eyebrows. "What do you mean, 'a person dressed in man's clothing'?"

"Just listen to the damned story, Donegal, and you'll find out! Anyway, I took one look and knew right off that person was the spittin' image of Mary Fraser herself."

Joshua, startled, said, "Mary Fraser? In a man's clothing?"

"Well, I didn't guess it was actually her, not until much later. But what I noticed was that the lad had a smooth complexion, with no beard on his face and the exact same shade of copper hair like Mary. I never forgot about that from the old days."

Donegal nodded. "Aye, it is lovely, and many a young soldier would dream of it."

"Anyway, Kirkwood said the redheaded man was his valet. Then he and I talked until it was time for us to march off. The 'valet' stood a distance from us and never said a word." McNabb looked at his listeners. "A week later I was leading a detail from our company at the camp in Glasgow, and we marched past the house which was the 42nd headquarters. And suddenly I see Kirkwood and a copper-haired woman, dressed in a green gown and a bonny hat, entering the front door. I hadn't seen her for thirteen years, and I was more'n forty feet away, but I was damn sure it was nobody but Mary. Then right away it became clear to me that must have been her on the road with Kirkwood. Nothin' else but that made sense."

The sergeant took a deep drink. Then he looked at his listeners. "Two days later I was in McPhie's Tavern in Glasgow, and I bumped into Ian Tavish."

"Tavish the piper? From the 42nd? I remember him," said Joshua.

"Aye, the same. And now he's Colonel Stirling's piper and the senior piper in the regiment."

Donegal nodded. "He was great friends with Kirkwood."

"You're right about that. So I asked him what was going on with Mary Fraser, and that's when I found out she had been made the matron of the hospital in the regiment."

Joshua asked, "Matron of the hospital? What the devil is that?"

"It's like the head nurse. Leading and training all the rest and doing some of the paperwork and keepin' track of the apothecary supplies. That kind of thing. Leastways, that's what Tavish told me." He paused to think a moment, then went on, "Tavish said none other than General Lord Murray, the proprietary colonel of the 42nd, appointed her and authorized her to get an ensign's pay and a ration."

"Well, I can understand part of that," mused Donegal. "Mary's the best nurse I ever knew. But what I no ken is why she left her position as a governess. That's what she always wanted to do."

"I asked Tavish why she would be wantin' to come with the regiment. He didn't want to tell me at first. But I fed him a couple more drinks of rum, and finally the story came out, at least a bit of it." He paused and looked at the two. "It seems the master of the manor she was working at had died, and the mistress remarried a year later. The new master liked Mary. Liked her so much one night when he had too much to drink, he tried to have his way with her."

Donegal exclaimed, "The bastard!"

"Aye, that he was. But it seems Mary took care of the problem with her dagger. And left him lying dead in his own blood on the floor of her bedchamber."

Joshua nodded. "Sweet as Mary is, she ain't going to let any man take advantage of her."

"Yes, she can handle herself. But the master's relatives were at the manor and accused Mary of seduction and then murdering him because he wouldn't pay her off, or some such thing. Mary knew what would happen if she trusted the king's justice and went on the run through the Highlands. I don't know the whole story, but Tavish said Kirkwood somehow found out and went to help her. He discovered her hiding at old Sergeant McCulloch's place in a village near Perth. Then he got her down to Glasgow and convinced Stirling and Major McDonald to help her. They agreed and then persuaded General Murray to appoint her matron and allow her to sail with the 42nd. "

Donegal said, "The poor lass. But I don't doubt what you said is true. Major McDonald always had a soft spot for Mary in his heart. He recruited her father and kept an eye on her after she was orphaned. And Stirling knew her story well enough."

McNabb shrugged. "Well, that's all I know about Mary. I was never that close to her, since I was in another company, but I hope she fares well with the regiment."

Donegal held up his cup and said, "We'll drink to that."

An hour later Donegal and Joshua, a bit unsteady on their feet, walked out of the camp. Lieutenant Collins was sleeping on a blanket near the guard tent. The sergeant of the guard woke him up, and Donegal told him of the results of their mission.

Collins said, "Well, I'll take that back to Lewis. Frankly, he didn't expect you would have much success, so it won't be any surprise."

Joshua asked, "Now, Lieutenant, what will they do with these Highlanders?"

Collins responded, "The plan is to obtain their parole, then break the two companies up into small groups and have them help farm families out in the backcountry, where there's a shortage of manpower because so many men have gone to the army. If an exchange is set up, they'll be traded back to the British."

Then the lieutenant went over to discuss a matter with the guard sergeant before they left.

Baird and Donegal went to their horses. Joshua said, "Wait till Wend finds out that Mary is back on this side of the Atlantic."

Donegal reached out and grabbed Baird by the arm. "No, Joshua! Wend must never know about this!"

"Now why would you say that?"

"Don't you see? He's got too much on his mind, with all that's goin' on with the company and his family. He must not be distracted by thoughts of Mary, after so many years. You know he loves her with all his soul. He hears about this, he'll not be able to keep her out of his thoughts."

Joshua stared at Donegal for a long moment. Then he slowly nodded his understanding. "You're right, Simon. I wasn't thinkin' straight. It must be held back to keep him from bein' disturbed."

"Yes. And there's more: You're going home when we march north to the main army. Don't you say a damn word about Mary to Alice. *Not a word*. You know she and Peggy are thick as thieves. You tell Alice, and Peggy will find out for sure." He sighed deeply. "And then there will be the devil to pay on Eckert Ridge."

"Damn, you're right! Peggy's fiery jealous about the other women in Wend's life. God knows she exploded when she found out Wend saw Abigail during Dunmore's War in '74 and brought Johann back from the Mingo village. She wouldn't talk with Wend for months. She knows all about Wend's love for Mary, and if she finds out she's back in the colonies, she'll never rest easy."

"Now you take care to remember all that when you've had a bit of whiskey. Don't let yourself spill it to Alice without thinkin'."

"Simon, rest easy. It ain't gonna happen."

"Just you see that it doesn't."

—⚏—

Wend woke up abruptly and shook the sleep from his eyes. It was still dark, but he felt the dampness in the air that presaged the onset of morning dew. Around him slept the men of the company, their fires burned down to the embers. A sentinel stood at the perimeter of the camp, silhouetted by the last light of the moon, now low on the horizon.

He tried to shake off the effect of the dream that had visited him. It had been intensely realistic. It was an old dream, one he had had uncounted times in the past. But this was the first time it had come in several years, and he had begun to think it had faded from his mind. *It was the dream about Mary Fraser.*

It had first visited him after he had returned from Pontiac's War, when he had thought Mary was dead from the wound she received at Bushy Run and lay buried in an unmarked grave at Fort Pitt. He was still single and living in his stepparents' house at Sherman Mill in Pennsylvania. It was a simple dream, illogical, as most tend to be, but also glaringly realistic, as they so often are. It invariably started with him marching along a forest track as part of a company of the 77th, with Captain Robertson in the lead and the faces of familiar soldiers striding along around him. But soon he would realize that some of the soldiers were ones who had died at Bushy Run and shouldn't be with them. It was just as he discovered this that suddenly Mary would appear beside him, seemingly out of nowhere, swinging along with the company, dressed in her marching outfit of cast-off Highland uniform parts, with an ankle-length kilt pieced together from those she had taken from dead soldiers. They exchanged happy conversation for some time, and then Wend would find himself puzzled and say to her, "But Mary, you shouldn't be here; you have passed on."

And she would look up at him with that beguiling smile, laugh out loud, and say, "Don't you know that I am not dead? Can't you sense that I am alive and will always be with you?"

He would answer, "Yes, I do feel you close to me sometimes. But I know it can't be real, for your body lies in the ground at Fort Pitt."

Then she would laugh at him again and respond, "No, Wend, I am very near to you. All you have to do is follow your heart, and you will find me where I belong."

In fact, when he had first had that dream, she was actually alive and a mere eleven miles from Sherman Mill, in the regimental hospital at Carlisle. *She was indeed where she belonged.*

Months later, just a few days after he was married to Peggy McCartie, he had learned, because of a chance meeting with Captain Charles McDonald, then commanding Fort Loudoun on Forbes Road in Pennsylvania, the truth that Mary had survived her wound. Wend reflected, as he had many times before, that her words in the dream had proven true. And suddenly, as he sat in the damp night air, a thought hit him: *Was there some supernatural reason that the dream had recurred at this very time?* A shock ran through his body. *For God's sake, was Mary somewhere near?*

He shook himself. It could not be, for Mary was a governess in the Highlands, happily living her dream. Donegal had received a letter from her describing her life there, years ago. *Most likely she was married by now, perhaps with children of her own.*

Then his reverie was interrupted by the sound of a horse approaching, the pounding of its racing hooves fracturing the silence of the night. He threw off his blanket and stood up, just in time to see a draft horse carrying two riders appear and approach the sentinel. After a few words with the riders, the sentinel pointed in Wend's direction. The riders slid off the horse and strode toward him. Then he realized the first was the fisherman Jack Cowell, and looking to the other, he was astonished, and overjoyed, to see none other than Billy Wood.

Billy called out in an excited voice, "Mr. Eckert! Sir, they be comin'. Comin' this morning!"

In a more calm tone, Cowell said, "The British are on the Bay heading this way. As we were hugging the coast on the way here, we saw HMS *Otter* leading a flotilla of small tenders southward from Hills Bay, all loaded with soldiers and marines, and your man says they plan to land near the mouth of Mobjack Bay."

Wend exclaimed, "Did you say Mobjack? Damn! That's to the south of Horn Harbor Bay. We're hours away from there."

Billy said, "Yes, sir, they plan to hit three plantations right in that area. They be comin' ashore when there's 'nough light to safely make a landing."

Cowell added, "That makes good sense for them. Those are middling-sized places, but prosperous. There'll be lots of good provisions for the British to gather up."

"Damn!" repeated Wend. "We're in the wrong position. It will take us hours to get there." He turned and shouted at the top of his voice, "O'beirne! Flannagan! Childers! Come here this moment!"

Soon the three men arrived, young Childers rubbing sleep from his eyes. Wend quickly apprised them of the situation. "We need to march immediately. Rouse the men—there's no time for eating."

The three nodded. Then Wend turned to Childers. "Saddle my horse, and ride to find Newkirk on the other side of Horn Bay. Tell him what we know and to do what he can to blunt the British. And tell him we're marching to join the fight as soon as possible but I don't hold much hope we'll be there in time to help him."

The ensign turned and ran to where Sonny was picketed. Wend turned to the others and said, "Get moving, and get the men out of their blankets. We march in fifteen minutes."

After Shay and Flannagan had departed, Wend said to Cowell and Billy. "Now tell me everything you know. How can we be sure where they are going to attack?"

Billy said, "Mr. Eckert, the morning after I went ashore, I saw a camp for one of the loyalist regiments. And I found the cook for the officer's mess and told her my story about being from a plantation and that I had been a house servant. And I also told her I was inoculated from the pox. All that made her and her helpers glad to see me. She made me a server at the mess, where I heard what was going on and them making plans."

Wend was astonished. "That was great luck. And great thinking by you."

"Yes, sir. And sir, it was the regiment run by that Major Welford. Anyway, yesterday they were making plans for the raid, and I heard it all." He grinned. "So last night I went to the beach right near the southern end of the island and with a candle lantern I stole, gave the signal for Mr. Cowell. And here we are."

Cowell said, "I was damned surprised when I saw the light; I didn't expect we'd see Billy again. But when I did, I got my boat in as close as I dared. Fact is, Cap'n, we put the bow into the mud right offshore."

"Yes, sir!" exclaimed Billy. "I was able to wade all the way to the boat without havin' to swim."

The fisherman said, "I was a little worried we'd be hung up, but Billy and I and my mate put our shoulders to it, and she came right off. Then we turned around and started rowing south along the coast a ways before we raised the sail. Just afore we landed here, I could see the line of British boats out in the Bay, comin' in this direction. So it seems sure enough Billy got it right."

As they were talking, Childers came up, leading Sonny. "Captain, Sonny's a powerful, spirited horse. I've always admired him. How hard will you let me push him?"

"Don't kill him, but take everything he'll give you. You know horses, so you'll understand how much you can demand from him." Wend ran his hand down Sonny's neck, just below the mane. "He's a youngster, just like you, full of piss and vinegar. I'm counting on you both to give us your best."

The ensign smiled broadly. "Aye, sir, that we'll do!"

And with that he sprang into the saddle, and the two were off. Wend watched them go and thought to himself, *That lad rides like he was born to it. Comes from years riding to the hunt.*

Now Wend became aware of the noise of the company being awakened by sergeants and corporals, the angry curses of men who had expected to sleep longer and have a meal before they marched, the sounds of accoutrement being gathered and slung in place for the march.

Wend showed Cowell his map of the area and pointed down toward the area of plantations where the British would raid. "You know the roads here. How long will it take us to get around the head of Horn Harbor Bay and down into that area?"

"The roads around the western headwaters are well inland from the bay itself. Probably will take you longer than you think."

"Well, can we march through the bush, right along the shoreline, to cut some distance?"

"That would be a hard passage, Cap'n. It's all scrub pine and heavy underbrush right up to the water's edge. I vow it will slow you down even more than takin' the road, long as that is."

Wend grimaced. "Damn! It means we're likely out of the fight. My first lieutenant will have to do what he can to hinder the British with just forty men."

Cowell looked at Wend with a knowing smile. "If'n you try to go around the head of Horn Bay, Cap'n, that's all true."

Wend looked sharply at Cowell. "You sound like you know something. Are you trying to tell me there's another way to get there?"

"Aye, Captain, there is. But you'll have to take a chance. You could lose some men along the way. But it could get you where you want much quicker if you dare to take the risk."

"All right, Cowell. I'm a desperate man. Tell me about this way to get south of Horn Harbor Bay."

Reese Newkirk stood looking eastward along the road, hoping to see his guide, Jared Brown, returning. He had sent him on a scout toward the coast while his tired soldiers sat beside fires along the wagon track, boiling coffee. He was hoping to get word if the British flotilla had been sighted or their raiding party was actually ashore. He reflected that it was now full light and if the British were coming today, they would probably be landing at this very moment. Then, to his surprise, he heard the sound of a horse coming fast from the west. He turned and looked up the road to see a rider in the distance, pushing his horse like he was being pursued by the devil himself.

Sergeant Tom Wilder, also seeing the rider, joined Newkirk on the wagon track. He stared up the road, then he exclaimed, "By God, sir! That's Eckert's long-legged hunter! No other horse I've known can fly like that!"

Newkirk put his hand up to shade his eyes and to his astonishment realized it was Edward Childers mounted on Sonny. "Damn, you've got good eyes, Tom. Indeed it's Sonny, and that's our own ensign riding him."

In a few moments, Childers had arrived and threw down from his mount. He said in a rush of words, "Mr. Newkirk, Mr. Newkirk! The British are on the way!" He looked up at the sun, now visible just above the horizon. "They may already be landing, sir!"

"Edward, calm down and speak slowly! Where are they headed? Where are they going to land?"

Childers pointed eastward. "Just north of Mobjack Bay." Then he remembered to say, "We got the word from Billy Wood. He came to our camp before dawn with that fisherman Cowell."

"Good. Now what is Eckert doing?"

"He was preparing to march when I rode out. They'll be around the head of the bay as soon as possible."

Newkirk shook his head. "They can march as fast as humanly possible, but it will be too late. If the British are landing now, or soon, the rest of the company won't get here in time to help." He took a deep breath. "We'll have to do what we can on our own."

Without orders, Wilder called out to the men, "Get up! Up now! Prepare to march! Form on the wagon track!"

Newkirk looked eastward again. "I wish Brown would get back with some information on the British. Hopefully he'll meet us on the road."

In less than five minutes, the detachment was on the march, moving eastward, route stepping at as fast a pace as could be sustained.

Almost immediately, they met Brown, half running, half walking toward them. Newkirk ran forward to meet him. "What do you have, Brown?"

The guide said nothing at first. Instead he bent over, hands on his knees, catching his breath. Meanwhile, Childers and Wilder joined them.

In a minute Brown stood up and said, "I ran into four men from a militia picket, running up the road. The British are ashore. They landed in a little inlet just north of the mouth of Mobjack Bay."

"Do you know their strength?"

"The militia didn't stop to count, but they thought there were one hundred or more ashore, marching for the plantations along Mobjack. Plus, there are marines and sailors guarding the boats and filling water casks from a stream which flows into the Chesapeake." He took a few more deep breaths. "It looks like they ain't worried about any opposition, sir. Militia say they've broken up into three parties."

"Three parties?"

"Yes, sir, that makes sense. There be three plantations, one after another, along the shoreline of Mobjack Bay. So looks like there's one party settin' out for each."

Newkirk nodded thoughtfully. "How far away from the closest plantation are we now?"

"That would be the Wilford place. Not much more than a mile, I make it, from where we stand. We just follow this road, and their drive meets it. The plantation house and farm buildings are down closer to the shore of Mobjack."

Newkirk asked, "How big a place is it?"

"I know the place and Richard Wilbank, the owner. It ain't a great-sized plantation, with one of them big mansions. But there is a comfortable house, and it is prosperous, sir. Goodly amount of livestock and food stores. British will find what they're looking for there."

Reese put his hand on his chin. "Well, if they've broken the landing party into three segments, we probably outnumber each one." He looked eastward. "We can fall on the party at Wilford Plantation with a good chance to ambush them. They'll be busy gathering goods, not expecting opposition."

Brown grinned. "I thought that's what you would do. So I left the militia hidin' in the scrub, in a good position to watch the Wilford place, and give us their strength." He stopped and raised a finger. "If we hurry, we can get there before the redcoats have a chance to do too much damage."

Wilder put his hand on Newkirk's arm. "Reese, we may able to take on that party at Wilford Plantation without too much trouble." He looked into the lieutenant's eyes. "But as soon as the other parties hear firing, they're going to come to support their mates. Then we'll have our hands full."

Reese Newkirk sighed. "You're right, Tom. But we'll just have to deal with the raiding party at Wilford's fast, then do what we can to hold off the others if they do come. But we must simply do our best, and maybe we'll be able to hold out until Eckert can relieve us." He turned and called out to the column. "All right, lads! The enemy is ahead of us, and we have a chance to surprise him! Let's march!"

—ɯ—

Breakfast was always early at the Wilford house, for Richard and his eldest son, John, ran the farm operation themselves with no overseer. Eleanor, his wife, minded the house with the help of three servants and insisted that the two younger children, Walter and little Jenny, got out of bed at the same time as everyone else. So all the members of the family had just sat down to the meal when the butler, an ancient African named Joseph, hurried into the dining room with a distressed look on his face.

"Mr. Wilford, Mr. Wilford!" He said in an urgent tone. "There be soldiers comin' up the drive! Sir, they be redcoats. I'm thinkin' they're the governor's men!"

Wilford, a wiry-framed man in his early fifties, stood up and looked at his wife. "Well, we knew this day might arrive. Eleanor, take the young ones out into the scrub and hide until this is over. John and I will stay and deal with these people."

Eleanor Bright Wilford, who was ten years younger than Richard, shook her head and said in a determined voice, "Richard, I'm staying here. We've done things together since you took me away from my parents' plantation, and we'll do this the same way." She turned to the middle-aged African woman who had been serving breakfast. "Delia, you go with the children. We've talked about where to hide."

Delia nodded. "Yes, ma'am." She grabbed little Jenny's hand and literally pulled the five-year-old, still holding a piece of bread in her other hand, out of her chair. Walter, who was seven, rose from his place, and the three ran out the rear door into the pinewoods that began about fifty yards from the house.

The three remaining Wilfords and Joseph walked out to the porch just as the British column arrived in front of the house.

A young officer walked up to them and said, "Good morning, sir. I am Captain Foster of the King's Loyal Virginia Legion. Might I ask to whom am I speaking?"

"My name's Richard Wilford, and this is my place. What business do you have with us?"

"I am here to requisition supplies for His Majesty's loyal forces, in the name of your rightful governor, Lord Dunmore."

"And what specifically is it that you desire?"

"We intend to take flour, molasses, whatever foodstuff you have in your storage buildings, cattle, fowls, and hogs. We shall also borrow wagons or carts to carry the material to our waiting boats. You can retrieve those at our landing site after we depart with the goods." Then he added, "And we shall visit your slave quarters and, under the authority of the Governor's Proclamation, invite any of your Africans who desire to join our cause." He waved his arm around, taking in all the farm buildings. "In short, sir, we will appropriate anything which can be of use to us."

Wilford looked over at his wife, then back to the captain. "And what if we decline to provide you these items?"

"Let me be clear, Mr. Wilford," He grinned broadly and waved his hand toward the waiting soldiers. "we will take what we need, and the choice is not yours." Then he turned to the soldiers. "Sergeant, send a detail to find wagons and horses. And send parties to collect the livestock and such stores as they have. And a sergeant to speak to the Africans."

The sergeant called out orders, and the soldiers broke ranks and spread out, moving toward the barns, storehouses, and the quarters of the field hands.

Eleanor screamed out, "You are nothing but damnable thieves! Captain, we know Dunmore. We've been to the palace in Williamsburg! You tell that damned Scotsman that Eleanor Wilford considers him no better than a captain of common thieves! A common thief, do you understand? And if I'm ever in his presence again, I'll spit on his face if it's the last thing I do!"

Foster threw back his head and laughed. "At the first opportunity, Mrs. Wilford, I will convey your heartfelt sentiments to Lord Dunmore."

But he would never have that opportunity. For at the instant he finished speaking, his head exploded into a mass of blood and brain tissue and his lifeless body crumpled to the ground. A second later the report of the rifle echoed around the farmyard.

Then a loud voice called out from the pinewoods, "First squad, fire together!"

The crack of a volley ensued, and several of the soldiers fell. Some screamed in agony. Others just lay still on the ground. Then the voice called out again, "Second squad, fire!" Another rippling volley crashed out, and more soldiers fell. "Third squad fire!" More soldiers fell to a rain of balls, and there were virtually no soldiers remaining on their feet.

A young officer, on his knees, one arm hanging useless at his side, raised his other arm and screamed, "Quarter! For God's sake, quarter! We surrender! Cease your fire!"

The voice in the woods shouted, "Hold your fire, men, but keep your firelocks on them!"

Wilford looked over at the tree line, and a man of medium height, dressed in a hunting shirt, brown breeches, and a black hat, emerged holding a pistol in his hand. Other men dressed in the same manner began to come out of cover, weapons aimed at the surviving loyalist soldiers. The man called out to the wounded officer, "Have your men drop all their weapons immediately." He walked up to the lieutenant. "And you can hand me your sword, grip first, if you please."

The young officer did as he was told.

Then the man walked up to where the Wilfords stood, made a slight bow, took his hat off, and said, "Good morning. I am Lieutenant Reese Newkirk of the Frederick County Light Foot. I assume you are the Wilfords?"

Eleanor said, "Oh, may the Lord bless you, sir! You have saved us from ruin!"

Richard nodded. "Indeed, sir. We are most appreciative."

Newkirk put his hat back in place, then said, "Mrs. Wilford, as we were approaching, we found your children and a servant." He turned and called out, "Mr. Childers, bring your charges out."

Soon Childers emerged, escorting Jenny, Walter, and Delia. Eleanor ran over and embraced her children.

Newkirk said, "Mr. Wilford, we have a problem. Regrettably, this action is not over."

Richard looked puzzled. "I don't understand, sir. What do you mean?"

"I believe that the sound of our firing will bring other loyalist troops. Probably in numbers which will outnumber my detachment. I'm going to deploy my men in the band of trees at the end of your drive, to hold them off. If things work out as I hope, my captain and the rest of our company will arrive to relieve us. Unfortunately, they have to march around the headwaters of Horn Bay, and it may be several hours until they arrive. We may have trouble holding out that long. In any case, your plantation is going to become a battlefield."

Richard Wilford's face turned grim, but then he nodded. "I understand."

Newkirk motioned toward Eleanor and the children. "You may want to take your family and retire to safety in the pines to the west, until the hostilities have finished."

Richard's son spoke up. "We've got firelocks. Father and I will help."

"My son's right. We ain't going to run away from the plantation while others defend it."

Newkirk responded, "All right, sir." Then he looked at the wounded loyalist soldiers on the ground. "They may be our enemy, but it's only humane to treat their wounds. And I'll need every man who can handle a firelock on the firing line. Do you have anyone who has medical knowledge?"

Eleanor spoke up. "Delia and I will take care of them, Mr. Newkirk. You just get your men ready to fight."

CHAPTER SIXTEEN

THE SHORES OF MOBJACK BAY

Reese Newkirk had ordered Sergeant Wilder to deploy his men in the wide band of pine trees between the wagon track from the Chesapeake and the open fields of Wilford Plantation. There soldiers were spread on both sides of the drive into the plantation, using cover as much as possible, waiting about a hundred yards down from the entrance gates, ready to intercept the British raiding party as they entered the plantation to investigate what had happened to their compatriots.

The men had just taken their positions when Jared Brown, accompanied by four other armed men, came running down the drive. "Lieutenant! Lieutenant Newkirk! They be coming!

Brown and the other four gathered around Newkirk. Reese said, "All right, Brown, slow down. Where are the British?"

"Just about a quarter mile down the road, sir! Me and these militia men been watching them. There be eighty, maybe ninety of them. All from that loyalist regiment—the King's Loyal Legion."

One of the militiamen said, "Aye, that's the truth. They gathered up all the different parties, and the whole lot will be at the entrance to the drive in just a few minutes."

Reese thought a moment. Then he called out to Edward Childers, who was in position with one of the field squads. "Childers! Come here immediately!"

The ensign came running up. "Yes, sir?"

"What's the condition of that horse—Sonny?"

"Well, sir, I used him hard getting here. Right now he's down in the Wilford's stable, resting. I gave him some grain right after we arrived, but he's only had a little time."

Newkirk gritted his teeth. "Well, it will have to do. We've got to press him into service again. I need you to saddle up and find Eckert. Tell him our situation and explain he's got to drive his men as fast as he can. Tell him we're outnumbered at least two to one. He'll under-stand and realize we can't hold out for long."

"Right, sir. I know Sonny will do his best."

"Now listen. You've got to ride him hard. You can have no sympa-thy for him; push him right to the point of exhaustion. And if he goes down, you keep going on foot till you find Eckert. Do you understand? You *must* get to Eckert."

"Yes, sir. I know what has to be done."

"All right, get going! And you'll have to lead him out through the woods to the west to get to the road, because I expect the British will be at the drive any minute!"

Wilford, who had been standing nearby with his son, said, "Lieutenant, there's a rough trail along the shoreline. It runs for a half mile west, then turns northwesterly to the road. That will get you out of here safely!" He turned to his son. "Johnny, you help Mr. Childers!"

The boy nodded and said, "Come along, Ensign! I'll help you get saddled and then guide you along the trail!"

It was just a few moments before Wilder called out from his po-sition with the squad next to the drive. "Newkirk, there are British coming down the drive! Should we start firing?"

"Wait! I'll join you. We don't want to fire until the last minute." Reese ran to Wilder's position and took cover behind a small scrub tree. Looking down the drive, he saw a group of soldiers walking in loose formation, led by a tall officer. Suddenly the British officer raised a hand, and Reese saw that he was holding a white handkerchief.

The officer called out, "Parley! We call for a parley! I want to see your commander!"

Wilder looked at Reese. "You gonna talk to him? Or should we answer the bastard with a volley?"

Newkirk thought for a long moment. Then he grinned at his sergeant. "I'd like to answer with a hail of balls, but prudence says I go out and parley with him. It will buy time, and that's what we need more than anything else." He handed his pistols to Wilder. Then he called out to the British officer, "I'll talk to you, but only if you hand off your pistols and have the men of your column ground their muskets."

There was a moment's pause, and the officer's voice called out, "Done. Please show yourself."

Newkirk turned to the sergeant, "Well, Tom, we shall see what we shall see." Then he stepped from the trees onto the drive and walked toward the Britisher.

The officer was in the uniform of the 60th Foot. He touched his hat in signal of salute, then said, "Good morning, sir. I am Major Reginald Welford, currently in command of the King's Loyal Virginia Legion. And to whom am I speaking?"

"Lieutenant Reese Newkirk, of the Frederick County Light Foot, at your service, sir."

"Well, Mr. Newkirk, I am informed that you hold a number of my men prisoner as a result of this morning's action. I would like to arrange an exchange."

Newkirk cocked his head. "You say exchange? I'm not aware of what you have to exchange for those prisoners. Incidentally, most of them are wounded."

Welford said, "That makes it all the more urgent, Lieutenant, since we would wish to provide adequate medical care for our men. And on the subject of what I have to use in exchange, why, it is nothing less than you and your men."

Astonished, Newkirk responded, "Excuse me, Major. I find your statement puzzling. How can you claim to use us as exchange for your men?"

"Quite simple, sir. You are essentially prisoners. I am quite aware, because of the report of two of our men who escaped your ambush, that you have perhaps forty men at your disposal. Thus we outnumber you two to one, with troops here in your front, and I have at my disposal a strong party of Royal Marines back at our landing site who could be called on to reinforce my command. Sir, prudence mandates that you must surrender or perish."

"I don't see it that way, Welford, but lay out your proposal."

"Well, if you surrender to me, I will take possession of my men who you hold, and then I will grant you parole. You can march off, quite safe."

"And if I decline your offer?"

"Then we will be forced to attack and destroy your command." He shrugged. "Sir, you must see what is the obvious choice for you."

"Indeed I see my obvious choice. We came here to protect our people from your depredations. So I shall defend our position and this plantation, and I will now advise you that I anticipate reinforcements under the command of my company commander, Captain Eckert, at any minute now. So I suggest that your clear path is to retire to the shoreline and take boat back to Gwynn's Island."

Welford's face took on a look of astonishment. "*Eckert?* Did you say your captain is named *Eckert?*"

"Quite so, sir. Captain Wendelmar Eckert of Frederick County, commander of this company of light foot."

"Mr. Newkirk, this not the time or place for a very poor jest. What you have said is quite impossible: Eckert is dead. Dead by my own hand in a raid on his farm in March. I repeat, *dead by my own hand.*"

Newkirk laughed out loud. "You're the man who led that raid? And shot at Eckert?"

"I am indeed; I put a ball in his head at point-blank range and witnessed him drop like a sack of flour to the ground, with blood pouring out. I do not know what your game is, sir, but it will get you no credit with me."

Still grinning, Newkirk said, "I regret to disenchant you, Major, but Eckert lives. Your ball only scratched the side of his head. I am quite familiar with head wounds, and the truth is they bleed profusely, even when relatively minor. Let me restate the situation: Eckert is on the way with reinforcements, and when he arrives, sir, we will drive you into the sea, or you will surrender. Now that is what faces you."

Welford stared at Newkirk for a long moment. Finally he said scornfully, "I do not credit anything you have said. It is a desperate attempt at deception. It is my judgment that the only reason you intercepted our party this morning is your commander has spread out small detachments along the coast, and it is unlikely there is another close enough to support you. And as for Eckert, I am quite certain you are lying, sir. Lying, do you hear me? The man was dead before his body fell to the ground."

Newkirk shrugged his shoulders. "Well then, I believe there is no need for further discussion. I will retire to my lines and await your action, sir." He touched his hat. "Good day, sir." He turned and walked off, leaving Welford to stare after him.

When he arrived back at where Wilder crouched in the bush, he said, "Well, they'll be at us shortly."

The sergeant said, "All right, I've got one squad on the western side of the drive and two squads spread out in the scrub and bush along this side of the farm. And I've got a full squad behind a shed back there toward the house, ready to either reinforce the forward squads or meet an advance by the British somewhere we don't expect."

Newkirk nodded. "That's good, but pass the word for the men to fire only when they have a high chance of hitting their target. Don't take any quick shots at men moving through the woods. We've got to preserve our ammunition; that will be our biggest problem."

Wilford was still with them. He said, "Well, your young officer got off all right, and he'll come out on the road where the British won't see him." Then he continued, "If you need more powder, I've got a keg. I'll fetch it."

"What about balls? You won't have the right size for our muskets or rifles."

"True, but we have a lot of shot. We use it against fowl and small game. Perhaps you can start firing that."

Newkirk sighed. "Yes, bring it out. It's better than nothing, if we get to that point."

Wilder motioned toward the loyalist column. "Reese, they're deploying—spreading out wide. They're going to come at us on a broad front, moving through the bush."

"That's encouraging. I thought that major might have decided on a quick rush at us in column along the drive in an attempt to overrun us just by weight of their numbers."

Wilder said, "He knows that would cost him a lot of men. I suspect he wants to keep his losses down."

Reese nodded. "I'll wager you're right. But he's playing into our hands; a drawn-out exchange of fire is more to our advantage than a charge." He grinned as he thought of something. "Not to mention that we're facing a bunch of tidewater and Norfolk loyalists. Our back-country boys are far better at this kind of fight." Then he motioned to the sergeant. "All right, go tell the men what I said about firing only when they've got a good bead. And tell them to be careful to stay under cover. We've got to preserve our men even more than powder."

—∽—

Harbridge tapped on the door and entered Dunmore's office in the Grymes house. "My lord, Sir Robert and Mrs. Eden are waiting outside."

Dunmore grinned. He was very fond of Maryland's governor and even more fond of his elegant wife, Caroline, the daughter of Charles Calvert, 5th Baron Baltimore, the proprietor of Maryland. "Well, don't keep them waiting! Show them in!"

Sir Robert Eden entered, with Caroline in hand. Dunmore walked forward, extending a hand to the governor, then bowing to his wife. "I am so glad to see both of you have arrived safely. I trust you were treated well on the *Fowey*."

"Captain Montagu and all his officers were most hospitable. And I thank you for sending the vessel so promptly, John," answered Eden. "Things were getting quite uncomfortable in Annapolis, and although everyone was quite polite and diplomatic to us, I'm not sure that that condition would have persisted much longer now that the Rebel Congress in Philadelphia has declared independence from the king's rule."

Dunmore was taken aback. "Independence? They've actually taken that step? We'd heard they were debating it but not that a decision had been taken."

"Yes, John, they voted on the second of this month, and every one of the colonies voted for it, even New York, which had been hold-ing out. Then a written declaration was signed on the fourth. We were relieved that the *Fowey* arrived in the harbor just after word was received in Annapolis. It allowed us to leave promptly and avoid any unpleasantness from the radical mob."

Caroline added, "The Council of Safety were so kind as to provide a cavalry escort to prevent any interference by hotheads. And I can tell you, among the common folk, there was considerable unrest. But all went well, and that young captain of the *Ann Arundel Light Horse*, Warren Bradley, was so very courteous to us. It was almost like he regretted how things had turned out."

Eden looked at his wife. "Well, Bradley and his men have often provided my escort. And we must recall that his father was close to your family. Young Bradley may be committed to the rebel cause, but family friendships do count for something."

Dunmore said, "Well, Caroline, I suspect the fact that you are a native of Maryland and a member of one of its most prestigious families had a good deal to do with the courtesies you received for the last year and in the instance of your departure."

Caroline's eyes looked wistfully into the distance. "Yes, it is so sad to have to leave all one's closest acquaintances. I do love England, but it's just not the same as home, and I hope that when all this unpleasantness has been resolved, we can return."

Dunmore said in a reassuring tone, "My dear Caroline, I would submit that General Howe is at this very moment making plans which will soon facilitate your desire."

Robert Eden raised a finger. "Indeed, John, we received word just before we left that ships of our navy are off New York in significant numbers and troops are being landed in strength on Staten Island."

Dunmore answered, "Now that is good news. And I should be surprised if they didn't break up that ragtag army of Washington's before the end of the year." He turned back to Caroline. "So you see, my dear, you may find yourself home in the governor's house before next summer."

Eden nodded. "We can all hope. But may I ask how soon we may expect to begin our voyage to England?"

Dunmore sighed, looked over at Harbridge and then back to Eden. "Well, the *Fowey* will carry you when the time comes. However, I regret to say it may be at an indeterminate date in the future."

Eden looked askance at Dunmore. "Oh, we had hoped to sail with little delay. Pray tell, why the wait?"

"Well, there are two reasons, sir. In the first instance, we are expecting some attempt by the rebels encamped on the shore across from the island to attack our positions. Captain Hammond of the naval squadron wants to keep the *Fowey* available since, with her twenty guns, she is the second most powerful ship in his force. And the second is that I am expecting word back from Howe any day now in response to my request for reinforcement. When I get word that regular troops are on the way, I shall be commencing offensive operations against the enemy ashore, and once again the *Fowey* is required for support." He looked at his two guests. "When things are satisfactorily underway, we will expedite your voyage across the Atlantic."

Disappointment spread across both Robert's and Caroline's faces.

Harbridge cleared his throat. "In the meantime, we will make you as comfortable as possible on the island. Since accommodations here in the Grymes house are limited, the governor has decided to move back aboard his flagship so that you may take his rooms." He added, "And I think you will find the Grymeses most congenial hosts."

Dunmore nodded. "Yes, and in any case, since we are expecting some kind of action soon, it makes more sense for me to be where I may direct matters as they progress."

Caroline looked at her husband, then smiled graciously at Dunmore. "John, in any case, we are *so* grateful. We shall patiently pass the time until arrangements can be made for our voyage."

Reese Newkirk wiped his brow. Things were getting hot. The July sun was raising the temperature as the morning progressed. And the firing along the front line was also heating up. The British were attacking all along his skirmish line, with shot flying heavily. Already two of his men had serious wounds, and they had been taken back to the Wilford house, where Eleanor and her cook were ministering to them.

Even worse, though his men were husbanding their ammunition, he calculated that they were at least halfway through their supply. As he leaned up against a tree, watching for a glimpse of an enemy, Tom

Wilder approached, half walking, half crawling to take advantage of cover.

"Reese, they're trying to flank us on our right." He took a deep breath. "They got enough men to overreach our line, and I think they may be going to try a rush."

Newkirk nodded. "I've been waiting for them to get impatient enough to do that."

Wilder motioned along the line. "We're stretched out as far as we dare. I don't see any choice but to bring up the reserve squad and put them on the right flank."

Newkirk nodded. "Yes, go yourself to fetch them, and choose their positions out there. I'll keep my eye on the line here."

Wilder just nodded, then pushed himself to his feet and left at a run. Newkirk thought, *One way or another, this will end in about an hour. We'll be out of ammunition.* He started thinking about his options. There only seemed to be two: he could either abandon the farm, and attempt to slip away through the pines to the west where he could try to link up with Eckert as his detachment approached along the road, or he could simply surrender. He mentally shook his head. *That would not do.*

He thought about how to execute the withdrawal. First, have Wilford and his family flee up the trail that Childers had used earlier. Then break off a squad at a time to follow, with one remaining squad staying in position until the last minute to amuse the British and hold them in place. The wounded in the house would have to be left behind to the mercies of Welford. *Not much of a plan, but all I have. At least it provides a chance to save most of my men.* He consoled himself with the thought *And if we can unite with Eckert, it might be possible to regroup and hit the enemy as they are withdrawing to their boats.*

He looked back and saw Wilder leading the reserve squad as they ran to take up positions on the flank. A few minutes later, a young rifleman, Dowty, came running up.

"Lieutenant, Sergeant Wilder told me to let you know the British are forming for an attack on the right. He expects it any minute."

Newkirk bit his lips. "Dowty, get on back and tell Wilder he must stop them, even if it comes to bayonets. Do you understand?"

"Aye, sir. Use bayonets!" He turned and ran back along the line. As he did so, a burst of loud, repetitive firing could be heard from Wilder's position.

A few minutes later, the crack of firing, almost like a volley, was suddenly audible to the west, from across the drive, where one squad was positioned. It had been relatively quiet in that sector. Newkirk thought, *Damn, are the British going to attack on both flanks at the same time? We can't withstand that. And if they came in force from the west, they will block the retreat I have been planning.*

Fear began rising inside him. *Will I lose my entire command in the first battle I've ever led on my own?*

As he was contemplating that, private Ben Howell, crouching over, came across the drive and went down to his knees beside Reese. "Lieutenant, Corporal Blaine says something is happening over on our side, and he can't figure it."

"I heard the firing. Are the British moving forward to attack you?"

"No, sir. The new firing wasn't from the British, leastways not the ones in front of us. It sounds like it was coming from down where the drive joins the road." He shook his head. "Sir, it's a puzzlement. It's like from *behind* the enemy."

As they were talking, Blaine himself arrived. "Sir, it's the damnedest thing. Them redcoats in front of us are pulling back and moving out. One by one, they're crossing the drive, falling back eastward in the direction of the shoreline."

"What?"

"Yeah, sir, it's like they're retreating. That's what I don't understand. They had us in a pretty hard spot."

Newkirk moved to where he could see the drive. And no sooner was he in position than he saw two enemy soldiers scuttle across, heading east like Blaine had said.

Blaine said, "Now listen close, sir. There's that shooting coming from up on the road. It's hard to hear with all the other firing."

Newkirk cupped a hand to his ear. And then he heard it. There was the distinct sound of firing in the distance, and Blaine was right, it was out on the road.

Blaine said, "It don't make any sense, but it damn well sounds like someone is firing into the rear of the British."

Newkirk realized Blaine was right. *But who could it be? Eckert was too far away; he wouldn't arrive for hours.* Then he had a thought. "Perhaps it's some local militia that mustered up after they heard all this firing?"

Blaine responded. "Well, whoever it is, they're sure disturbin' the hell out of the redcoats. Look at that, Lieutenant!" He pointed to the drive.

Newkirk looked up to see a squad-sized group of British crossing at the run, including an officer.

The corporal exclaimed, "They look like the devil himself is after them."

Howell said, "Hey, suddenly it's all quiet over there across the drive."

Reese listened carefully. "Damned if you're not right. Perhaps all the British there have gone."

A split second later Blaine burst out, "Sir, will you look at that!" He pointed down the drive.

Not fifty feet from where they crouched, a man had walked out into the drive. He was tall, with powerful shoulders, and burley chest. He was dressed in a hunting shirt and black hat and carried a long rifle in his hands.

Blaine laughed. "For Christ's sake, sir! It's that loudmouthed ass Jensen!"

Newkirk stared in disbelief. "Corporal, you're right." Then it hit him. "He's with Eckert's party! I don't know how, but they're here! It's our own men who are doing that firing!"

As he spoke, Jensen turned around and motioned in the direction of the scrub behind him. He yelled to unseen men, "Get out here, you bastards! Form skirmish line!"

His squad emerged from the pines and formed into a loose line.

"All right, you musket men, fix your bayonets! Now let's go, let's drive those redcoats! Keep them running all the way to the Bay."

The entire squad crossed the drive and disappeared after the running British.

Blaine looked at Newkirk. "Lieutenant, how can our men be here? How could they have made it so fast?"

"Damned if I understand, Blaine. I just know they're here, and thank God for it."

Just then Wilder come hurrying up. "Reese, the British have broken and are running! Running like foxes chased by the hounds! All down the line. What's going on?"

"Look up the drive, Tom." Newkirk pointed. More men of the company were flowing across the drive, heading into the scrub on the other side. "Eckert's here, but I can't tell you how."

He called out to Wilder, "Have your men cease firing until I find out what's going on. Some of Eckert's men may already be in front of you."

Wilder nodded, then ran through the pines calling, "Cease fire!"

Newkirk stepped out into the drive and immediately saw Shay O'beirne standing about halfway down the drive, grinning at him. "Shay, glad to see you! What's toward?"

"Eckert says we're going to drive the British into the water. I've got all our squads moving to keep herding the bastards to the east."

"How did you get here so fast? We thought you were still hours away."

Shay grinned even more broadly. "I ain't got time to tell you now. And you wouldn't believe me if I did. Eckert will explain." He pointed eastward. "Now I've got to keep all these men moving." Then he ran into the scrub after the field squads.

Newkirk looked up the drive again and saw Eckert hurrying toward him, with Billy Wood behind him carrying the company standard and the fisherman, Jack Cowell, trailing behind.

Newkirk called out, "Captain, I'm damned glad to see you." He touched his hat in salute. "We didn't expect to see you for hours. How the devil did you get around Horn Bay so fast? Or did you walk on water?"

Eckert laughed. "Not on the water, Reese—only the Good Lord can do that. And I'm no Moses to part the water. No, we waded *through* it."

Extraordinarily puzzled, Reese said, "Sir? *Through* it?"

"Exactly." Wend turned to Cowell. "Please explain to Mr. Newkirk."

"Sir, these little bays shallow up very fast, once you get a bit from the Chesapeake. If you stand on the edge, looking at the water, you think it's plenty deep. People in boats who don't know the area, they get hung up all the time. Fact is, Mr. Eckert's camp was just a couple hundred yards from Horn Harbor Bay. And at that point, it is very narrow, less'n a hundred yards across. And it don't get deeper than a man's waist or maybe his chest in a place or two. Since I was a lad, I've waded out in the water in that spot and sometimes all the way across, gatherin' shellfish."

Wend explained, "We got to the bay, and it looked so narrow you could throw a stone across. We had the men take their shoes and stockings off and put them in their packs. Then they put their cartridge box belts around their necks. With Cowell leading us, and knowing where the deep spots were, we were able to wade across in single file holding our firelocks well out of the water."

"My God, so you cut hours off the march."

"Yes, and we hadn't gone far on this side when Childers arrived to tell us your situation. So we dropped our packs and came on as fast as we could!" Wend looked around. "But right now we have to concentrate on pushing these raiders to the shoreline." He pointed back to the wagon track. "Childers is moving along the road with two squads. O'beirne is moving in a skirmish line through the woods to the south of the road with four squads. I know your men have been fighting for some time, so form them up to act as our reserve, and then follow on behind the rest of the company as soon as you can. If the British rally, I may have to put you back into the fight."

Newkirk said, "Wend, there's something you'll want to know. The leader of the British is Major Welford—the man who led the raid on your farm—and he says he's the one who shot you."

Wend's head snapped around toward where the retreating enemy would be. Then he answered in a grim tone, "Well, it's not so important that he shot me. But I hold him responsible for the death of Donegal's wife and Hecht's son." The muscles tightened on his face. "Welford will not make it back into the boats if I can help it."

As he spoke, the sound of firing could be heard, first a few scattering shots, then heavy firing. Wend said, "That will be O'beirne making contact with the retreating British."

Reese answered, "Aye, sir. I'll be moving out as soon as possible. But I must mention that we have almost a score of prisoners, mostly wounded. They're down at the plantation house. And two of our men are there also, with serious wounds."

Wend bit his lip. "All right, leave one squad behind under a responsible corporal to watch the prisoners and wounded."

Newkirk turned and started down the drive, calling over his shoulder, "Right, sir. We'll be close behind you."

Wend soon caught up with O'beirne and the skirmish line. Together they kept the men moving forward, pushing the British relentlessly. It was advance, take a position in cover, shoot, reload, and then move forward. The loyalist troops seemed dispirited and put up little resistance. Wend had lost track of time as they passed the next plantation after the Wilford place.

Then they had crossed the drive for the next plantation in line when Cowell put his hand on Wend's shoulder. "Cap'n, this is the last place afore we reach the Bay. The Chesapeake shoreline ain't but a few hundred yards ahead. Less'n a quarter of a mile, I'd say."

Just then O'beirne called, "Eckert, they've stopped retreating and are forming to make a stand. Looks like forty or more, spread out in the woods under cover. We're taking fire from them."

Wend moved up close to the Irishman. "I suspect they're trying to hold the line to buy time so the rest can reembark on their boats. They probably plan for this line to slowly withdraw until they're near the shore, then run for the boats."

O'beirne nodded. "Aye, it sounds right to me. We'll push them hard."

Wend responded, "Yes, keep pressing them—keep them busy. But we need to break this line and get to the beach before they can load their troops." He gritted his teeth. "I damn well mean to destroy this entire raiding party." He turned to Billy and ordered, "Get back and find Newkirk. Tell him to come fast and form on O'beirne's right. I want him to overlap these British and hit them on their flank. You understand what I'm saying?"

Billy said "Yes, sir!" and turned and ran off to find Newkirk.

Wend called to O'beirne. "I'm going to find Childers and get him in position to strike their other flank. They'll not be able to stand with attacks on both sides as well as you pressing their main line."

O'beirne waved. "We'll keep them busy until you're ready to attack."

Wend found Childers and his two squads moving along the road, not facing much opposition. He stopped them and explained the plan. Then he said, "We'll not attack until we hear Newkirk go into action on the other flank."

The young ensign nodded. "I understand, sir."

"What have you encountered so far?"

"Sir, we haven't had much opposition at all. When we did, they ran off in the direction of the shore and left two wagons full of plunder deserted, sir. Full of chicken carcasses, flour, bags of grain, and other foodstuffs. And we just passed a creek where they had been filling water casks. They had abandoned them also."

"Thank you, Edward," Wend responded. "Now let's get your men ready for the attack. Move your squads up until you're on the flank of the British." He pointed to give Childers an idea of where they enemy had their line. "Use cover, so they don't know what we're up to, then have your men go to ground and wait until you hear Newkirk attacking to go in."

"Aye, sir! We'll move right now."

"And when you get into position, have your musket men fix their bayonets." Wend put his hand on the ensign's shoulder. "Now lad, if the British are stubborn, it will have to be close work. Cold steel and pistols. But you must be determined and dislodge them."

Childers's face took on a determined aspect. He said quietly, "Yes, I understand, sir."

Wend quickly moved along the line to the other flank and arrived just in time to meet Newkirk leading his men up. He explained the situation quickly, then said, "Now I know you're men are tired, but you're going to be the main attack force. Mass your squads, fire a volley or two, then go in with the bayonet. O'beirne will be pushing in on the center, and Childers will be on the other side. He'll attack when he hears your firing. Swing left, and squeeze the enemy up against Childers's men. I think when they realize that we're on both flanks, they'll break and run for the beach. Then we can shoot them down as they flee."

Newkirk nodded.

Then Wend moved back along the line and gave final instructions to Shay. As he was speaking, he heard volley fire erupt from Newkirk's detachment.

Shay heard it too and immediately ordered his men to step up their firing.

Wend said, "The moment you sense they are wavering, get at them with the bayonet," then he hurried toward Childers's position to ensure he advanced as required. But when he got there, he found that he need not have worried. Keyed by Newkirk's firing, both squads were advancing to the attack, bayonets gleaming in the sunlight, the ensign in the lead.

It all lasted less than ten minutes. Attacked on three fronts simultaneously, the last organized element of the King's Loyal Virginia Legion soon broke and ran for the shore. The bayonet attacks by Newkirk and Childers were more than the poorly trained loyalists could withstand; those facing Newkirk's men began running at the sight of the mass of advancing blades. The ones on the other flank were made of somewhat sterner stuff, and Childers's men actually had to engage in close combat for a few brief moments before the royalists turned and fled. With both flanks collapsed, the center crumbled and the men began streaming for the rear, many dropping their muskets to more easily move through the scrub. Others turned to face the advancing Virginians and grounded their muskets in a sign of surrender.

After the company, shouting and yelling at the top of their voices, had chased the running mob for about a hundred yards, Wend called a halt to re-form the line. It was difficult, for the Frederick County men now had their blood up and wanted to plunge ahead. But with the help of the officers and sergeants, shouting orders and sometimes grabbing men by their shirts to stop them, order was restored. Wend took a few minutes to brief the leaders, detach men to deal with the prisoners, and form a wide skirmish line. Then they began a measured advance to the shoreline. Wend went ahead with O'beirne, Cowell, and a small party to scout the way.

The pinewoods ended abruptly at the beginning of the sandy beach. Wend and the others took cover at the edge to observe the British. A protective line of redcoated marines with bayoneted muskets stood ready, and behind their line the demoralized remnants of the legion milled about, mostly without arms. Wend sighted Welford moving around, waving his sword and shouting orders in an attempt to restore some kind of order among his men. He was having little success. Meanwhile, a party of sailors was frantically unloading supplies from a row of boats drawn up on the beach. They were throwing flour bags, produce, and animal carcasses onto the beach, where other piles of plunder had been stacked waiting to be loaded. Wend could see more boats coming in to the shore from HMS *Otter*, which rode in the distance.

Wend turned to Cowell. "They're desperately trying to get the boats ready to take off their men. Can the *Otter* get in closer to use her guns on us when we attack?"

"No, Captain. She's got too much draft. The shallows go a long way out. Her guns can't reach us here."

Wend turned to Billy Wood. "Go tell Mr. Newkirk to bring up the company in skirmish line but to stop at the very edge of the bush."

Billy nodded and ran back to find the lieutenant.

Shay looked over at the marines. "Those are the first regular troops we've encountered." He grinned. "It will be entertaining to go after them with the bayonets."

Wend shook his head vigorously. "No bayonets if I can help it. I don't want to lose men. We'll shoot them down from the edge of the bush, and there will be no rush until there's only a remnant."

O'beirne made a face. "Damn shame. I was looking for a chance to use my sword on one of those lobsters."

In just a few minutes, Newkirk arrived and went to his knees in the bush beside Wend. "Company's taking position now."

Wend turned to him. "Quick! Bring the two rifle squads here to the center of our line. Tell them to target the sailors manning the boats. Kill them, and the rest can't get away."

In a few moments, twenty riflemen began picking off the sailors. Soon men were lying still or bleeding in pain on the sand while other bodies were floating lifeless in the water.

Welford was moving along the beach exhorting his men to rally and form a line of resistance. Wend pulled a pistol from his belt, then, allowing his anger to guide him, stepped out from the scrub.

O'beirne called, "Eckert, what are you doing? You'll be hit!"

Wend ignored him. Immediately he felt the disturbance as a ball whizzed past his head. He ignored it and called out, "Welford! Look here!"

The major turned and stared at where the shout had come from. A look of horror came over his face.

Wend shouted, "Welford, you bastard, it's Eckert! Wend Eckert! You missed me, you ass! Now you're the one who will die!" Wend raised the pistol and fired.

It was a long shot, but the ball struck Welford high on his chest. He put a hand to the wound, then stumbled and fell to the sand. He lay there, writhing in pain, trying but failing to get up.

A marine, who had been sheltering behind a pile of flour sacks, jumped up, ran to the major, and started to drag him toward the sacks.

Wend called out, "I need a rifle."

Jensen came up. "You can use mine, sir."

Taking the rifle in hand, Wend quickly inspected it, then cocked the hammer. He looked up to see another man had joined the marine to help drag Welford. Wend aimed rapidly to get in a shot before Welford was shielded. It was difficult with the officer being dragged rapidly along the sand. He fired and was gratified to see Welford's body twitch violently just before it disappeared behind the flour sacks.

Shay said. "Nice shooting, sir." He waved his arm along the beach. "By the way, most of the sailors are down."

Wend shouted, "You riflemen! Aim for the officers and sergeants of the marines! And let's have musket fire by squad volley!" He pointed toward the shore. "No one leaves the beach!"

The words were hardly out of his mouth when the entire company opened fire. Most of the officers and many of the marines in the line fell immediately. The others ran for the boats.

In the brief silence after the first volley, Shay said, "Now my dear captain, I might point out that the British are going to be quite unhappy with you. Targeting officers is considered very unsporting."

410

Wend, keeping his eyes on the action on the beach, replied dryly, "They're in America now. They better get used to it."

Shay didn't respond. Instead he pointed to the waterline. "Look, there are some marines and others climbing into the boats."

Wend shouted out to the company, "Try to get those men at the boats!"

However, there was a near lull in firing—most of the company was reloading, Shay pulled out a pistol and snapped off a shot, but it was hopeless at the distance. Wend watched as twelve, maybe fifteen, men were able to get into two of the boats and quickly shove off.

Finally, with some men having reloaded, a burst of shots rang out before the boats pulled out of range, but the range was long and there was no indication of any of the men in the boats had been hit. They pulled away rapidly toward the *Otter*.

Shay said, "With them bouncing around so much on the waves, it would be a miracle if anyone could hit them."

Wend answered, "You're right. We'll not stop them." He thought a second. "It may be useful for us. They can tell Dunmore how we deal with loyalist raiders. Maybe they'll have to end these incursions."

O'beirne gave wend a glance. "Or be smarter and trickier how they do it. Perhaps they'll raid further up the Bay where we can't respond."

As he spoke, another round of firing rang out from the company. There were few British on their feet now and many lying on the sand, either dead or wounded. Suddenly one voice on the beach started shouting, "Quarter! Quarter! For God's sake, stop firing!" The remaining men dropped their weapons, raised their hands, and picked up the shout for quarter. Some who had been hiding behind boats or piles of plunder stood up and raised their hands too.

Wend called out to his company, "Stop firing!"

The officers and sergeants echoed his words, and it was suddenly very quiet on the shoreline.

A wounded marine who had blood running down his arm but still able to stand stepped forward and said, "We got many men what are hurt. We need a surgeon."

Wend called out, "We don't have any medical people. But some of our men will try to help, and we'll send for help back to the plantations to see if any of the women have experience."

Wend waved the officers and sergeants to join him. "We've got to get organized to guard the prisoners and provide medical assistance to both our own men and the British." He turned to Childers. "You make the rounds of the plantations and see if you can find some women who will help with the wounded."

O'beirne spoke up. "Now I'm not pleased to be the bearer of inconvenient news, Captain, but the wounded here on the beach are not all we have to worry about. I must say you have left a *very long and messy* battlefield. There are undoubtedly dead and wounded men in the woods all the way back to the Wilford place. We're going to have to go search them out. And there are muskets lying all over the place."

Wend thought a minute. "You're right: it's going to take a while to clean all this up." Wend looked up at the sky. "It's just a little after the noon hour. We have a lot of work to do for the rest of the day, and we'll have to camp right here for the night." He turned to Childers. "Edward, when you go to the plantations, select a detail to go back with you and pick up the company's packs."

"Aye, sir. Right away."

Wend looked at the others. "All right, let's begin cleaning all this up so we can start back to Gwynn's tomorrow."

The officers hurried off to get started. Wend walked down the beach toward the stack of flour bags where the marine had pulled Welford. The body was stretched out, face to the sky, the sightless eyes peering upward. Welford had been hit in the chest and on the side. Blood was all over his torso and had stained the sand around his corpse. Then Wend was surprised to see a young boy—he looked to be twelve or thirteen—sitting with his back against the bags. He was dressed in the blue coat and white breeches of a naval officer. Tears were running down his cheeks.

Wend asked, "Who are you?"

The boy looked up, startled at seeing Wend. A look of fear came over his face. He wiped away the tears and said, "I'm Midshipman Thomas Thorne, of the *Otter*, sir." He looked down at Welford's body. "Are you going to shoot me like you did Major Welford?"

Wend laughed. "No, lad. The battle is over. We don't shoot people after the surrender."

O'beirne came over and looked down at the body. "So that's the infamous raider of Eckert Ridge?"

"Yes, Shay. Major Reginald Welford, late of His Majesty's Guards, late of the 60th Foot, late of General Gage's staff, and now dead commandant of the King's Loyal Virginia Legion. And an insufferable bastard."

"Well, I learned long ago that being an arrogant snot is one of the requirements for an officer of the guards." He looked over at Thorn. "Hello! What do we have here?"

Wend answered, "He says he's a midshipman. I'm not familiar with the term. Is he considered some kind of officer?"

"Yes, my dear captain, my understanding is that in the naval service, he is both a minor officer and a trainee. A rough equivalent of an army ensign." He looked down at the youth. "And the navy does start them young."

Wend nodded and said to the boy, "Mr. Thorne, it's time to wipe away the last of those tears. It seems you must be the only king's officer left alive here on the beach."

Thorn rose to his feet and straightened out his uniform coat. "Yes, sir. What do you plan to do with me?"

"It's not what I'm going to do with you; it is what you are going to do for us and your compatriots. You will take charge of the prisoners and make up a muster list of the survivors. And you will keep a tally of your dead as we gather them up. You will report all that to our ensign, Childers, who will be back here presently. Do you understand?"

The youngster touched a finger of his right hand to his forehead. "Yes, sir. I can do that."

"Well, then, Mr. Thorne, I suggest you get started."

The two men watched the midshipman hurry away, and Shay shot Wend a wink. Then he said, "Newkirk has set some of the men to digging a common grave for all the dead British. I'll have someone come down and get Welford's body."

A hard look came over Wend's face. He shook his head. "No, Shay. There will be no burial for Welford. Leave him lying here in the sand for the seabirds to peck at his eyes and these land crabs to eat his flesh. And soon enough the tide will wash his remains out into the Bay, where the fish will feast on him. That's a proper end for his body."

And with that he turned and walked up the beach, leaving Shay O'beirne staring after him, eyebrows raised in astonishment.

Chapter Seventeen

THE DECLARATION

With the afternoon sun low in the sky, Colleen McGraw watched as Edna's son Charlie pulled the loaded wagon into the pasture near her tent. "Did you get everything on the list?"

"Yes, ma'am. But it was hard, what with all the people heading to Manhattan for the big celebration. It was good I got downtown early, 'cause a lot of shops was gettin' ready to close."

Colleen wrinkled up her face. "What celebration?"

"Why, there's a proclamation from the congress, ma'am. Everyone says it's about independence from England. And people are sure excited."

Edna joined them and had heard her son's words. "Are you sure about that?"

"Yes, Ma. They're talkin' about it all around the town."

Colleen sighed skeptically. "Congress has been debating it for weeks now; it's hard to credit that they've finally made up their mind. And I wonder if they are really going the whole way." A thoughtful look came over her face. "Perhaps it is just a letter to the king threatening to become independent if he and parliament don't give the colonies more power to govern themselves. I've always presumed that was how this would work out in the end."

Just then Edna pointed down the road. "Well, will you look who is coming? And he's in that fancy carriage again."

Colleen turned to see Geoffrey Fairfield arrive in the carriage he had used the night they had gone to supper. The rig was driven by Sergeant Quinn, he of the half ear, and was escorted by two outriders.

The lieutenant raised his hat in greeting and stepped down from the vehicle. "Good afternoon, my dear Mrs. McGraw." He turned and bowed to Edna. "And to you, Mrs. Farley."

Colleen acknowledged his greeting with a bow of her head. "To what do we owe the pleasure of your visit, Lieutenant?" She grinned impishly. "Would you like to visit with one of my girls?"

Fairfield returned her grin. "There's only one *lady* here with whom I desire to visit. And I thought perhaps you would let me escort you to hear the reading of the proclamation from congress. It will be done on the common at six this evening, and General Washington himself will be there."

"Precisely what is in this proclamation? We get the news rather late out here, and all we have heard was that something was to be announced, although there are certainly rumors about the content of this document."

Fairfield grinned. "Well, then, it is my pleasure to bring you the exciting details. Our esteemed Continental Congress has voted to declare full and complete independence from England. They voted on it a few days ago, and the commanding general received a copy just yesterday. He has ordered that all brigades hold a parade at which it will be read to the men by their commanding officer, and there is going to be a formal reading for the headquarters troops and the good citizens of New York this very afternoon." He grinned and added, "The whole town is turning out. I thought, Mrs. McGraw, that perchance you would like to don one of your elegant gowns and accompany me to the ceremony."

Edna glanced at Colleen. "Why don't we load everyone into the wagons so they can see it? The girls have been working hard—they could use a day off without having to entertain men."

Colleen turned to Geoffrey and gave him her brightest smile. "I'm beginning to understand that this will be a truly memorable occasion, Lieutenant. And of course I should be honored to accompany you."

"You have made me a happy man, Mrs. McGraw. I shall wait until you have prepared yourself."

Colleen waved toward the canopy in front of her tent. "Please seat yourself in the shade, sir, while I dress. And one of my girls will bring you a libation." She looked at the waiting soldiers. "And they'll also bring some refreshment for Sergeant Quinn and his men."

Edna asked, "Should I tell everyone to get ready and have the men hitch up the wagons?"

"Quite right, Edna. We shall make a holiday of today."

An hour later Colleen sat beside Geoffrey as they rolled toward downtown Manhattan. She turned to her escort. "Well, we've not seen much of you for the last fortnight. I presume you have been busy."

"Indeed, I and my whole troop have been quite engaged. We've been keeping an eye on the British and also serving as couriers."

"Oh yes, I had heard that there were several British warships lying in the outer harbor."

"Well, Colleen, it's gone considerably beyond that. There are now many more warships, and convoys of troop transports have arrived. But even more serious, they are landing men."

Colleen was surprised. "They have come ashore? I had not heard that."

"There are now many redcoats on Staten Island—perhaps as many as ten thousand. They're making it their base for the future offensive." He looked at her. "We've been scouting them and providing reports back to Washington."

"That's a lot of British. But Geoffrey, I'm told that Washington has nearly twenty thousand men now. And that militia are coming in from the surrounding areas. Surely we should be able to fend off that number of the enemy."

"My dear Colleen, this is only the beginning. Yesterday we captured four British soldiers from Staten Island. They say additional convoys are coming, with both English battalions and mercenaries from the Germanic states. Sympathizers in Canada report the British have even more troops sailing down from Halifax. We shall soon be confronting as many as twenty-five or thirty thousand enemy soldiers."

Colleen shrugged. "Geoffrey, you sound very pessimistic. I'm sure Washington has a plan to defend the city, else he would be making preparations to withdraw."

Fairfield turned to her with a grim look on his face. "Now I'm going to tell you something in the strictest confidence: Washington would like nothing better than to retreat. He believes the city is indefensible. The area is so cut up with waterways that he cannot consolidate his forces and must defend numerous separate pieces of land. And the British fleet can move their troops around the various parts of the city and up the Hudson at will to attack where they desire."

"For God's sake, Geoffrey, if that's the case, why is the army still here?"

"Congress has mandated that the city will be defended. Washington must comply."

"But that makes little sense! If what you say is true, it will be a waste of lives."

"Indeed. But the practice of politics leads to strange outcomes." He lowered his voice as if relating a secret. "This Declaration of Independence could not have happened unless all of the colonies agreed. It needed to be unanimous."

"I don't understand. How does that relate to fighting a battle which can't be won?"

"My dear, the Colony of New York has many loyalists, or at least a considerable number of wealthy families who are quite hesitant about making a complete break with the king. It has been the most adamant holdout in the vote to break our ties with England. Washington won't say it out loud, but many on his staff whisper that the price for New York's vote in the affirmative is the defense of this city. So Washington has vowed he will make the British pay a heavy price to take the city." He shrugged. "And our cost will be high as well."

Colleen sat silent for a long moment. Then she said, "So because of a political deal, many men, from various places besides New York, are about to sell their lives to pay for the vote of one colony."

"You are a businesswoman, Colleen, and logically you have stated things in terms of commerce. And I should have to agree with you. But of course, it would be more *diplomatic* to say they are fighting for the ideal of independence and getting New York's vote is simply a necessary step along the way."

The two rode in silence for a while. Then Geoffrey said, "Look, here we are at the common. And what a crowd!"

Colleen stared at the grassy common area. Several regiments were drawn up in formation. A platform had been constructed, with a lectern on it for the speakers to use. And as Fairfield had said, there was a mass of civilians standing before and on either side of the stage—men, women, and children. A thought occurred to her, and she turned to him and asked, "I don't see your troop. Why aren't they here?"

"We are excused from this formation. As I said earlier, a goodly number of my men are posted to watch Staten Island under Sergeant McCrae. They're with pickets of both regular and militia, ready to act as couriers to warn of any movements by the enemy. And the others are in our camp to rest and graze the horses." He looked over at her and smiled. "I read the declaration to those men who are in camp this morning."

"Well, that's certainly fortunate for me, since it enabled you to be here as my escort." She grinned at him. But then she looked at the crowd size. "But I doubt we're going to be able to get close enough to hear clearly."

"Fear not, Mrs. McGraw! Do you have so little confidence in my good offices? There is a place reserved for our carriage just behind the platform, and my men are also protecting a space for us right in front of the platform."

She gave him her most coquettish smile. "Geoffrey, you are always so thoughtful."

Quinn maneuvered the carriage into a spot where two cavalry-men stood guard, and after they came to a stop, Geoffrey jumped to the ground and then handed Colleen down. He waved to the two dismounted troopers, and they opened a way through the onlookers at the base of the platform and led them to a spot near the podium.

Colleen looked up. "Well, this is marvelous, Geoffrey. You have indeed thought of everything. We will not miss a word. And how exciting it will be to see General Washington with my own eyes."

"Yes, I rather thought you would like that."

Looking around at the assembled troops, Colleen asked, "What is that company right behind us? They are all well uniformed, whereas most of the others don't have uniforms."

"My dear Mrs. McGraw, those are the general's Life Guards. They have been established to escort and guard Washington both at his headquarters and in the field."

Colleen looked more closely at the unit. Then she nodded toward the officer standing in front. "I'm sure that's one of the officers who visited upon us when we were having supper at Fraunce's place. Captain Gibbs, if I am correct."

"Yes, that's Caleb Gibbs, captain of the guard. Quite a coveted position. In addition, he manages all the events which Washington attends and also governs his 'official military family.' He's done much of the planning for this event."

Just then they heard cheering from some distance away.

Geoffrey said, "That will be Washington and his retinue arriving. It would seem that the ceremony is about to begin."

The cheering sounds became louder, reaching a crescendo in a few minutes, then dying down slightly. Momentarily, several officers appeared on the stage.

Fairfield whispered, "Washington's staff."

Colleen said, "Yes, and I recognize young George Baylor from the night at Fraunces'."

After the staff had taken their places, the general ascended the steps and stood on the stage.

"My God, the general is tall! He towers over everyone," Colleen exclaimed. "And I must admit he looks just like you think the commanding general should—very dignified."

"Yes, Mrs. McGraw, if there's only one thing you could say about Washington, *dignified* is the first word which would come to mind." He smiled and added, "*Humorless* is the second, I would say, at least in my experience." He thought a minute and then said, "Although I must relate that his immediate staff insists he appreciates a witty jest when in private and is known to make a joke."

As they spoke, an officer stepped forward to the podium and raised his arms to signal silence.

Geoffrey said, "That's Colonel William Grayson—he's the general's chief secretary."

Grayson announced, "The commanding general, His Excellency George Washington, will speak a few words."

The crowd noise died down as Washington stepped forward, a piece of paper in his hand. He laid it on the podium and looked out on the crowd of civilians below him. As he did so, his gaze momentarily rested on Colleen, and she found herself looking into his eyes. She gave him a broad smile and a nod of her head. Washington raised an eyebrow, stared for a moment, then raised his face to the soldiers drawn up in ranks behind the crowd and began to speak.

"Soldiers of the army and people of New York, I have extraordinary news for you. The Continental Congress, meeting in Philadelphia, has just a few days hence moved to dissolve the connection between this country and Great Britain. We are in possession of a document which declares that the United Colonies of North America are now, and forever more, free and independent states." He paused, moving his glance around the assembled citizenry. "I emphasize, we are now no longer *colonies* but *independent states*."

He paused and a round of huzzahs, orchestrated by the officers of the various regiments and the guard, resounded. They were augmented by spontaneous cheers from the civilians gathered around the platform.

Washington stood waiting until the cheering died down, then said, "Now, the commanders of the regiments paraded here will read to their men the document which we have received. Colonel Grayson will read the document for the hearing of those civilians here assembled."

Washington stepped back, and the captain resumed his place in front of the podium.

Colleen leaned over to Fairfield and said softly, "Lord above, I hope this isn't going to be a long, drawn-out thing with flowery words which will be hard to understand."

"It's not that long. And my men found it quite arresting when I read it to them this morning."

Grayson cleared his throat and began to read. "In Congress, July 4, 1776. A Declaration by the Representatives of the United States of America, in General Congress assembled." He paused, and Colleen realized that the crowd, for the first time since they had arrived, was absolutely silent. Then Grayson resumed. "When, in the Course of human events, it becomes necessary for one people to dissolve the political bands which have connected them with another, and to assume among the powers of the earth, the separate and equal station to which the Laws of Nature and of Nature's God entitle them, a decent respect to the opinions of mankind requires that they should declare the causes which impel them to the separation."

He paused, looked around the crowd, then resumed reading. "We hold these truths to be self-evident, that all men are created equal, that they are endowed by their Creator with certain unalienable Rights, that among these are Life, Liberty and the pursuit of Happiness.— That to secure these rights, Governments are instituted among Men, deriving their just powers from the consent of the governed,—That whenever any Form of Government becomes destructive of these ends, it is the Right of the People to alter or to abolish it, and to institute new Government, laying its foundation on such principles and organizing its powers in such form, as to them shall seem most likely to affect their Safety and Happiness."

Colleen eyed the assemblage and realized that the people were enthralled, their faces glued to Grayson.

Then she turned back and heard that Grayson was now reading a list of grievances that the colonists ostensibly had with the king's government. Now the crowd began to murmur in agreement, as Grayson read the items, occasional voices shouting, "Here, here!" or "Aye, and that's the truth!"

Grayson continued reading the list, and when he came to one item that mentioned unfair taxation, the assemblage raised the greatest clamor of approbation that had occurred in the reading.

Finally he finished the list and came to the conclusion of the declaration. "We, therefore, the Representatives of the united States of America, in General Congress Assembled, appealing to the Supreme Judge of the world for the rectitude of our intentions, do, in the Name, and by Authority of the good People of these Colonies, solemnly publish and declare, That these United Colonies are, and of Right ought to be Free and Independent States; that they are Absolved from all Allegiance to the British Crown, and that all political connection between them and the State of Great Britain, is and ought to be totally dissolved; and that as Free and Independent States, they have full Power to levy War, conclude Peace, contract Alliances, establish Commerce, and to do all other Acts and Things which Independent States may of right do. And for the support of this Declaration, with a firm reliance on the protection of divine Providence, we mutually pledge to each other our Lives, our Fortunes and our sacred Honor."

There was another round of cheering. Grayson held up his hands to quiet the crowd, and when a reasonable silence had been achieved, he read the names of the men who had signed the document.

Colleen looked over at Geoffrey. "Well, the part about their lives, fortunes, and honor may well come true. That list of names will be seized upon by the British if they are triumphant. And I have no doubt the gallows will be a busy place."

Fairfield nodded, then said, "The word around the staff is that three men were most involved in drafting this document: John Adams of Massachusetts, Benjamin Franklin of Philadelphia, and Thomas Jefferson of Virginia."

Colleen wrinkled her face. "Well, everyone has heard of Franklin, and I've seen Adams's name in newspaper articles about the debates in congress, but I've never heard of this Jefferson fellow."

"It's a name I'm not much familiar with either. But George Baylor, who is from Virginia, knows him."

Colleen laughed. "Oh yes, we know Baylor well. After visiting us at Fraunces, he has often visited the Red Vixen. He likes to spend time with the girls."

"Yes, knowing George, I don't doubt that. At any rate, he says this Jefferson is a wealthy plantation owner in the western part of Virginia and was an active member of the House of Burgesses before being appointed to congress. He's a lawyer and reputedly quite adept with the spoken and written word."

Colleen was about to respond when Grayson came back to the podium and ordered the troop commanders to take their men back to the camps, essentially marking the end of the ceremony. Then Washington and all the members of his staff departed from the platform. Orders were shouted in the military formations, and the soldiers began parading back to their quarters.

This had no sooner begun than members of the crowd raised shouts of "Let's get King George! To the Bowling Green!" It was taken up by many more, shouting it rhythmically. Then the crowd rushed out onto Broadway and flowed down toward the harbor like a river of humanity.

Colleen, puzzled, looked over at her companion. "What's going on? Where are they rushing?"

Geoffrey shook his head. "I have no idea." Then he smiled. "Let's get back to the carriage. We can follow them and see what is toward." He signaled to his troopers to take the lead, then took her arm. "In any case, I want to take you down to the harbor to see something with your own eyes."

They arrived at the carriage, and Quinn aroused the horses from their reverie. He carefully guided the rig down Broadway, picking his way through the crowd. Presently they arrived at a grassy park with a statue of a man on a horse. The mob had surrounded the statue.

Fairfield pointed to the statue. "In case you're not aware of it, that's a statue of our now former sovereign, the less than esteemed George the Third."

"Listen—they're calling for it to be torn down!"

"Yes, my dear Colleen, and some of them have come prepared." He pointed to a small group of men.

"Why, they're carrying ropes, hammers, and other tools!"

"Exactly, Colleen," responded Fairfield dryly. "This clearly has been well planned in advance."

As they watched, one of the men pulled himself up the high stone pedestal of the monument, and another man tossed him one of the ropes. The climber crawled up onto the statue itself and looped the rope around the figure of George. Then several more ropes were tossed up, and he did the same with them.

"Why, they're going to try to pull down the statue!" Colleen looked over at her companion. "Do you think they can manage it?"

"We shall soon see."

Men came forward eagerly to grab the ropes—soon there were many pulling on each line. At first they had little success, but then one man took charge, coordinating their efforts. He called out a cadence so the gangs on all the ropes pulled in unison, and almost immediately the statue began to move. Soon the metal base was being lifted off the stone pedestal, and with a few more strong pulls on the lines, the whole figure leaned over and then crashed down to the ground.

There was a resounding uproar from the crowd.

At once a pair of men approached the statue and using a sledge hammer and chisels, began cutting at George's neck.

Colleen laughed. "By God, they're going to behead him!"

It took a while to cut through the heavy lead, but presently the head was severed from the body. One of the men held it up high to another deafening cheer from the people. Then another man appeared carrying a heavy stick. It was inserted into the hollow head through the severed neck, and the man held it high to approving shouts from the crowd. He yelled to the crowd, "We'll parade the king's head through the town!"

Then he turned and headed up Broadway carrying the head like a standard. A large part of the assemblage followed him, singing and chanting as they went. However, a large number of people remained behind, and Colleen could see they were starting fires.

Fairfield said, "Look, my lady, jugs have mysteriously begun to appear. Undoubtedly they contain intoxicants."

"Yes, obviously this is going to turn into quite a party."

Geoffrey said, "Indeed it will." Then he called out to Quinn. "Take us down to Fort George." He turned to Colleen and said, "There's something I want you to see."

It was a very short drive to the old fortification at the edge of the harbor waters, and the sergeant pulled up the vehicle close to the ramparts.

Fairfield stepped down and helped Colleen out of the carriage. "Come on, we're going right to the water's side."

"What do you have in mind, Geoffrey?"

"As I told you, there's something I want you to see."

They walked around to the front of the fort, and he led her up the stone stairs of a small outer work.

Colleen said, "It is a lovely view, Geoffrey, particularly in the evening light, with the sun so low. Very thoughtful of you."

"Yes, but beauty is not why I brought you here." He raised a brass telescope that he had brought from the carriage and peered down to the south for a long minute. Then he handed it to Colleen. "Put this to your eyes and let me guide where you look."

She obliged and felt Geoffrey move the glass slightly as she peered through it. Then she saw what he obviously intended. There was a mass of ships anchored close together in the distance, their masts looking like a dense forest. "My God, Geoffrey! The British ships. There are scores of them!"

"Very true, my dear Mrs. McGraw. And when I glanced through the glass just now, I realized many more arrived today. Undoubtedly a new troop convoy." He moved the glass slightly to the west. "That land you see is Staten Island."

"Why, there are many little boats moving back and forth."

"Yes, putting troops and material ashore. I wager there are far more than ten thousand soldiers now on the island."

"Geoffrey, if you intended to make me anxious, you have succeeded remarkably well."

"Yes, well now I'm going to give you some advice. Don't get too settled in your camp."

"But our location has been very profitable for us! We have to replenish our stock often, and being close to the town is very convenient for that. More importantly, we're located within easy walking distance of several regimental camps. And it's a short travel time for those quartered down here in lower Manhattan."

"Colleen, the British are soon going to outnumber us vastly. And they can move and land their troops by boat essentially anywhere they want. Washington's forces are spread out trying to defend the whole area; I fear the British can cut off segments and destroy them at will." He gave her a serious look. "And you must understand, this is an island and the British can cut off ferry service with their fleet. It is well within their capability to isolate Manhattan. If that occurs, order may collapse in an instant. I urge you to spend some time calculating various routes to get away, and as I said, be ready to flee in a hurry."

"Geoffrey, I know you said Washington thinks New York can't be defended. But aren't you being a bit too gloomy? Things will develop over time." She had another thought. "And even though that congress in Philadelphia has declared independence, there's still a lot of talk about a peace commission from the British. I think there's a fair chance there actually will be no further conflict."

Fairfield put his hand on her arm, gripping it tightly. A fierce look came over his face. "Now listen to me! Listen, I say! Washington is in no mood for peace. None! He may not be able to defend the city, but he is determined to battle it out with the British. He will put up a fierce fight here, making them pay a deadly price, then he will withdraw to more favorable territory. I've seen enough of the man these last few weeks to know his sentiments." He motioned back to the park where the celebration was in full swing, with men and women dancing around the fires. "I hope the people of New York City enjoy this moment, for I believe soon they will be once again under the rule of the king's minions. And none of us can foresee how all this will end."

The grim tone of Fairfield's words sent a chill through Colleen's body. "All right, Geoffrey, I will take your advice. We shall be prepared for any eventuality."

"Excellent. Now, my dear lady, I must escort you back to your encampment, for early tomorrow I am ordered to ride with my troop to scout out the British positions. We must try to obtain some idea of their current strength at Staten Island."

—⁘—

In the morning light of a sunny day, Wend walked over to the headquarters of the 7th Virginia from the company's camp across the wagon track. In actuality, it was now also General Lewis's headquarters, for he had arrived on horseback with his staff at dusk the night before. Wend had been summoned by an aide to report the results of the fight at Mobjack Bay directly to the general.

Lewis and Daingerfield were sitting at a table under a canvas fly, surrounded by aides and subordinates. Wend came to attention and saluted Lewis. "Reporting as you requested, sir."

Lewis motioned down to the table. "Eckert, I've been reading your report of the recent engagement against Dunmore's raiding party. Damn, sir, I must say you were fortunate. Splitting your force, then wading through chest-high water of a bay, then rushing headlong into a fight with a numerically superior force. Suffice it to say, you took great chances. If the enemy had been more skillfully deployed, you could have been destroyed in detail." He raised an eyebrow and sat silent, inviting a reply.

Wend looked from the general to Daingerfield. The colonel had raised his eyes to the sky with a noncommittal expression on his face. "Well, sir, I didn't see any choice but to split my company above and below Horn Harbor Bay if we were to provide an adequate resistance to a possible raid. In the end, we smashed the King's Loyal Virginia

Legion, taking forty-six prisoners—many of whom are wounded—and killing thirty-nine men of the legion outright. And we killed seven marines and wounded five. Only a handful of marines, sailors, and legion men escaped in two boats. That is against losses of two dead and five wounded. And the people of the plantations in the area got most of their goods back. I'd say the chance paid off, General."

"Yes, in this case it did, Eckert. You were successful, and you have my compliments and the gratitude of the Virginia Convention. But I'll say this straight out: Don't count on riding your luck forever. Do so, and sooner or later it will lead you and your men into catastrophe."

Wend stood silent for a moment, a tight smile on his face. "That may be true, General. But then there are stories told in taverns all over Virginia of a certain Captain Andrew Lewis taking daring risks and bold movements while leading rifle companies and rangers on the border during the French War." Wend stared at the general for a moment. "Are those stories not true, sir?"

Daingerfield's face broke into a grin, and he held up a hand to his mouth to hide it while he looked sideways at Lewis.

Lewis looked like he was going to explode. His face reddened, and the muscles of his face stood out. But he calmed himself and said, in measured tones, "Well, Eckert, you are still a saucy one. But just *remember* my advice. And since you are so eager for action, I have a job for you and your men." He added, "A train of artillery will arrive here tomorrow. We've located two naval eighteen-pounders and six six-pounder field guns. Right now my artillery commander, Captain Arundel, is supervising work building emplacements along the shore of Milford Haven so that we can bombard the British ships anchored there and the forts on the north and southern ends of the channel." He looked toward Gwynn's Island. "When we've sunk or chased off the ships and silenced the British forts, I plan to launch a landing force on boats to take the island." He pointed at Wend. "You and your men will be in the first wave. I anticipate there will be stiff resistance from Dunmore's forces. You will likely be crossing under heavy musket fire and perhaps any artillery they can still muster." He looked back at Wend. "Now, Captain, what do you think of that? Is that enough risk for you?"

The eyes of all the staff officers were on Eckert. With the unexpressive face he was known for, Wend said in a steely and formal voice, "General, the men of the Frederick County Light Foot will be ready for whatever duty they are ordered to face." Then he pulled himself up to his full height and asked, "Is that all the general wished to tell me? If so, I'll return to my camp, make preparations, and await the call to action."

And without waiting for Lewis's response, he turned and strode back toward the company's bivouac, leaving the assemblage staring after him.

—m—

Lord Dunmore sat at his desk in the great cabin of his flagship, looking over some letters that Dudley Fellows had prepared. The secretary himself stood before the desk, describing and discussing each piece of correspondence as the governor looked it over. They were interrupted by a knock on the door, followed by the entrance of Aubrey Harbridge. Dunmore looked up to see that Captain Hammond was with him.

The governor asked, "Well, Andrew, I hope you are here to report the return of the raid."

Hammond said, "Indeed we are, sir. The *Otter* has returned."

Dunmore sat back in his chair. "Well, what news do you have?" A look of irritation came over his face. "And where is Major Welford? I distinctly asked to see him once the raid was over."

Harbridge and Hammond exchanged glances, then Harbridge cleared his throat and said, "I fear there is some discouraging news regarding the raid."

Dunmore looked at the two men. "Discouraging news? Pray tell, what on earth do you mean?" A look of puzzlement came over his face. "Did we have unsatisfactory results in gathering provisions?"

Hammond replied, "I'm afraid it's much worse than that, my lord. The rebels intercepted the force we landed." He paused and sighed deeply. "I regret to say the landing party, including both the King's Loyal Virginia Legion and the detachment of marines, has been in large measure destroyed."

Harbridge added, "To be accurate, it appears that the King's Loyal Virginia Legion has ceased to exist."

Shock immediately registered on Dunmore's face. "Destroyed? No longer exists? What the devil do you mean?"

"Sir, the landing force was ambushed. Most of the party was captured or killed. Less than twenty were able to escape the rebel attack and return to the *Otter*. And all but two of the boats accompanying the *Otter* were lost."

Dunmore jumped to his feet. "And Welford? What of him?"

"I'm afraid, Your Lordship, I must convey the sad news that the major is dead, his body left behind on the beach."

"If he was left behind, can we be sure he's dead?"

"There's a witness, sir."

Harbridge spoke up. "One of the survivors saw Welford die. A marine corporal. Hammond has brought him along; there's something he has to say that you'll want to hear."

Hammond motioned to the door. "He's just outside; shall I summon him?"

Dunmore, visibly shaken, merely nodded.

Hammond went to the door and escorted the young marine into the cabin. His uniform was dirty and streaked with blood. The man had a bandage around the upper part of his right arm. He saluted as he stood before the governor.

Hammond ordered, "Horsely, this is Lord Dunmore. Relate to him what happened to Major Welford."

"Well, your lordship, the legion had broken, and what was left of them came runnin' out of the woods onto the beach. Them rebels was right behind, shootin' our men down like dogs. We formed a line and tried to stop the enemy, but they took cover at the tree line and began shooting everyone who was on the beach." He looked over at Hammond. "Soon all the officers was down; they was the first to be shot."

Dunmore raised his hand to stop the marine's story. "You say they were deliberately targeting the officers?"

"Sure thing, sir. We heard rebel officers say to do it."

Dunmore shot an angry glance at Harbridge and then Hammond. "By God, that is a crime!" Then he told the man to continue.

"Well, sir, then they commenced the hottest fire I've ever seen, just sweeping the beach with balls." He paused and took a deep breath. "No way could we stand up to that. Men was falling all over. We broke and ran for whatever cover we could find, behind piles of provisions. I ended up behind a stack of flour bags, sir."

Hammond interrupted. "Tell him about Major Welford."

"Well, sir, the major was about the only officer of the legion left. He was movin' fast up and down the beach, tryin' to rally the men. Then a man came out of the trees holdin' a pistol. He shouted at the major, who turned to look at him, then the rebel shot him right in the chest." Horsely shook his head. "It was the most perfect shot I ever saw. Welford sagged down onto the sand and couldn't get up." He bit his lip. "Then young Midshipman Thorne, who was hidin' next to me, says, 'We've got to help him.' So the two of us ran out and grabbed the major and started draggin' him back behind our flour bags." The marine shook his head. "But as we was pullin' him across the sand, another ball hit him in the side, and he started bleedin' heavily. He started cryin' out and kickin' his legs in pain."

Fellows, with tremors in his voice, asked, "But he was still alive? Did you get him to cover?"

"Yes, sir. But like I said, he was bleedin' god-awful heavy, sir. And he was fadin' out fast and gasping for breath."

Hammond raised a hand to stop the marine. "Now, Horsely, tell the governor what Welford said before he died."

"Oh yes, sir." He looked around at the faces of the other men. "The major grabbed Mr. Thorne's arm, real tight and desperate like, and said, 'It was *Eckert*. Tell the governor it was *Eckert*. He's alive.' And then he passed out and died." Horsely shook his head. "He just lost too much blood, sir."

The captain nodded to the marine. "That will do, Corporal. You may retire."

Dunmore stood shaking but finally found words. "I have no doubt Welford was accurate in saying Eckert was shot in the head during the raid. But apparently the man has a supernatural ability to survive. And he is becoming my nemesis. It appears he has returned to haunt me."

Hammond said, "Well, regardless of this fellow Eckert's survival, we must face the fact that we have lost one-third of our military force.

It was unequivocally a disastrous outcome. We are in a much worse position today than yesterday."

The governor said in a flat tone, "Yes, yes, Hammond, you are quite correct."

Fellows, noting the governor's distress, stepped over to the sideboard. "My lord, would you care to take some rum?"

Dunmore was standing stone-still, his eyes again staring into the distance. Without looking at his secretary, he said, "Yes, make it a large cup."

Fellows poured the drink and handed it to Dunmore. Then Harbridge waved to Fellows and Hammond, and the three quietly left the cabin, leaving the royal governor of Virginia to his own thoughts.

—◊◊◊—

Wend, surrounded by his officers and sergeants, stood in the trees near the shoreline and looked across Milford Haven to the flat expanse of Gwynn's Island. Donegal and Baird were with them, having returned from Williamsburg with Lewis's column. Anchored on the far side of the channel were the *Dunmore* and to the south of her, HMS *Otter*, which had recently taken the position previously occupied by the *Roebuck*.

Also standing with the group was the waterman Jack Cowell. Cowell had sailed in his boat up to Gwynn's, towing the captured British boats from the beach down near Mobjack Bay.

Wend was trying to figure out the best way to cross the channel and land on the island. "Cowell, General Lewis wants us to land along the southern part of the channel. A company of the 7th will land to the north." Wend pointed to the island. "Where is the best place to go ashore?"

"Ain't no real good place, Cap'n. You drew the hard lot in this job. There's plenty of shallows, and the whole coastline of the island is cut up into little coves and bays. That means boats can't get right close to the land and you're goin' to get your feet wet going ashore." He waved to a tree-covered part of the land next to them, where scores of canoes had been gathered. "That's why we've collected all these dugouts lying there in the woods. They got as shallow a draft as you can find. They'll help you get in close, almost to the dry land, afore you got to jump out." He waved down the coastline. "We also got a collection of small fishing boats and all those British boats we captured in the raid. They're beached in a small cove a little down to the south where we're holdin' all of the craft; we'll bring them up when you're ready to make the crossing. We'll use them in a couple of places where the water's a little deeper inshore."

Shay, looking through a glass, pointed to the island. "He's surely right about that shoreline being broken up. If we land along a broad front, we'll be cut up into small groups without the ability to communicate until we get farther inland."

Newkirk looked at Wend. "He's right. Maybe we should make sure we land close together at one point."

Wend stared at the opposite shore, working things out in his mind. "No, gentlemen, I believe it's better if we do go ashore in a wide front, groups going into different little coves. That will make it harder for the British to mass forces against us. And Billy learned from his time on the island that Dunmore doesn't have a lot of men. Certainly not enough to cover the entire shoreline."

Shay laughed. "And after the fight down at Mobjack Bay, he's got a lot fewer."

Wend answered, "That's right. So if we land at separate points, they'll not be able to stop us all. It's a better gamble that most of us can get ashore safely."

Donegal looked at the canoes, then at the channel waters. "I na fancy bein' in a small boat for all that distance. If the British are smart, they'll have marksmen stationed along the shoreline picking us off as we paddle across. We'll have no choice but to just take the fire."

Wend answered, "Yes, we'll just have to accept the losses."

The officers and sergeants stood silently contemplating that thought.

Then Wend pointed to the little inlets along Gwynn's coastal line. "We'll go ashore in four groups, each led by one of the officers. Then each detachment will leave the beach and push inland until the terrain allows us to join together."

Wend waved toward the small British battery protected by earthen fortifications at the southern point of the island. "Lewis wants us to capture that battery as our first objective. So once we have assembled, we'll move to take it from behind."

Newkirk, who had taken the glass from O'beirne, responded, "If the British are smart, they'll evacuate it once they see we're success-fully ashore. It's oriented only to cover the Bay and the channel. I can't see any defense line covering its rear."

Wend nodded. "I hope you're right, Reese. But first we've got to get safely ashore." Then he said, "Let's go back to camp. I've got a rough map of the island, and we'll do what planning we can."

As they walked toward the camp, they observed much work being done to prepare for the artillery bombardment. The guns had arrived earlier in the day, and gunners were preparing for action. The two eighteen-pounder naval cannons had been taken out of their carriages and transported from Williamsburg on wagons. The artillerymen had brought a wooden derrick along on another wagon and were setting it up in preparation for lifting off the heavy cannons and remount-ing them on their carriages. Wend saw a young captain inspecting the emplacements that had been prepared for the guns. Each of the two positions were protected by an earthen embankment with an embrasure for the gun. The ground within the emplacements had been planked over to facilitate the movement of the guns forward and back during the actual firing.

Suddenly Edward Childers spoke up. "Why, that's Dohickey Arundel! The artillery officer over there!"

Wend said, "Yes, he's the commander of the gun batteries. How do you know him?"

"Why, I met him in Williamsburg while I was still at William and Mary. He's a Frenchman, a former artillery officer who came to America. It happens we spent many a night in the taverns of Williamsburg, along with other friends from my college days." The ensign hurried over to greet his friend. Wend and the others waited for Childers, and took the opportunity to watch the unloading of the naval guns.

Newkirk pointed to a wagon sitting nearby. "Do you see that piece of equipment on the wagon? It looks like a mortar. But it can't be one—it's made of wood with iron bands holding it together like a cask. What on earth is it?"

Wend stared at the device. Then he said, "Perhaps it's made to fool the British into thinking we have mortars. Such a weapon would be ideal for attacking the two artillery positions over on the island."

Shay smiled. "Now, lads, I'd say that's just what it is—a 'Quaker gun' since it looks like the real thing but can't do any harm."

As they were contemplating it, Childers brought his friend over to meet them. He said, "Captain Eckert, I'd like you to meet my friend, Captain Dohickey Arundel. He's in charge of all the artillery for General Lewis."

Arundel offered his hand to Wend and smiled broadly. "I'm called 'Doe' for short, sir."

Edward laughed. "Just like a female deer. I fear we have teased Captain Dohickey about that, especially after a few drinks."

Wend responded, "Glad to meet you, *Doe*." Then he pointed at the mortar like object. "What is that—a device to fool Dunmore's men?"

Arundel's face took on a very serious expression. "Why, it's nothing of the sort. It's a mortar which I intend to use to bombard that fort on the north end of the island. I designed it myself and had explosive shells specifically cast for use with it."

Wend was stunned. "Let me be sure I understand: You plan to put a charge of black powder in that, load it with an iron shell full of more powder, and then you intend to set it off? And you expect that it will stand up to the explosion and actually launch the shell?"

Arundel looked at the 'mortar' with pride in his eyes and responded, "Yes, sir. That is precisely what I plan. I have mathematically calculated the force of the explosion and reinforced the wood with those iron bands, which are of the proper width and thickness to withstand the pressure."

There was a deep silence as all the men looked at the device. Eckert, Newkirk, and O'beirne exchanged looks of disbelief. Finally Wend asked, "Have you performed test firings of this mortar?"

"Well, there wasn't time. I just finished it before we were summoned to travel up here."

Wend pointed to the mortar. "And you expect someone to stand near that and ignite it with a slow match?"

"I intend to perform the function myself, at least the first time it is fired."

Wend stared at Arundel. "I should like to watch that event—from a safe distance."

The young captain looked up at the weapon. "Yes, Captain Eckert. I would be most happy for you to observe."

Wend motioned to his officers. "Come. We need to make our plans for the crossing." Then he turned to Arundel. "It has been very *instructive* meeting you, sir."

"I look forward to seeing you when we begin the bombardment, Mr. Eckert."

Wend started walking back toward camp, his officers in company. Childers said, "Doe is considered quite brilliant by everyone." He laughed, "Both for his advanced mathematical skills and his ability with the ladies."

Wend looked at Childers and asked, "Is he married?"

"No, sir. But he told me he has been courting a young lady whose hand he intends to seek in marriage once this battle is over."

Wend walked for a couple of steps, then said, "Well, she'll have to find another suitor."

"Sir, I don't understand."

"Edward, I have never been to college. And I have no facility in higher mathematics. I'm just a gunsmith who learned his trade at the knee of a master. But I know one thing for sure: if the esteemed Captain Arundel touches off that mortar, he'll never be a married man."

CHAPTER EIGHTEEN

THE ASSAULT

Wend stood watching as the artillerymen prepared to begin the bombardment of the British forces. All the company officers and sergeants were with him near where the two gun batteries were emplaced. In addition, at Lewis's request, the company's riflemen were hunkered down in the woods just behind the artillery emplacements. The plan was for them to harass the sailors on the ships with long-range sharpshooting to distract their efforts to return fire.

Close by Wend were Jack Cowell and Edward Childers. The young ensign was excited and eager to see how Arundel and his guns performed. The wooden mortar was set up behind its own protective earthen redoubt.

Cowell pointed to the two large ships anchored in the channel. "We're fortunate in the direction of the wind; it's coming from the northeast. See how the ships are riding with their port quarters to us?"

Wend nodded. "Yes—why is that so much in our favor?"

"Well, that means it's hard for them to use their batteries against us effectively." He pointed to the *Otter* with her row of gunports. "If that ship could turn beam onto us and present her full batteries, she'd be able to rake us with heavy fire. But it looks like under the conditions, she'll only be able to bring a fraction of her guns to bear."

Childers spoke up. He pointed to the battery of large naval guns. "Bo says he is going to aim and fire the first gun himself. That will be the signal for all our guns to open up. He's going to concentrate on the ships with his eighteen-pounders while the battery of six-pounders will aim for the British fort at the narrows to the north."

Donegal, who was sitting with his back against a tree, asked, "What are those little boats with sails which are moving around the channel?"

Cowell looked back at the Highlander. "Those are tenders, or guard boats with crews of sailors, off the *Roebuck*. They're armed with little swivel guns, and they're meant to warn off any landing attempt or stop any boarding party we might send out against the ships. We may have to deal with them when we cross. That's a reason we're bringing up the bigger boats."

Childers called out, "Look, Doe is getting ready to fire!"

Wend turned his attention back to the eighteen-pounder battery. Arundel was standing behind one of the long guns, a slow match in hand. He bent over, aligning the gun on the *Dunmore*. First he sighted over the barrel and had the men on the adjusting ropes move the rear of the gun back and forth until he was satisfied. Then he attended to the proper elevation, putting in a wooden wedge to slightly lower the gun's muzzle.

Wend said to Childers, "The ships are only a little over two hundred yards away. He shouldn't have much trouble getting a hit."

Childers responded with a grin. Then he said, "Yes, sir. That's true. But he wants to send Dunmore a special message. He figures the Lord's cabin is at the rear of the flagship. He's trying to put the ball right into his windows."

Wend was skeptical. "Good luck with that."

Moments after he spoke, Arundel moved around to the side of the long gun and applied the match to the touchhole. A split second later, flames erupted from the muzzle and the gun jumped rearward.

All eyes focused on the *Dunmore*, watching to see if Arundel had scored a hit. Momentarily they had their answer. The cannon ball hit the side of the *Dunmore* just forward of the gallery windows. Wend could see debris flying upward and outward, then dropping into the water. When the cloud of material subsided, a large hole was visible in the side of the flagship.

A great cheer erupted from the mass of men along the shore and the artillerymen of the two batteries. Arundel doffed his cap in acknowledgment of the cheers. Then in a few seconds, the battery of six-pounders opened fire at the British fortification near the northern end of the channel.

As the gunners worked to reload the gun just fired, Arundel walked to the second eighteen-pounder and carefully aimed it, this time at the *Otter*. In a few moments, he fired it and scored a hit amidships on the upper bulwark of the ship. Wooden splinters flew in all directions. Another cheer resounded along the banks of the channel.

Now both batteries began their work in earnest. Wend could see that Arundel was concentrating the fire of the two long guns on the *Otter*, which was the most powerful of the ships, with its six-pounder guns. They were scoring hit after hit on the warship, which as Cowell had predicted was unable to return effective fire because of the way she was lying in the channel.

After the bombardment had been underway for less than a half hour, O'beirne came over and pointed to the *Otter*. "Captain. It looks like Arundel has stirred up a hornet's nest. Look at all the men runnin' around on the *Otter's* deck and climbin' up into the rigging. And there are signal flags flying from the rear mast of the ship."

Wend saw that Shay was right. He answered, "Yes, something's up—they're making preparations for some sort of movement. Perhaps they're going to try to use the sails to swing the ship into a better position for firing on our batteries." He turned to Cowell. "Is that possible with the current wind conditions?"

Cowell licked his finger and held it up to test the wind, then he looked at the flags flying on the ships. "The wind's not very strong and not really in a good direction for that." He made a face. "I don't know why they didn't moor the ships with a second anchor out from their stern—that would have held them parallel with the shoreline so that they could keep their guns bearing, whatever the wind or current conditions."

O'beirne interrupted. "Take a look at the *Otter*. There are men getting into the boats moored alongside."

Wend took out his telescope and eyed the side of the frigate. What he saw was puzzling. "They're manning all those boats." He turned to Cowell. "What could that mean?"

Cowell stared for a long moment. "Most likely they're taking them to shelter—maybe on the other side of the ship, so that they won't be hit by cannon fire."

O'beirne said, "Well, something's going on. All those little tenders are heading for the *Dunmore*."

Wend shrugged. "I don't understand what precisely they intend, but we have an opportunity here." He motioned back to the riflemen sheltering in the woods. "Shay, get them out into positions along the shore, and try to throw some balls at the *Otter*. Aim for the men in the rigging and the boats."

Shay looked skeptical. "Pretty long range—there'll be very little accuracy."

"Yes, I know. But at least we can distract the British and maybe hinder them in whatever it is they are trying to do. The sailors will not appreciate a shower of balls dropping around them."

Shay went back and brought the rifle squads up to the shore between the batteries, and they soon commenced firing at the warship and the boats.

Wend looked back at the *Otter* in time to see another shot from Arundel's long guns hit the side of the vessel. He scanned the ship and suddenly became aware of activity at her bow. He adjusted his glass and saw they were working with the anchor cable. In fact, as he watched, the end of the cable dropped into the water. Meanwhile, sailors were working to get some of the smaller sails set. Suddenly it dawned on him. The *Otter* was trying to get out of the channel and out of range of the guns! He turned to Cowell. "Unless I'm very wrong, the *Otter* is trying to escape our bombardment." He handed the waterman the glass.

Cowell looked over the ship with the telescope. "By God, sir, I believe you're right! Our fire is too hot for them! They're trying to get out of Milford Haven." He lowered the glass and pointed at the three masted vessel. "The current is taking them southward toward the mouth of the channel. I'll bet the boats are going to help guide her so that she stays in deep water and gets safely out into the Bay."

Wend said, "I can't believe the *Otter* is going to leave the governor and his ship to the mercy of our guns."

Cowell stared at the channel and the ships for a moment. "They're not! Look, some of the boats are heading for the *Dunmore*. And so are all the tenders. I say they plan to tow her out!"

Cowell was soon proven correct. The boats and tenders were rapidly hooked up to the *Dunmore*, and immediately the flagship slipped her anchor cable. The sailors in the boats began rowing and soon pulled the ship's bow around to the south. Then the ship slowly picked up speed, moved by the combined effect of the towing boats and the current. Arundel kept his battery firing on the two ships as they ponderously moved southward. But his artillery crew, mostly novices, were not as successful against the moving targets. Few shots hit the escaping vessels.

In less than a half hour, both ships were safely out of Milford Haven. Dohickey Arundel then concentrated the fire of his two guns on the small battery at the southern end of the island.

Suddenly Childers said, "Doe's going to try the mortar now! He pointed to the large battery at the north end of the island. "Earlier today he aimed it for that fortification."

Wend watched as Arundel approached the wooden mortar, slow match in hand. He said to his compatriots, "I think we're far enough away, but I recommend taking cover." They moved back inside the tree line and found shelter where possible.

Childers said, "I don't know why you are so worried. Doe has proven his abilities through the shooting of his long guns. A man who could calculate the flight of the balls so well has undoubtedly made accurate calculations about the explosive powder in the mortar."

Wend answered, "Yes, I'm sure he is a genius. But just in case, get down, Edward."

Childers complied. Wend looked back at the mortar just in time to see Arundel make a final check of the weapon, then carefully apply the match to the touchhole.

The result was spectacular. There was a massive explosion, with shards of wood flying at lightning speed in all directions. A flying splinter impaled itself in the tree behind which Wend was crouching. Others flew through the wood, but luckily no one was injured.

Doe Arundel was blown into the air and smashed against a large stump about twenty feet from the mortar. His clothing was flaming.

Wend and many others jumped up and ran to where Arundel's remains lay against the stump.

Edward Childers was the first to arrive. His face broke into a look of absolute horror, then he dropped to his knees and vomited onto the ground.

Wend arrived and saw what had led to his repulsion. Arundel's body was burnt and blackened by the flames of the explosion. In fact his clothing was still on fire in places. But that wasn't the worst of it. His left leg had been amputated just below the knee, and his right hand was also missing. In his upper torso were impaled two large, fire-blackened splinters of wood. The eyes were wide open and staring into oblivion, showing stark white against the blackness of the charred skin of the face.

Childers was on his knees before the body, sobbing. Meanwhile, Donegal and Baird arrived. They were carrying Arundel's severed leg and hand, which they dropped beside the body.

Donegal said, "At least all the parts can be buried together."

Wend put his hand on the ensign's shoulder. Childers looked up, tears running down his cheeks. "I'm sorry, sir. I couldn't control myself."

Wend said, "Don't be ashamed. I reacted the same way when I saw a man die like this. It happened to be my best friend, twelve years ago, and he was burnt to a crisp defending his family from a Shawnee war party. Their cabin was burned down. He was lying by the door, where he had been guarding, and his mother and sister where inside burnt to death like him."

Joshua added. "Yeah, I thought Eckert was going to spit out his very guts, he was puking so hard." He looked around at the crowd standing by the body, then said, "Now listen, Ensign, you are gonna see worse in this damned war. You'll see bodies torn asunder by cannon balls and cut to pieces by bayonets. So steel yourself to it. You're gonna have to live with it all."

Childers looked up at Wend and shook his head. "I don't understand how Doe could have been so wrong. He was so brilliant and educated in mathematics at a French university. How could he have miscalculated?"

Wend was trying to think of a diplomatic, soothing answer for the ensign when O'beirne spoke up. "Hell, lad, we all get things wrong and do stupid things." He looked around, then said, "But to my experience, really stupid things get done by people who are so educated they figure that they can't be wrong. *Arrogant* stupid can be the worst kind."

Childers rose to his feet and wiped his face. His face was red with extreme rage. "Damn you, O'beirne! How dare you speak of the dead in such a tone, with a smile on your face?" He reached out to grab the Irishman.

Wend stepped forward and took hold of the ensign by his shirt, pulling him away from O'beirne. "Now listen, and listen *well*, Edward. I know you admired Arundel. But here's the truth of it: *he made a big mistake.* He did a magnificent job directing the artillery here today. He drove away the British ships, and his guns have done damage to the batteries on Gwynn's. If he had left it at that and not insisted on firing his damned mortar, he would be recognized as the hero of the day. But Shay is right. Arundel ignored the cautions of people with common sense because he had to prove the brilliance of his mind and his invention. So instead of being a hero, he's dead and in the end will be remembered only for his pigheadedness."

Wend released Childers and spoke to all the other officers and sergeants standing around. "Now all of you, listen to me! Soon we will be making an assault on the island. We will be taking on a foe who may outnumber us when we land. We must work together, or we will face defeat and death. So Shay and Edward, let us put this argument behind us."

He had just finished when General Lewis approached. He took a moment and looked at Arundel's remains. He shook his head. "I told him last night that infernal wooden mortar wouldn't work." He sighed. "Somebody take care of the body and give him a decent burial."

Wend said, "Mr. Childers here knew Arundel in Williamsburg. He will direct the detail."

Lewis nodded, then turned to Wend. "Eckert, this bombardment is having a definite effect on those shore batteries on the island. But it's getting toward evening. We'll hold off the crossing until early light tomorrow, then we'll make the assault. So everyone get a good rest tonight and make sure you are ready to take to the boats at dawn on the morrow."

—⚏—

Wend stood at the edge of the water at first light, looking out on Milford Haven. He couldn't see much of the channel, because a dense morning fog lay in sheets over the water. There was little wind, so the mist was hanging motionless over the surface.

Behind him, sitting or kneeling, were the men of the Frederick County Light Foot. Interspersed among them were thirty or so canoes, which they had just finished retrieving from the grove of woods where they had been stored. Grounded at the shoreline were three pulling boats, all of which had been captured from the British during the recent raid. Jack Cowell and other watermen had just brought them up from a cove to the south and beached them along the shore.

The watermen were hunkered down around the boats, ready to launch when the command was given.

Cowell approached Wend and said, "We're all ready to go when you give the word, Captain."

Wend replied, "I'm waiting for Lieutenant Colonel McClannahan, of the 7th Virginia, to order the assault. He's in command of the crossing and action on Gwynn's when we get there. Last I saw, he was up with Posey's company, which will cross to the north of us."

Cowell waved toward the channel. "Well, he better do it soon. It will be better if we can cross before the sun burns off this fog—Dunmore's men won't know we're coming until we get close to shore. I don't fancy bein' shot at, and it's hard to take cover while you're rowing a boat."

The waterman had barely finished speaking when McClannahan arrived. He called out, "All right, Eckert. Let's get moving." He motioned northward. "I'll ride across with Posey. Now remember your orders: Taking that southern battery is your first priority. Drive off any of the enemy you meet, and get there fast."

Wend nodded. "I understand."

"After you get the battery, swing around and sweep along the bayside coast. We'll be doing the same from the north, and we'll aim to link together at the Grymes House, which is on the northern part of the shoreline of the island." The colonel thought a minute, then said, "Our pickets saw some movement of Dunmore's troops last evening after the bombardment ended. Possibly small bodies of solders moving through the woods. Then, after full darkness, there were lights seen to be moving about. We think they may have been repositioning to better receive an assault. It seems likely there will be resistance at points along the island's shore when you try to land."

Wend said sardonically, "Sir, you are the bearer of such good news."

"I'm just telling you what we believe has occurred." He looked over at the island. "Good luck, and we'll meet at the Grymes House."

Wend answered, "Right, sir. See you there." Then he called for his officers. When they had arrived, he said, "All right, we're going now. Move across as fast as possible. Keep some men in each canoe ready to fire if necessary when we get near the far shore. And use the fog to your advantage as cover." He pointed to where the battery was intermittently visible through the fog. "As we planned, I'll be landing with my detachment nearest to the fortification. We'll advance directly to its rear and try to keep the garrison contained until the rest of the company arrives. O'beirne and Childers, with their groups, will go inland until they are clear of all the little coves and bays, then hurry south to join us. Finally, Newkirk, with the northernmost detachment, will be the rear guard. He'll pivot south and round up anybody who has straggled or otherwise gotten lost. When everybody is assembled, we'll assault the battery from the rear."

Everyone nodded. Joshua grinned and spoke up. "Shit, Wend, we been talkin' about it all night. Everyone knows what to do. Let's just do the damn thing."

All the officers laughed.

Wend sighed. "Joshua's right. Let's put the boats in the water and get it done."

Donegal called out to the company, "All right, pick up your canoes and get them into the water. And watch you keep your firelocks dry!"

The men had been sitting on the ground, the tension building as they waited for the crossing. Now, at the order to move, they sprang into action. In mere moments all the boats were in the water, and they began boarding them and pushing off.

Wend, Donegal, Baird, and Billy climbed into Cowell's boat, and the sailors pushed off, then jumped in themselves and took their places at the rowing thwarts.

Wend called out to the men in the canoes carrying his detachment: "Follow me and stay close so we can land together. And no shouting or other noise!"

With the canoes following, Cowell steered the boat toward the island. He said to Wend, "The current is moving southward; I'll have to keep adjusting course to the north, or we'll land too close to the battery."

Wend nodded. "With this fog, its good we've got the help of you and the other watermen, or this whole crossing could turn into a real mess."

Cowell didn't respond directly but said, "I'm aimin' to put you ashore about two hundred yards north of the battery. There's a firm piece of land there for you to land on, and you'll have an easy march through the woods to the battery."

Wend looked up and saw that the island's shore, specifically a pine-scrub-covered spit of land, was becoming visible through the mist. He thought, *That would be a perfect place for marksmen to be hiding.* He steeled himself for a volley of shots.

Cowell had the oarsmen increase their pace, and Wend saw that the following canoes matched their speed. The faster they got to the beach, the shorter their time of exposure to shooters.

But to his surprise, there was no burst of fire from the woods; there was only stillness and silence. And then, perhaps thirty feet from the shore, the boat abruptly grounded. Wend almost fell, saving himself only by holding on to the thwart.

Cowell called out from the stern, "All right, Eckert, that's as far as we go! Time for you to start wading."

Wend looked around to see the canoes, with shallower draft, sliding past them. He turned to Joshua and Donegal. "Well, let's go!" And with that he climbed over the gunnel and dropped into the water, which he found to be just above his knees. He started moving toward the shore.

By now most of canoes had also grounded, most of them almost at dry land. The men, firelocks in hand, were rapidly debarking and heading into the trees.

Wend ran across the narrow beach and into the scrub. He looked around. Everyone was out of the boats. He called out, "Donegal, get everyone to form a defense line and take cover!"

Quickly the men sheltered behind trees and bushes, and Wend surveyed the woods in front of him. All was quiet. Clearly they had landed in a place where no British troops were waiting. After a moment he called out, "Joshua! Schreiber! Take four men and scout ahead to the battery! Scout it out, and the rest of the detachment will follow!

Joshua, a wide grin on his face, rose to his feet. "Well, now this feels familiar! Come on, Schreiber, let's take a little walk!" And with that he led off, followed by the rifleman and four privates selected by the corporal.

Wend ordered the rest to form a column and begin a cautious march toward the southern point of the island. He turned toward the water and waved to Cowell, who was with his crew on the beach; they had their firelocks in hand.

The waterman waved back and called out, "We'll keep the boats ready in case them British chase you off the island!" He laughed heartily.

Wend shouted back, "Don't make a wager on it! Alive or dead, we're here to stay!" Then he turned to Donegal. "Let's head for the battery, Simon!"

They advanced cautiously through the bush. Although it was early, Wend could sense it would be a hot day. He looked upward and could see that the sun was strong and beginning to dispel the ground fog.

It took less than ten minutes for them to reach the end of the island and tree line behind the battery. Wend had expected Baird to be waiting at that point to brief him about the enemy's strength at the battery, but neither the scout nor the others were anywhere to be seen. Puzzled, he motioned for the column to go to ground and wait. Then he said to Donegal, "Come on, let's go take a look."

The two walked until they were at the edge of the scrub and could see the battery. And there they met with a shock.

The battery was there. Four field guns on their carriages, protected on the channel side by an earthen work, with gaps for the guns to fire through. Behind that was a campsite.

And everything was deserted. The camp had been hastily abandoned, with discarded items of equipment lying around. The coals of cooking fires dotted the area. Some tents remained in place.

But there was no human occupation whatsoever. None except for Joshua and the other men of the scouting party, casually lounging at the top of the earthen berm, taking in the sights.

Donegal said, "The bastards have flown the coop!"

Wend replied, "You're right!" He stood up and walked out of the trees. Joshua sighted him and called out, "Hey, Sprout! What took you so long!"

Eckert walked through the camp to where the scouts sat. "Did you see anyone as you approached?"

Baird shook his head. "Nary a one. And they be gone a goodly time." He pointed to the camp. "Them fires is just cold ashes." He pointed to one of the field guns. "They're all spiked. Them British left in a hurry."

Wend thought a moment. "Those lights McClannahan told me they saw last night—that wasn't the British making preparations to receive us. By God, they were pulling out."

Joshua nodded. "Here's the way I figure it: That bombardment convinced them we would be coming over afterward. They didn't have enough men to defend the whole shoreline of the channel, so they pulled back inland."

A realization came over Wend. "You're wrong, Joshua. They didn't just pull back; I think they've left the island."

Donegal said, "You don't think they've withdrawn to a point where they can defend? I'd be thinkin' they could consolidate all their men to make a stand at the plantation homestead down the shoreline."

Wend shook his head. "If they were doing that, Simon, they'd have taken the cannon with them. No, I'm wagering they're gone and in a hurry. And they left the field guns here because they didn't think they had time to get them out to the ships."

Just then Jensen pointed to the tree line and called out, "Here comes O'beirne!"

Wend looked around to see the Irishman leading his detachment onto the beach. Then he was immediately followed by Childers and his men.

O'beirne came up to Wend and waved his hand to take in the berm and the guns. "Looks like you didn't leave anything for us to do."

Wend pointed out toward the Chesapeake and explained the absence of the British. Then he said, "Have your men sit down and rest. We'll march to meet with McClannahan once Newkirk gets here."

In about ten minutes, the first lieutenant appeared with his column. He approached Wend, who told him the situation.

Then Newkirk said, "We had no problems, and like you wanted, we advanced along a wide front to make sure to gather up anyone who was lost in the bush. There weren't any such, but we did stumble onto something else. Something quite grim."

Wend cocked his head. "Indeed, what was that?"

"A pair of bodies, rotting and partially eaten by varmints. By the remnants of their uniforms, they were Africans of Dunmore's Ethiopian Regiment." He paused, then continued, "From what I could read from the corpses, they died of smallpox. I suspect they were dragged there by their mates or other loyalists. Perhaps before they were even dead." He looked away for a moment and repeated, "It was a grim sight."

Wend sighed and responded. "I wonder how bad the pox is among the blacks. Many of them just off the plantations won't have been inoculated or built up any resistance to the contagion."

The lieutenant responded, "You're right, and I have no doubt we'll find more victims."

Wend turned to Billy Wood. "How far is it up to the plantation house?"

Billy responded, "Not far, sir. A little more than a mile. But along the way is the hospital where they treated the people with pox, sir. And then just before you get to the house is the camp of the King's Loyal Virginia Legion, where I spent most of my time."

"All right, Billy. Now take your standard and walk out to the very tip of land beyond the battery, and try to attract Jack Cowell's attention back at the boats. I want to give him a message to take back to Lewis about what we found."

449

"Right, sir." He headed off for the beach.

O'beirne, who had climbed to the top of the earthen rampart to look around, called out to Wend, "Now my dear captain, if you would care to join me, there's something you'll be interested to observe."

Wend made his way to the earthwork and climbed to the top. "And just what is it you want me to see, Shay?"

The Irishman pointed out onto the Bay. "Now take a look at that, my captain. As pretty a little ship as you would like to see."

Wend shaded his eyes and looked at the vessel, which was quite near and under full sail, moving swiftly toward the British anchorage. "I'm not familiar with ships. I know that those with two masts are often called 'brigs.' Is that what that is?"

"Now, my captain, I've been around enough to know what they call some of these little ships. And that, my dear Wend, is not a brig, but what the sailors call a 'schooner.' You can tell because of the lowest sails on the two masts. You see they are what they call 'fore and aft' sails instead of square sails."

Wend replied, "I'll take your word for it."

"Now, I would also point out the flag flying on the after mast. That's the ensign of the Royal Navy, so it's quite clear that another vessel has been added to Lord Dunmore's squadron."

Wend watched silently for a moment. "I wonder where she has come from?"

O'beirne looked at the vessel. As he did so, a string of small flags was hoisted on the after mast of the schooner. "Well, wherever it might be, she seems quite excited. It appears her captain has something to say." He shrugged. "But we'll never know what that might be."

—⁊⁊⁊—

The flagship *Dunmore* rode to her anchor at the south of Hills Bay, just off the northern shore of Gwynn's. Nearby were HMS *Roebuck*, the *Fowey*, and the *Otter*. Behind the naval ships were the scores of vessels that bore the loyalist refugees of the floating colony. The *Raven* had anchored in close proximity to the naval vessels.

Northcutt and Lieutenant Proctor carefully descended the ladder and boarded the *Raven's* gig.

Proctor ordered the cox'n, "Make for the *Dunmore!*" Immediately the oarsmen took up their rhythmic beat and pulled the boat rapidly toward the flagship. As they approached, Proctor pointed to the ship's stern gallery. "Look, Northcutt, they've taken a hit! Obviously by cannon fire. The gallery windows are all smashed!"

Barrett saw what the lieutenant was pointing to, then swept his eyes over the length of Dunmore. "They've suffered other damage. I see the marks of shot in other places along the hull."

Proctor nodded. "Aye, clearly there's been a fight. The rebels must have brought up artillery. But then we'll find out about that soon enough when we board her." He motioned toward the *Roebuck*. "Before we left the *Raven*, I received a message that Hammond is meeting with Lord Dunmore aboard the flagship, so we can simultaneously inform both about the results of your mission."

Northcutt didn't answer; his mind was busy going over the unwelcome news that he had to present to Dunmore and trying to formulate the words that would put the adverse decision of General Howe in the most acceptable light for the governor.

In a few minutes, they were alongside the flagship and ascended the ladder to the main deck, where they were greeted by the master, Jacob McCabe. Immediately he escorted them to the entrance of the great cabin. The master opened the door and entered, then momentarily returned, accompanied by Harbridge.

The counselor smiled and said, "Barrett, your arrival is truly timely! And I hope you have favorable news, for to be honest, the governor is in dire need of it."

Northcutt, a sense of foreboding rising within, asked, "Good God! What has happened?"

"We've been forced to withdraw from the island. Things are in complete disarray. We are meeting to discuss the way forward."

"I don't understand. What could have happened?"

"Against all expectations, the rebels brought in heavy guns and drove the *Dunmore* and the *Otter* out of the channel. They couldn't fight back because the direction of the wind was keeping them from using their batteries to full effect. And then the rebel artillery caused major damage to Fort Hammond at the northern end of the island and also bombarded the battery at the south end of the channel. Afterward, it became clear they were massing to assault the island, and we simply did not have enough troops to repulse them." He sighed. "So the governor ordered the abandonment of the island overnight."

"Not enough troops? When I left, our land forces would have amounted to five or six hundred. Surely, if they were arrayed on the shoreline, that would have been enough to repulse a boat attack, when the enemy would be vulnerable while crossing."

"I'm afraid the situation has deteriorated since your departure. The Ethiopian Regiment has been decimated by the smallpox and other contagions. That left only the Queen's Loyal Virginians and the 14th Foot, plus a few marines and artillerymen to man our defenses. It was simply impossible to resist."

"You forgot to mention my regiment."

Harbridge and McCabe exchanged glances. The counselor said, "Northcutt, it is my sad duty to inform you that the King's Loyal Virginia Legion has essentially ceased to exist."

Stunned, Barrett stared at Harbridge. Then he exclaimed, "God above! But what could have happened?"

"A strong force of rebels intercepted them while they were raiding ashore for provisions. They attacked the regiment while it was broken up into small details. Most were killed or captured. All that is left is about twenty men, mostly those who didn't go on the raid, and of course, the camp followers." He paused a moment and looked into Northcutt's eyes. "And I regret to inform you that Major Welford was killed in the action."

Northcutt stood speechless.

After a few moments, Harbridge said, in a gentle tone, "Barrett, I realize you are grieving at the loss of your friend and trying to absorb the shock of your battalion's destruction, but I must ask, is your news from Halifax favorable? Is Howe sending reinforcements? It is superfluous to say we are in dire need of them."

Northcutt shook his head. "The answer is not as we would desire. I will explain Howe's position directly to Lord Dunmore. He will not be happy." He waved to the door. "Let us not delay longer."

Harbridge led the way. Northcutt was surprised to see that the room was crowded with people standing around the governor. Hammond was there, as were Ellegood of the Queen's Loyal Virginians and Byrd of the African regiment. And of course Harbridge and McCabe had entered with him. He was also surprised by the presence of Sir Robert Eden, the governor of Maryland, along with his wife, Caroline, who was seated in a comfortable chair next to where her husband stood.

Barrett was shocked to observe the condition of the cabin. The shot had done major damage. One whole side of the gallery windows had been demolished and was now patched with wood and canvas. Some of the furniture—including most of the chairs—had been smashed and the wreckage piled in one corner. Northcutt thought, *That explains why everyone is standing.* Then he noticed that the governor's china cabinet was splintered, and although an attempt to sweep the deck had been made, he could see shards of porcelain lying near it.

Dunmore was the only one beside Caroline who was seated. He was semireclining in a chair with his right leg bandaged and resting on a stool. A glum expression resided on his face. But then he saw Northcutt, and his face brightened.

"Ah, Barrett! You have arrived. I can say we have missed you."

"Sir, would that I could have returned more swiftly. And I am greatly distressed to see the turn of events which has occurred."

Dunmore stared out one of the remaining windows. "Yes, the last few days have most definitely not been in our favor." He waved around the room. "Those damned rebels, with their artillery, managed to put the very first shot into this cabin." He gritted his teeth. "You can see the damage to the gallery. And damn them, they destroyed the china! The elegant serving china which has been in the palace at Williamsburg for decades and we took such care to save when we departed." He sighed deeply. Then he pointed to his leg. "And a large splinter of flying wood did this to me."

Northcutt said, "I am deeply sorry for what has occurred."

Dunmore put his hand to his forehead, and his countenance turned to pure grief and he took a deep breath before continuing. "But the worst, Northcutt, is that the same ball took the life of young Dudley Fellows."

Shocked, Barrett exclaimed, "Fellows is dead? I am so sorry to hear of that, sir. He was a promising young man and quite devoted to you."

Dunmore sighed. "Indeed he was both of those things. And now his earthly remains are consigned to the waters of the Chesapeake. So sad."

A silence hung over the cabin for a long minute. Then the governor said, "We are glad to see your return, Barrett. And what news from Howe do you bring? We pray it is positive in our cause."

Northcutt looked around the room. All eyes were on him, and the silence hung heavy in the cabin."

"My lord, General Howe is most gratified at your defiance of the rebels and assured me that he realizes the importance of Virginia in the effort to hold the colonies for the king. He was quite impressed with what our limited forces have been able to accomplish."

Dunmore's face brightened. "So he is indeed dispatching troops? Pray tell, how many? And when will they arrive?"

Barrett sensed an air of anticipation around the room. All were looking at him optimistically, except for Harbridge and McCabe, who knew the truth. He said quietly, "My lord, I regret that is not the case."

"Are you saying that Howe has refused to send us reinforcements?'

"Yes, my lord."

"And precisely why? I am certain you made a strong case. Does the man not know the military value of this colony to the Crown's cause? It is the geographical center of the colonies and a major producer of foodstuffs and material to the rebels!"

"Sir, he understands all those things very well. But he pleaded the limited resources he has been allocated by the king and the fact that military operations already in progress or planned demand all the assets he possesses." Northcutt looked around the cabin. "Specifically, he pointed out the expedition to South Carolina which is even now in progress and his own imminent descent on New York City. He says Washington is gathering strong forces and he requires every battalion he can muster to overpower him."

Dunmore pushed himself up in his chair and grimaced in pain as his wounded leg moved. "Damn it! How can he deny us a *single* battalion. That is all we asked for to hold the colony! For God's sake, one miserable battalion to hold the largest colony! And Northcutt, did you not point out to Howe that if we hold Virginia, the rebels will be cut off from the south? That alone should have swayed him!"

"I pointed out the situation on maps, Your Lordship. But it seems that Howe and his other generals feel that if they take Charleston, both Carolinas and Georgia will be taken out of the war without the need to immediately subdue Virginia. But even more consequential, Howe considers New England the heart of the insurrection and he feels cutting it off from the middle colonies by taking New York will force the rebels to come to terms." Barrett held out his hand toward Dunmore and said, "So Howe is agreeing with your idea that the colonies must be split from each other, but his focus is on doing it in the north, sir."

Harbridge spoke up. "And what does Howe expect us to do while he is subduing New York?"

Northcutt replied, "A very relevant question, Aubrey." He looked at Dunmore. "Sir, he directed that you hold your position on Gwynn's Island, as a presence representing the Crown. Given the shortage of military resources, he directed that you abstain from activity in the field. He felt that once he had carried out his plans in the north, the rebel congress would have no choice but to begin serious negotiations. You, at your station at Gwynn's, would be well positioned to return to Williamsburg when peace and royal governance were restored."

Harbridge sighed. "Well, of course, now that we have withdrawn from the island, that strategy is no longer viable."

Dunmore stiffened and slammed his right fist down loudly on the small table beside his chair. "Aubrey, that is off the mark! The fact is, we are still here in the Chesapeake, and by God, here we will stay!" He looked around defiantly at the assemblage. "There are other places we can occupy in the tidewater. Places even more suitable for our purposes and more secure from rebel attack than Gwynn's!" He turned to Hammond. "Andrew, send out the *Otter* to find such a place! The site of our base may change, but we shall carry out the spirit of Howe's orders and keep the Union flag flying! We cannot waste a day!"

Dunmore's outburst was met by silence from all in the cabin. After a prolonged moment, Captain Hammond cleared his throat and began to speak.

"My lord, we all admire the spirit of your words. Were we able, we would choose to take the action which you advocate." He paused and took a deep breath and exchanged glances with the other military officers present. "However, we have jointly conducted a review of our readiness, and we agree that we cannot recommend continuing the campaign here in Virginia."

Rage crossed the governor's face. "What? What! I do not believe what my ears are hearing. We *must* carry on in the king's name! Virginia cannot be left to these deplorable rebels!"

"My lord, the truth is our forces are seriously depleted. My ships have been constantly in service for over a year. All are in need of dockyard time to renew cordage and canvas, and in some cases they require being hove down for bottom cleaning. Even routine maintenance is lacking because so many sailors have been detached to man ships of the refugee fleet. The *Fowey* is due back in England for extensive work. And all are short on naval stores and provisions. Moreover, our land forces are greatly diminished. We lost most of our field artillery and all the accumulated supplies from raids in the precipitous withdrawal from the island." He looked over at Captain Leslie and motioned for him to speak.

Leslie said, "Sir, my detachment of the 14th is essentially unfit for further service. We were sent here when we were due to return to England to be reorganized and rerecruited after long years in the West Indies. When we reported, there were more than one hundred and fifty men in the three companies. Now I can muster less than one hundred fit for duty. In other words, our companies are at less than a third of their full strength. And our clothing and shoes are near worn-out, sir."

Byrd of the Ethiopian regiment spoke up. "My lord, I have no more than two hundred of the Africans fit for duty and more are going down due to the pox every day. I believe that toll will increase now that we are back aboard ship. Moreover, sir, the number of Africans coming in to enlist has fallen off drastically. We received very few in the last raids. I'm afraid the word has spread of the high number of deaths, and they are dearth to join us."

Dunmore turned to Ellegood of the Queen's Loyal Virginians. "And what about your battalion?"

Ellegood said, "We are, as always, ready for service to you and our home of Virginia." He shrugged. "However, my men have become discouraged at the lack of recruits from the colony who are willing to join them in the service. And we have had a high frequency of fevers, from the climate on the island, and this is detracting from the number of men fit for duty."

Hammond resumed speaking. "Sir, I must reemphasize that our ability to support you is in rapid decline. I fear we don't have enough troops to hold any significant land, whether an island or a peninsula." Then he held up a finger. "And all this is not to mention the condition of the refugees on the ships. Quite frankly, their physical condition is declining because of the difficulty in providing adequate foodstuffs. And fever and the pox continue to run through the ships. It is clear that even finding a base which will suffice to our defense needs will not rectify their condition and provide for their welfare." He shook his head. "In summary, I believe, and most sincerely recommend to you, that we should withdraw our forces from Virginia. And having done so, we must find a suitable place for the loyalist refugees to reside until their property is restored to them by the action of Howe's army."

Frustration and anger spread over Dunmore's countenance. He gritted his teeth and finally spoke. "I can hardly credit what I am hearing! Officers of His Majesty's army and navy ready to give up the most important colony in America to a mob of rebels! I refuse to countenance this! We must recruit, reform, and reorganize. That is our way forward!"

Hammond stiffened. "Sir, until now I have supported you in every way possible. But my recommendation stands. I feel we must, at least for the present, withdraw from the contest. And if you order me to remain in support of you, I will accept that order, but I will report my condition and recommendation to the flag officer commanding the North American station who has the ultimate decision as to the employment of my squadron."

Dunmore gripped the arms of his chair and pressed down as if attempting to rise. But the effort obviously caused severe pain in his leg, for he immediately gave up the attempt. His face turned red, and he looked like he was about to explode.

Harbridge interrupted before the governor could give voice to his anger. The counselor looked at the naval captain and raised an eyebrow as a signal. "Captain Hammond, I believe it would be beneficial for you and the other officers to withdraw and enable the governor, his immediate staff, and Governor Eden to discuss the situation in political terms." He added in a conciliatory tone, "We appreciate your submitting your frank assessment of the situation from a naval and military perspective and will inform you of the governor's final decision."

Hammond made a small bow and said, "Of course I understand there are considerations beyond the purely military aspects of the situation which must be taken into account. We will stand by to receive the governor's decision."

And with that, all the officers and the master, McCabe, filed out of the cabin.

Dunmore sat fuming in his chair, the muscles in his face working. Northcutt expected him to explode in rage at the military men in an instant. He thought, *I must do something to calm him, to cool his anger so that he can think rationally, to realize that the game is over.* Barrett exchanged glances with Harbridge and realized the senior counselor was of the same mind. He prepared to speak to Dunmore.

But before he could do so, Caroline Eden looked up to her husband and said, "Robert, pour a large cup of rum for the governor." Eden quickly did so, and meanwhile the lady rose from her chair and said to the governor, "John, you need a drink, and you need to consider things rationally. Above all, you cannot give way to your anger, justified though it may be."

Caroline took the cup from her husband and walked over to where Dunmore sat. She leaned close to him and put one hand on his shoulder and handed him the drink with the other. Then she said in a calm, soothing voice, "John, you have performed miracles here in Virginia. No one could have achieved more given these difficult circumstances and the limited resources you had at your command. Everyone must recognize what you have done against all odds—General Howe, the secretary of North America, Lord Germain, and, I am sure, even the king himself."

She bent down closer to Dunmore. "But John, we must recognize that for now, withdrawal from the colony is the only viable option. It *really* is beyond your control. To continue fighting with exhausted troops and with dedicated loyalists suffering on their ships from disease and lack of nourishment would be doing great disservice to those who have sacrificed so much to support you. You cannot ask more. It is now not for you to make the decision; events have made the decision for you."

She stood up and looked down at Dunmore.

Dunmore took a long drink from the cup, then bowed his head and covered his face with a hand. He remained in that pose for a long minute as silence in the cabin deepened. Then he looked up at the lady beside him and said in anguished tone, "Caroline, my heart wrenches in pain at your words, but I must admit that you are right." He took a deep breath and looked around the cabin. "Gentlemen, we must make plans to withdraw from Virginia." He shrugged and asked, "But where shall we go?"

Northcutt quickly responded, "Sir, I say you and your staff must sail for New York. That is now the center of events, and you can volunteer your service to Howe. After all, you have been governor of *both* Virginia and New York. You have intimate knowledge of the two colonies and familiarity with many people of substance and influence in both. I believe the general will be most grateful for your counsel."

Dunmore brightened and said, "Yes, yes, Barrett, that makes sense."

Northcutt continued, "And being close to Howe, you will be well placed to resume your duties here in Virginia once our army has humbled the rebels. And we can rest assured there will be much work to do to put governance back in proper order."

Dunmore was nodding as Northcutt spoke. He turned to Harbridge. "Aubrey, what do you think of that?"

Harbridge quickly looked over at Northcutt, then turned back to the governor. "Yes, Your Lordship, I think New York is the proper move. If nothing else, it will give you a chance to ensure that Howe clearly understands what strong efforts you have made to hold Virginia and your ideas for bringing it back to Crown control."

Dunmore put his hand to his chin. "But what shall we do with all the refugees? We would do a disservice to General Howe if we were to present him with thousands of people needing food and shelter at the same time he must support a large army."

Harbridge held up a finger. "I have had some discussions about this development with both Hammond and leaders of the loyalists."

He paused and cleared his throat. "I believe the loyalist fleet should sail for Florida. There is considerable room for them to establish a settlement, perhaps near Saint Augustine, and they are agreeable to that. And Hammond is prepared to provide a naval escort for them."

A flash of anger crossed Dunmore's face. He said in an irritated voice, "So you have been planning all this behind my back? As if you had already decided we would withdraw from Virginia?"

Northcutt feared that the governor would burst out in rage at his senior adviser. He quickly said, "My lord, Aubrey was clearly doing his duty to *you*. It is his role to be prepared for any contingency. I am sure it was in that vein that he explored these measures."

Harbridge quickly agreed. "Sir, Barrett is quite correct. I must be ready to provide you with options for whatever eventuality arises."

Caroline Eden defused the situation. "John, that sounds like a reasonable solution."

Dunmore thought a moment more, then nodded. "Yes, it makes sense."

The lady looked over at her husband. "And now, with your permission, Robert and I will go to our quarters and allow you gentlemen to your work."

Dunmore nodded. "Of course, Caroline, we do have much to do."

Robert Eden took his wife's arm, and the two left the cabin.

After they had departed, Harbridge said, "My lord, with your agreement, I shall go and brief Captain Hammond and the other military officers regarding your decision. Then they can make necessary preparations for the coming movements, which I urge we undertake immediately."

Dunmore waved toward the door dismissively. "Yes, yes, Aubrey. Please take care of it. The fleet should sail as soon as possible." He pointed to Northcutt. "Remain, Barrett. I have something to discuss with you."

When they were alone, the governor held out his cup and said, "Pray, fetch me another. I need it this day. Rum eases the pain." He added, "It eases *both* the pain in my leg and that in my soul."

Barrett handed Dunmore the cup. "You said you had something to discuss?"

The governor took some of the rum and momentarily closed his eyes as it went down. "Indeed, Barrett. Are you aware that Welford was killed in the battle which destroyed your regiment?"

"Harbridge told me."

"Did he tell you how Welford died?"

"Not specifically. I assume he was shot by musket fire from the enemy's force."

"You assume wrong. He was killed by aimed pistol fire by Wend Eckert."

Northcutt, who had been pouring himself a rum, stood frozen at the sideboard, cup in hand. Then he said, "By *Eckert*? But he died in the raid on his farm. Welford saw him hit in the head."

"Welford was *wrong*. The man *somehow* survived. I found out a few days ago from the Crosswells—the couple who own the plantation from which the raid was launched. Eckert and a band of men burned out their property and made them refugees. They came here for succor and carried a message for us from Eckert himself."

"A *message*?"

"A *threat*. He told them to say that he was coming with a hundred men at his back for revenge against you, Welford, and myself. And two days later, your battalion was wiped out and Welford murdered."

"My lord, how can we be sure it was actually Eckert?"

"There was a witness. A marine who was with Welford when he expired. Welford, with his dying words, told him to tell me that Eckert did it." He took a sip of his rum. "So Eckert is alive, he is here, and he is the captain of a company of foot."

Northcutt took a deep drink, then exclaimed, "Damnation! The man seems to have more lives than a cat. We set him up last year for an ambush by Richard Grenough and his men, and instead it was they who disappeared. And now Welford is gone."

"That is precisely what is on my mind. I tell you, Barrett, sleep has been difficult. I have a persistent dream of awakening to find him by my bedside with knife and pistol in hand. He stands there with that damnable stone-faced expression of his, evil in his eyes, silently preparing to strike. It has visited me every night since I heard about Welford."

"We shall have to be on alert, sir. But keep in mind, we will be in New York, in the midst of an army, in a time of war. Probably close at hand to General Howe himself. I hardly think we must fear Eckert when we have thousands of soldiers around us."

"That is my only solace, Barrett."

Northcutt suddenly felt the need to be somewhere where he could think. He said, "My lord, I beg permission to leave you for now. I should see what arrangements Harbridge has made with Hammond for the withdrawal."

"Yes, do so. And I do need some time alone to ponder the situation."

Northcutt left the cabin, ascended the companionway to the main deck, and walked over to the rail. There he stared out over the waters of the Bay, beyond which he could see Gwynn's Island. As he watched, he caught sight of a column of rebel soldiers marching purposely along the beach of the island. He could see the Grymes house through trees and wondered if they were heading there.

As he watched, Lieutenant Proctor joined him. "Well, Colonel, I'm off again! Hammond wants me to track down General Howe, whether he's still in Halifax or New York by now, and apprise him of what has occurred here in Virginia."

Northcutt extended him his hand. "Well, good luck in your mission, Wesley. Thank you for all the courtesies you extended to me on your ship. Perhaps we'll see you in New York."

The young captain grinned. "Stranger things have happened." Then he turned and was off to descend into his boat alongside.

Northcutt mentally focused on the future. He pushed thoughts of Eckert and his threat to the back of his mind. He was actually delighted about the prospect of returning to New York. It was where he had started his career in the colonies and had extensive property. Moreover, he knew many influential people in both the city and the colony. Once the war was concluded, which he expected would occur in a few months, he could work at repairing his financial situation, which frankly had deteriorated during the years in service to Dunmore. But beyond repairing his wealth, there was a more important reason he was excited about the return to New York and becoming associated with Howe's army. For there, in the ranks of a certain Highland regiment, was the auburn-haired beauty who more than anything else had dominated his thoughts since Halifax. He had despaired of encountering Mary Fraser again, but now Dunmore's loss was his gain, for once with the army, he would find some way to locate, court, and ultimately win the favors of the beguiling lady who had become his ideal.

CHAPTER NINETEEN

DRUMS AT WILLIAMSBURG

Wend led the company, walking in open order, along the beach. As expected, it was deserted. They saw no sign of the enemy.

They had gone a few hundred yards when Billy pointed to a grove of large pines. "Mr. Eckert, the hospital is behind those trees. There were a lot of people with the pox and the fever in there. It's a couple of old huts, and they put up some canvas canopies to provide shade for the people, 'cause they couldn't all fit into the buildings."

Wend said, "We'd better go take a look." He signaled for Newkirk to hold the company in place. Then he called for men who had been inoculated to raise their hands. He knew that Billy, Joshua, and Donegal had had the procedure, but he didn't know who else in the company had done so. Only a few men held up their hands. O'beirne was one, so Wend took Billy, Baird, and the Irishman along with him. They left the beach and walked up a path toward the hospital.

After a few steps, the hospital came into sight. There were numerous people under the canvas tarps, lying on blankets on the ground. Some were obviously alive, while others lay very still. Wend noticed something else: the unmistakable smell of death.

They had nearly reached it when an African woman appeared in the door. She had a bucket in her hand and had her hair up and wrapped in a cloth. Even at a distance, Wend realized she was of stunning appearance: narrow, high-cheekboned face, tall, willowy body, and most startling, a lighter than normal complexion.

O'beirne said, "Hello! What do we have here?" Then he said in a quiet voice to Wend, "There's undoubtedly more than just a wee bit of white blood in her veins."

Wend nodded. "Yes, but I wonder what she's doing here?"

Suddenly the girl looked up and stared at the soldiers, and then a great smile spread across her face. She shouted out in obvious joy, "Billy! Billy Wood! My God, you've come!"

Billy dropped the standard and ran for the girl. "Meli! I thought I'd never be see'n' you again! I thought you'd left with Dunmore! Praise God you're here!"

He arrived at the door; the girl dropped the bucket and threw her arms around him and laid her head on his chest.

O'beirne cleared his throat, looked over at Wend, and said, "My esteemed captain, I daresay our Billy hasn't told us *quite everything* that happened while he was on the island."

Wend looked at the Irishman and grinned. "Shay, you've just proven yourself a master of the obvious." Then he turned to the couple. "Billy, you need to tell us who this is and why she's here."

Billy disengaged himself from the girl. "Mr. Eckert, she was the cook for the officers of the King's Loyal Virginia Legion. The morning I landed, she took me on as a servant for the mess. That's how I was able to find out about the raid."

O'beirne raised an eyebrow. "But the question is, why did she help you? Did she know you were spying for us?"

"Not at first, Mr. O'beirne." Billy bit his lip, and tried to figure the words to explain.

The girl put her hand on Billy to quiet him. "I'll tell them." She stepped in front of Wend and said in good English, "Captain, my name's Melinda. I was a house servant and cook at Hallowell Plantation, which lies between the Piankatank and Rappahannock. When the British raided, I went with them."

Wend said, "I understand. You wanted your freedom"

"Yes, but not the way you are thinkin'." She pointed to herself. "My ma got pregnant with me by the master when he was young. And now the master's son, by the mistress, was startin' to lookin' to have his way with me."

O'beirne interjected, "Ah yes, a chip off the old block."

Meli nodded. "Yes, sir. And I didn't want none of that. So I went away with the British." She shrugged. "When they learned I was a maid and a cook, they put me in charge of cookin' for them."

Wend asked, "But why did you help Billy?"

"I saw what was happenin' to the blacks who joined the British. They do their fightin', but the British can't take care of them when they get the pox, and they end up dying. I decided to bide my time and try to leave if I got a chance. Then Billy came along."

Wend asked, "How did you find out he was on Virginia's side?"

"He said he was a house servant from the Blakewell Plantation; it be close to ours, and I been there many times, and I ain't never seen him there. So I knew he was makin' up a story, and when I told him that, he told me the truth."

Wend said, "You took a chance, Billy."

"No, sir, it weren't much of a chance. From some things she'd already said, I realized she wasn't happy with the British. And she helped me listen to what Welford and his officers were sayin' about where the raid would go. Fact is, she's the one who heard them say it would be to the south near Mobjack Bay. And then she helped me get down to the beach unseen so Jack Cowell could pick me up. She kept the sentinel they had watching the shore busy."

Shay said, "It appears she's a woman of many talents."

Wend thought of a question he should have had earlier. "Melinda, why didn't the British take you with them to their fleet?"

"Cap'n, they was in such a hurry to get off the island, there was so much confusion everywhere. I just slipped off. Ain't nobody lookin' out for one African girl. I was runnin' down the beach from the camp when I saw the surgeon and his mates comin' up from the hospital, hurryin' to catch a boat to the ships. That's when I realized they had deserted the hospital." She shrugged. "I hid in the pines from them, and when they'd passed by, I figured I'd do what I could for the sick people. That was last evening, and I been here ever since."

Wend looked at the girl. "You're a brave woman, Melinda. Aren't you afraid of contracting the contagion?"

She pulled up the left sleeve of her shift to show the unmistakable scar of an inoculation. "The master, he had his whole family and all the house servants inoculated. I was just a little girl then."

Wend said, "But in any case, by staying behind, you have to know you'll be taken into custody and sent back to your plantation. It means a whipping for you at the very least."

The girl shrugged. "I just know'd I didn't want to go with the British. I figured I'd get away somehow."

O'beirne said, "That was a forlorn hope. The only way off the island for her is by boat, which means she'll be taken into custody."

Melinda sighed. "I wasn't thinking of that. I just didn't want to go with the British."

Billy looked at Wend with beseeching eyes. "Sir, Mr. O'beirne is right. There be only one way she can stay free. She got to come with us."

Wend stared at the lad. "What do you mean?"

"Sir, she could be a cook. She's really good. At least till we get up north. Then she'd be safe."

O'beirne grinned. "Now that's an idea. Much as I appreciate Mrs. Flannagan's efforts, her cooking leaves more than a wee bit to be desired. Perhaps we should give Miss Melinda a chance to cook for the officer's mess."

Wend thought quickly. "I'm sympathetic. But we'd be harboring a runaway slave. The law has strict punishments for that."

Billy looked like he would cry. "But sir, you can't make her go back to the plantation! There'd be a whipping! And worse, the young master would just be biding his time!"

Baird, who had been leaning up against a tree and listening, said, "Hell, Wend, we've broken more serious laws than that. And besides, with this war on, nobody's going to be suspicious of an African woman cooking for a military company. There ain't much chance of it bein' a problem."

Shay looked at Billy and then at the girl. "Now, my good captain, I might suggest to you that we owe the two of them a favor, seein' as how they helped us take down Welford and his lot, which as I recall, you were most keen on doing. If anyone starts asking about her, I'll claim she's my servant. That will put an end to it."

Joshua, who had left to explore the hospital and its surroundings, came back from behind the two shacks. "Wend, there's something here you should see." He pointed to the woods behind the shack.

Wend followed the scout. The others came along behind. He had gone about twenty steps through the scrub to where Joshua stood. And then he saw it.

The ground under the trees was filled with bodies. Some just dumped in piles, more lined up in irregular rows. Most bloated almost beyond recognition. Clouds of flies hovered over the lines. As they approached, the stench became unbearable. Everyone pulled their handkerchiefs out and put them over their nose and mouth.

Wend said, "Good God! There are scores of them."

Meli spoke up. "No, sir. I'm figurin' there be near two hundred. I ain't too good with numbers, but that's the way I count. I walked out there to see if any was alive, 'cause one of the men back in the hospital said some of them had been dragged out while they were still movin'."

O'beirne had walked along one of the rows of bodies. "Some of these bodies have been here a while. The animals and birds have been feeding on the flesh."

All of them stood staring in silence, profoundly shocked by the sight of it.

Finally Billy broke the silence. He said in an angry voice, "They ran off and joined the British because they thought they was goin' to get their freedom. But the British used them, and then in the end, all they got was death."

Wend stared at the lines of decomposing bodies. And as he did so, a thought came to him. He turned to Billy and said, "You're wrong about that, lad. They *did* get freedom. Just not the *kind* they expected. What they got was freedom from the pain and hardships of life on earth. Here at Gwynn's Island, they found the freedom of eternity."

They all stood in silence for long minutes, looking at the rows of victims, trying to grasp the enormity of it. Then, one by one, they turned and left, leaving the remains to the silence of the pine scrub.

The sun was low in the west, and the company was bivouacked in front of the Grymes house, along with Posey's company of the 7th Regiment. Colonel McClannahan was using the sitting room of the mansion as his office. Wend and his officers were gathered around a fire, finishing up their supper. The men were doing the same around squad fires.

Just as they were finishing, Childers pointed down the beach. "Look, Captain, people coming up the beach."

Wend stared. There were several soldiers, but the one in the lead looked familiar. Joshua, sitting at the next fire, was the first to recognized the man. "That's Lieutenant Daniel Collins. Lewis's aide."

Wend realized Baird was correct. He said to Newkirk, "I'll bet he's carrying orders from the general."

Collins and his party approached, and seeing Wend, called out, "Captain Eckert! Where is Colonel McClannahan? I have dispatches for him from General Lewis."

O'beirne said, "Good guess, Captain."

Eckert waved to the house. "He's inside. Probably having supper, like we are."

Collins nodded, then hurried up the steps and through the front door.

Newkirk had been staring out at Dunmore's fleet. "Wend, it looks like the ships are getting ready to sail."

Wend stood up and scanned the fleet. He could see boats being hoisted aboard ship and seamen in the rigging, working on the sails. On some ships the furled sails had been loosened in preparation for getting underway. As he watched, the little schooner that he had seen arriving earlier in the day hoisted her anchor and set sail, heading down the Bay.

As he was watching, there was a shout from the front veranda of the house. "Captain Eckert! Colonel McClannahan wants to talk to you!"

Wend looked at Newkirk. "Reese, I don't like the sound of this."

The first lieutenant grinned. "It can't be good news."

Wend rose, walked over to the house, and entered. He found McClannahan, Posey, and Collins in the parlor. The colonel was sitting at a table reading papers; the other two were standing.

When Wend entered, McClannahan looked up. "Eckert, I've got orders for you from General Lewis." He held up a piece of paper. "You need to break camp immediately and get back to your boats. You are to recross the channel and join with Lewis."

"I don't understand, Colonel. What's the urgency?"

"Lewis, the artillery, and most of the troops are leaving for Williamsburg tomorrow. The 7th Regiment is to stay here and guard the island. You are to march with Lewis's column."

Wend was puzzled and disturbed. "Colonel, we were formed to join Washington's army. Our presence here was to be only until the emergency was over, and then we were to march northward. In fact, our year of enlistment doesn't start until we report to Washington. I protest these orders and maintain that we should be allowed to leave for New York."

McClannahan reddened and said in a heated tone, "Damn it, Eckert. You are in the army now. In *Virginia's* army. I follow Lewis's orders, and so will you. In any case, you will depart here as soon as possible to cross Milford Haven and join Lewis. And if you want to protest to him, that's your business! Now I suggest you return to your company and carry out the orders."

Wend sighed. "All right, colonel. I will do that. But what about the smallpox hospital? I reported to you that some of my company are down there taking care of infected people. We can't just leave them."

McClannahan looked up at Collins. "Lieutenant, I sent a messenger to request a surgeon and medical orderlies. Have you heard anything about that?"

"Yes, sir. The general's response is in one of those dispatches. A surgeon and his men were getting ready to cross the channel when I left. They may already be at the hospital."

McClannahan looked back to Wend. "There you are, Eckert. Rouse your men and head back to the channel, and pick up your people at the hospital along the way."

"Aye, sir." And with that, Wend turned and walked out of the parlor.

Less than an hour later, the company was marching down the beach. Shortly they arrived at the hospital. Joshua walked up the path to the hospital and came back in a few minutes with Billy and Melinda. However, Melinda was unrecognizable as a woman. She was dressed in a man's outfit of clothing, which had been put together from the contents of various backpacks among the company and included a floppy hat loaned by Joshua, who was for the moment hatless.

Wend asked Billy, "Any problem about Melinda with the surgeon or his mates?"

"No, sir. They hardly looked at us, and soon as they saw all the sick people up there, they got right to work."

All the officers and sergeants had gathered around. Wend looked up at the sun, which was low in the sky. "All right, gentlemen. Let's press on to where the boats are and get across the channel. And then perhaps we'll learn more about what the esteemed General Lewis has in mind for us."

———ɯ———

A line of gleaming carriages, each pulled by matched teams, stood before the entrance walk to the Governor's Palace, waiting to discharge their passengers. Andrew Horner pulled the wagon in behind the rearmost rig. Wend sat on the seat beside Horner, wearing his dress blue Virginia uniform. The other three officers of the Frederick County Light Company, dressed in like fashion, rode in the wagon bed.

Shay O'beirne remarked, "Well, as judged by the quality of our conveyance, we seem to be the poor cousins of the guest list. I am quite surprised we weren't directed to drive around to the back of the building." He looked at Newkirk and Childers. "Damn shame we couldn't manage a carriage of some kind."

Wend turned around. "Shay, if you were so worried about appearances, perhaps you could have arranged the hire of a more elegant vehicle out of your own pocket."

"Well," responded the Irishman, a broad grin on his face, "unfortunately, it happens that at the moment my purse is somewhat embarrassed."

Newkirk said, "As are we all. Hence our travel in Horner's work wagon."

Wend, changing the subject, asked Childers, "Edward, while you were at William and Mary, did you have the opportunity to attend entertainments here at the palace?"

The ensign grinned. "Of course, sir. I have many pleasant memories of dancing in the grand ballroom. It is quite a sight all decorated and lighted with hundreds of candles."

Shay said, "Of course you did." He winked at Newkirk. "And if I might ask, can we expect to find interesting and attractive young ladies present?"

"Certainly, sir. Williamsburg has many charming and virtuous girls." A mischievous look came across his face. "Of course, sir, I'm aware that your taste runs more toward willing tavern maids, such that young Jenny Croft you were keeping company with at the Golden Buck just before we left Winchester."

Eckert and Newkirk exchanged winks at the lad's baiting of O'beirne.

Shay coughed into his hand and replied with aplomb, "Tavern maids have always been a specialty of mine. However, I am also considered quite handy with ladies of more elevated position. And I've never particularly valued virtue in the fair sex."

Newkirk said, "Indeed, I don't believe Shay has ever let the marital status of a woman stand in the way of his attentions."

Edward grinned broadly at O'beirne, "Well, I'll wager you will have a chance to demonstrate your prowess to us tonight, sir. I would be quite surprised if numerous unattached ladies were not present for this affair."

"Gentlemen," responded the Irishman, "I will point out that, regardless of their situation, I only direct my attentions to woman who are *willing*, who constitute a special category."

Newkirk laughed and said, "Then we shall have to see how you fare tonight."

Shay looked behind them. "Now, lads, will you look at that line of rigs. There are more carriages arriving every moment. It seems that all of Williamsburg is turning out for this ball."

Wend said, "Well, it's not every day we celebrate independence from Britain and the birth of a new nation."

Newkirk nodded. "Yes, this will be a night to remember."

Wend added, "Did you see how attentive the men were when I read that declaration from congress? They listened closely to every word. And they were genuinely excited at the end. Those were honest cheers when I finished reading."

Newkirk nodded. "Well, it certainly clears up any ambiguity about what we are fighting for."

Meanwhile, they had arrived at the front entrance, and Wend slipped down to the ground. The others jumped down from the rear of the wagon. Wend turned to Horner. "Wait for us at the nearest tavern. We'll find you there when this is over."

The young gunsmith smiled. "Don't hurry yourself on my account."

They entered the palace, walked through a foyer, then down a hallway that opened into the ballroom.

As they passed through the entrance, Childers remarked, "This ballroom was not part of the original mansion. It was added years later."

As they emerged from the hall into the ballroom, Wend reflected that the ensign had been quite right about the elegance of the room. Wend had never seen so many candles in one place. Despite the fact that many more people were flowing in, the place was already crowded. An orchestra was playing, and servants were circulating with refreshments on trays.

They had no more than entered when a feminine voice called out, "I don't believe it! Edward Childers is here!" Wend saw a group of five or six young girls, dressed in beautiful clothing, standing together. The call to Childers had come from a lovely young lady with golden locks. Next to her stood a brown-haired girl who waved to Childers and said, "Edward, you must come join us! We haven't seen you for months!"

The ensign, grinning ear to ear, looked at Wend. "Sir, may I?"

Wend motioned toward the girls. "Of course, join your friends."

The lad was hurrying toward the bevy even before Wend had finished answering.

Shay said, "Well, our young ensign seems to have returned to his natural habitat."

Newkirk replied, "Would that he knew his way around a drill field as well as the ballroom."

Wend grinned. "Well, let's remember he did his part at Mobjack Bay."

Then a server presented a tray of wine glasses to the officers, and O'beirne picked one up and said, "And now, my dear captain, I believe, with libation in hand, I shall perform an exploration of the room and its guests, particular those of the fairer persuasion."

In a moment Newkirk also went off, having seen an acquaintance at the other side of the room. Left to himself and feeling very much out of his element, Wend sighted a table with plates of hand foods. He walked over, picked up a small plate, and took a sample of the fare. He stood at one end of the table, looking around the room as he slowly ate.

Then he was surprised to see Jean Moncure Wood, James's wife, who was talking with a young woman. Relieved at finding someone familiar, Wend finished off his plate, set it on a small table, and walked over to greet Jean.

Jean saw him as he approached and, smiling, said, "Wend! I was hoping to encounter you tonight."

He replied, "I'll admit I'm surprised to see someone from Winchester."

"Well, I came down to be with James, since he's spending so much time here. And in any case, I love Williamsburg and was glad for the excuse to journey here."

Wend said, "I must ask you if you have seen my family recently."

"Rest assured, all is well with everyone. And just before leaving, I spent an afternoon at Glengarry Plantation with Anna and Peggy. We had a grand time visiting together." She reached out and put her hand on the arm of the dark-haired girl. "And I must introduce you to Miss Dorothea Dandridge, of Hanover County. You should be aware that Dorothea has just become betrothed to our new governor, Patrick Henry." She paused a moment and said, "Dorothea, Captain Eckert is a very good friend of James and myself. And he commands Frederick County's company of light foot."

Wend, struggling to say the proper thing, bowed slightly and said, "It is my pleasure to meet you, Miss Dandridge. The governor is a very fortunate man to be marrying such a lovely lady."

Dorothea nodded to him and said, "Well, thank you, Captain. I am looking forward to living here in Williamsburg. I've visited many times, but the thought of taking up residence, particularly in this mansion, is exciting."

Wend, looking over the girl closely for the first time, suddenly recalled James Wood's comment about Dorothea resembling Peggy. He couldn't resist remarking, "It may be a bit forward, Miss Dandridge, but I must say you remind me very much of my wife when she was your age."

Dorothea cocked head and said, "Indeed, sir?"

Jean quickly looked at the girl and then said, "I hadn't thought of it, but he is quite right! You have the same raven hair and slim figure. And you should feel very flattered, Dorothea, for Peggy Eckert is considered one our foremost beauties in Frederick County."

Wend quickly said, "As is Mrs. Wood."

Jean laughed and said, "You're very gallant, Wend, but your words are quite welcome."

A little embarrassed, Wend asked, "Miss Dandridge, when are the nuptials?"

Dorothea raised her hands, palm up. "That is entirely up to my father. He and Mother are trying to determine a proper date. But one thing has been decided: it won't be until sometime next year." She waved a hand, taking in the mansion. "And actually, time is needed to get this place ready for us. Dunmore left the residence upstairs in quite a disarray when he fled."

Wend was about to speak when Lieutenant Collins appeared at his elbow. Jean said, "Oh hello, Daniel. It's nice of you to join us."

Collins said, "My regrets, ladies; would that I could dally with you. However, I am here to fetch Captain Eckert to meet with the governor. He and General Lewis have some business to discuss with him."

Jean's face broke into visible irritation. "Business? Tonight of all nights, when we are celebrating our independence from the Despot of London and the final flight of Dunmore?"

Dorothea laughed. "I have already discovered that the business of government is never very far from Patrick's mind."

Wend gave in to an impish urge. "Miss Dandridge, perhaps when you marry the governor, you will be able to distract him from such constant attention to matters of the state. I, for one, would appreciate that."

The girl laughed again, and a devilish look crossed her face. "Captain, I assure you that I am already working on that object."

Wend bowed to the ladies and followed Collins. He led on back out the entrance hall, then took a right into a small room. Collins knocked, then opened the door and ushered Wend inside.

There sat several men at a table. Patrick Henry was at one end, flanked on the right by Andrew Lewis. Also at the table was James Wood. There were three other men, none of whom Wend had ever seen before. Smoke from pipes and cigars floated in the air. Collins walked over to a side of the room and leaned back against the wall.

Nobody offered Wend a seat, so he remained standing near the door. It remained quiet for what seemed a long time, the men all staring up at him. Wend, feeling uncomfortable, took the initiative. "Good evening, Mr. Henry. Congratulations on your election to the governorship. And congratulations also on your engagement to Miss Dandridge. She is a lovely young lady. You are a fortunate man."

Henry nodded. "Thank you, Eckert. I heartily agree with you about Miss Dandridge. However, we didn't bring you in here for social discourse."

"I rather thought you hadn't. Every time you ask to speak to me, I find myself either in trouble or about to be sent off on some distant and disagreeable service."

Wood chuckled openly, Henry smiled crookedly, and Lewis covered his mouth with his hand. The three other men at the table displayed puzzled looks. Collins was expressionless, his arms folded in front of him.

Henry said, "Well, Eckert, I see you do have a saucy mouth. However, on this occasion you are essentially correct." He looked around at the others, then said, "I'll be direct with you. Washington is preparing for a major fight at New York City. The British are massing a huge expedition there. The Continental Congress and Washington have been beseeching us to send all the troops we have in hand. Most of the rifle companies we sent last year ended up with the campaign in Canada. As a result, there are virtually no Virginia troops with the main army. And until now we have not been able to comply with their request to send more because of the need to fight Dunmore."

Lewis added, "Dunmore has sailed from the Chesapeake, destination unknown. And now that he's gone, we can release our regiments for service outside the state. But it's going to take time for them to get fully outfitted and to march the long distance to New York."

Wend asked, "So how does the Frederick County Light Company play in all this? I remind you, we were recruited for service with the main army but were sent to the tidewater temporarily to combat Dunmore."

Henry pointed at Wend with his cigar. "Exactly, Eckert. And so now we are going to send you onward as rapidly as possible to join Washington." He motioned toward Lewis. "The general says your men are the most-disciplined and best-trained troops in our forces."

Astonished, Wend stared at Lewis with questioning eyes. "General Lewis said *that* about my company?"

"Indeed he did. He cited your work in the Gwynn's campaign, particularly how you smashed a large contingent of troops who were raiding in the Mobjack Bay area."

James Wood interjected, "Wend, Frederick County is proud of our company. You have rightly earned the reputation as the best in Virginia's army."

Henry said, "Yes, and since you are our *premier* company, we intend to send you north to be representative of the quality of Virginia's forces and as the vanguard of a significant contingent of troops to soon join the army."

Wend said, "Well, Governor, if you wanted my company to get to Washington rapidly, why did you order us down here to Williamsburg from Gwynn's? We could have been well on our way by now if we had marched north directly from the island. If I'm now to march north, you've just added a good many days to our journey."

Lewis, who had been drawing on his pipe, exhaled and said, "Eckert, it's my pleasure to say you're wrong in this case. We're going to speed your arrival in New York much faster than you could anticipate. And you won't have to march north from here."

Henry said, "That's right, Eckert. When you march, it will be southeasterly. A very short distance southeast. You'll be going to the port of Yorktown. And there you will board ship. We're sending you by sea to Philadelphia. A relatively short voyage. And that will put you only a few days' march from New York City."

Wend was momentarily speechless. Then he asked, "What about the Royal Navy? They might have something to say about your plan. I don't fancy the idea of spending the war as a prisoner."

"The Virginia Navy—yes, Eckert, we do indeed have a small one." Henry took a deep drag on his cigar and then looked around the room with a broad grin on his face. "And I take pride in claiming the title of its founder." He turned back to Wend. "The Virginia Navy, Captain Eckert, has found that the British have withdrawn most of their warships to support the movement of troops from Halifax down to New York. For the moment the seas off Virginia are largely clear. A Virginia warship will escort your transport, and once you get around the Virginia Capes, it's only a short distance up to the Delaware Bay, where there's even less chance of being intercepted."

Wend responded, "I pray you are right on this occasion." Then he thought quickly. "I need provisions. We've used up most of those we brought from Winchester. Once I have those, we'll be ready to go to Yorktown."

Lewis said, "We have stocks in a warehouse here, and they'll be delivered tomorrow."

Henry said, "And tomorrow you will also receive your written orders and dispatches to Washington from me. Dispatches explaining how many troops we can send and when they will arrive."

Wend contemplated all he had been told. "If all that happens as you say, my company will march early morning the day after tomorrow."

Lewis nodded. "We could ask no more."

James Wood spoke up. "Wend, we are confident you will be of great service to Washington and continue to burnish the reputation of Frederick County and her men."

Wend responded, "That is my greatest desire." Then he looked around the room and said, "If there's nothing further, I will return to my company and begin preparations."

Henry waved in the general direction of the ballroom. "Well, Eckert, I admire your eagerness. But at least allow yourself to enjoy tonight's celebration."

Wend, who had his hand on the doorknob, turned back to the group and said, "We're celebrating words on a piece of paper which proclaim our independence. That *decision* is certainly something to celebrate. But the words will not mean anything unless we drive out the British army, and that will be a grueling, bloody challenge. And the outcome is by no means certain." Wend paused and looked around at the men around the table, all of whom were staring at him. "So Governor, you celebrate; I will prepare."

Henry raised his eyebrows, looked around at the other men with an ironic smile on his face, and responded, "In that case, we have nothing further to discuss. And Godspeed to you and your company."

—𝔪—

Dorothea Dandridge awakened in her bed in a second-floor room of Weatherburn's Tavern and Inn. She glanced out the window and saw that the sky was showing the first hint of light. She sighed deeply, pushed herself up on an elbow, and nudged the man asleep beside her.

"Patrick, Patrick! It's coming on light. Servants will be up and moving around soon. It's time for you to get back to your own room."

Henry came awake and said sleepily, "Yes, my dear, I know." He sighed deeply. "Would that we could dispense with these clandestine visits."

"Next year, Patrick, next year. After the ceremony there will be no need. But do hurry."

"I have found that the servants here at the inn are quite discreet. I am too old and disinclined to be rushed. I will go but fully intend to preserve my dignity in the matter."

The governor sat up, stretched his arms, and then got to his feet. He walked over to a chair where his dressing gown lay and shrugged himself into the sleeves.

Just at that moment, the profound stillness of early morning was broken by the beat of drums, barely audible but growing in loudness.

Dorothea sprang out of bed and ran around to the window. "Soldiers? Marching through the town at this time? Who could that be?"

Patrick had to think a moment, then he smiled. "Unless I'm far wrong, *that*, my dear, is our first contingent of troops to depart for New York. They are marching to Yorktown to take ship."

Dorothea quickly put on her night coat, pulled up her long black hair, and hurriedly pinned it into position. Then she went over to the window and threw it open. She looked up toward the sky. "The light is getting much brighter." Then she said, "Oh, Patrick! I see them coming down the street!"

Henry joined her. He noticed that she was right: the light was quickly spreading across the sky; he would indeed soon have to get back to his own room. However, he felt compelled to linger to watch the troops pass.

"That company," said Dorothea, "looks very impressive in their hunting shirts and black hats. And they all wear their accoutrement in the same way. All very proper." She watched for a moment longer. "And to my eyes, the way they march is as good as any redcoat company I've seen on parade. All so different from all the rest of our troops."

"That, my dear, is the Frederick County Light Foot. Their company sergeant is a Scotsman named Donegal, who was in a Highland regiment for many years. He has indeed drilled these men to the standard of regulars."

She stared at the marching soldiers for a moment. "And those men in the ranks—Patrick, see their faces: there's a look of hardness about them I'm not familiar with."

"Ah, yes, my dear Dorothea. They are western-border countrymen. Men of Ulster and German heritage. Hunters and farmers steeled by years in the forests and the field." He pondered for a few seconds. "In literature, down through the years, they are referred to as 'the sturdy yeomanry.' And mark my words, they, and men like them, will be the soul of our army."

She pointed toward the women and children walking along behind the company. "My God, Patrick, I wonder what life is like for them. I cannot imagine how I would fare, living as they do."

Henry said, "I learned, in my brief time as colonel of the 1st Regiment, that the camp women are indeed a strong and independent breed. They're as hardy as the men. They march long miles with them, sleep in the open, prepare meals for the messes, wash and sew clothing, and nurse the wounded in battle." He laughed. "And you do not want to cross them in any way, because they will instantly find a way to make you aware of their displeasure." He looked at his young fiancée. "I fear, my dear, although you are quite strong and adventurous in your own way, you would never prosper in their life."

"Patrick, I should never try, and I do hope fate never puts me in their situation."

Then her eyes ran over the column, and she pointed at the man who rode a powerful black horse at the front. "I know that man—that's Captain Eckert. I met him at the ball. Jean Wood introduced us."

"Yes, and just what did you think of him?"

"He was very polite, but I must admit a little intimidating."

"Intimidating? Interesting that *you* should say that. How so?"

"It was his face. It's handsome, but his visage is quite unexpressive and somewhat fierce-looking; he has what they call a stone face. You would say he was cold, if it weren't for the eyes." She was silent for a moment. "But for the eyes—they are lovely and very expressive. That was the only part of him that reacted to conversation, except for the corners of his mouth, which would turn up just a bit when he smiled. Indeed, the eyes compensated for his face and actually gave me a feeling of warmth about him." She considered for a moment. "I think he's very thoughtful and intelligent. But also quite determined in his demeanor, for lack of a better word." She reflected a moment, then said, almost to herself, "His look was very much like a sailor I knew once, in Fredericksburg—a merchant captain—who also had that look in his eyes, and he was indeed a very determined man."

Henry grinned at her. "You and a sailor, my dear? I find myself jealous."

Dorothy smiled at her fiancé. "A mere passing fancy, I assure you."

Henry grinned, "Of course, my dear." Then he looked out the window at the company. "Eckert is all that you say—particularly determined—and I must admit that he has been very useful to me. Last year he stopped a conspiracy by Dunmore to raise the Indians against the border settlements which could have been very bloody and harmful to our cause. And just a few days ago, he conducted a daring battle in which his company eliminated a large part of Dunmore's force, an outcome that was undoubtedly instrumental in compelling our former governor to give up the fight so easily." He again looked out at Eckert, now well past their window. "Quite frankly, I am convinced he is the most effective officer presently in Virginia's army. Men follow him willingly, and when assigned a task, he will not give up until he completes it, even in the face of the most daunting challenges. Lewis, who, for some reason I don't fathom, has little warmth toward him, grudgingly believes the same thing. Eckert doesn't know it, but among the dispatches he is carrying, I have included a private letter to Washington which conveys my feelings about him and recommends that the general place him in a responsible position, a position of independent command if possible."

"That is a very high recommendation indeed." She stared out at Eckert for a moment. "Do you suppose he will rise to become a general?"

Henry exclaimed, "Good God, I hope not!"

Dorothea stared at him in puzzlement. "But my dear, I do not understand. You just said he was the best officer we have. Why would you not want him to rise to a high rank?"

"Dorothea, my dear, practically *anyone* can serve as a general, if he has a modicum of common sense. A general can plan and issue orders, but there must be hard, practical men under them who get things done. Those men are too important to be generals. Without them the army won't work. And that is precisely the kind of man Eckert is."

Dorothea again stared out at the passing column and the man at its head. "Yes, I think I understand what you are saying."

Henry said, "And there's one other thing that recommends Eckert to me. Something I consider very important."

"Oh, and what would that be?"

"His overwhelming desire is to get this fight done and then return to his family, his farm, and his workshop. James Wood tells me his greatest pride is in his craftsmanship and doing a job well. He has no wider ambition beyond that. James tells me that the Winchester Committee of Safety essentially had to bribe him to accept a commission."

"Patrick, you frequently puzzle me. Why is a man's lack of ambition so important to you?"

"My dear, think on it a moment: I am a politician, and I readily admit to having a *great* amount of ambition. I intend to leave my mark on this state and the nation which is even now being created. And it is comforting to me that a man of many talents like Eckert has no similar desire. As time goes on, I am convinced, he will continue to be useful to me and this state. But successful as he may be, I can be confident that he will never seek to rise to the status of a rival or political adversary." He smiled conspiratorially. "Because, my dear girl, I already have far too many of those here in Williamsburg."

Dorothea smiled in admiration at her fiancé. "Patrick, how *clever* you are. I am so fortunate that I am to marry a man of such intelligence and vision. I only hope I have the talent to help you reach the success you desire."

"Of course you do, my dear. I saw that when I first laid eyes on you. I am certain we will move forward as one and climb the heights together."

Dorothea rose up on her toes and kissed her man on the cheek and then said, "Indeed we will. And now you *must* go before someone sees you leaving my chamber, or we shall have a monstrous scandal on our hands. And that will *not* do at all for Virginia's most famous orator and new governor." She went to the door and opened it.

Patrick Henry grinned at her words and bent down to lightly kiss her forehead. Then he slipped out the door, leaving Dorothea smiling to herself. She pulled her housecoat tight around her against the chill of the morning as she stood there, recalling the intimacies of their night together and contemplating what would undoubtedly be a most promising future.

The End
Of
Freedom At Gwynn's Island

HISTORICAL NOTES AND ACKNOWLEDGMENTS

The opening period of the Revolutionary War in Virginia is one of the most sparsely covered subjects in the history of that conflict. Although Virginia was the largest and most wealthy colony, the story of the campaign to eject the royal governor of the colony, Lord Dunmore, is often treated as a footnote to the war. But in fact, there were several consequential actions that could have changed the course of the revolution if they had played out as Dunmore planned. An earlier volume of this series, *Pursuit Through Chaos*, provided a fictionalized account of how Dunmore's plot to start an uprising of the Ohio Indian tribes, supported by loyalist militia and the British Army, was thwarted. This novel has striven to provide an account, entertaining but largely accurate, of the final act of Dunmore's campaign, wherein he attempted to set up a base of operations from which an offensive campaign could have been carried out.

Notes and comments on the historical military aspects of Dunmore's campaign.

The Loyalist Ground Force. The Governor's order of battle on the ground generally amounted to the following:

> (1) Royal Marines from the ships of Hammond's Royal Navy squadron augmented by an extra detachment sent by General Gage. Total available for field operations at any time about 100–120.

(2) Detachment of the 14th Foot, three companies, not exceeding 150 regulars at any point.

(3) The Queen's Loyal Virginia Regiment, effective strength in the vicinity of 100–150 men.

(4) The Ethiopian Regiment. Although 2000 or more Africans were liberated and joined the ranks, the effective strength ranged only from 200-500, and usually toward the lower number due to the ravages of Smallpox and other contagions. The former slaves, having lived most of their lives isolated on plantations, had scant natural immunity.

Thus Dunmore's typical field strength was never more than 400-600, and often less than that. However, it is safe to say that Dunmore's force, in modern terms, "punched above its weight." Its significance was recognized by Patriot leaders. The following shows how Washington felt about the danger of Dunmore. In a letter to Richard Henry Lee, he wrote:

> "If, my Dear Sir, that Man (*Dunmore*) is not crushed before Spring, he will become the most formidable Enemy America has—his strength will Increase as a Snow ball by Rolling; and faster, if some expedient cannot be hit upon to convince the Slaves and Servants of the Impotency of His designs. I do not think that forcing his Lordship on Ship board is sufficient; nothing less than depriving him of life or liberty will secure peace to Virginia."

Unquestionably, the most important effect of Dunmore's force was to tie down several battalions of Virginia troops from marching to join Washington's main army for what would become the New York City campaign. Prior to the defeat of Dunmore, only two Virginia rifle companies had joined Washington, and these had been sent in the Summer of 1775. In the Spring of 1776, Washington was desperate for every trained soldier he could muster as he prepared to face the large and growing British expedition which was forming to take the city. He was sending correspondence to the various colonies, and particularly Virginia, requesting battalions to round out his force. In the end, because of Dunmore's presence, Virginia's troops were not able to join the Continental Army until the New York City campaign was in its last stages, and they were of no material assistance to the commanding general.

The Royal Navy's Participation in Dunmore's Campaign. The Royal Navy squadron which was assigned to assist Dunmore was obviously the cornerstone of his operations. Their participation represents an excellent example of how sea power can effect and in truth enable events on land. The squadron provided the mobility and firepower support which allowed the movements of Dunmore's ground forces and to a significant degree the manpower and seamanship expertise which made his floating colony possible. While I have specifically focused on three ships in the narrative, HMS *Roebuck*, *Fowey*, and *Otter*, others were active at various times during the campaign, arriving and departing as events progressed. Of course, the dispatch schooner HMS *Raven* is fictional, but is typical of the vessels used for such service during the period.

Notes on the history vs fictional elements of the novel.

African Soldiers and Smallpox. The high loss of life among the Africans of Dunmore's Ethiopian Regiment due to disease was tragic. The scene in the narrative wherein Wend and his companions come upon the smallpox hospital and find the massive number of dead and dying, although fictionalized, is based on fact. Captain Thomas Posey, of the 7th Virginia Regiment landed on Gwynn's Island as part of the assault after the British withdrawal. He recounted the following:

> "I cannot help observing that I never saw more distress in my life, than what I found among some of the poor deluded Negroes which they (*The British*) could not take time or did not choose to carry off with them,

they being sick. Those that I saw, some were dying, and many calling out for help; and throughout the whole island we found them strewed about, many of them torn to pieces by wild beasts—great numbers of the bodies never having been buried."

Dohickey Arundel's Mortar. Captain Arundel was a French professional officer who came to America as the rebellion was breaking out. Appointed as head of Virginia's artillery, he did indeed conceive and build a wooden mortar. There's little information regarding where he got the idea, or what convinced him that it could work. But it is fact that he died in the act of firing the weapon. He was the only fatal casualty among the Virginia forces during the attack on Dunmore at Gwynn's Island. On the other hand, the relationship between Arundel and Ensign Edward Childers presented in the manuscript is fictional, and was intended to personalize the story.

The Captured Highlanders. Unlikely as it may seem, the story of the 200 Highlanders of the 42nd and 71st being taken prisoner by Virginia forces is actual history. The capture of the two companies at sea by an American privateer, their recapture of the transport from the prize crew, and the sailing to the Chesapeake is accurate. As recounted in the narrative, the Convention did attempt to have them defect to the Patriot cause. The Scotsmen were having none of it, however, despite the numerous inducements offered. As mentioned in the novel, they finally were broken up into small detachments and housed in rural Virginia. Eventually they were exchanged and were able to return to their regiments. Upon learning of the incident, I couldn't resist using the situation to involve Simon Donegal and Joshua Baird and thus provide a means for the two to learn about Mary Fraser's return to the Black Watch and to America.

Dunmore's Requests for Reinforcement. Dunmore's military correspondence shows numerous appeals for additional troops and other support, both to Howe and Lord Germain, the Secretary for North America. In the early days of the campaign, John Connolly was in fact sent by ship to Boston to get General Gage's approval of the plan to raise the Indians in the Ohio Country and to request the support of British troops for the operation. Gage responded by sending the 100 extra Royal Marines and the detachment of the 14th Foot to Virginia. He also authorized detachments of British regulars from the forts on the Great Lakes to accompany Connolly's planned Indian-Loyalist force from Ohio as they marched on Virginia from the west. Their purpose was to provide a disciplined backbone for the column. In light of this, Barrett Northcutt's trip to Halifax aboard HMS *Raven*, although fictional, would not have been illogical or unprecedented.

Dorothea Dandridge and Patrick Henry. Dorothea was born in either 1757 or 1755, with the former date the most frequently reported. The only known portrait of her was made when she was elderly. However, there is a drawing of her eldest daughter as a young lady, who was supposed to bear a striking resemblance to her mother. If that is accurate, Dorothea was indeed a beauty. In the narrative, I have advanced the historical timeline somewhat in the case of her relationship with Patrick Henry. In reality, the betrothal was not announced until early 1777. The marriage ceremony occurred October 8, 1777, shortly after her (probable) twentieth birthday. Several articles about her life mention the courtship by John Paul Jones and it is a major subplot in the 1959 movie *John Paul Jones* which starred Robert Stack as Jones and actress Erin O'Brien as Dorothea. However, at least one reference is skeptical that the relationship actually took place.

In addition, there is another serious, almost unbelievable twist in the story. Before Patrick took an interest in Dorothea, she was *actually* being courted by Henry's oldest son, John, who was deeply infatuated with her. Then John joined the army, and was sent to serve as an artillery officer in General Gates northern army. He left expecting to return and ask for Dorothea's hand. Meanwhile, the elder Henry met and became enamored of the dark haired beauty and negotiated the betrothal with her father, Nathaniel Dandridge, who obviously considered that marrying his daughter to a governor was more advantageous than to an artillery captain. Young John learned of the situation about the same time as the battle of Saratoga. Shocked, he sank into deep despair and disappeared after participating in the battle. Patrick, in a confidential and emotional letter to George Washington, appealed to the general to use his good offices and military assets to locate John. In 1778, the younger Henry was found in Elizabeth, New Jersey, despondent and financially broke. Washington, through army channels provided resources to John, who eventually made it back home. There was some form of reconciliation, and Patrick gifted John 1000 acres of land to build his own plantation and start a new life.

Even though the marriage of Patrick and Dorothea was an arranged affair, it appears there was considerable passion between the two. The alliance produced eleven (!) children, a prodigious number even in an age of large families. Reportedly Dorothea was a loving mother not only to her own children, but to the youngest three of Henry's six children by his previous marriage.

By all reports—and despite her youth—Dorothea, beautiful, smart, and endowed with the polite manners of the gentry, carried off her duties as first lady of Virginia in a capable and gracious manor. She was held in much esteem throughout the state.

Andrew Lewis. The ejection of Dunmore from Gwynn's Island was General Lewis' last military action. The veteran border warrior, who had fought in the French and Indian War, Dunmore's War in Ohio, and other backcountry conflicts was already in declining health during the Gwynn's Island campaign. He resigned from the army in early 1777, citing his health, but did subsequently serve in the Virginia House of Delegates and in other political posts in Virginia government. However, while traveling home from Richmond in 1781, he contracted a fever and died on September 26, 1781.

Robert Eden, Governor of Maryland. The incident of the governor of Maryland joining Dunmore at Gwynn's Island is true. However, it is uncertain whether his wife, Caroline, was with him. Some accounts imply she was present whereas others say she sailed for England before he left Maryland. I have chosen to assume she was present, and found appealing the idea of a female, in gentle tones, consoling and persuading the reluctant governor to understand that no more could be done in the aftermath of the withdrawal from Gwynn's Island.

Incidentally, the Edens returned to Maryland after the war and became permanent residents of the state. Caroline was a Calvert—that is, she was a member of the proprietary family of Maryland, and thus more comfortable in America than in England.

Camp Followers in 18th Century Armies. While literary and historical books concentrate on the actions of the soldiers in the American colonial period wars and the Revolution, people collectively known as "Camp Followers" had an important place with the army. There were three distinct classes of civilians who traveled with the regiment:

> (1) "The ladies"—wives of the officers. Financially supported by them.

> (2) The enlisted wives (and children), officially supported by the regiment. They received rations and were transported and provided shelter at army expense.

> (3) The "true" camp followers, people not part of the regiment but there for profit—sutlers, peddlers, craftsmen, prostitutes. This class also included common law wives and other women unofficially attached to soldiers.

The enlisted wives marched with the regiment and were expected to provide beneficial auxiliary services as laundresses, seamstresses, cooks, and nurses with the regimental hospital. They shared the rigors of the men and they and their children necessarily became hardened and street savvy. If their husband was killed in action, the wife instantly lost her ration and those of her children. So out of necessity she was likely to remarry immediately to another soldier, romance not being a factor.

While some officers' wives accompanied the regiment into the field, more often they secured genteel quarters in towns near where the regiment was operating and didn't actually march with the unit unless it was shifting its area of operations. Obviously Colleen Alison McGraw and her Red Vixen Sutler Company fitted into the third category, and are included to illustrate the function played by this type of camp follower.

Selected References Related to Dunmore's Campaign and Virginia in the Revolution. These works were of significant assistance to me in the writing of the novel, and are recommended for those who desire to read further about the revolution in Virginia.

A Universal Appearance of War: The Revolutionary War In Virginia, 1775-1781 (Heritage Books, 2014). Michael Cecere

The Revolution in Virginia, 1775-1783. (University of Virginia Press, 1988) John E. Selby

Dunmore's New World: The Extraordinary Life of a Royal Governor in Revolutionary America (University of Virginia Press, 2013) James Corbett David

Lion of Liberty: Patrick Henry And The Call To A New Nation (Da Capo Press, 2010) Harlow Giles Unger

Whispers Across The Atlantic: General William Howe and the American Revolution (Osprey Publishing, 2017) David Smith

Acknowledgments. I'm grateful to many individuals for assistance in producing this third novel in the Rebellion Road Series. Bryant White extended permission for the use of his painting, *Route Step* for the cover and promotional activity. My son Michael and cousin Francis Tananis served as "Beta" readers of the draft manuscript and provided much useful feedback. I am particularly indebted to the *Elite Authors* publishing organization, whose members performed the design work for the cover and interior, the copy editing of the draft and digitally formatted the finished product for upload to the online booksellers. Their professionalism and production values are superb. Above all, I want to thank the loyal readers of the Forbes Road/Rebellion Road Series, many of whom have contacted us on the Rebellion Road

Facebook page or the Forbesroadbook.com website to express their appreciation and support for the content of the novels.

Robert J. Shade
Sunshine Hill Farm
Madison County, Virginia
October 2022

www.ingramcontent.com/pod-product-compliance
Lightning Source LLC
Chambersburg PA
CBHW051935020726
47501CB00001B/136